Tom De Haven

=

Sunburn Lake

PENGUIN BOOKS

PENGUIN BOOKS
Published by the Penguin Group
Viking Penguin, a division of Penguin Books USA Inc., 40 West 23rd Street,
New York, New York 10010, U.S.A.
Penguin Books Ltd, 27 Wrights Lane, London W8 5TZ, England
Penguin Books Australia Ltd, Ringwood, Victoria, Australia
Penguin Books Canada Ltd, 2801 John Street,
Markham, Ontario, Canada L3R 1B4
Penguin Books (N.Z.) Ltd, 182–190 Wairau Road, Auckland 10, New Zealand

Penguin Books Ltd, Registered Offices:
Harmondsworth, Middlesex, England

First published in the United States of America by
Viking Penguin, a division of Penguin Books USA Inc. 1988
Published in Penguin Books 1990

1 3 5 7 9 10 8 6 4 2

Grateful acknowledgment is made for permission to reprint excerpts
from the following copyrighted works:
"Rockin' Chair" by Hoagy Carmichael. Copyright © 1929,
renewed 1956, Hoagy Publishing Co.
"Bruised Orange (Chain of Sorrow)" by John Prine. Copyright © 1978
Bruised Oranges (ASCAP)/Big Ears Music, Inc. (ASCAP).
Administered by Bug Music. All rights reserved.
Used by permission.
"The Last Letter" by Rex Griffin. Copyright © 1939 by
Hill & Range Songs Inc. Copyright renewed and assigned
to Unichappell Music Inc. International copyright secured.
All rights reserved. Used by permission.

LIBRARY OF CONGRESS CATALOGING IN PUBLICATION DATA
De Haven, Tom.
Sunburn Lake/Tom De Haven.
p.   cm.
Contents: Clap hands! Here comes Charley (1936)—He's all mine
(1987)—Where we'll never grow old (2028).
ISBN 0 14 00.8549 1
I. Title.
[PS3554.E1116S86   1990]
813'.54—dc20   89–36584

Printed in the United States of America
Set in Primer
Designed by Julie Quan

Many thanks to the
National Endowment for the Arts
for their support during
the completion of these stories.

For Santa,
and for the De Havens of Eraho Lodge,
with love.

Contents

Clap Hands! Here Comes Charley (1936)

He's All Mine (1987)

Where We'll Never Grow Old (2028)

Clap Hands!
Here Comes Charley

(1936)

1

Lifebuoy Presents
Leo Bender

I'd promised my sister Dotty that I'd come for supper, but it was freezing out, plus I'd had a tooth extracted the day before—a molar—and my gums were still sore, maybe infected. I felt like ringing her up to cancel. If I did, though, she'd turn clipped and sulky on the telephone, and I'd only end up changing my mind and going anyway, so why bother to call in the first place? You understand me, I didn't want to hurt her stupid feelings.

I gave my scalp a sixty-second workout with Vitalis, combed my hair and put on a fresh shirt. By ten of six I was ready to go. Almost. Standing at the kitchen table, I emptied a box of Wheaties into a crockery bowl and picked out the premium, a Jack Armstrong magnifier and compass, for my nephew. I pocketed the doodad, then went out the door and down the stairs, five long flights, humming something torchy that Connie Boswell sang.

It took me a good twenty minutes to creep through the Holland Tunnel, another half an hour to cross the Hackensack meadows. By then it was quarter of seven and my stomach was gurgling, but I would've bet a dollar that she didn't have the supper ready, or even started, when I got there. I could just see her, stretched out on the sofa by the radio. Well, let me get cracking, she'd say when I walked in, famished. Just relax, Charley. Do you want a vermouth?

I'd say no, like I always did, and finally she'd rattle around in the
pantry and busy herself at the stove, making either franks and kraut
or chopped meat in tomato sauce, what she called slum-gullion,
and meanwhile—meanwhile she'd be talking a blue streak. That
Dotty.

Stuck in traffic on Route 1&9, I read a couple of lighted bill-
boards, one advertising Ipana toothpaste, the other Father Coughlin
on WOR. Alongside the highway was a a brewery complex with
huge long-neck bottles on the rooftops. I wished I had a beer right
then, and a package of cigarettes, and while l was at it, I wished
that Dotty wouldn't talk so much. It was a fact, I didn't care to be
told everything she did. The more I knew about her shenanigans,
the harder it was to feel any sympathy.

Maybe, I thought, she'll tell me about going to a matinee at the
Branford downtown, or about looking for a job again, again without
success, at Public Service and the Pru, at Bamberger's, Wiss Cutlery, a cocktail lounge. And blah-blah-blah. I meant to pay for it,
Charley, really I did, I just forgot I even took it off the shelf, but
try and tell that to an Irish cop! And Charley, please listen Charley,
it sounded like a sweet deal, Charley. Double my money back in
four weeks' time. He guaranteed it, Charley. Thirty days. So all
right, I was stupid, but he seemed like a real good egg, Charley,
he was nice like you. . . .

That's what I figured I was in for, more Dotty babble. Which
would only make me crazy. I wouldn't let on, though, I never did.
I was no buttinsky. I'd just eat my supper and listen with half an
ear tuned, and end up tomorrow chewing pepsin gum, all day. Dotty
wasn't a bad person, she was just . . . dizzy. Well, she was more
than dizzy. She was silly and thoughtless, and a big conniver—a
pain in the neck! But worst of all, she counted on me. Always had,
all her life. Could you loan me twenty dollars? Would you come
with me to court next Wednesday? I was Dotty's Rock of Gibraltar.
Don't laugh, that's what she called me. The Rock of Gibraltar. And
Charley, I'd go jump off the Pulaski Skyway if you turned your
back on me. I would, I would, I would. The thing was, I knew she
wouldn't. She was all phonus-balonus, my little sister Dorothy.

She and her boy, Leo, lived in Newark's Ironbound District, on the top floor of a three-family house that badly needed painting. The rent was seventeen dollars, which I paid, and, believe me, that hurt. Counting salary and commissions, I made only two thousand per. That's all. And I worked hard for it, too hard, driving all over creation. I was not what you'd call a natural-born salesman.

My sister hadn't had a job in three years, three solid years, and the only reason why I hadn't moved in with her to save money was because I couldn't stand her boyfriends. I could not stand her boyfriends, I'm sorry. She accused me of needling them, and I won't deny it. I can't deny it. I did it, sometimes. But what a tribe! Monkeys and bums and married men!

I parked the Ford out in front of Dotty's house, then trudged up her walk, fighting a wind and holding on to my hat. This was a mostly immigrant neighborhood, with freight yards and a few small factories close by. I could hear a train whistle blow. The air stank of cleaning fluid and sweet glue, and there was a wobbly hound on the front lawn sniffing at the garbage cans. It reminded me of Fuzzy—you know, in the funny papers?—only this animal looked half-dead, on the brink of starvation. It skittered away with an oleomargarine wrapper clenched in its teeth, poor thing. The bell didn't work, so I opened the door and climbed the stairs, catching bits of "Amos and Andy."

On the landing outside my sister's flat was a tall pile of her movie-star magazines and romance pulps. I couldn't believe there was one actually titled *Thrilling Marriage*. I knocked and waited, remembering Dotty's last birthday, in October, when all of a sudden she'd got red-faced and weepy, saying, I'm thirty years old, Charley, I got a twelve-year-old kid, who's going to marry me? Who's going to marry me? I'm crazy worrying all the time—who's going to marry me? *Thrilling Marriage. Sweetheart Stories. Complete Love.* I knocked again, and finally heard somebody come across the kitchen linoleum. "Posty?"

"It's me, Dot."

She said my name with a big question mark, then opened the door. Her yellow hair was brushed silky, her lipstick was on. She was wearing a tweed skirt and a snug cashmere sweater. "Charley? Is something wrong?"

I gave her a hard look and walked in. Then I unraveled my scarf and took off my coat, put my hat down temporarily on the steam radiator. The oven was on, and the kitchen was blissfully warm. I smelled lamb, a leg of lamb. "Dotty," I said, "you asked me to supper. You asked me last weekend."

"I did?"

"When you called me about Leo's Christmas bazaar, remember? Jesus Christ! About if I'd buy a chance book?"

And right away, she put on her dizzy doll act, rolling her eyes and nailing herself with a right to the chin button, and generally going on about how sorry she was, how stupid she felt, meanwhile giving me that crooked chastened smile that I'd seen a million times before. "Who's Posty?" I said.

"Joe Post."

"Yeah? So who's Joe Post?"

"Oh, don't make a face."

"I'm not making a face." Then I said, "Well, can I stay?"

"Of course you can," she said without hesitation, but her eyelids flickered.

"He's from Newark, this guy?"

"There you go, this guy. His name is Posty. And yeah, he's from Silver Lake. He's kind of quiet, and he's very nice, Charley."

Aren't they all? I thought, flipping down the breadbox door. Inside was a loaf of Sunbeam with the end seal missing. I took it out, sat down at the table and ate half a slice. Dotty was bent over, peering into the oven. Her skirt was tight across her can. "What's he do?"

"Don't breathe through your nose," she said, straightening up. "But he works in a filling station."

I didn't breathe through my nose, but I sure wished to heaven I'd stayed home. Another boyfriend. Dotty and her boyfriends. This year alone there'd been several. I'd met Phil, I'd met Frank, I'd met Nick, I'd met the one called Sandy that Dotty had thought looked so much like Alfred Gwynne Vanderbilt, though I hadn't seen the resemblance, myself. And I tried to recall which of them it was that stole her good Bulova watch. It wasn't Phil—he was the goof who'd lost his job at the Submarine Boat Company and just sat around the flat all day reading the New York tabloids, entering their dream-house contests. And it wasn't Frank; he was the nut who worked at the Waterman plant, who'd brought Leo bottles and bottles of blue-black ink, and gave my sister one beaut of a shiner before he'd stopped coming around, finally. Maybe it was Nick, the assembler of electric light bulbs. Maybe Nick took the watch. I remembered Nick once claiming that the chemistry of a Pepsi-Cola could burn through even baked-on enamel. He swore he'd seen twelve spilt ounces of the stuff positively ruin the paint job on a new Packard motorcar. No, it wasn't Nick at all, it was Panico. Panico the egg man. *He* took the watch, and what the hell did it matter, anyway?

"So how you been, Charley?"

"Fine," I said. "Nothing's new." Nothing ever was. "How about yourself?"

"Can't kick," she said. That's what she always said: I can't kick. Though it was usually followed by an emphatic *but*. *But* I was in Military Park yesterday and this shoeshine boy stuck out his lips at me. I felt like smashing him! *But* that milkman of mine is getting pretty darn fresh! *But* that Leo. He's always talking back. "I guess I can't kick," she said, opening the cutlery drawer and taking out flatware for me. I waited for some kind of *but*, only tonight there wasn't one.

"How's Leo?"

"All right," she said. "I guess. He's writing his own radio programs now, honest to God."

"No kidding."

"You should ask him to put one on for you. He won't for me."

"There's money in that," I said, and Dotty snorted.

"Yeah, well, I don't figure he's quite ready yet for a career at the Blue Network."

"I know this guy named McIntyre, who's made a pile writing for the radio. And he got started when he was only sixteen."

"How do you know him?"

"From the bowling alley," I said, meaning Radio City Bowling, where I used to work four nights a week respotting pins. "He used to come in every Tuesday."

"Married?" she said, and we both laughed. Then I remembered the cereal premium that I'd brought. While I was thinking of it, I dug it out and passed the magnifier lens slowly over the slice of bread I was eating, as if that bread were the clue of clues in a bloody homicide and I was Doc Savage or the Phantom Detective. Dotty caught me and poked me between two ribs, teasing. "You boys and your premiums," she said.

Directly behind the kitchen was the parlor, and off the parlor were two small bedrooms. Leo's was the one with the Buck Rogers calendar tacked on the door, December's picture a bulbous rocket ship hung with holiday tinsel and garland. I found my nephew lying flat on his stomach across the bed. In dungarees and a brown-and-white polo shirt, the skinny-belink was deciphering that afternoon's "Radio Orphan Annie" secret message—consulting a decoder card, then jotting a letter of the alphabet underneath a numeral: H below 16.

His skin was pale, almost white, and his eyes—not brown like his mother's, but very pale green—were heavily shadowed. He had his father's wavy carrot-color hair. Dotty was still a Kackle, but Leo was a Bender. Leo Bender. And his father was Billy Bender. Occasionally, he'd still ask, Where is he? and I'd say, Nobody knows. But Dotty would say, Timbuktu. Then he'd ask, Is he ever coming back? And Dotty would reply, Are the dinosaurs? But I'd say, There's always that chance.

At last, he looked up from his decoding. "I didn't know you were coming. Supper ready?"

"Not yet. We're still waiting for your mom's friend."

"Wait'll you meet this one, Uncle Charley," he said, cracking more code: E below 10.

"What's the matter with him?"

"He's always swallowing, like he's got a sore throat or something.

And he's always talking about cars, but you gotta see the hunkajunk he drives."

I shrugged. "Mom tells me you've been writing radio programs. For what show?"

"My own," he said, blushing a little.

"What's it called?"

Leo shook his head, sticking the decoder card into his shirt pocket. Then he mumbled something.

"What?"

"The Leo Bender Show," he said hotly. "It's called the Leo Bender Show and it's sponsored by Lifebuoy." Then he rolled off the bed and scooted past me, right out the door and into the bathroom. Christ, he was the moodiest kid. Some days he'd practically talk your ear off, other days he'd glower and sulk and treat you like the furniture. His father's temperament, exactly. Said his mother. And I always felt like asking her, Yeah, how would you know? But I never did.

I stood there sucking on my front teeth, and noticed that Leo had covered one of his knotty-pine walls entirely with pictures of gangsters torn from his detective pulps. Dillinger and Machine Gun Kelly. Herman and Lloyd Barker, Baby Face Nelson, and some other, lesser desperadoes that I didn't recognize. On his desk sat a Junior G-Man Portable Crime Lab with the top open. Inside were neat stacks of aluminum inner seals and Cocomalt labels, bread flaps, box tops and ice-cream cup lids, the lot of it redeemable for club badges, shaker mugs, adventure booklets and code-o-graphs, bright junky things of cardboard, ceramic or tin. His lamp shade was studded with dozens of tiny premium buttons, pins, badges and tabs. I realized I was still holding on to that goddamn compass-and-magnifier, that it was squeezed tightly in my fist. Before plonking the device on Leo's bed, I took a reading. Due north was the bedroom window.

The latest big moment in Dotty's life—*Posty*, for crying out loud!—finally arrived at ten minutes of eight, saying he'd got lost and ended up driving all over nigger town. He was in his middle twenties, lean and long-waisted with thick black hair and a pencil-thin mustache. He reminded me of Smilin' Jack. He was wearing a five-dollar wool suit and heavy black shoes, and his hands were rough, callused, nicked with tiny cuts. His teeth were almost supernaturally white. And Leo hadn't exaggerated—he kept swallowing, clearing his throat. I imagined him in coveralls saying, That'll be fifty-five cents, please. And I imagined myself checking the pump's money totalizer, just to be sure. "Very nice to meet you, Posty," I said. He said, "Likewise." And taking his car coat, Dotty said, "Everything's ready. Charley, you want to call Leo?"

I was encouraged to see that Posty washed his hands before taking a seat at the table, that he didn't eat with his fork upside down, that he even paid some attention to Leo, asking him,"So how's school?"

"School's all right," said Leo, already playing with his food.

Posty didn't ask me any questions, though, but whether that was deliberate or not, it was hard to tell, since Dotty monopolized the conversation, as usual, talking about stuff that she'd read in the tabs, junk straight out of Walter Winchell's column, who was dueting with whom, all that malarkey; talking about the society girl who'd married the governor's son yesterday, what a gown, what a beautiful, beautiful gown; talking about how it was so funny, wasn't it, Mary Pickford getting married the same day as Jeanette MacDonald. "Charley, how old is Mary, anyhow? She has to be in her forties, right? Early forties?"

When I said that sounded about right, she glanced across the table at Posty. His gaze was concentrated on her face. His eyeballs were steady, his eyeballs were wet. He looked like he wanted to flop her, right then and there, on the supper table. Another monkey, I thought, another bum. He cleans your windshield, he checks your oil. That'll be fifty-five cents, please.

"You know," Dotty was saying now, "I read that Hitler wants to marry Leni Riefenstahl. Boy, that'll break a lot of hearts in Germany, don't you think? Somehow, I always figured him for Pola Negri."

Posty finished eating and took out his cigarettes, tamping one gently against the table edge.

"Pola Negri, I think, is much prettier than Leni, but Pola's been married I don't know how many times, and I guess Hitler has to take that into consideration."

Pola, Leni, like she knew them both, like they were old school friends. It was a wonder she didn't call Hitler Adolf. Standing on her bedside table was a framed silvery-brown picture of his nibs, the Führer, which she'd torn out of a Saturday rotogravure. A picture of Hitler! She was goofy about Hitler and his Nazis. The men are so handsome, Charley, she'd say, and all the girls look so scrubbed. Bums aren't tolerated there. They got national purpose, Charley. And what do we got? Shiftless men.

Right, shiftless men. And she'd dated most of them.

"Goebbels thinks she's a Jew, Leni Riefenstahl," said Dotty. "I read that he wouldn't even stay at the same party she was at. Is she a Jew, Charley?"

"I wouldn't know," I said.

Leo shoved his chair back. "May I please be excused?"

"You may," said Dotty, without looking at him. He jumped up and carried his plate and milk glass to the sink, then checked the wall clock and fled. "Cling peaches?" said Dotty. "Raisin cake? You can have both. Who wants both?"

While she was pouring the coffee, Posty met my eye squarely, for the first time in maybe half an hour. "Dotty tells me you're a salesman," he said. "What's your product?"

I told him, "Newspaper features," but he gave me a blank stare, so I said, "Embarrassing moments? Sewing patterns? Crossword puzzles? Comic strips? That sort of thing. Features."

"Charley drives all around," said Dotty, taking her seat again. "To all different newspapers."

"You get your gas paid for?" said Posty. "Your tires and such?" When I nodded, he thumped the table hard with an open hand. I wasn't expecting that, and I flinched. "That sounds all right to me," he said, very enthusiastic. "I could see myself doing that, something along those lines. I like the whole idea of traveling."

"I don't go all that far."

Turning to Dotty and folding his arms, Posty said, "A Chrysler

came in the station today. It had Texas plates. Last week I seen
one that had Washington plates, the state of Washington plates."
Then he turned back to me. "Every week I make a list in my head
of what license plates I see. And on Friday, I figure out which car
I gassed since Monday came the farthest. Well, I bet you that
Chrysler is this week's big winner, and we still got three full days
left. I could sure take going from here to Texas, from here to anyplace. Standing still is murder."

"Well, I never go too far," I said. "Just as far as Pennsylvania.
I'll tell you something, though—Posty. I get sick and tired of driving. Maybe you don't know it, but every place is pretty much the
same." I smiled—pleasantly, I thought—but all at once this Posty
character cocked his head and was squinting at me. He looked
almost offended, and Dotty kicked me under the table.

"I'd like to go to Florida," she said. "And from there I could take
a nice white ship to Cuba. You know that big leader they got there,
that Batista? He's always dating American girls that come on a
ship. Not that I'd go out with him. Not on your life! But I sure
would like to go to Cuba. On a cruise."

"You know where I'd go?" said Posty. "Texas. I'd go tomorrow.
I'd go tonight. I'd go in a minute. It never bothers me to sit in a
machine, so long as I'm under the wheel."

"I'd come along for the ride," said Dotty. "I love taking rides. But
I'm no driver. You remember when I was a girl, Charley, how I
used to hitchhike? Just out to the Oranges and back. Remember,
Charley?"

I said I remembered, and I did—I remembered, all right. But it
wasn't just out to the Oranges, I can tell you. There was that time
she'd got stranded at High Point with ten cents in her pocket, and
I had to take a bus up there to bring her home. Another time it
was Atlantic City. Another time it was Lambertville.

"It's funny, though," said Posty, "but I really can't think of a
single city in Texas."

"I can't, either," said Dotty.

"Abilene," I said.

"Abilene," Posty said. "Abilene, Texas." He laughed. "Sure."

And then I said, "Dallas. El Paso. Fort Worth. Houston. Dallas."

Posty stuck his cigarette into the ashtray. "You already said Dallas. You said Dallas twice."

"Did I? And what's that little border town?"

"I don't know."

Dotty gave a little cough and glared at me.

"Brownsville," I said.

"Brownsville. Yeah, right," he said. "I forgot Brownsville."

"And Corpus Christi."

Posty cleared his throat, a couple of times, then leaned across the table, and I felt a sudden twinge of anxiety, thinking of Lenny Tyner, yet another dipsy-doodle friend of Dotty's. One night—what, two years ago, almost exactly—I'd been sitting right where I was sitting now, getting ready to go out with Dotty and Tyner to join the repeal celebration. We were just gabbing, about dirigibles, about Alcatraz Island, finally about that monster fish everybody was talking about, the lake thing in Scotland thirty feet long with two big humps. Well, I'd asked Tyner if he really believed in that dinosaur fish. Seriously? I said. Oh, come on, Lenny! And he'd turned and looked at me—how Posty was looking at me now—and for no good reason whatsoever, he'd stabbed me in the shoulder with his cake fork! Superficially, but still!

Posty kept staring, and swallowing hard. He picked a shred of tobacco from a canine tooth. I was sorry I'd opened my big fat mouth—but imagine him not being able to name even a single town in Texas! A third-grader could do it. "Your brother sure knows his geography," he said.

Dotty looked relieved. "Oh, Charley's a great reader," she said, as I started to clear the dessert stuff from the table. "He's always staying up late, reading his Zane Grey."

"You can leave my coffee cup," Posty said to me then. "I'm not quite finished. But you can take the bowl."

Well, he thought he was such a wise guy, didn't he? Treating me like a busboy! I wanted to sock him right in the nose. But of course I didn't. I wouldn't spoil things for Dotty. If she liked this monkey, that was her business.

"Charley, just leave the dishes," Dotty said, a bit snappish, when I got out the soap flakes and started filling the sink. But I said it was okay, I didn't mind. Then I said, "Whyn't you go sit in the parlor, you two, I'll take care of this. I'll join you later. Go on." I shooed them out.

Whenever I had a meal at Dotty's, I almost always did the dishes; I just did. Sometimes I even ran the carpet sweeper, or baked with Bisquick. And because I did, she'd cracked on several occasions that one of these days I was going to make some lucky man a splendid wife. Very funny, I'd said every time, knowing full well that she wondered whether I might be a queer, since as far as she could tell, I'd never romanced a woman. That was true enough, though not strictly true. There was that chambermaid I'd met when I was still hopping bells at the Governor Clinton, almost five years ago. Carlene. I'd taken her out a few times to the pictures. I'd kissed her and petted her, entertained concupiscent thoughts about her, but never slept with her. For that sort of thing I'd always gone to a plain and inexpensive whorehouse in New York, though in the last couple of years I'd been there no more than—what?—three or four times. Because two dollars was two dollars, and because— well, because my urges hadn't seemed all that imperative. If they'd ever been.

"Charley?" They were back again, Frick and Frack. "Charley, when were you thinking of going home?" said Dotty. Posty was leaning in the doorway with his arms jauntily folded, like he thought he was William Powell. "Did you want to get home early?" she said.

"Why?"

"Well—Posty was just saying maybe we could go out, to the pictures or something. If you're not in a big rush, would you mind staying with Leo for a couple hours?" Stay with Leo? He was almost thirteen years old—what was he going to do, play with matches?

"I'm a little worried about the snow," I told her. "I don't want to have to drive back in the snow."

"It's not snowing," Posty said. "It's not doing anything."

"They're saying three inches. It was on the radio."

"Forget it," said Dotty. "It was just an idea."

But finally I agreed and said all right, okey-doke, I'd stick around, no problem. I've always been that way. I'll grump a little, but do the favor. What can I tell you? I'm just a pushover. Dotty smiled happily and said, well, in that case, she'd just, you know, check her lipstick and comb her hair, grab her hat and coat and tell Leo she was going. "Be ready in a jiff!" she said.

As soon as she left the kitchen, Posty lit another Camel and said, "Waco."

And I said, "Galveston."

Once they'd gone off together, those two beauties, I washed and stacked the rest of the dishes, wiped the tablecloth and swept the kitchen floor. By the time I was done, it was almost nine-thirty.

I found Leo at his desk, memorizing a list of vocabulary words. I asked him if he wanted to play Chinese checkers, or a board game—listen to the radio? But he said no, thanks. Big test tomorrow. He mumbled, "Kayak: a narrow Eskimo boat," and told me to close the door, please, on my way out. So I went and flopped down on the sofa in the parlor. Right away, I jumped up again and put one of Dotty's recordings on the electric phonograph. Mildred Bailey with the Goodman Orchestra.

Spilled open across the coffee table was the New York *Daily News*, and I settled back with that, its pages full of benzine bombings and lewd-film racketeers, breach-of-promise suits, aviators and sugar daddies. I glanced at pictures of Chiang Kai-shek, of Pope Pius, of Marlene Dietrich in trousers. No Hitler today, for a pleasant change. The King of England, naturally, and Mrs. Simpson. WILL THEY WED? THE WORLD WAITS. PLAYBOY NEAR DEATH IN STAG BARBECUE BRAWL. ILLINOIS BANK ROBBER SLAIN IN NEW JERSEY HIDEOUT. REBELS ENTER MADRID, and Dick Tracy was blowing some crook's brains out in a hospital room, while Orphan Annie hawked flowers on the poor side of town.

With only a few weeks left till Christmas—fourteen shopping days, according to the little box on page two—the tabloid was glutted with advertisements, for everything from candid cameras and rayon undies to printed slips and fielder's gloves. Maybe Leo would

like one of those. But probably not. Then how about a case of
Kellogg's Corn Flakes? And for Dotty? For Dotty, an unmarried
Catholic with a steady income; a civil-service employee. I figured
that she'd probably give me an Arrow shirt or another sweater-vest.
And from Leo I could expect the usual bottle of Aqua Velva.

I started thinking about other Yule times, when I was a boy and
we lived in Kreischerville, on the southern tip of Staten Island. I
would gild walnuts and pierce them with tacks, then string them
all up on a tree that almost scraped the ceiling. I remembered my
father standing on a ladder and clipping candles to the branches,
my mother rolling out stollen dough and scoring it deeply, filling
the scores with melted butter and granulated sugar. My father's
friends from the Turnverein would visit on Christmas eve. They
were huge men. They ate poppy-seed pudding and threw baby Dotty
high into the air. . . .

I finished looking at the paper and picked up one of my sister's
romance pulps, read part of a novelette about a lumberjack and a
blind French-Canadian schoolteacher. It was pure goop and nearly
put me to sleep. Then, along about ten, Leo appeared in blue pa-
jamas. He scurried across the parlor to the kitchen, barefooted.
When he came out, he was carrying a five-pound sack of flour, a
nutcracker, two walnuts, and a miniature wooden Indian that was
actually a candlestick. I said, "Whoa," and with a straight face he
just stood there telling me it was all stuff he needed for a science
project. "It's homework," he said. I didn't believe that for one second. Science project? Did he think I was an idiot? But I let it pass,
and he skedaddled right back into his bedroom.

With a sigh I tossed Dotty's magazine off my lap, reached up
and turned out the floor lamp. I sat in the dark wondering whether
or not it was snowing. I thought of taking a peek through the front
window, but couldn't motivate myself. Then I wondered if Dotty
had really gone to the movies. Or if right now—right that very
second—she was flat on her back in some motor court along Route
22. It was none of my business what she did, of course, but for her
sake I sure hoped that whozzits carried rubbers. He must, I thought.
Christ, even I did. I'd had the same three in my wallet since 1934.

My head drooped, I was half-dozing, when, clear as a bell, I heard Leo say, "There's big trouble in Newark tonight as Leo Bender, the boy manhunter, finds himself face to face with Ma Gruesome and her gang of toughs. Let's listen in: I told you before, Ma, if you think you can scare me with those cow-brain palookas of yours, you're making a big mistake!"

As quietly as I could, I tiptoed over to my nephew's door, dragging a footstool to sit on. Leaning forward and squinting through the keyhole, I saw Leo at his desk with his hands wrapped around the stem of the candlestick. It was tipped toward him, and he was speaking into the Indian's war bonnet. But this was radio, so I closed my eyes and just listened.

He was speaking now in a cackly high-pitched voice, saying, "Kid, let me show you how it feels to be dead. Show 'im, fellas!" And right away, there was a loud smacking sound, obviously his breast being struck a ferocious blow. Leo grunted and groaned, and slapped himself silly. Then crack! crack! Obviously the walnuts. Then something—the flour?—went bump on the desk, then bump on the desk twice more. And the fight was over. Speaking once more in his regular voice, crowing, Leo said, "Who's laughing now, Ma Gruesome? A kid can take care of himself pretty good, if he has to, and if he eats right, packs heat and keeps clean with Lifebuoy."

That, apparently, was it, the entire episode. His bedroom light clicked off, and I carried the stool back to the sofa, switched the radio on and listened for a while to a dance band. Leo didn't come back out to say good-night. The boy manhunter! God in heaven.

A few months ago, I'd read one of his short stories, which had filled three and a half sides of loose-leaf. "The Innocent Wraith." About a slum kid named—I forget: Benny? Johnny?—something Lewis, whose father gets the electric chair for a killing he didn't do. When the old man comes back from "the other world," seeking vengeance, he and Benny, or Johnny, set out to find the real murderer. They snoop around a couple of dives "near the river," and their sleuthing eventually takes them to a seedy rooming house, where the killer is hiding out with a big dumb redhead.

Johnny, or Benny, shoots them both with a Colt revolver, and his father's ghost delivers their souls—described as resembling "dirty shirts without sleeves or collars"—to a horned demon. In the last paragraph, father and son shake hands and go their separate ways. Leo had asked me what I thought, and I'd told him, well, you got a real flair for writing, kid, but your stuff's a little, I don't know, cold-blooded. He'd sneered, and snatched back his ring binder. . . .

At half past eleven, I put away the supper plates that I'd left out to dry. Cups and saucers to the pantry, middle shelf, left-hand wall. And that serving platter belonged in the hutch. I decided I was hungry. Well, not really hungry—I just felt like eating something, tasting something, something sweet. Like a prune-jam danish or Streusel Küchen. I didn't find anything like that, of course, in Dotty's kitchen and had to settle for a piece of her store-bought raisin cake. I washed it down with flat seltzer-water. All right, Dotty, I thought, you can come home now.

"Uncle Charley?" Leo was standing in the kitchen doorway with his pajama top unbuttoned. "Uncle Charley?" he said. "I don't feel so good."

"What's the matter—you going to be sick?"

"Maybe."

I reached and touched his forehead with the back of my hand. He didn't feel warm. Well, maybe a little. "Go on into the bathroom," I told him, and walked him there, my hands lightly on his shoulders. He bent over the toilet, but didn't vomit. Meanwhile, I went searching through the medicine cabinet for children's aspirin.

"I hate getting sick, Uncle Charley," he said, whiny. "I hate having sweat dreams."

"You don't look all that sick. Maybe you won't have any."

"I already did. I was in the yard and there was a man. He was coming to grab me and I couldn't get back in the house. His clothes were all wet. They were black and soaking wet. And the door was locked."

"You're in the house," I said. "You're in the house now. Chew an aspirin."

I took him back to bed, then dragged over his desk chair, offering to stay a while. But only a few minutes. "You want me to read you a story?"

"I'm thirteen years old!"

"Not yet, you're not," I said, thinking suddenly of my father and of how he'd used to read to Dotty and me at bedtime, in German. *Aber wehe, wehe, wehe! Wenn ich auf das Ende sehe! Ach, das war ein schlimmes Ding, wie es Max und Moritz ging!* He had a big red face and bony yellow fingernails, my father. A barber, he always smelled of bay rum and talc and hair tonic. *Eins, zwei, drei!—eh' man's gedacht, Sind zwei Brote d'raus gemacht.*

"Uncle Charley?" Leo had turned over on his side and was jacked up on the heel of a hand. "What time is it?"

"Late," I said. "Go to sleep."

"If it's so late, how come she's not home?"

"She's probably on her way."

"Did you see how that guy kept swallowing? What'd I tell you?"

"I really didn't notice," I said. "Now, go to sleep."

"You hear the one about the traveling salesman that needed a hearing aid?"

I said, "What?" Then, when he laughed, I said, "Leo, cut out the gab, really and truly. I thought you were supposed to be sick."

"Uncle Charley—do you like being a bachelor?"

"I'm not a bachelor. I just haven't married anybody yet. I thought you were sick."

"If you got married, would you move far away? I guess you would."

"Nobody's moving," I said, "nobody's getting married," and he flopped down on his stomach. Nearby, a factory whistle blew, and downstairs, Mrs. Meatro's new baby started crying.

"Uncle Charley?" he said as I was on my way back into the living room. "What do you think of Leo Bender?"

"Leo Bender?" I said. "Oh, him. Well, he sounds like a pretty tough cookie."

"He is," said Leo. "He really, really is."

Quarter of one and still no Dotty. I'd finished the raisin cake, finished the seltzer and had a cup of tea; I'd finally looked out the
window and it hadn't snowed—so they couldn't have gotten stuck.
That Dotty! I was stretched out on the sofa with my hands folded
on my belly, fuming and fretting. Was she all right? Was she okay?
And just who was this Posty character, anyhow? Where'd she meet
him? How? I couldn't help it, I thought about a wreck on the
highway, her murdered corpse in the meadows. That sister of mine!
She'd been causing me anxiety of one kind or another since I was
eight years old. And she was four.

Remember when she let herself out the front door, I thought,
and just wandered away? Remember? Dear Christ, everybody figured she was dead. They'd even started dragging the Kill Van Kull.
But I'd found her—me!—playing in wet leaves under the stoop
behind a Lutheran church, scarcely two blocks from home. And as
a teenager she was always running away, then coming back home
a day later, sometimes scared and disheveled, other times defiant
and scornful, but never once offering an explanation or an apology.
By then we were living in Newark and my father was dead—he'd
died at forty-seven, of heart disease, same as his father before him—
and my mother would say, Talk to her, Karl. You always been close.
Talk some sense into that girl. She goes around with boys so stupid
they buzz, she quits the piano lessons, she cuts her beautiful hair.
Karl, talk to her, talk to your sister. And, reluctantly, I would, saying,
Dotty, you'll get a reputation. Saying, Dotty, if you need a little
spending money, just ask me, don't go helping yourself. Saying,
Dotty, what do you mean *in trouble*? You can't be in trouble, you're
only seventeen! I'll kill that Bender! And she'd said, If you can find
him, Charley, go ahead, be my guest. . . .

I dozed off finally, and dreamed I was calling on an editor, a
client, except that the place didn't resemble any newspaper office
that I'd ever been in; it was more like a living room. And my client
was curled up in a blue upholstered chair with his shoes off and
his shirttail out and his suspenders down. There was coal burning
in a grate, and a woman asleep on a leather couch. She was using

a sealskin coat as a blanket. Her freckled white shoulders were partly uncovered.

All of a sudden, she sat up, showing everything—dark rubbery nipples on little chubby breasts, a surgical scar across her abdomen, heavy white thighs and brown hair between her legs. Her knees were dirty. And she looked fit to be tied. Oh, for the love of Christ! she bellowed. For the love of shit! Who's this monkey? she said, meaning *me*!

She buttoned up her coat and started toward the door. My client stretched out his right arm, palm up, like a traffic cop. Wait! But she wouldn't. She banged the door closed behind her, rattling the cups and saucers on a lacquered black teapoy. For several moments, my client just sat there, blinking. Then he spat in my direction, jumped up and ran out. I could hear him trampling down a flight of stairs. On his desk, the telephone bell started ringing. I walked to the window and held back the drapery. The woman in the black coat was chasing barefooted after a taxi cab. My client appeared, on a high stoop directly below the window. He shouted—"Texas? What do you mean, Texas?"—and I woke up.

I felt achy all over; I'd been sleeping awkwardly, with my left arm folded under my chest. The floor lamp was on, but I knew that I'd turned it off. I sat up, alarmed, and saw Leo in the easy chair by the radio, leaning forward, elbows on his thighs, pajama top plastered to his skin. His hair looked wild, it looked damp, and his eyes were shut tight. He had the telephone receiver gripped like a war club in his left fist.

2

Charley Kackle at the House of Doom

I'd been traveling with Leo since Tuesday, motoring through Wayne, Pike, and Lackawanna counties in northeastern Pennsylvania. Four days, practically forever. At each new town and small city, he'd browsed the five-and-dimes, or stopped into a food market to buy cereal and caramels for the premiums and coupons, while I'd called at *Gazette*s and *Tribune*s, *Sentinel*s, *Eagle*s, *Standard*s and *Post*s to present my latest budget of features and to pass out gift-wrapped bottles of Ancient Age whiskey. Merry Christmas from King Features! And from yours truly, of course! Being cheerful, let me tell you, was no lead-pipe cinch. But I did the job.

We'd spent Thursday night at the Tamarack Motor Court, outside Honesdale. After supper, Leo had tried listening to his favorite radio programs on the midget set he'd brought from home, but neither the Kingfisher nor the Green Hornet could enthuse him, and by nine o'clock he was tossing and turning in the rollaway bed, asleep. I'd sat hunched over a bridge table all evening, toting up expenses with my Vacuumatic pen, then finishing a long story in a western pulp. I finally turned in around midnight, but kept waking up every twenty, thirty minutes, having dreamed briefly of Dotty—of her lighting a stove burner with a book match, of her eating cinnamon toast and reading an air-mail letter, of her biting thread, threading a needle, sewing a button on a pair of greasy coveralls. Eventually, I put the light back on and swallowed a couple of Bayer tablets.

I got Leo the log up at twenty past eight Friday morning, and we had breakfast in a café. Sweet coffee and two scrambled eggs with bacon for me; for the boy manhunter, a bowl of Post Toasties. The counterman was kind of friendly, so before we left, I offered to pay him four bits if he'd write a postal card to his local newspaper. No big deal, I assured him. Just say you'd like to see Frances Drake's Golden Horoscope every morning. But he shook his head, no. Fortune-telling, he said, was against his religion. So then I asked him his religion, and he said Catholic. I said, me too, and *I* read *my* horoscope every day. I'm Taurus. And he said, well, Taurus, you ought to be ashamed of yourself, and Leo guffawed. By ten of ten, we were back on the highway, and by eleven we were crossing the Delaware River Free Bridge into New Jersey timberlands.

U.S. 206 was macadamized there, but only for a short stretch. After turning sharply to the right, the roadbed changed back to concrete and began a steady, winding climb up through the Kittatinny ridge. I gave the electric air-horn a good smash every few seconds, just in case there was another machine that I couldn't see yet speeding down at us from the opposite direction and on the wrong side of the road. I've always been a careful driver. Let it be said.

Directly in back of me, Leo sat bolting dry wheat flakes by the handful, eating his way toward the premium at the bottom of the cereal box. As soon as he found it, a tiny G-man whistle, he blew it. Then he blew it a second time, and Leo, for Pete's sake, cut it out, I wanted to snap, but didn't. He'd grow tired of it soon enough. Until then, I'd just have to—cheeeep!—square my shoulders and clench my teeth.

We drove through Montague, then on through Hainesville, where the land, now dipping and rising, rolled away from the forested mountains; rising in small hills, then dipping abruptly into valleys cleared for grazing, clumped with big red milk houses. Tuttles Corner, Normanock, Kittatinny Lake, and suddenly my ears popped, making the clinking and jingling of the tire chains—and the skirling of Leo's whistle—sound all that much louder. Maybe I should start a conversation? But all week long, day after day, mile after mile, I'd been trying my best to do just that, to make small talk, safe talk, asking Leo's opinion of boxers and ballplayers, popular songs and motion pictures, even current events—What do you think of that crazy king of England? What a monkey! No matter the topic, though, my nephew had only shrugged, sometimes with a smile, more often with a scowl.

"Leo—see those funny-looking mounds?" I lifted a hand from the wheel and pointed. "They were left there by a glacier, a million years ago. That's glacier junk."

He chewed and swallowed more Wheaties. Then blew that goddamn whistle again.

"Glacier junk—that's pretty good, Charley," I said. "Thanks," I said, then shut up.

It was snowing flurries when we arrived in Newton. I parked at a penny meter in front of a pillared white courthouse opposite the town square and a good three or four blocks from the *Sussex News*, where I had an appointment. My habit is always to park in the first legal spot in a client's general vicinity, the simple reason being I like to walk. It's good for the heart.

At Main Street, I insisted on waiting for the light to go green before crossing. With his hands deep in his pockets, Leo pushed out his lips, conveying mockery without words. I felt like swatting him. On the opposite corner stood a commercial bank whose great clock had Roman numerals. A big Packard automobile with pontoon fenders and a rounded grille was parked in front. At last the light changed, and I said, "This should take only half an hour, maybe not even. Then it's just Dover and Morristown, in and out. Sound good to you?"

Leo shrugged, moistening his lips.

"I'll have us back in Newark by six. Five-thirty if we're lucky."

"Will she be there, Uncle Charley?"

"And I'll pick up some fish for supper."

We walked along Spring Street, past a radio sales-and-repair, past the Woolworth's and a pressing shop, then past a drugstore with a blue fountain-service sign and a Christmas window display of Prince Albert tobacco in glass humidors. "Do you have Prince Albert in a can?" I said. "You do? Well, for heaven's sake, man, let him out!" and Leo, unamused, said, "I hate fish."

"You hate fish, you hate eggs, you hate pork chops. What do you like? You like cornflakes."

"I like other things. I like steak."

"It's Friday."

"I'm not *asking* for steak, I'm just telling you what I like. You say I don't like anything. I like steak."

"Well, good for you, Leo."

By this time, we'd arrived at the *Sussex News*, a three-story buff-colored stone building in between a luncheonette and the telephone exchange. "Here's where I'll be," I told him. "In case you get pinched by a truant officer." I hadn't been letting him call with me at client papers. Because, for one thing, I was supposed to be alone, and for another, I didn't care to make explanations. What could I tell people, anyhow—this is my nephew, the cornflake? His mother's in Texas?

Nodding toward the lunchroom, I said, "How's about we rendezvous there? You can sit down and have a cup of tea. Do you have pocket money?"

He nodded, drawing a deep breath, and went moseying across the street, oblivious to automobile traffic. I watched him disappear into a smoke shop, in front of which stood a life-size wooden Indian chief. Then a liveried telegram boy stepped out of the newspaper building and held the door for me. I thanked him, but trotted after Leo.

It was a very narrow establishment, the smoke shop, three times longer than wide, and I walked quickly down its only aisle, between showcases filled with pocket knives and gift candy, cigars in boxes, pipes and pipe tobacco. Leo was standing below a Bulova clock, browsing through the periodicals. He had a copy of *Black Book Detective* in his hand, open to an advertisement that claimed: *Your Imagination Can Make You Rich! Write Stories in Your Spare Time! Write Love Stories! Write Crime Stories! Write to Sell!* "Uncle

Charley," he said, "what's the matter?" and I said, "Fish, Leo, fish! Because it's Friday, we'll both have fish for supper!"

Startled, his face went white, then red, and he gaped at me looming there with my feet planted wide and my chest thrust out and my satchel in one hand and the bottle of liquor in the other. "Fish," I said again, suddenly breathless. "Flounder maybe." I pivoted around then and left the shop in such haste that the tobacconist leaned halfway over the counter to see whether I'd swiped something.

My appointment was with Horace Langtree, the managing editor, but he wasn't around. One of the advertising solicitors told me that he'd just gone upstairs to see the publisher. "He'll be right back," she said, primping her hair with a yellow pencil. So I spread a week's worth of "Your Sew Right" and a sample of Ida Kain's new diet column on Langtree's desk, and took a seat.

After a few minutes, though, I began to fidget; I never could stand the ringing of telephones and the constant racket of typewriters. I stood up and walked to the window. By then it was snowing in earnest, the small flakes dropping heavily. A Silvercup bread truck went by, and its driver was wearing alpaca earmuffs. Across the street, a chunky redheaded man in dungarees and a black pig-grained jacket was trying to light a match. A large woman in a shadow-plaid jacket stepped sluggishly out of the cigar store. She said something to the man, and he gestured irritably, then ducked behind the wooden Indian to get out of the wind.

"Sorry I kept you waiting so long, Charley."

I said, "That's okay, Horace," and we shook hands. Langtree was a once-brawny Irishman gone lumpy, going gray. He had on a blue serge suit, the fat knot of his crepe tie yanked below his third shirt button. He pointed me to a chair and we both sat down. I asked him how he'd been, how were his wife and kids, all that token baloney, and he said he was fine, they were fine, everybody was fine and dandy. Then he casually moved a framed photograph from one side of his desk to the other. A youthful picture of himself, stripped to the waist and caulking a rowboat.

I leaned forward, starting my spiel with Ida Kain's diet column. Twenty minutes later I finished, with "Dr. Sabina H. Connolly's Daily Quiz." Throughout, Langtree had steepled his fingers, sipped at his coffee, hummed softly or ticked his front teeth with polite indifference. "So," I asked him, "what looks interesting?"

"Nothing, really," he said. "But if you'll leave that Sew Right thing, I'll take a second look at it Monday, show it around. Give you a definite yes or no by New Year's. Okay?"

What, could I say that it wasn't? "Sure it's okay," I said, starting to gather my stuff. "Now, one last thing, Horace. Dare I mention a certain name to you?"

"If the certain name is Derby Dugan," he said, "no, you dare not," and his smile faded, like I'd just put the touch on him for twenty bucks.

"Oh, give it another shot, why don't you? It's a good strip. It deserves a second chance."

"It's mediocre and does not. Besides, we're carrying *Orphan Annie*."

"*Orphan Annie* is *Orphan Annie*. *Derby Dugan* is different."

"A kid and a dog."

"Orphan Annie's dog doesn't talk."

"Big deal. Nobody hollered bloody murder when we dropped it. Maybe we got one letter."

"One letter you have to figure is worth a hundred readers that feel the same way. You get two more letters, why, in a manner of speaking, that's practically half your circulation," I said, and probably shouldn't have. It was only a little joke, but he gave me a sniffy look.

"When the complaints start pouring in, Charley, we'll talk about it again," he said, and I made a face, deciding to let it just lie there for now. It was already twenty of one and I was starting to feel anxious about Leo. What if he'd got lost, wandering around? What if he'd hurt himself? What if—I don't know, what if he'd fallen down, banged his head and got a serious concussion! Or amnesia!

I was just about to give Langtree his bottle of whiskey when all of a sudden I heard a gleeful whoop of horror, followed by a school-girl shriek. It was the two switchboard ladies all stirred up, their

hands fluttering around their faces and their hair nets. You'd've
thought Boris Karloff had just lumbered in with all his sutures on,
but it was only the man in the pig-grain jacket I'd seen earlier
trying to light a cigarette. He was avidly waving a couple of stained
linen napkins like they were parade flags. The backs of his hands
were tattooed with blurred serpents, a Maltese cross, even a tiger's
head in the petals of a red rose. Somebody took his picture with a
flashlight camera. "Good Christ," said Langtree, "the local hero
strikes again."

"Couple more, Mr. Dix," the photographer pleaded, and the man
leaned against a filing cabinet, striking a casual, Sears Roebuck
pose. His lips were chapped and his eyes looked as though they
weighed a hundred pounds apiece. The whites were completely
bloodshot. Pop! Then Dix pulled a lumberjack shirt from a paper
sack. Holding it by the yoke, he shook it loose, almost like a barber
snapping a hot towel. There were holes in the body, the placket,
the collar and the sleeves, too many to count and each one surrounded by a dark, crusty bloodstain. My heart kicked, let me tell
you, and my eyes snapped wide open. "Hero?" I said, and Langtree
grunted.

"Mr. Dix—one last one? This time whyn't you hold up that letter. And let's get your wife in." The photographer looked around.
When he spotted the fat woman standing by a cigarette machine,
he motioned to her. But already she was crisscrossing her hands
and shaking her head no, being emphatic about it. Dix, in the
meantime, had unfolded a letter typed on good bond paper with
an official-looking seal at the top. He said, "Forget her, she's
camera shy," then touched the letter to his mouth and mugged
that he was kissing it. I looked back at the wife. I guessed she
was around thirty, and must've weighed, oh, about two hundred
pounds. She was big all over, except her feet. They were tiny. It's
a wonder, I thought, she don't just topple over. Our eyes met
in the vending machine mirror, and we smiled. Then pop! the
flashlight went off again, and I saw blue wheeling spots for half
a minute.

Finally, that Dix character stuffed the shirt and napkins back into his paper bag, and with a wink to the switchboard ladies, brusquely escorted his wife out the door. He walked a crooked line, she carried herself very, very stiffly. I looked at Langtree, and he said, "Idiot's been in here almost every day for a week and a half. God bless us!" Or maybe he said idiots, plural. "You know about Lester M. TenEyck, Charley?"

I said, "No, Lester who?"

"The bank robber. Oh, come on. From Illinois? They shot him last week at Sunburn Lake. Down the road?"

"I know Sunburn Lake. Couple times every summer I'd go up for the day—they still run excursions?"

"No, that stopped."

"There was an amusement park."

"Loy's. But it's gone. Anyhow, that's where they shot TenEyck. He was hiding out in a little cabin."

"Killed?"

"I'll say! I seen some pictures you would not believe. Little moron deserved it, I'm sure, but what galls me is this Raymond Dix. It was him that called the state cops. And yesterday he gets a letter from the Governor of Illinois. They're giving him a reward. Three thousand bucks! And he's nothing but lake trash! He owns a road-house on 206." Langtree opened his top drawer, rummaged briefly and brought out a napkin edged with rust-brown stains. "Dipped in the blood of a bona-fide public enemy," he said and reached it across the desk. I only looked, though. I wouldn't touch it, not on your life. "Dix must've brought fifty of these to the turkey shoot. I swiped this one the last time he was up. For the grandkids."

We both sat there for half a minute gawking at the napkin on the blotter, then Langtree chuckled, and I stood up, feeling a little sick at my stomach. Turkey shoot! I wished Langtree a merry Christmas and gave him his whiskey, which he didn't bother to unwrap. He just stuck it in his bottom drawer and tossed in the napkin after it. "Think about *Derby Dugan*, would you?" I said.

"And a merry Christmas to you, too, Charley," he said. The monkey.

———

Leo wasn't in the luncheonette, so I plopped down on a bolted stool, to wait for him. Scarcely half the quartet tables were occupied, and those mostly by geezers who'd been loafing there, I'd bet you, since nine or ten o'clock. Down at the far end of the counter was a young state trooper in a spotless French-and-dark-blue uniform. He was a handsome kid with a ruddy, freckled, impassive face. His harness squeaked as he reached for the catsup and poured it on his Spam. A picture of Dick Powell was tacked up alongside the chalkboard menu, a radio was playing back in the kitchen. You could hear the rumbling organ and distraught voices of a noontime drama.

At last, the waitress came over. She was a thinnish blonde with vermilion lipstick and a slight pot belly. I said I'd have just coffee, then asked her if she'd seen a kid in a wool cap. She said she hadn't, then went off to draw my coffee. I watched her rear end shift and slide.

When she returned, I directed her attention to a pen and a postal card that I'd taken from my coat and laid on the counter. "Would you do me a little favor?" I said, giving her my friendliest smile. "I'm willing to pay fifty cents for just ten words and your signature. All you have to do is write a short note to the editor of your local paper. That's all!" I said. "I'll even tell you what to write. Two sentences."

She lifted both hands, like I'd pulled a gun, and leaned away from me. "I don't sign nothing but checks."

Just then, the lunchroom door opened and shut and she glanced away. This has to be Leo, I thought. Only it wasn't. It was that local hero again, him and his portly wife. She was steering him by an elbow—until the waitress recognized him and said, "How you doing this afternoon, Mr. Dix?" Then he pulled away, squared his shoulders and colored proudly. Everybody in the place, even the state trooper, lifted their heads. The wife looked embarrassed, but not just that. Rankled, too.

"Know who that is?" the waitress asked me in a whisper, and I nodded, watching them take stools next to the trooper. When they sat down, though, he stood up, giving Dix a look that was too vague to call unfriendly, but with just a cut more squint to his eyes, it would've been. It would've been contemptuous, even. After he'd walked out, Ray Dix called down the counter to the waitress: "Tacky in the kitchen today?"

"Sure is," she said.

"Tell him I'm here, would you, sweetheart? I got something to show him."

She knocked at the pass-through, and a moment later, the cook stuck out his head. He could've been Jimmy Durante's twin brother, I swear. He had the same big schnozzola and bulging forehead, the same long jaw and stick-out ears. When he spotted Dix, he grinned, then disappeared from the window and two seconds later came pushing through the kitchen doors with his hand outstretched. "I heard the news, Ray! Congrats! When're you gonna get your money?"

"I don't know. Soon, I hope."

I couldn't see the wife—Dix was in between us—but I heard her say, "May we have some coffee, please?"

"Yeah, sure, Edith," said the cook, and he motioned at the waitress. "A pair of drawers, Mary Jane." Then he leaned down and planted both elbows on the counter. "How're you gonna spend it all, Raymond? Think about that yet?"

"Not really. It's all kind of sudden."

"Sure!"

"But there's a guy at Budd Lake sells house trailers," said Dix. "I might take a run over there next week and have a look."

The cook shook his head, laughing. "Jesus! A house trailer! What do you think about that, Edith?"

She didn't reply, but she must've made some kind of face, because the cook said, "Well, maybe he'll change his mind," and started laughing again. Then he said, "So, you get Lester's shirt? Troopers give you his shirt yet?"

Dix held up the paper sack. "Want a peek?"

"Could I resist? But in the kitchen, okay? People are, you know, eating."

And off they went through the swinging doors. Then I heard Mrs. Dix tell the waitress, "Take away the milk pitcher, would you? I think J. Edgar Hoover should drink his strong."

"Been doing a little celebrating, has he?"

"Yeah, a little. Is it too late to get scrambled eggs?"

"You want eggs?"

"Please," said Edith Dix.

The waitress cracked open one of the kitchen doors—"Tacky? When you get a chance, spoil a pair?"—and I caught a glimpse of Ray Dix. He was grinning from ear to ear and sticking an arm into a sleeve of that lumberjack shirt. Then Leo appeared, climbing onto the stool next to mine.

He smelled of damp wool and there was snow twinkling on his cap. "Sorry," he said, not sounding it. "I kind of lost track of the time." He'd bought more breakfast cereal—Kellogg's Pep, this time, a red burst on the front trumpeting a free baking-soda frogman inside.

"I thought you'd been kidnapped," I said.

"Hardly." He gave a little snort and leaned the Pep against a napkin dispenser, so he could study the back panel.

"You want lunch?"

He shook his head, lips twitching as he read all about how to fill the frogman—there was a plug in its back—to make it swim like sixty in bath water.

"I thought you'd had an accident."

"You said an hour."

"I said *half* an hour."

He wedged three fingers under the tuck flap and pulled, breaking the seal.

"Why don't you have something to eat? Do you want me to get you a bowl? I'll get you a bowl and a glass of milk. At least you can have a bowl of your cereal."

He shook his head again, plunging a hand through Pep flakes, fingers searching for that frogman, and I gave up.

Dix and Tacky returned from the kitchen then, Tacky saying, "It's impressive, Ray. Very impressive. You got yourself a god-blessed museum, all right." Leo's eyes flicked to them both, but flicked away the moment Tacky noticed him and winked. Dix sat down on his stool.

"Can I get some milk?" he said to the waitress. She was up our way, impatiently jiggling the toaster knob.

"Drink it brunette," Edith told him. "I'd like to get home in one piece, if you don't mind."

Dix expelled an irritated breath, then dropped off his stool and came charging up the counter. He glanced at me, then grabbed the milk pitcher that I'd used and carried it back to his seat. He turned his coffee almost white.

"But, Ray, you know what I think?" said Tacky. "Forget about a trailer home. You should hire an orchestra, soon as you can. All that stuff about you in the newspaper, now this museum you're putting together—you're famous! You bring an orchestra into the Elephant, you'll be turning people away at the door. Whyn't you get Paul Whiteman? Maybe he'd even let Edith sing with him."

"Paul Whiteman," said Ray, slurping at his coffee. "How in hell can I afford Paul Whiteman?"

"You can use some of that reward money, is what I'm saying. That's what I'm trying to say. You'll make it back. It'd be nice to meet Paul Whiteman in person."

"I suppose I *could* hire Paul Whiteman," said Ray. "Now that you mention it. I could, couldn't I? He'd probably tell me to call him Pops."

"You bet he would," said Tacky, and the way that he said it, you could just tell, or at least I could, that he was having Dix on, that he was pulling his leg. But Dix didn't seem to notice. Thick as the vault at Fort Knox. Well, I guess I knew his type. I guess I did. "You bet he'd let you call him Pops," said Tacky.

"I'm sure he would, too," said Dix. "But do you think I'd let Edith sing with Pops? I would not." He half-turned on his stool to face her. "No offense, honey. But I couldn't ask Pops to put you on stage with him. This is Pops Whiteman, Edith, this isn't Harry Seltzer. We're talking about the King of Jazz!"

"You stink," she said. "Drop dead." Then she got up from her stool, made a beeline to the door, and slammed out.

Dix gave a throaty chuckle and made a spiral at his temple with a pointing finger.

During all this folderol, Leo had only gaped. But once I'd paid the tab and we'd left and were back on the street, he said, "Who were those nutty squirrels?" and I made the mistake of telling him what Langtree had told me. His breath, you should've heard it, came whooshing from his mouth like radio wind, and he jiggled up and down on his toes. Was I kidding? Was I *serious*? Holy cow! Holy cow! he kept saying, all the way up Spring, across Main, and through the monument park. Holy cow! Ray Dix! "FBI on the Air" had been all about Ray Dix last Sunday night. Ray Dix, the Suspicious Tavern Owner. And Lester M. TenEyck, the Mad Dog Bank Robber. Holy cow! Was Sunburn Lake around *here*? Still spluttering, he clambered into the back of the Ford, and we took off.

Leaving Newton, we saw Edith Dix again. She was on the curb in front of a private hospital with her thumb stuck out. The Suspicious Tavern Owner's Disgruntled Wife. I didn't stop, of course. Picking up hitchhikers was strictly against company rules. Grounds for immediate dismissal. But I felt for her. I did. She looked so—grouchy.

On 206 again, motoring south, we got stuck behind a county dump truck cindering the road. I probably could've passed it, but didn't want to speed up and maybe go into a skid. The snow was spinning, swirling every which way, ticking against the windshield. I had to be careful I didn't get hypnotized. Other machines kept passing me *and* the truck, all in one go, but that was their business, it was their funerals. "Leo," I said, "quit your sulking, would you? I'm not going to stop. It's snowing. Look at the stuff, it's coming down."

But he wouldn't answer me.

We went by a gray stone monastery called the Little Flower Shrine, and I noticed two Benedictine monks in overcoats standing on the lawn, their brown habits flapping above their trouser cuffs. Each of them was holding a plaster lamb—I supposed for a crèche, but didn't see one. We passed under a high railroad embankment, and the road began to wind again, climbing into more hills. On our left suddenly were the remains of a British fort made of bluestone. "How about that, Leo," I said. "It must be two hundred years old."

"Uncle Charley, it's coming up, it's up ahead, it's four miles. I see the signs. Five minutes, Uncle Charley—please? Can't we stop?"

"Leo, it's not my idea of a good time to go see where some bum gangster was shot to death. It's gruesome."

"It's interesting."

"It's snowing. Why would you even want to see such a place?" I looked at him in the mirror. His forehead was stretched tight, his mouth hung open. He looked excited, annoyed, a little stupid, all at the same time. In a tizzy. Dotty's expression. Oh, Charley, I'm feeling all in a tizzy. "What's the big deal?"

"I read about him, Uncle Charley. He must've robbed about ten banks, all by himself."

"What do you mean, by himself? These guys have gangs, don't kid yourself."

"Not Lester!"

"Oh, it's Lester now, is it?" I said, and he breathed through his nose. "Did he ever kill anybody?"

"You don't get to be a public enemy without killing somebody. Sure he did! He killed a whole bunch of people."

"A bunch?"

"He didn't shoot them all at the same time," Leo said, as though talking to a real ninny. "Three miles, Uncle Charley! There's another sign. I bet we could find the house."

"Leo, cut it out."

"This is the crummiest week of my life!"

"Is that so? Well, it hasn't exactly been my favorite, either."

"You should've left me home."

"By yourself? What if your appendix burst?"

"My appendix!" he said, driving his hand deep into the Pep carton.

We were going through Andover then, and I wondered if I should tell him about the old forge, the famous ironworks that used to be there. Would he be interested? Of course not. In Scranton the other afternoon I'd gone out of my way to show him a coal mine and he'd responded by fluttering his lips, doing like a motorboat. Coal, schmoal.

At the far edge of town, where the highway crooked around an old church, I spotted her. I could hardly believe it, but it was Edith Dix, all right, gallumphing along with her head bent against the wind. I slowed to a creep, then cranked down my window, stuck out my arm and gave the right-turn signal. We stopped about ten yards ahead of her. She took her sweet time catching up. "I thought you were going to pass me again," she said—not Thanks! not Hello!—when she'd climbed in up front.

I said, "Again?" But right away I said, "Well, this is a company car. I'm not supposed to have riders."

She scrubbed at her wet face with a coat sleeve. "Then I don't know if I should tell you this," she said, "but there's somebody in the back seat."

"That's Leo," I said. "And he's not a rider, he's my nephew."

"Only kidding," she said. "Gee." She removed her hat with both hands and brushed off the snow. "And you're uncle who?"

"Charley."

"Uncle Charley," she said. "Well, I'm Edith," and finally she thanked us for stopping.

"How'd you get down here so fast?"

"Oh, you're slowpokes." She leaned against the door. I checked that it was locked. "We passed you boys way back. Me and the lady in the new Plymouth. But you'd think she could've taken me the last two miles on such a day. I said as much when she dropped me off, and she got mad. I won't tell your company, Uncle Charley, I promise." She put her hat back on, then said, "There's a little parking circle up ahead, on your right. It's just past a sign that says World's Largest Hot Dog. I'll let you know."

And all of a sudden Leo blurted, "Were his fingertips really blank?"

I said, "There's that sign already."

"There it is," Edith said, her forehead puckering into a frown. She turned around and looked at Leo. "Absolutely," she said. "They were absolutely blank. And his skin was bad. And he smoked Camel cigarettes." Then she faced front again, telling me,"We're here, Uncle Charley."

She pointed, and I signaled again, steering into an empty parking circle, the tires crunching gravel. I braked in front of a long clapboard roadhouse with a plywood elephant, painted candy pink, displayed on its flat roof. The elephant's trunk was curled around a musical note, a G. There was a CLOSED sign on the front door. "That's the famous roadhouse," said Edith, "where we saw him smoke his Camel cigarettes." Directly behind the building was Sunburn Lake, frozen the color of tin and spanned by an arching wooden footbridge. I remembered that bridge very well. Edith said, "I appreciate the lift," and reached for the door latch.

"Do you know the house?" said Leo. "Could you tell us how to find it?"

I said, "Leo, button it."

"I could tell you, sure," said Edith. "I could show you, even. If you really want to see."

"We really don't," I told her, glaring at Leo, who just glared right back.

"It's only a ten-minute walk," she said.

"See? It's only a ten-minute walk, Uncle Charley! Ten minutes, please?"

So I fumed for a moment, but finally gave in. What'd I tell you about that? "All right, Leo," I said, "you win. But if we go, you have to promise me something."

"Oh God. You want me to eat fish, don't you?"

"I already mentioned flounder. We don't have to have flounder, but it's sort of nice. It doesn't taste like fish too much. Fried flounder," I said. "You promise?"

"Yeah, yeah."

"You don't bake flounder?" said Edith.

"I fry everything."

"You should watch that, Uncle Charley," she said. "Too much oil is bad."

After we'd all climbed out, I leaned against the Ford's bonnet and looked around, glimpsing several chimneyed, snowy rooftops on the far shore. It was a Christmas-card scene. "Which way?" I asked her.

"Well, we could go over the bridge," said Edith, "but that'll take longer. It's easiest just to walk straight down the lake."

"You mean on the ice?" said Leo, before I could. "Is it thick enough?"

"Absolutely. It's absolutely thick. I went skating yesterday." Then she added, as though he'd made an incredulous face, which he hadn't, "Sure, I skate. I might be stout, but I have good ankles. They're strong. And, I might add, they're well-turned, though that probably doesn't interest you."

Well! You should've seen him blush, from his hairline to his muffler. Then he took off at a sprint across the gravel and out to the end of a long, skinny boat dock. "He's only twelve," I said, and Edith smiled, wrinkling up the corners of her eyes.

When Leo saw us coming, he jumped off the dock, hit the lake, bounced once and went sliding, tipping his skinny body this way and that, for balance. Going under the footbridge, he reached up, exuberant, and slapped the cantilevers. "That's far enough, G-man!" I shouted. But he just laughed and ran ahead.

"How come he's not in school?" Edith asked as we started up the lake together.

"Oh, it's a long story."

"Meaning don't snoop, Edith. All right," she said, "I get you."

Along the shore were little cottages, exactly like the ones in magazine ads for Seagram's V.O., the kind that people arrive at late on Friday evenings in the summer with a few groceries and some easy books to read. They looked pretty cozy. But over the lake hung a dreary silence, which made me think of funerals, then of church, then of Dotty.

On the telephone the week before, drunk and giggly and claiming to be engaged, she'd reminded me that Leo was supposed to go to the nine-o'clock Sunday mass. Don't forget, she'd said. He has to sit with his class, she'd said. Otherwise they make him stay after school on Monday. And don't be too sore at me, Charley, please? Pretty please? Pretty please with butterscotch sauce? And I'd said,

Dotty, this is nuts, I don't think it's charming. You're not a movie star, you're not Mrs. Simpson, you're somebody's mother—you can't just run off and get married. You don't even know this . . . person. What're you going to do about clothes? What about money? What about Leo? I have to go away next week! What am I supposed to do with Leo? But she'd already hung up. . . .

"His mother's in Texas," I said.

"Texas!" said Edith. "She didn't win that trip, did she? There was some trip you could win to the Alamo. You had to write a jingle about spinach."

"No," I said, "she didn't win any contest, she just went."

"I never been there, myself. I went as far as North Carolina, once. You ever heard of Greensboro? There. One time we drove straight down from New Haven, Connecticut, to Greensboro, North Carolina. I thought I was going to die on that stinking bus." She nibbled a moment on her bottom lip. "I used to be a singer, in case you're wondering."

"With a band?"

"Harry Seltzer's Carbonated Rhythm Orchestra," she said, and laughed. "That's how come I ended up being called Soda Wauters, with a *u*. It was a cute joke." I smiled, and she said, "But you never heard of me, right? That's because I never made a recording. These days, if a singer don't do recordings, she might as well, I guess, be a mute. She's a mute. What do you do, Uncle Charley?"

"I'm a salesman."

"I guess I figured that," she said. "The way you talked about your company car." Then she said, "Spending every day with sixteen men on a fumy old bus wasn't any picnic, let me tell you. I'm not the most beautiful creature in the world, but still—it wasn't easy. Well, you can understand. You can imagine."

I nodded, imagining—imagining this fat, pretty woman staring morosely through a bus window, just as she was staring now up the lake after Leo, her lips a thin, straight line, her shoulders slumped. I could imagine, all right. But understand? Understand what?

"I had to buy my own gowns," she said. "I had to pay for the dry cleaning, I had to pay for all of that stuff. And I wasn't any big

attraction, just another canary. But don't get me wrong," she said,
"I loved to sing. It's just I didn't like all that driving around."

"I know what you mean."

"I know you do, Uncle Charley." Then, a moment later, she said,
"Do you like Connie Boswell?"

"Oh sure. Who doesn't?"

"Well, my husband, since you asked. But Ray has screwy taste
in music. Take that Paul Whiteman," she said, and her eyes looked
suddenly all charged up, weirdly bright. "Paul Whiteman! He's not
the real thing, he's just a copy cat."

I shrugged, because I had no opinion, really, about Paul Whiteman, and because—well, just because.

"She's one of my two or three favorite singers, Connie Boswell.
Did you know she was in a wheelchair? But I just love her," said
Edith. "She can really break your heart, can't she? That's how come
Ray doesn't like her so much. He says they should arrest her for
general mopishness. But what's he know? Paul Whiteman wouldn't
come play here on a bet! What's your favorite Connie Boswell song,
Uncle Charley?"

"Oh, geez, I don't know. Let me think."

"You like 'Time On My Hands'?"

"Yeah, that's nice."

"Would you call that mopish?"

"Not at all."

"I used to sing that one. Professionally." Then she said, "I have
no desire to see Texas, none. I'm just interested in getting to New
York City. That's where all the good records are made, you know."

Leo had clambered onto a rock island that wasn't much bigger
than a pitcher's mound. When we came parallel to it, he rejoined
us. "Over this way," said Edith, and we rounded a jutting point of
land, coming into a back cove. On a ridge that overlooked a sand
beach was a deserted construction site: lumber and bricks, roofing
shingles, wheelbarrows tipped on their sides, tubs for mixing cement. And maybe a dozen barracks-style buildings.

"There's our little Nazi camp," said Edith. "Or will be, next
summer. You read about that? About our Nazi friends?" She pro-

nounced it *nah-zees*, and clearly with distaste. "They're building a stinking beer garden down here. Can you imagine?"

Leo glanced at me, and I prayed he wouldn't blurt something he'd picked up from Dotty—Jesus, I thought, please don't let him quote one of her stupid remarks about handsome young men. He just frowned, though, and stared at the buildings. Edith was saying, ". . . big stink, I can tell you, when Mr. Loy sold 'em those ten acres. Even Ray threw a fit. But what can you do? They shouldn't let those stinkers build so much as an outhouse, if you want my opinion. But who's asking me?"

And then Leo was off again, scrambling up the beach to one of the more finished-looking billets. A minute later Edith Dix and I joined him at the window. Inside, it was raw—no hanging swastikas yet, no portraits of the Führer, just a dropcloth spread on the floor, a workman's lunchpail, a sawhorse, a coffee can full of tacks. Edith clucked, then turned abruptly and trudged on through the bund camp, heading toward a road that bent away sharply into a pine thicket. I put my hands on Leo's shoulders, giving them a gentle squeeze—let's go, kid—but he twisted free with such violence that his cap flew off his head and landed in the snow.

After he'd snatched it up, he looked at me kind of sheepishly. Then he said, "Mom took me to a place in Jersey City once, where some Nazis were having a picnic. It was exactly like the Fourth of July, except they sang a bunch of songs in German. They even played baseball. Remember that friend of hers, Mr. Barsch? He took us. And you know what happened? Somebody threw a stink bomb—over this wall, from the street. Mr. Barsch figured it was a Jew."

"You never told me about that."

"Mom said not to. She said you don't like Hitler."

"Of course I don't like Hitler. And I don't care if Pola Negri hears about it, either."

"Yeah, Pola Negri," he said. "That was pretty dumb." He gazed across the compound, at a yellow frame building with a squat clock tower. "What about Mom?" he said. "You like her?"

"At the moment, Leo, not very much."

"Do you hate her?"

"I'm angry with her."

He gave me a slow, disgusted look. "Do you think she really married that cowbrain?"

"Don't call people cowbrains. And how am I supposed to know what she did or didn't do?"

"I want her to be home when we get there, Uncle Charley, and I don't. Maybe she'll never come back."

"Don't be silly. Of course she will."

"I wouldn't really mind," he said. "I really wouldn't mind if she didn't."

I said, "Well, *I* would!" Trying, you know, to be funny, and it worked. He laughed in spite of himself, then pushed away from the wall, and we hurried on through the camp to catch up with Edith.

Mr. Barsch. Which cowbrain was Barsch? I thought, then suddenly I was thinking back to an August Sunday in 1923, when I'd come up to this very lake on a Lackawanna railroad excursion with Dotty and her newest boyfriend.

We'd all stretched out on the beach, this Billy Bender saying he'd seen a jazz band at the Adams Theatre the night before that used, get this, cowbells, then saying how he'd heard it wasn't apoplexy that killed President Harding the other week, it was poison, and meanwhile he kept sneaking looks at Dotty's bosom. She was seventeen. Billy was a year or two older. Woolly red hair, straight teeth and a muscular build. Dotty thought he was pretty swell, the tiger's spots.

He was, she felt, about as American as the touring sedan. He even had a personal motto, adapted from a Positive Thinker he'd once heard at Redpath's Chautauqua: "Bender, get out and get to it!" He was going to be somebody. And that meant rich. Wasn't he taking Business Barometers at the University of Newark? And didn't he study the stock market page every morning in the newspaper, jotting a check mark beside American Telephone and Telegraph, an asterisk next to New York Central? So what if he only worked for the Lionel Company, assembling scale-model locomotive en-

gines? Someday he'd be rich. Dotty was sure of it. And Charley,
guess what? she'd said. Every Friday on his lunch hour, Billy runs
down to this brokerage house on Raymond Boulevard and buys
himself three shares of United States Steel!

I'd never have dared risk my own money like that. Never. Mine
I'd kept safe in coffee cans, like my father before me. Bender, I'd
thought. What kind of name is Bender? When we met finally, I
asked, and he replied, American. Right off the bat, I didn't trust
him.

After we'd all had enough sunbathing, we strolled down to Loy's
Funland, where I tested my strength of grip—on a scale of Weak-
ling to Hercules, I rated Stalwart—and Billy fired baseballs at a
Negro's head stuck through a canvas backdrop. The African Dodger.
Then he took Dotty on a circular airplane ride. I stood at the railing
and watched them go 'round and 'round. A few minutes later, Dotty
burst through the fence gate, her cheeks blushing with pleasure.
Billy thinks I'm cute, she said. He just told me so. Cute as a button
or cute as a bunny? she asked him then, point-blank, brazen and
trying to embarrass him. But he wasn't embarrassed, I was.

What next? said Billy, looking all around. What next? All of a
sudden he was in charge, leading me and squiring Dotty, into the
flea circus, the House of Thrills—but let's skip the Choir Celestial,
shall we? Sounds deadly. He bought Dotty hot roasted peanuts,
crushed ice drizzled with Coke syrup; he bought her a package of
King Tut chewing gum. He bought her tickets for the Shoot the
Chute, the miniature railroad and the dodgem cars. He even paid
for her challenge at the Weight Guess, where the guesser, a short,
leering fat man in a derby hat, prodded my sister all over with his
pointer, estimating her body mass. Dotty laughed when he guessed
wrong, and she won a box of soda crackers.

Billy stopped next at a shooting gallery. He picked up a rifle and
fired pellets at mechanical ducks, rabbits, grizzly bears and fish
leaping across the target area. A fair shot, he scored enough hits
to win a bottom-shelf prize, his choice of either a straw hat or a
wooden cane. But he wanted a plaster kewpie, so down he slapped
another nickel. And made my sister bend and kiss the rifle sight,

to bring him good luck. That bothered me, and when Billy read the displeasure in my face, I felt like a fool and my alien father's son. He grinned, took aim, and fired. Got the Kewpie. Dotty said it was junk, but thanks.

Then he pointed at a circus wagon plastered with crude and garish posters and draped with a tasseled banner: CUT IN HALF, SHE LIVES IN A BUCKET! Let's, said Billy, but I said, No. Oh, let's, said Dotty. Let's. And then Billy was buying admission tickets—Two, please—but impulsively I tugged at his shirtsleeve, telling him, You go ahead if you want, but it's not the sort of thing for young ladies. Billy pushed out his mouth with the tip of his tongue. Oh, don't be such a Prussian, he said quietly, then tore up the tickets with a fury that startled me.

Afterwards, they strolled ahead together, chatting and laughing—at me?—and Billy slid his arm around Dotty's small waist. She leaned readily against him. My skin was wet and my shirt was sticking to my back, and I was miserable. Cut in half, I lived in America.

Between the dance pavilion and a high plankboard stage where the Beautiful Grandmother pageant was being juried stood a red-and-white-striped tent, whose sign promised, YOU FULLY RELIEVE YOUR PRIMITIVE INSTINCTS HERE! DESTROY! DESTROY! SEE HOW MUCH DAMAGE YOU CAN CAUSE! And the moment I stepped through the flap, reluctantly following Billy and my sister, someone tugged at my vest bottom: a dark-haired woman in her early twenties, my age, offering me a tin bucket full of hard white balls that were like golf balls without dimples.

There were half a dozen or more pine cabinets set flush against the canvas walls, and arrayed on the shelves were cheap platters and glassware, cups and saucers, soup bowls and tureens. Treacherous debris covered the ground. Some crunched underfoot as I took a step. Ten cents the pail, said the woman, whose forehead gleamed with perspiration and whose throat was pebbled with a summer rash. And no wonder! The tent was suffocating.

How many? she asked me, and Billy answered, One please. For

our friend Charley, here, who's feeling especially primitive this afternoon.

Is he now? the young woman said with a laugh. Well, goody!

And I'm sure that I blushed. I'm sure of it.

My first pitch I threw wild, and the ball struck nothing except the back of the tent; it bounced once on a shelf, then dropped to the dirt, clicking breakage. But the next one! The next one flew straight and blasted a pyramid of drinking glasses into a slew of chips. Billy gave a loud, hiccuping laugh, and the young woman said merrily, Nice shot! Manslaughter in the first degree!

Every time I shattered something else, she passed another exclamatory remark. There goes his spine! That's one satisfied lady! I got my captain working for me now! When I pulverized a casserole, she clapped and clapped. Send for the coroner! Goliath is dead! I smiled at her. She crinkled her mouth and eyed me craftily— she did!—and my stomach folded right in half. She was very pretty. I was having fun. I hadn't expected to, but I was. I hauled off and threw another fastball, shattering a tulip cup. We need a stretcher! Call an ambulance! Call the cops!

As soon as my pail was empty, she stooped and dragged a big carton full of novelty candlesticks—Indian-chief candlesticks—out from under the counter. Although they seemed to be entirely identical, she carefully sorted through the lot of them, and finally selected one, which she handed up to me. If you want a pair, she said, stay and break some more legs. And I laughed, admitting that a pair would make sense, wouldn't it? Since candlesticks always came in twos. Another pail? I was tempted, and looked around for Dotty and Billy Bender, to see how they'd feel about my staying just a little while longer, but they were gone. They'd sneaked off— ditched me! The woman noticed my frown, and frowned herself. I'd like to stay, I said, but. . . .

But what? she said. Was that your girl?

No, my sister.

With a little shrug, she took a pushbroom that was leaning against the counter and started to sweep up.

You bet I'd love to break some more legs, I said then. Four, count 'em! Four broken legs! I said. Call the orthopedist! She didn't laugh, though. She wasn't paying me any more attention, and suddenly I felt ridiculous. What had I thought before—that she was flirting? You big dope, you big stupid Dummkopf. Without another word, I turned and left.

With my mouth full of spit and that stupid Indian chief clutched in a fist, I trekked from one end of the amusement park to the other, sticking my face into every arcade and pavilion, the photography booth, a tattoo shack, dashing from the slot cars to the Ferris wheel, even waiting for the miniature railroad to come tootling around. I went back to the swimming beach. But still I couldn't find them, and probably never would have if I hadn't bumped into a fellow I'd known at Barringer High School. He'd seen Dotty, yes. With a redhead, right? Going across the bridge. That way.

So off I went and crossed the footbridge myself, and for the next three-quarters of an hour I wandered around the lake, following paths that kept leading me down to either a vacation house or a lilypad cove.

I kept meeting families laden with hampers and blankets and towels, and the air was filmy with the smoke from charcoal fires. From time to time through the trees I glimpsed a lovely green or red canoe out on the lake. Jealous, I watched a man carry a suitcase into a log house that had a fieldstone patio. I heard a door slam, a dog bark. Then I heard a woman say, And don't forget, a packet of yeast! Moments later, a little girl of eight or nine came trotting around the side of the house, a dollar bill clutched in her fist. I felt it wise not to smile at her, because I was a stranger, a prowler, and didn't belong there.

Eventually, I came to a granite spillway. Beyond the spillway, the path simply ended. A swamp began. And twenty or thirty yards in was an abandoned automobile, an old Marquette, its tires gone, its chassis listing. Under the wheel, pretending to steer, sat my teenaged sister Dorothy, naked. From behind some highbush, Billy Bender appeared, stepping over a rotten log, then wading through muck. He was shirtless and shoeless and he'd rolled up his cuffs almost to his knees. His shins were muddy, splattered. He carried an armload of thick brown punks, and he'd stuck one through the unbuttoned fly of his trousers. Dotty laughed, made some filthy crack about circumcision, and I was holding that candlestick, I could've run out there and clubbed them with it, bloodied them both, but I didn't. Instead, I just hung back, not breathing, crouched there, watching. My father would've throttled the pair of them. He would've, but I only watched. There goes his spine! Send for the coroner! The woman is bleeding!

Finally, I sneaked away, and later on they came across the footbridge and met me at the railroad station. Their faces were sunburnt, their clothing damp. They'd been out pedaling on water bicycles, they said.

On the train ride back to Newark, Billy Bender told college jokes and talked securities and commodities. Cuban-American Sugar. Kelly Springfield Tires. Dotty read a magazine. I buried the candlestick in the picnic basket. . . .

"So what about Mildred Bailey?" said Edith. "You like her?"

I said, "Oh sure, Mildred's good. Mildred's very good."

"Did you know that she was part Cherokee Indian? I used to sing a lot of her songs too. Before I got stuck up here."

And Leo, God bless him, said, "This house is where, exactly?"

"It's exactly where it's always been," she replied. "Keep your shirt on, kid. We're coming to it." And so, with Edith Dix reciting Mildred Bailey song titles, the three of us followed the road out of the camp. " 'What Kind O' Man Is You,' " she said. " 'Squeeze Me,' " she said. " 'Give Me Liberty Or Give Me Love.' " I walked with Edith, but Leo trailed behind, snacking on Pep.

We passed a small pink house on stilts, then a black-log cabin nearly hidden in fir trees. Smoke was rising in wisps from both their chimneys. Then, as we topped a small hill, I noticed, down by the lake, a young man in denims carrying firewood in a bushel basket. " 'Nobody's Baby,' " said Edith. "That too, but I kind of got sick of it."

"You wouldn't think there'd be so many people around," I said. "At this time of year."

"What? Oh, yeah, but it's only hobos. They come up every winter, for the empty houses. And some of these guys are really brazen. They turn on the water, they even use the electric."

"It's how Lester did it," said Leo. "He was making believe he was a hobo, just till he got back on his feet again."

"They don't bother nobody," said Edith, "and nobody bothers them. Except maybe the staties once in a while. And they usually clean up real nice before they leave in March."

Leo said, "He was broke. He had bronchitis."

"He paid for his sandwiches. So he wasn't all that broke," said Edith. "And it was influenza."

"That's what he told you? They said bronchitis on the radio."

Edith squinted at him, then pointed off the road, at a mailbox on a mounting post. The name Englehardt was pasted on in block letters. Behind it, a hill clumped with boulders climbed to a fenced patio of blue slate. The house was made of tarred logs and had a fieldstone chimney. The door and front windows were boarded up with fresh plywood.

"There? That's it?" said Leo, frantic suddenly. "Where did the troopers stand? Were they lying on their bellies, or what? There's not much cover," he said. "There's not much cover here." He went bounding up the hill and onto the patio, swinging his head this way and that.

"Maybe I'm not in the same league as Connie and Mildred," said Edith, "but I'm not half bad. If you closed your eyes when I'm singing, you'd swear I weighed a hundred pounds." Then off she went, swinging her arms and calling to Leo, "If you want a closer look, I bet you we can get in."

"Can we, Uncle Charley?" he asked, peering down over the fence. "Say yes."

"No, of course we can't. This is private property."

"Oh, let's just make believe we're hoboes," said Edith, raising a section of latticework at the side of the house. She braced it with a fence picket she'd found lying by the propane tanks, then ducked underneath and disappeared. "Do you boys want to see this or don't you? It's okay! Really."

Leo, flying down off the patio, went next. And finally, reluctantly, me.

Walking crouched, bent low from the waist so I didn't split my skull on the overhead beams, I smelled wood rot and turpentine and last summer's paint cans. A pair of men's blue swimtrunks and a railroad lantern were hitched on a cleat in the wall. Some rusted tools and gardening implements lay scattered in the soft red dirt. "Uncle Charley? Are you still with us?" Edith called down the cellar stairs. Through an open trap, I glimpsed Leo's wet shoes and the damp cuffs of his woolen trousers. "This is known as trespassing," I said, coming up into the living room. "Just in case anybody's interested in the legal term."

I guess I'd been expecting to find, oh, a lot of broken glass on the floor, furniture overturned, everything in shambles. The glass had been swept up, though, and every stick of furniture was standing, smartly arranged—a brown slipcovered couch with roll cushions, a padded rocker, a white wicker lamp table, a writing desk, a ladderback chair. Off the living room were two bedrooms, both doors shut. The knotty-pine walls were splintered and bullet-pocked in a hundred places. Through an archway I could see the end of a rustic dining table.

Leo grabbed a pillow from the couch, inhaled it, put it down. Then he stooped and pulled a tabloid newspaper from the wood carrier by the fireplace. The New York *Daily Mirror*. KING EDWARD ON THE BRINK. "This is from last week, Uncle Charley! This is what he was reading, I bet you, the day he died! And look at this—he did the word scramble! Bleat! Cornet!"

Leo turned the paper toward me, so I could see the crossword grids filled in with soft pencil, then he tossed it away and started to pace, his eyes solemn, pensive, sweeping the floor—was he looking for shell casings? Bloodstains? Well, that's what I was looking for, though I hoped not too obviously. Looking for bloodstains and thinking vaguely—then less vaguely—about old Mrs. Schaeffer, who'd lived up the street in Kreischerville, when I was a boy. Mrs.

Schaeffer, who'd said she'd had a visitation from the Virgin Mary.
Who'd said the Virgin Mary had appeared in her tiny backyard,
floating on a radiant cloud. . . .

My mother would often drag me there with her, to Mrs. Schaeffer's yard, on sunny afternoons. Clutching rosary beads or a tatty
novena booklet and holding my new baby sister in the crook of an
arm, she'd join other women gathered around the flowerbed, everybody speaking German and waiting eagerly for the Virgin to reap-
pear. I'd also waited, as eagerly as anyone, trying to anticipate the
color of the Virgin's hair, and its length, and wondering if she'd be
slight or stout, and if she'd have conspicuous breasts; waiting,
becoming impatient, and wishing that Dotty would just quit bawling, then blaming her and the gulping, shrieking racket that she
made when the Mother of God, time after time after time, failed to
show. That Dotty!

"So what do you say, Leo? Should we head back?"

He was lost in a kind of trance, though, and just kept pacing,
exploring, plopping down alternately on the sofa, the rocker, and
the ladderback chair. He opened one of the bedroom doors and
poked his head inside, then monkeyed up the ladder to a sleeping
loft. That did it. "Leo," I said, "for God's sake! You want to break
your neck?"

"I wish we had a camera," he said, swinging off the ladder onto
the balcony floor. The enclosure was made of logs, the bark un-
stripped. "Be neat if we had a camera!"

"Well, we don't. Get down." He'd found a *Huckleberry Finn* straw
hat, the sort you can win at carnival games, and now he stuck it
on his head, right over his wool cap. "And take that off. This is
somebody's house. In real life," I said, "this is somebody's house."

"The Englehardt sisters," said Edith, who'd parked herself in the
rocker and was paging through the *Daily Mirror*. "They're school-
teachers. From Yonkers. You should've seen them last week, poor
things, when they had to come up here. As it is, they're always
having their little nervous breakdowns. If you knew them, you'd
know what I mean by their little nervous breakdowns." She'd reached

the comics page, and before she could turn past it, I said, "Oh, there's *Derby Dugan*! That's always been one of my favorites." Then I said, "But I guess you don't follow it."

"Follow it?" She closed the tab and stood up.

"*Derby Dugan*. I'm just saying it's kind of a shame that you can't read it. Because it's not in your paper. It used to be, but not anymore. They dropped it."

"Are you talking about the *Sussex News*? That's not my paper, Uncle Charley. I wouldn't call that rag my paper. I'm used to real newspapers. I lived in Chicago, you know. Before I got stuck up here."

As soon as Leo vanished through the archway, I went after him. For all I knew, there might've been a hole in the dining room floor. Jesus! even a dangerous hobo skulking back there. Don't laugh. Not every hobo on the road is like Pete the Tramp. Don't kid yourself. Edith tagged along, saying, "That stupid rag. They printed Ray's picture four times! And now they're going to do it again. Five times! Like he was a big swindler or cured polio or something."

"*Derby Dugan*'s my personal favorite comic strip," I said, sticking a hand into my coat for a postal card.

"You know which funny I like? *Winnie Winkle*. I think she and Bill are really going to get married this time."

"I don't handle Winnie."

"Well, let's hope not. She's a very respectable young lady. What do you mean, handle?"

I found Leo at the back of the house, in the L-shaped kitchen, squatted by a laundry mangle. He'd picked something up, a semi-circle of white porcelain, the broken handle of a dime-store teacup. He dropped it into his cereal carton, then flinched when he realized I'd come in. "It's only a piece of junk," he said. "It's only a crummy piece of junk."

"I just hope all this doesn't give you bad dreams, mister. It better not!" I said. "Your mother'll brain me."

"Don't worry, I seen where Dutch Schultz got killed and nothing happened."

"I'm not so sure about that."

He ran his tongue across his top lip, then squeezed between me and the kitchen table and scooted out.

"I can never understand the big deal people make over souvenirs," said Edith. "Sailor hats and corncob pipes, all that stuff." She crossed her arms and leaned against the sink.

"Well, he's only twelve."

"I'm just saying, I'm not criticizing. Look at Ray! I'm just saying I can't understand the big deal." Then she reached over and twisted the cold-water tap. It coughed, spat once, then ran in a gush. "I wonder if there's gas. We could have a cup of tea, if there's gas," she said. "And if there's tea." She turned a burner knob and sniffed. "No luck. I guess he didn't do any cooking. Lester, I mean."

"I guess not."

"If he did, maybe he'd still be alive. Not that I care one way or the other. I guess he was pretty much of a stinker. Although he was always civil enough to me. But his big mistake was having sandwiches every day at the Pink Elephant. You wouldn't see me going out for a sandwich, not if I was wanted dead or alive." She sat down at the table and began to pick absently at the oilcloth. The nails on both her pointing fingers were long and sharp, the others not. The others were chewed. She had no neck and chipmunk cheeks and three or four permanent worry lines. She gazed out the side window and down a wooded slope to the lake. Pretty eyes, though. She looked around at me again. "Oh, don't fidget so much, Uncle Charley. Nobody wants *us* dead or alive. Sit down."

So I did.

"I'm having fun," she said. "Aren't you having fun? What do you mean, you don't handle *Winnie Winkle*?"

"I don't happen to sell that particular strip. That's all I meant. She belongs to the Trib Syndicate."

"You're a comic-strip salesman!"

"Not *just* comic strips," I said, and named some of the other stuff that I drummed. Then I brought up *Derby Dugan* again and mentioned my trouble with Horace Langtree—how he'd canceled the strip and all, for no good reason. Edith said that he sounded to

her like a big dumb cluck. "Well, I don't like to call people names,"
I said. "But I do think he's made a mistake. It's very popular. Henry
Ford reads it!"

"I used to read it myself."

"But now you can't. It's a shame."

"Well, I don't look at that paper, anyway. Like I told you."

Then I thought, Oh, why not? "Could I ask you to do me a favor?"

"You didn't say *Edith*. You just said, could I ask you. You don't
call me anything," she said. "Do you realize that? Not once since
we met."

"Edith."

"For a while, people used to call me Soda, like in everyday conversation. What's the matter with you, Soda? You look down in the
dumps, Soda. Speed up the tempo, Soda. It was kind of silly. Not
that I've ever been crazy about the name Edith. I don't know whatever possessed my mother to call me that. Edith! You remember
Edith Wilson, the President's wife? So, what's the favor?"

When I'd told her, she opened her mouth and laughed. "Ray
would kill me! Him with his picture in that stupid paper and his
own wife saying she won't buy it no more." Then she said, "Gimme
the pen."

"On second thought, maybe it's not such a hot idea. I certainly
wouldn't want him to kill you."

"Don't be so funny. I meant have a conniption, Uncle Charley."
She took the pen and uncapped it. I slid her the card.

"If you want, I could tell you what to say."

"I can do it myself, you don't mind."

While she was composing, I went to check on Leo and caught
him in the act of unscrewing the lightbulb from a table lamp. "Put
that back!" I said, and he jumped. "Put it back!" He did, but he
sure made a big puss. God in heaven, he'd be dragging the sofa
out the front door, next.

"You're gonna love this," Edith said when I came back. She
nudged the card toward me. "No beating around the bush."

Where is he?! she'd writtten. *What have you done with him?!
Where is my boy and his dog that talks?! You stink! You stink on*

ice! Bring them back or face the consequences!!! Signed *Edith Dix*.

Her script was crimped and finicky, almost like printing, and she'd dotted every *i* with a tiny bubble. Also, every question mark and exclamation point. It made the message look, well, carbonated.

"How do you like it, Uncle Charley? How do you like that part about facing the consequences? It's punchier than just saying I won't buy his stupid newspaper anymore. Let him stew. Let him think he's got a desperate woman on his hands," she said, getting up from the table, and we both laughed. There were gold fillings in several of her teeth, and she'd had some bridgework done. Her face was about six inches from mine.

"Thank you, Edith, very much."

"You said Edith."

"I did."

"Now can I ask *you* a little favor, Uncle Charley? You can say no, all right? But would you give me a lift to New York?" Just like that! Would I give her a lift to New York! "You're blushing all over," she said.

"I don't doubt it."

"So will you?"

"You're not serious."

"I am, too! I'm dead serious."

"I'm not going to New York."

"So take me where you *are* going and just drop me off. I'm not asking you to take me home—is that what you're thinking?"

"I'm not thinking anything. Except maybe I'm kind of wondering what brought this on."

"What brought it on? You seen Dix, you heard him. It's like that every stinking day of my life, only usually worse. Oh, forget it. If you can't give me a lift, you can't." She turned away, and her hair brushed my face. "I still got a little pride left," she said. "So I'm going first. I've thought about this, believe me. It's not anything spur of the moment. If I don't go, he will, as soon as he gets that money. You bet he will! I just thought—since we kind of like the same singers."

When I didn't say anything, she said, "But it's okay, Uncle Charley, don't worry. I can take a bus. I came up here on a bus, I can leave the same way, and I will. Just don't think I'm a complete idiot," she said. "Just don't, because I'm not."

And that was that. I'd said no, and for once I'd stuck to it. But I'll tell you something. I sure felt lousy about it. So lousy, I knew if I stood there very much longer, I'd start wagging my head and sucking on my front teeth, chuckling spit, and going, We-e-e-ll. . . . So I just walked away. I gave a little shrug and just walked away. Why on earth I should've felt so lousy, though, was beyond me. Who was this Edith Dix, anyhow? Nobody in *my* life.

Leo was kneeling at the fireplace now—inside the hearth, if you can believe it, with half his scrawny body up the flue. I startled him, and he smacked his head on a blackened field rock. Before he turned around, he grabbed his Pep carton from the fender and, quick, jammed something into it. "Just a little piece of cement," he said. "It was loose." There were gray soot licks on both cheeks and along his jawline. "It was already loose," he said and blushed, looking guilty as sin. Then he glanced away, and the two of us watched the soft crown of Edith's hat disappear through the floor trap.

"Let's go," I said. "We're leaving."

"Uncle Charley?"

"What now?"

"Do you think it hurts when you get shot dead? Or do you think you don't feel anything?"

"Jesus H. Christ, Leo, how the heck should I know? Write the Answer Man!"

He screwed up his mouth and looked at the ceiling, then went on down the trap. And there I was, standing all by myself in the very room where a public enemy got his. Big deal! I only wondered who'd cleaned up the mess. Somebody had to. Somebody had to get out the mop. Somebody always has to get out the mop. I guess I felt sorry for the Englehardt sisters, whoever they were. I pulled the trapdoor closed behind me.

As soon as Leo and I came back outside, Edith snatched away the picket, and the lattice banged against the house. It was still

snowing. Without anybody saying a word, we all started back down
the hill, me first. But halfway down, my scalp tightened. Because
standing in the road was the big hero of Sussex County, himself.

"How's everybody?" said Dix, sounding much too jolly and clearly
still drunk. "All finished? Give 'em the grand tour, Edith? That's
so nice." He played with the mailbox flag, thumbing it up and down.
"I was worried about you, baby. Geez, I didn't know *where* you'd
went to. I'm real sorry if I hurt your feelings before. Honest. You're
a good singer, honey, I didn't mean to say you weren't."

"For Christ sakes," she said, "don't start, Ray."

They walked in silence ahead of Leo and me, the two of them
puffing on cigarettes. At the bund camp, Dix said, "So what do you
fellers think of this place? There used to be an amusement park
here. But that's been gone, must be eight, nine years. Then it was
just a private beach, now it's this." He pointed up at the handcarved
sign hanging by a wire over the gate: ZU DEM JUNGENLAGER. To
the children's camp. "It had a Ferris wheel and everything." He
crossed his arms over his chest, blandly surveying the parade ground
and barracks.

As he mused, Edith caught my eye. Her expression was sulky
and hostile, and I felt a pang of—something. Irritation? Pity? Something. Then Dix was saying, "These tats I got? See these?" He
pulled off a heavy glove. "This is where I got 'em. Right here, when
it was an amusement park. Every time I went home with a new
one, the old man knocked me flat on my ass. But I kept on going
back for more, you couldn't stop me. If you love how they look, you
love how they look," he said, dropping his cigarette and grinding
it out. "That's how I recognized Lester. From his tat. From his
tattooed heart. I got the same thing, different spot. Same thing,
don't I, Edith? But in a different spot."

She said, "His was nicer."

"Man burns off his fingerprints and leaves a tattoo. Is that smart?"
He winked at Leo. "That sound smart to you?"

Leo was noncommittal, pressing his lips together and fumbling a hand into his Pep carton. But I said, "If you love how they look, you love how they look," and Edith laughed.

Dix said, "What?"

"I'm just thinking maybe he couldn't stand to have it taken off. His tattoo, I mean. You love yours, he loved his, maybe."

"He could've had it changed into something else," said Dix, inspecting my face. Guaranteed, though, he didn't find a smirk there, not even a trace. I'm usually very careful. "A good tattoo man could turn a heart into a rose," he said, "or anything else. It was stupid, him leaving it there for anybody to see."

I said I guessed so, and he nodded several times, staring at Edith till she turned red in the face and finally struck off through the camp. Then he said, "Mrs. Dix is a very good singer. Really. She had a job singing with an orchestra once—she tell you? They played up here, couple summers ago, and we fell in love. What'd you do, you give her a lift?"

I said, "Well, she was standing out in the snow."

He pulled his glove back on. "I'm seeing you all over the place today. I seen you at Tacky's, right? And up at the newspaper. You work there?"

I shook my head. "Salesman."

"What, door to door?"

"Town to town."

"Boy always come with you?"

"No," I said. "This week is kind of special."

"I didn't know *where* she went. I looked all over Newton. I got worried." Then Dix didn't say anything else till we'd caught up with Edith on the lake. Then he said, "I never been a salesman, per se, but I done my share of traveling around. I been in maybe twenty states, all together. I like it. Edith don't. You get Edith talking about her traveling days, she goes a little crazy. She hates traveling."

"I never said that."

"Oh come on, Edith."

"I never said it."

"And not just once, either. You said it lots of times. You did.

Don't make me look foolish, Edith, honey." He shook his head, amazed, or more like it, pretending to be. "I know what you like and what you don't. I should! If I don't, who does? You like Connie Boswell, you like Elsie Carlisle, you're not so crazy about Dolly Dawn. Ruth Etting is a big phony, in your opinion. Am I right?"

"You're drunk," she said, and he slapped a hand to his chest, melodramatically.

"Now, hold on. Let's not get nasty, Edith. Hold on—this all started because suddenly you're telling these nice people that you like to travel. This is news to me. And I'm your husband. This is big news! Since when do you? Since when?"

"Ray, shut up. Please?"

"Ray, shut up, please?" he said, squeaking his voice. "You're drunk, Ray. You're this and that. Goddamn, Edith, I looked all over Newton for you. I'm sorry, honey, but I'm losing patience with you. I am."

"Fine. Lose patience. Just lose it quietly, okay?"

He gave her a long, slow look, letting his eyes move over her face. "You come up here so jittered you can't even walk a straight line. Miss Soda Wauters. You can't even sing your dopey songs, hardly. And you said—believe me, Edith—you said you couldn't take any more traveling around. I wish I had a witness. You said nix to any more traveling. And then you said you bet I was the man you could meet. First you said the one thing, then you said the other."

Edith's lips drew away from her teeth.

Dix looked at me. "Edith used to have this bit of business she'd do on stage. She'd kind of close her eyes. Almost like she was praying. Then she'd say, 'This is for the man I could meet,' and start to sing 'All I Do Is Dream of You.' It was nice. It was real nice. It was classy. If you got to know Edith better, she'd be telling you all about it. She tells everybody in pants. She even told Lester M. TenEyck. It was her trademark, is what it really was. 'This is for the man I could meet.' "

"Shut your mouth!"

"It ought to be a song by itself," said Dix. "Sounds like one already, don't it? The man I could meet? Lots of rhymes there, Edith. Sweet. Heat. Feet. Feet's a good one. He'll knock me off my feet. The man I could meet. I'm not drunk, Edith. Really, I'm not." He squared his shoulders. "But I'm trying to celebrate. I'm trying good and goddamn hard to celebrate!" He suddenly pointed a finger at Leo, who flinched and grabbed hold of my coat sleeve. "The governor of Illinois wrote me a very complimentary letter. And I bet you I get one from J. Edgar Hoover, too. Before Christmas, even. Now, there's the man I'd like to meet."

Whirling around, Edith walked off across the lake. Ray watched her go, his eyes drawn into slits. He pinched the skin at the bridge of his nose. "Don't anybody feel embarrassed," he said. "It's all right. This don't mean nothing." Then he cupped his hands around his mouth and shouted, "Treat! Sweet! *Cheat!*"

We left Dix there, mumbling and snuffling, and continued up the lake. Leo kept looking at me sidewise, like he expected me to say something. So finally I did. I said, "When you grow up, Leo, stick with soft drinks." It was the best I could do.

"I thought you were going to say don't ever get married."

"That's your business."

He lifted one shoulder in a half-shrug. Then, as we passed under the footbridge, heading in toward the Pink Elephant bar and that boat tie-up, he said, "Uncle Charley?" and pointed.

Edith Dix was climbing into the company Ford.

Well, you may laugh, but I didn't think it was funny. Not one tiny bit. I'd had more than my fill of these queer country fish, and when I got to the car, I told her as much—I used that very expression. "So get out," I said, yanking open the back door. "Right now."

"I wrote your stinking postcard," she said. "I showed you Lester's house. Be nice."

"Get out, Mrs. Dix."

"Oh, boy. That's worse than calling me a fish."

"Would you please get out?"

"I need a ride."

"No."

"Please?"

Leo tugged on my jacket. I looked around, and sure enough, Ray Dix was on his way over. "For the last time, Edith, will you please get out of there?"

"No. I'm fed up."

"*You're* fed up?"

"Well," said Dix. "Well, well."

"Would you kindly remove your wife from my car?"

He took a short step backwards, rubbing a hand all around his face. "Geez, I'm afraid if I try that, I might accidentally wring her stupid neck on purpose—you know?" But then he moved abruptly, shoving me aside and plunging at Edith with both arms stretched out, elbows locked, fingers scrabbling. She slapped at his face, and he grunted. "Then live in there!" he said. "I don't care. You're too fat, anyway! And you sing off key!"

I said, "Dix, if that's your best shot, I'll handle this myself, thank you."

He bent out of the sedan, and the next thing I knew, the monkey belted me right in the nose. Then he hit me again, that time in the shoulder, and he kept hitting me and calling me—get this—a son of a bitch bastard, till a piercing whistle stopped him cold. Then he cracked up laughing. "Jesus Christ," he said, "it's Dick Tracy!"

Leo spat out his G-man whistle, and plunged a hand into the Pep carton. With a great rustling of wheat flakes, he withdrew a small blue revolver. My nose was bleeding and I guess I was kind of slap-happy, and—well, it didn't dawn on me that it was anything but another one of his silly premiums. Not till he said, "My name is Leo Bender, cowbrain," and fired twice.

3

The Soda Wauters Story

"Up the flue," said Leo. "In the chimney. And can you *believe* those cops? What a bunch of townies! Who trained *them*? What'd it take me to find it, what? All of ten minutes? Every bad guy worth his *salt* keeps spare heat."

"I'll give you spare heat. Why in hell didn't you *say* something when you found it?"

"You would've made me put it back."

"Jesus Christ, you might've killed Mr. Dix! Are you mental or something?"

"Mental, you're mental! I didn't even *point* it at him."

"He's telling the truth, Uncle Charley. I seen everything."

"Edith, I'm not talking to you. And quit calling me Uncle Charley."

"I'm only saying I seen everything. *Charley*. The kid fired at the elephant."

"Sure, I did! What do you think I am, some big dope? You always give a couple of warning shots. It's standard police procedure. Except in the case of mad-dog killers. Then you just blaze away."

"You scared the man half to death!"

"Charley, you're talking about my husband. He's no mad-dog killer, okay, but don't make me laugh."

"Mrs. Dix, either you shut up right now, or I'm putting you out."

"*I* think you should be grateful, Uncle Charley. He was beating you up."

"You too, Leo Bender. Just shut up and let me drive this stupid car."

In Dover, I mailed Edith's postal card, then called at the *Afternoon Democrat*. But I didn't bother with any sales spiel. I still couldn't think straight—could you, with a loaded pistol stashed in your coat pocket? I just left a bottle of Ancient Age, shook some hands, and wished everybody a merry Christmas.

In the lobby, after I'd bought a package of Pepsin Beechies, I ducked into a telephone box, dialed the operator and told her I wanted an exchange at Sunburn Lake—the Pink Elephant restaurant and bar, please.

It rang seven, eight times, nine times. Come on, Dix—answer, you monkey! After twelve rings, I hung up, then called the *Morristown Advertiser* and canceled my appointment. The editor didn't seem let down.

When I got back to the car—I'd parked it just around the corner, for once—I found Edith sprawled out across the back seat, reading the Pep box. The daylight was poor, and she squinted. Leo was slumped against the front passenger door. And what a puss on him! What a sourpuss! You should've seen him earlier, though, right after Dix had taken off running across the parking circle. Leo had looked anything but surly then. His mouth had split into a grin so wide that half an inch of pink gums showed all around. Smug, I can tell you. Downright smug. I could've clouted the stinker. He said now, "Are you ever gonna gimme back my gun, or what?"

"*Your* gun."

"Yeah, mine. I found it! And I saved your skin! I was saving your life!"

"I'm sure Uncle Charley appreciates that, Leo," said Edith. "He's just a little upset."

I said, "Mrs. Dix? That'll be enough from you."

On the way out of town, I stopped at a gasoline station for a fillup, which entitled me to my choice of either a five-pack of razor blades or a *Skippy* comic book. I took the *Skippy*, as a peace token to Leo, but he only gave me another withering stare and tossed it behind him, into the rear footwell. "We're not bothering with Morristown," I said. "We're going straight home. Okay?"

"Anything you want," said Edith. Then she said, "Do you handle *Skippy*, too?" She'd picked up the comic book and was flipping through it. "I can never understand the jokes. But maybe I'm dense."

"And you I'm dropping off in Newark," I said. "You can take the Hudson Tubes. If you want to go to Manhattan."

"Whatever you say, Uncle Charley."

It was still snowing, and I mean really snowing. It was half-dark already, and there was slush in the road. Twice on the way home the Ford went into a long skid. My eyes burned and I had a splitting headache, and my nose throbbed and my stomach was churning—and, well, I don't want to sound like a big bellyacher. But it was a rotten trip. It was one very crummy trip.

As we were coming down South Orange Avenue, Leo twisted around in his seat and looked at Edith. "You could probably send your story to *True Detective*," he said. "Lady? You could probably write up your story and send it in." I caught her startled expression in the rearview mirror. "I don't guess he ever told you anything about his bank jobs—did he?"

"Lester? You got to understand, honey, I didn't know the man as Lester TenEyck. He was always Harry Spangler to me. It's what he called himself. And he said he was a, I forget what he said he was. A welder. A tool-and-die worker. Something like that. But on the bum."

Leo said, "Harry Spangler? That's a new one. That's a new alias. I never heard that one before. George Comstock he used a lot. And Fred Mitchell. Alex Williams."

"Harry Spangler," said Edith, "from Columbus, Ohio. That's what he said. That's who he was."

"Was he friendly?"

I said, "Leo, enough. You're too nosy to live."

"Oh, I guess you could say he was friendly," said Edith. "He was a little crude in his speech, but he was all right. He was courteous. He'd come around every afternoon, we'd talk a little. My husband kept telling me to quit blabbing, or else make him buy something more than a sandwich."

"White bread?"

"White bread," said Edith. "Toasted, sometimes."

We got to Newark a few minutes after five, and the downtown traffic was a purgatory. Red, green, white and blue lights glowed in the big department stores. The trees in Military Park were decorated for the holidays. A harness cop blew his whistle, hailing me through an intersection, Broad Street and Raymond Boulevard.

"Penn Station's right up here. Mrs. Dix?" We were stopped again, so I hitched around and looked at her. She was in another world. I could've passed my hand in front of her face, she wouldn't've blinked. "You feeling okay? Do you want to call your husband? If you've changed your mind, I can't drive you back."

"Call my husband?" she said, snapping out of it. "I left him, remember?"

"It just crossed my mind that you might want to call. See how he is. See if there's a warrant out for Leo's arrest."

I pulled to the curb in a No Standing zone across from Penn Station and set the hand brake. Edith handed Leo back his cereal box, and I jumped out and opened her door.

"You're a gentleman, Uncle Charley."

"Do you know where you're going?"

"The Hudson Tubes, you already said."

"No, I mean—after. You have some friends?"

"I'll get on. I know my way around. You're looking at me funny."

"Edith, you don't even have a suitcase!"

"You never just walked away from something?"

"No," I said, "I guess I never did."

"Well, it's not the end of the world. It's never the end of the world, Uncle Charley."

"Well, good," I said, "very good," and stuck out my hand. I know a man isn't supposed to offer a woman his hand to shake, unless she first offers hers. I know that, but I did it anyway. So what? Edith didn't seem to mind.

"Thanks a lot," she said. "And take it easy." I nodded, but then watching her trudge away down Raymond Boulevard, I suddenly felt—it's hard to describe, exactly. Disappointed, I think. I'm just telling you what I think I felt. I think I felt disappointed. But about what I couldn't say. After Edith had crossed Raymond Plaza and gone into the station, I slid back under the wheel.

"So," I said, "let's go buy some fish, shall we?"

With a hand mechanically dipping into his cereal box, Leo stared at me in disgust. Then he looked startled, plucked out a five-dollar bill and said, "Uncle Charley!" Then he said, "Hey! Where're you going? Gimme that! Uncle Charley!"

Edith hadn't gotten far. I caught up to her in the main lobby. She was reading a wall poster advertising Rudy Vallee on the radio, and didn't seem all that surprised to see me.

"We can't accept this," I said. A colored shoeshine man and his customer watched me wave the bill around.

"You gave me a lift."

"You wrote a postcard. Take it back, please. You'll need it."

"I'm not broke," she said. "I always carry a few bucks." Then she lightly touched my arm and said, "Listen. At the moment I can't think of anybody in New York I could stay with tonight. Can you recommend a decent hotel? Not too expensive."

I hesitated, but finally said, "Oh, for goodness' sake, stay with us tonight. It's snowing. I'll run you back here in the morning."

"I like you, Uncle Charley," she said. "You can take a hint."

"We're having flounder."

"You already told me—fried."

"It's how I always make it."

"Well, baked, I think, is better. But you're the chef." Almost as an afterthought, she took back the fin.

Leo was standing alongside the car when we came across the street together. He held the door open for Edith, like a chauffeur, and like a chauffeur, he closed it gently behind her. Then he looked peevishly at me over the roof. Then something distracted him, a loud noise, a bus, and he glanced away. The woman had no place to stay. It was a week till Christmas. It was Christmas time. We liked the same singers. Oh, I don't know.

Down Neck, I stopped at a fish market and bought the flounder, then ran across the avenue and into a grocery store for half-a-dozen eggs, a handful of string beans, a bag of yellow cornmeal and a stick of butter. On the way out, I noticed a phone box, and, after a moment's hesitation, went in, sat down, and called Dix. That time he answered on the third ring.

"Mr. Dix?" I said. "It's Charley Kackle."

"Who?"

"Charley Kackle? We met this afternoon? I have your wife in my car?"

"Jesus," he said, "you have your crust, calling me. So what do you want?"

"I guess just to explain about my nephew. He was only trying to protect me. His mother's in Texas."

"Texas? What the hell is that supposed to mean? Where'd he get the gun?"

"Where do you suppose?"

"At the house? Really? It's Lester's?"

"Listen, you haven't called the police or anything, have you? Because I should warn you, if you press charges, I'll do the same thing. You could've broken my nose."

"Fuck your nose."

"Mr. Dix, this is all your fault. Do you think I want your wife? What am I supposed to do with her?"

"She want to come home?"

"It doesn't seem that she does."

"So what am I supposed to do, then?"

"What do you mean, what're you supposed to do? She's your wife. She's your responsibility."

Then he said, "About that gun. Would you be interested in selling it? Twenty bucks," he said, "and I'll even take Edith off your hands."

I hung up, thinking that maybe Dotty was right about shiftless men. They got national purpose over there, Charley. And what do we got?

When we arrived at Dotty's house, it was ten to six. I could see Leo's jaw go rigid, also his posture. He was wondering, of course, whether his mother was home. Me, too, but since there were no lights on upstairs, I was pretty certain that she wasn't. But what if she was? What would she think when I walked in with a two-hundred-pound woman? A singer who'd left her husband because he'd shouted rhyme words at her? She'd think I'd lost my wits, that's what. And she'd tease me the first time she cornered me alone. I almost hoped—I *did* hope, God forgive me—that she was still gallivanting around Texas, or wherever, with what's-his-name. Posty.

Coming in, I called hello, then switched on the kitchen light. Nobody'd been there since we'd left on Tuesday—my note was still on the table, propped against a milk bottle. I went into the parlor, tossed my coat on the sofa, turned on a couple of pole lamps and the space heater. Then I stuck the gun into an old vase of my mother's in the china closet, and walked back to the kitchen, sorting through the mail I'd brought up from downstairs. Several bills, a radio premium, the diocesan newspaper, and two deckle-edged picture postcards.

The postcard with the diamondback rattlesnake on the front said, "The weather is crummy. See you soon. Love, D." The other one—the one with a half-dozen red-cheeked couples in cowboy hats dancing on a flagstone patio—said, "Beautiful here, but lots of bugs. Bought Leo a loaf of Mickey Mouse white bread. Never saw it before. Love Dot/Mom."

"Leo," I said, "these are from your mother." He was busy shaking a rocket badge from a padded brown envelope. "Leo?"

Finally taking the cards, he glanced briefly at both messages. Then he wrinkled his forehead. Then, without saying a word, he picked up his suitcase—actually, his G-man portable crime lab—

and walked off to his bedroom. "Edith," I said, "I'll be right back. Excuse me."

I went across the parlor and stood in Leo's doorway, watching him open a National shoe box. The tip of his tongue poked out one side of his mouth. He put the lid down on his desk and scooped up a double handful of badges and whistles, cowboy spurs, signet rings, scarab rings, pedometers. "Everything still there?" I said.

He clapped the lid back on. "I don't think she's coming back."

"She bought you a loaf of bread! Jesus Christ, Leo, would she buy you a goddamn special loaf of bread if she wasn't coming home?"

"I don't want her stinking special loaf of bread."

"She thinks she's doing you a favor—you like Mickey Mouse."

He glared at me, and I wasn't in any mood to be glared at, so I said, "I'll start dinner," and turned to go. But then I stopped, noticing the rogues gallery on Leo's wall.

"Lester is there," he said. "On the left, beside that picture with all the circled heads."

I went over and looked. It was an FBI poster with two blurry photos of TenEyck, one profile, the other full face. Wanted for general depredation, banditry and the murder of this guy, that guy and a special agent. Five thousand for the capture of, three thousand for information leading to his arrest. I leaned closer and read the tiny print. Alias George Comstock. Alias Fred Mitchell, Alex Williams, Dick Idris. But no alias Harry Spangler. Leo had been right. Harry Spangler was a new one. Age, thirty-one. Height, five feet, eight and a half inches. Weight, one hundred seventy. Distinguishing marks, acne scars and a tattooed heart. Nationality, American.

"*There's* your cowbrain," I said.

"Yeah? Well, at least he had some guts."

"Guts," I said, "aren't everything." Then I said, "I'll call you when supper's ready."

"How long is *she* gonna stay?"

"Just overnight."

Leo said, "Yeah? I heard that one before."

Edith had already unwrapped the fillets, dipped them in egg and rolled them in cornmeal. I cut the ends off the string beans and threw them into a pot. Then once the fish were in the pan and frying, I said, "Is it possible your husband might call the cops? I mean, on account of the gun?"

"No, it's not possible."

"Really?"

"He wouldn't do that."

"He could make trouble for me, though. If he was to call up King Features, say, and tell them—whatever he felt like telling them. If he was to call up my boss—well!" I sat down, feeling groggy. "Maybe I could explain things. I probably could. But maybe not." With my elbows on the back of the chair, I watched her poke at the fish, then lower the flame under the beans. "I like what I do," I said, "I just wish I didn't have to drive so much. Three hours driving, fifteen minutes with a client. Then right back in the car again. Man whose territory I took died suddenly and there was a lot of scrambling around, lot of confusion, and I said, I'll take the route, and they said, no, you wouldn't stick with it, it's too far. I said, no, it really wasn't, I could do it. I wanted to make a good impression. You want to impress people these days. And it's a lot of driving, but it sure beats respotting pins. It sure beats hopping bells. Best job I ever had. Which I guess isn't saying much. But I do it all right. I get tired. Every week, of course, I don't have to go the same distance. I have shorter swings. I have some parts of New Jersey. I have two routes combined."

She was staring at me in open amazement. My face turned warm, and I said, "It's not a bad job."

"You got a very nice speaking voice, Uncle Charley. You could be in radio." When I laughed, she insisted, "You could so. You absolutely could so." She picked up a fork and lifted the fish from the skillet, laying the pieces neatly on a plate. "You can even be my announcer when I get a national sponsor. If you want it, the job's yours."

"Well, I'd kind of like to keep the job I have, is what I guess I've been trying to say."

"Oh, don't worry. He won't get you fired," she said, finally sitting down. "I'm sure he's glad to be rid of me. And besides," she said, "there's no reward."

At the supper table, there was hardly any conversation—Edith just remarked, once again, that she preferred her flounder baked, and Leo said that he preferred his uncaught. But he made good on his promise, and ate two fillets. All through the meal, he kept sneaking glances at Edith, his mouth open, his expression cranky and scornful. Once he'd finished, he pushed away his plate, wiped his mouth, excused himself and left.

"Edith, should I make coffee?"

"Yeah, that'd be good," she said. Then she said, "Charley? This sounds dumb, but I'm scared to death that my eyeglasses aren't in my bag. I just thought of it. If they're not, I'm sunk."

"Why don't you look?"

"I'm afraid to."

"I think you should look."

"Will you look for me?" She pointed to her dice-grained bag leaning against the foot of the radiator. "Please?"

So I did. I got up from the table and got her bag and snapped it open, and what a jumble there was inside! Kleenex and chocolate-bar wrappers, lipsticks, chiffon hankies, candy-coated chewing gum tablets, a plaid scarf, *two* plaid scarves, a change purse, and, way down deep, an eyeglass case, the hard kind. When I showed it to her, Edith sighed like a small child, then laughed. "I couldn't read a thing," she said. "I'd get headaches."

"Well, now you don't have to worry," I told her.

"That ever happen to you, your stomach just drops?"

"Very rarely."

A few minutes later, we carried our coffee cups into the parlor, where Leo was squatted in front of the cabinet radio, tuning it fitfully, jumping the needle up and down the lighted dial. He settled for a program of Christmas carols, by what sounded like a boys' choir, then sat Indian fashion on the carpet with his shoe box of premiums on his lap. "Oh, I remember that," said Edith, about a small pirate die cut that he'd just taken out. "It came in Wheaties."

He nodded glumly, identifying it as a pawn for the Smuggler's Cove game.

"And what're those?"

"My decoders," he said, loosening up. "This is the 1934 Radio Derby Dugan Secret Society Pin. The 1935 pin. And this is the new one, with a hidden compartment. And these are my Orphan Annies. These are Dr. Huer's Invisible Ink Crystals. They really work. And this is the Radio Derby Dugan Cocoatine Mug." Then I guess he remembered he was supposed to be out of sorts and threw everything back in the box.

"I was on the radio once," said Edith, settling down on the sofa. "I was interviewed on the radio. The program was sponsored by Pall Mall cigarettes. It was a classy show, a lot of people listened. Thousands of people. I sat there at the microphone smoking Lucky Strikes." She grunted at the sheer audacity of it. "The announcer smoked Luckies, too. He'd be advertising Pall Malls and meanwhile he'd be puffing away on a Lucky. I was interviewed along with a gossip columnist from a daily newspaper. Both men kept asking me if the rumors were true."

Leo said, "What rumors?"

She waved her right hand in a languid arc. "Oh, I was supposed to be romantically linked with a famous actor."

"Who, which actor?" he asked, belligerent as Mr. D.A., and I said, "Leo, they were only rumors. Mrs. Dix just told you that."

"Those radio microphones are big," she said. "They're as big around as cereal bowls."

"Leo wants to get into radio," I said. "That's what he wants to do."

"*Maybe* I do."

"It's a good field," said Edith. "Not that I know beans about it."

"He wants to write the programs."

"There you got me again. I don't know anything about writers, except aren't they pretty gloomy, though? You gloomy enough, Leo?"

"Well, I'd say he's gloomy enough. And he has a very good vocabulary," I said. "He's always getting hundreds in English."

I was trying to pay him a compliment, but holy mother of God, you should've seen how his eyes blazed—he was furious. Twisting a rubber band around his decoder cards and tossing the cards into his shoe box, he got up and stormed off into the kitchen. Half a minute later, he reappeared. "There's not even a cookie in this dumb place!" Then bang! into his room.

I looked at Edith and gave a little shrug. "His mother's in Texas."

"Of all places! Where's his father?"

"Timbuktu."

"So you're the breadwinner?"

"I guess you could say that."

"You and Winnie Winkle."

"Me and Winnie Winkle, right."

"What's in Texas?"

"Nothing's in Texas. This was supposedly an elopement. But I hope it's only a trip."

"You ever been married, Charley?"

"No."

"No?"

"Never."

"With Ray was my third time. And two other times I might as well have been. All that love, and here I am spending the night with strangers in Newark. No offense intended."

"Or taken," I said, and we both shut up and listened to carols on the radio. I kept waiting for "Silent Night," but they didn't sing it. That was disappointing. Every so often, I'd hear some mumbling and thumping through the bedroom wall, and wonder if the Leo Bender Program was under way.

"You're like his guardian, then."

"I'm his uncle."

"I mean practically speaking."

"Most of the time I don't live here, you know."

"I was brought up by my aunt. From the time I was eleven. I wasn't orphaned or anything. I just couldn't get on with my mother. We fought like sisters."

"You left your *parents*?"

"My mother, just. My dad left us both, long before that. You must think all I *do* is cut and run, is that what you think, Uncle Charley?"

I said, "You called your father Dad?"

She didn't reply, but leaned forward, clearing her throat. Then, raising her eyes, her expression turning thoughtful, sentimental, she sang, "My dear old Aunt Harriet, somewhere in heaven she may be, send me down your sweet chariot . . ." She broke off, laughing, her cheeks pink. "Her name really was Harriet. I had an aunt named Harriet. She paid for my singing lessons. Whenever I sang 'I Got My Captain Working for Me Now,' I put her in stitches."

Edith cocked her head, musing. A few moments later, she said, "I made a big mistake, marrying Dix. There was never any real chemistry there, just biology, and even that was on the high school level." She looked at me and smiled, and I smiled back. "I was in a bad way, though, when I met him. After fourteen months on a bus? I could be standing perfectly still, but it felt like I was moving. It was a trick of the blood, but it felt so real, Uncle Charley, so real that I had to hold onto something or else I'd be gone. I was sure I'd be gone. And when I was in bed? Or even on stage? The same thing, the same, same thing. Only then it felt like the whole stage was moving, every board, or the whole bed, like it was going to roll right out of that motor cabin, right out of that stinking Moose Hall, and just keep going. You understand."

"There's probably a name for that."

"There probably is—I could look it up. It's some condition."

"It might even be your ears."

"My ears?"

"It could be a balance problem. But I don't know."

"I'm perfectly balanced, Uncle Charley. It was a trick of the blood, that's all. You ever feel it, what I'm talking about?"

"I don't think so. But with me, I don't go so far, and I don't keep going. It's I go and I come back, and then I go again."

"Fourteen months straight. Almost fifteen."

"You could probably look it up in a medical book, like you say. That feeling. Maybe it's even called travel sickness."

"No, that's different. But I don't have it anymore, so it's moot. The whole thing is moot. Dix was good for something, at least. He cured me of that, at least." Then she stroked the sofa cushion beside her and said, "Why don't you come over here, Uncle Charley? I think we should keep our voices down."

"Why?" I said, suddenly alarmed. "What do you want to talk about?"

"Just come sit. There's room. I'm not so fat you can't squeeze in."

"You're not fat at all," I said. Then I went over and sat beside her, my thigh touching hers. I guess I looked a little suspicious, though, because right away she laughed again, reaching for my left hand and pressing it. "Thanks a lot," she said in a whisper. "Really, thanks a lot. You're a nice guy, Uncle Charley. You're a lifesaver."

"I'm not a lifesaver," I said, and then she kissed me on the mouth. I hadn't been up that close to another person's face since—since, I really couldn't remember when. Her pupils became small by contraction. There was the tiniest filament wart on her left eyelid. I tried to pull away, but she wouldn't let go of my hand, not immediately. "I'm only saying thank you," she said.

"Well, you're very welcome." I got up and collected our cups and saucers.

"You think I'm an awful person."

"That's not true."

"Well, I am! You know what I was thinking, actually thinking, just this morning? Before I saw you in that newspaper office? I was thinking I could stick around till Dix got his money and then I could run him over with the car. Make it look like an accident, you know? Wait till he got good and drunk, then run him over with the car some night. What do you think of that, Uncle Charley?"

"It's been done before. And they gave her the electric chair."

"They sure did."

"Eva Coo."

"Eva Coo," said Edith. "Eva Coo. With three thousand bucks, though, I could put together a nice little band. Lots of musicians out of work."

"Lots of everybody out of work. Including me, if your husband decides to make a stink."

"You hear what I been saying?"

"I heard."

"I'm just trying to tell you the kind of woman I am."

I nodded.

"So what do you think of me now?"

"I think you're full of beans."

She threw her head back and laughed. "Well, it's better than being full of baloney." Then she picked at the slipcover on the arm of the sofa and, pressing it between her thumb and first finger, made a little pleat. "He'd be all right," she said, "Dix would, if he wasn't basically such a nasty human being."

I nodded again, then went and rinsed the cups and saucers. When I returned, Edith was fiddling with the radio dial. Over the blat of stations, she said, "Is there anything special you want to listen to? I'm just slumming." She found a comedy program with raucous studio laughter, and left it. "Or maybe we could play records? Your sister has a very nice electric phonograph," she said, sitting back down and putting up her feet again. "I was just admiring it."

"Do whatever you like," I said, and looked out the window, into the backyard. There was six inches of snow on the flat garage roofs. A dog in the alley was standing on its hind legs, front paws against a trash barrel, rooting for scraps.

"Still coming down?"

"Yeah. But the flakes are pretty big now," I said. "It'll stop soon."

"When the flakes are big, that means it's going to stop? I thought it was just the opposite."

I said, "No," letting the curtain drop, and when I turned back into the room, Edith's mouth was quirked up.

"I'm trying to decide if I should tell you something," she said. There was a longish pause, then she said, "Just now I had this funny thought. Ready? That you and me, that me and you are just the types to get the electric chair. Couldn't you just see us both on page three? The fat canary and the traveling salesman?" I stared at her. "Your expression is priceless. It was only a thought! What, you never had crazy thoughts? I'm not saying we should *do* anything to get the electric chair, but just *suppose* we did, we'd get caught in a day. Don't you think?"

I said, "Yeah, I think. I definitely think so," and she nodded. Then she put on her glasses and bent over the end table, sorting through Dotty's magazines. She picked out a *Screenland*, and I put a recording on the phonograph.

"Connie Boswell? Your sister likes Connie Boswell? Well, she can't be all bad."

Edith listened to one torchy ballad after another with her eyes closed and her head back against the bolster, a sad, dreamy smile on her mouth. When the needle started lisping in the leadout groove, I got up to change it, and she said, "That girl can really break your heart. Can't she? Can't she?"

"She can," I said.

Leo never reappeared, and Edith flipped through a stack of romance pulps, and I kept yawning and dozing. Finally, around ten, I told her, "You can have Dotty's room."

"Oh, I'll take the sofa, Charley, it's fine."

"Don't be silly. You'll take her bed and that's that."

"She isn't by some chance a size fourteen-and-a-half, is she?"

"No, but I can lend you one of my nightshirts."

Edith said, "Oh brother."

While she was using the bathroom, I took out a couple of nightshirts from my valise and tossed one across the foot of my sister's bed. I grabbed the picture of Hitler from the nightstand and threw it in a dresser drawer. Then I found a set of sheets, a pillow case and a blanket on the top shelf in the closet. When Edith came back out, patting her face dry with a towel, I'd already made up the sofa for myself and was turning off the parlor lights. The neckline of her sweater was damp. "I used one of the toothbrushes in there," she said. "I hope that's okay. I promise I don't have pink gum."

"I put out that nightshirt. It's on your bed."

"Well, then. I'm set." She glanced toward the bedroom. "So. Good night, then, Charley."

"Good night," I said, and, after grabbing a fresh towel from the linen closet, stepped into the bathroom and shut the door. I examined my face in the mirror, rubbing a palm across one cheek. I didn't much feel like shaving, but I thought, oh, maybe I should. It was always easier to fall asleep when I didn't feel so—bristly. You know? But as I was reaching down a safety razor from the medicine cabinet—Dotty always had a few on hand—my heart started to flutter, then to race. It took my breath for a moment. Bending forward, I gripped the sink basin. Those sorts of things— those speed-ups, extra beats, sudden jumps in my chest—had been happening more and more frequently, every other day, sometimes. Well, I'd had coffee, maybe that was it. Shaving, I decided, was probably a bad idea. So I skipped it and just washed my face, then dropped my trousers and gave my lower parts a cursory swipe with a soapy facecloth.

Once I'd changed into my nightshirt, I went out and checked on the boy manhunter. He was sound asleep, or pretending to be. Dotty's bedroom door was closed, but not entirely. Edith still had a light on.

At last I got settled, but instead of falling asleep I kept remembering Leo in that ridiculous straw hat, and Edith writing out my postcard. *Let him think he's got a desperate woman on his hands.* Then I was thinking about Dix showing me his tattoos, and about Dix on the ice—*feet! heat! cheat!*—and about Leo drawing that revolver from his cereal box. Two shots that echoed. God in heaven!

Then suddenly I felt a sharp twinge in my shoulder. And I thought, Not shingles again, please! Miserable things! My father, shortly before he died, had had the same business. A line of red blisters following the path of a nerve. *Mizable tings!* He'd believed it was caused, like ulcers were caused, by catastrophe and persecution. So I'd always believed that, too, until last summer, when my doctor had set me straight. *Nonsense, Mr. Kackle, it's strictly a viral infection.*

And then I was remembering the time during the war when Hamburg Place, our street, had been rechristened Wilson Avenue, remembering my father making me sit and write, in good public-school English, his letter of protest to the Newark *Evening News*. *Don't mail it!* I'd pleaded. *Don't mail it, Papa.* I was fifteen, ashamed of his accent—like der Captain's in the "Katzenjammer Kids"— and appalled by his allegiance. At school, where my classmates and I were urged daily to collect scrap and to contribute peach stones for use in Allied gas masks, I'd told everybody they should call me Charley—not Karl!—and that Kackle was Anglo-Saxon, English. *Please don't, Papa. Don't mail it.* But he did, reckless man, and three weeks later he was arrested at his barbershop by agents of the Secret Service, then detained in Hoboken for almost a month on suspicion of being a saboteur for the Hun. A saboteur! Well, it had been his own stupid fault. I'd warned him. Keep a low profile. Mind your own business, you're an American now. *Als man dies im Dorf erfuhr, war von Trauer keine Spur. . . .*

Dotty's bedroom door opened, and Edith's big silhouette filled the jamb. "It was only a stupid thought," she said in a loud whisper. "I wasn't serious before."

"I didn't imagine you were."

"I'd never run Dix over with a car. I'm too chicken."

I sat up and said, "Sure, I know that."

"I think I'd scream like crazy, if they ever put me in the electric chair."

"But you know what I hear? They slip a little dope in your last meal, so it's not so hard. It's what they did for Eva Coo. Slipped her a little dope."

Edith came across the floor—she was still fully dressed—and sat in the chair opposite the sofa. I asked her if she wanted to smoke a cigarette, since we were both wide awake. "Yeah, sure," she said.

Then she said, "Charley, I don't guess you believe in ghosts, do you?"

"I guess I don't." Ghosts?

"It don't matter. Most men don't. I guess most men are about the same, regarding ghosts. Ray don't. Believe, I mean. But I can tell you, Charley, there are such things. There really and truly are such things. I saw one—for three solid years. You remember I told you about my Aunt Harriet? It was hers."

"Maybe we should put the light on," I said, and she laughed. Then I lit her cigarette and mine.

"When she died, I was by myself," said Edith. "I wasn't going back to Champagne," she said. "I was only seventeen, but I figured I could get on all right by myself. And I did. I found a waitress job at this restaurant, and every night when I opened my front door to go out to work? There she was. Always dressed for winter, no matter what season it was. Had her big boots on and a beret sort of hat. And it wasn't like she died in those clothes, either. She died in a hospital bed. It wasn't even winter when she died. It was May."

"Edith—"

"Hold on till I finish. She'd walk me to the streetcar. And later on she was there when I got out of work. To walk me back. This was every single night, Charley. She was still taking care of me, in her own way. I don't tell this story to everybody, don't get that idea. I almost told it on that radio program, but I stopped myself in time."

"Probably a good idea," I said.

"It wasn't scary, it was my aunt, why should I be scared? But she never said anything, and of course I never did, either. I mean, I'd be talking to myself as far as anybody on the street was concerned. And they put you in the loony bin for that. Nobody could see Aunt Harriet but me. She never talked, either, except once. And that was the last time she walked me to the streetcar. She said, 'There's a man you could meet, he'll make you happy. You could meet him,' she said, 'or you could miss him. But if you miss him, Edith, you're in for big trouble, my girl.' That's it, word for word.

"I was singing at weddings by then, on weekends, mostly. A few extra bucks here and there. I'd made friends with some musicians. Here, use my ashtray. And one of them had told me about a rent party where there'd be jazz music and he said I could go. I decided to. Well, I got out of work after midnight, and there's Aunty, like always. She walks me to the streetcar, I can see it coming, and that's when she told me about the man I could meet. There was nobody else around, thank God. Because I said, 'Who's this man?' But she didn't answer me, and I got on the streetcar, but then I got off again ten blocks later, a mile from where I lived. And I went to that party, and I met a fella there. I ended up going home with him, and later we got married. For six months I was sure he was the man that Aunt Harriet meant. He played cornet. He probably still does, but I've lost track of him."

My eyes had grown accustomed to the dark, and I could see Edith crush out her cigarette, then fold her arms on top of her head, elbows jutting like wings.

"So that's what that was all about," she said. "The stuff about the man I could meet. He's right, though. Dix is. It could make a terrific song."

"It could."

"If this was a movie, Charley, we could compose it right now. We'd get it in a Broadway show. I'd sing it. We'd be the toast of the town."

"I don't have a piano, Edith."

"You crack me up!"

"I'm a funny guy?"

"Don't you think you're funny? At all?"

"I guess. I can be a wiseguy. But not so much lately. These days, I'm a little worried about what happens to me if my sister don't come back."

"Would she do that? What's she like?"

"I don't feel like talking about Dotty, if that's all right with you." I'd already rubbed out my smoke, and drawn up my legs and covered myself with the blanket. "I guess I really don't feel much like talking at all."

Edith stood up. We liked the same singers, we both could take a hint. "I just wanted you to know I was only kidding around," she said. "That's all. Sometimes I give the wrong impression. I wasn't *really* saying we should kill Dix for his money."

After she'd gone back to the bedroom, I turned on a light and started reading a Cisco Kid reprint in one of Dotty's slicks. I put it aside, though, to get up and open the china closet and take out the big vase of my mother's. It was a heavy thing, with kind of a woozy garden scene painted on it, like a storybook garden, everything lush and pretty and soft at the edges. When I was a kid, I used to—all right, it's pretty silly, but I used to make believe I could shrink myself down and step right into that garden, walk around, nobody to bother me, all by myself. Karl in wonderland. On the bottom it said Made in Bavaria.

I stuck a hand in and lifted out the pistol, taking care that no finger went near the trigger. I was figuring to empty out the bullets, but I picked and picked at the loading gate and it just wouldn't open. So finally I gave it up and sat back down on the sofa, and imagined myself strolling into a bank to rob it. What do you do, I thought, do you bring a note, or do you just say what you want? And then I thought, My luck, there'd be a long line at every single teller—housewives in crest hats waiting to pay the mortgage. I'd probably turn right around and go. The heck with it! If there's one thing I can't tolerate, it's standing on a slow line. That drives me nuts. I chew my cuticles and later they sting like blazes. . . .

"Edith?" I'd turned off the lamp again, put on my robe and crossed the parlor. "Are you still awake?"

"What's the matter?"

"Nothing," I said. "It's just—did you want to get an early start in the morning? Or should I let you sleep?"

She didn't answer.

Then I said, "I didn't mean to cut you off like that before. I was rude. If you still want to talk, it's okay. Edith?"

I pushed open the door, felt my way inside, touched the bureau, found the clothes chair and sat down. It was pitch black. We didn't say anything for a couple of minutes, maybe even as many as five.

It sure seemed a long time. And I was on the verge of being sore at Edith. I mean, all day long she don't shut up, now she does. Finally, I said, "I'm pretty worried about what the two of us are going to do, me and Leo, if she don't come back. Though she *did* say there were a lot of bugs. Dotty can't stand bugs."

"Who can?"

"Why do we care for people we don't even like, I ask you. Why do we even *talk* to them, much less look out for them?"

"It's not everybody. Everybody's not like that, Charley. Take myself. When I don't like somebody, *really* don't like him, I just leave. Vamoose."

"I've thought of going to California," I said. "I mean, actually *moving* out there."

"Jack Benny broadcasts from California. Edgar Bergen, Charley McCarthy. On second thought, I'm not so sure about Edgar Bergen. When I think of California, I think of girls in cuffed white shorts. Don't you?"

"Ever been there?"

"No. Oh no. That's just the picture I get. Girls in white shorts. You *were* thinking of moving out there? Or you still are?"

"Well, I keep postponing it. I could probably get a job with the Hearst outfit in San Francisco. Probably."

"San Francisco. I was thinking of Los Angeles. So why don't you do it?"

"Dotty might starve to death. Family is murder, Edith."

"Family and everything else."

"But if I ever *did* move to California, I'd just sell what I have. Take one suitcase and go."

"By train? I wouldn't mind that. I could stand that."

I said, "She's bringing us home a stinking loaf of special bread. Can you imagine how stale it's going to be?"

"I can't figure you out, Charley. I can't figure out if you're shy or maybe you don't like fatties, maybe. Or, maybe, I don't know, maybe you think I'm the worst person in the whole world. Say something," she said. "Interrupt me."

"The thing is, Edith, I'm starting to feel like somebody in a traveling salesman joke."

She switched on the lamp. She'd gone to bed in her corset and Valkyrie brassiere. The nightshirt was still lying across the foot of the bed. "Thanks a lot," she said.

"See? See that? You were talking about your husband being so nasty. Well, I have a lot of potential there, myself. I could turn out to be the kind of guy that'd take some kid's pinkball when it bounced on his lawn."

"Not you, Charley."

"I could end up with a whole drawerful of pinkballs."

She fixed me with a puzzled frown, then smiled. "Somebody in a traveling salesman joke? Really?"

"Or in a crime magazine, for that matter," I said, picking up the gun from my lap. "The kind of guy, couple years down the road, you'll feel like running over some night with a car."

Edith looked at me, and I looked at her, and we cocked our heads to opposite sides. "So what're you saying, Charley, you really don't think you're the man I could meet? There's not even a remote chance?"

"I noticed she didn't sign Posty's name to either card."

Edith grunted, and switched off the lamp, and I saw her bulk slide down in the bed. The bedsprings whined as she turned over. "You know something, Uncle Charley?" she said. "You're lucky. You're a very lucky man. You got your family. I only got myself to blame."

I don't know why I didn't get up and leave then, but I didn't. I just sat where I was, tapping the gun barrel against my front teeth. I felt content, and comfortable, and didn't bother going back out to the sofa. Eventually, thinking about Edith's Aunt Harriet, I fell asleep in the chair.

It was still dark when the telephone rang. At first, I thought I'd let it ring till it stopped, but it didn't stop, and finally I got up.

Coming out of Dotty's room, I collided with Leo—we bounced off each other, then just stood there for a moment in front of the

bathroom, staring at each other in surprise. By the time I reached
the phone, the bell had stopped. "Maybe that was Mom," Leo said,
like he was accusing me of something. Then the phone rang again.
Numb with anxiety, I lifted the receiver off the hook.

"Harold?" said a man's breathless voice. "Put Ruth on. It's
mother. She died. Harold, did you hear what I said? Get Ruth."

"This isn't Harold," I said. "You've dialed the wrong number."

"Oh, Jesus Christ," said the man. "Jesus holy Christ."

"But I'm very sorry for your loss."

"It was so sudden! Totally unexpected. She's not even sixty-five.
She wasn't even ill. She was fine at supper. And my daughter is
supposed to get married the seventh of January."

"I'm so sorry."

"I suppose we can't have the wedding. What's the right thing to
do? I suppose we can't."

"I suppose not," I said. "But don't worry about that now—just
call Ruth and tell her."

"Do you know Ruth?"

"No—but that's who you said. You said you wanted Ruth."

"She's my sister, Ruth is my older sister. Are you in Newark? Is
this a Newark exchange?"

"Yes."

"Ruth's in Newark, too. She'll be so upset."

"Well, you just try and stay calm."

"I reversed digits, maybe. I'm calling from Pompton Lakes."
Then he said, "I'm sorry. You've been awfully nice."

"It's okay. But call her. That's what you should be worrying about
now."

"I must've reversed digits," he said.

I hung up, unsure whether he was still on the line.

"Cluck dialed the wrong number," I told Leo, who was standing
framed in his bedroom doorway, hands in his bathrobe pockets.
Behind him, some luminous premium glowed blue-green on the
study desk.

"Charley? Is there some trouble?" Edith had come out, wrapped
like a squaw in the bed blanket. "Is something wrong?"

"Go back to sleep," I said. "Please, Edith, just go back to bed."

"I have to use the bathroom." She went in there and shut the door. A moment later I heard water running in the sink.

I sat down on the sofa, and Leo came over, seeming to float through the gloom.

"You know what?" he said quietly. "You *really* give me a royal headache."

"Is that so?"

"Yeah, that's so. That's definitely so."

"Go back to sleep, Leo."

"My friends call you Andy Grump, like Andy Gump, but Grump. Because you always walk around looking so stupid and grouchy. Did you know that?"

"Is there anything else? You want to tell me I got halitosis?"

Edith switched off the bathroom light and came out. "Well, good night again," she whispered. "Just wake me when you get up. I'll make everybody scrambled eggs."

Leo waited till she'd closed the bedroom door, then he said, "Why'd you bring her here? And why'd you let her sleep in Mom's bed! She could be a Jew! Ethel Merman is. Mom says Ethel Merman is. What'd you bring that fat Jew singer here for?" he said, and I stood up and slapped him.

"I hate you, Uncle Charley!"

"No, you don't."

"I do!" Then he ran back into his bedroom and shut the door. I heard the lock click.

"Leo," I said, jiggling the knob, "let me in. I want to talk to you, come on."

"Go away!"

"I will not! Open up! Or I'm coming in!"

"Go away, I don't care! I hate you! Mom hates you! Whenever she says your name, she laughs, like you're screwy, like you're not all there!"

"I'm all here, Leo," I said. "I'm all here, all the time!" Then I said, "Stand back!" and shot out the lock. *Shot out the lock!* Have you ever heard of anybody doing anything stupider than that? The whole door had to be replaced, and the jamb. It was a real mess. It cost me almost fifty bucks, what with a new door, a new lock, the carpenter and locksmith. But Leo thought it was great. He got a real kick out of it. A real charge. Once the smoke cleared and he was over his shock.

Poor Edith, though! Poor Edith thought I'd committed suicide. Can you imagine that? Me, commit suicide?

I'm not the type.

He's All Mine

(1987)

Side One

This guy that Camille lives with? This guy Jacky? I told you about that guy Jacky Peek? He was in jail, three, four years ago? Well, I don't know how he swung it, but now he's a guard, like a watchman? At this weird new development they're building down behind Bayview Cemetery. Down Caven Point, behind the graveyard, on the beach. It's gonna be for rich people just, brokers and junk. There's gonna be, like, canals, like in Venice, is that a hoot, or what? Bunch of condos that'll go for half a million, at least, each with its own boat dock, so these mothers can hop in their boats every morning, zip across the bay to Wall Street. How do you like that, Rita? You like that? Hop in their fucking speedboats? I think it's a riot. It cracks me up. It's the future.

So anyway, he's a guard, this guy Peek. Gets to wear a gun even, to keep out the riffraff while they're building this goofy place. I didn't think you could have a gun once you'd been in jail, but what do I know? He was some kind of thief, I never got the whole story, I never asked. I think he's kind of wasted, myself. But Camille? Camille's nuts for him. I can't figure it. I see him, I don't see nothing.

She picks him up at one, every night. She drops him off at five, she picks him up at one. Only last Thursday? Her car don't start.

Ten of one, her car won't start, she comes up the front stoop and knocks at my door. Wants to know can she borrow mine. Maybe if I'd been asleep, I'd've said yeah, okay. But I was still up, still. Watching a movie I'd rented. So I said, I'll drive you. I think I insulted her, like she thought I don't trust her, but what the hell. I mean, I'm sure it would've been okay, she's dependable and all, she's a good tenant, she's my friend, but what it really was, I felt like doing something. I wasn't tired, I was bored. And the movie really sucked. I go, I'll drive you, Camille, I'll bring you both back.

So then in the car? She starts telling me again, she's always telling me, how she wants to marry this guy Peek, she wants to get married. I don't say nothing, Rita. It's better I should just keep my mouth shut. Camille's cool, I like Camille, but this Peek, in my opinion, is a real loser, not to mention a creep. I mean, he lives with Camille? But he's always going out with this other girl, this Jewish girl, except she's been in California the past two weeks. Camille knows about her, too, and puts up with it. She wants to get married. She goes, I'm twenty-eight years old, Franny, it's time.

Time. She wants kids, is what it comes down to. That's the real story. I felt like telling her, You don't need Peek for that, honey. You don't need anybody. I almost told her about Walter, I almost mentioned Walter, but I didn't. Walter. You know Walter, that guy Walter I was seeing, who sold his sperm to a sperm bank? Come on, Rita, I told you, you just forgot. This was around the time everybody killed themselves in Guyana, I remember we talked about it all the time. Once-a-month-Walter. Squirt! right in a jar. He did, I'm serious, for I don't know how much money. Nothing to it, he goes. Sperm is blood, he goes. People sell their blood, don't they?

Yeah, so. It's a little after one, I turn off Garfield, just past the park with the cannon? Before you get to the cemetery. Caven Point Road, that's Caven Point Road. Used to be, you could take it straight to the water, practically. Used to be you could park, get out, walk on the beach. It was a pretty shitty beach, lots of trash, people dumped, but you could sit there, at least, get a postcard view of New York. Now, you can't get near the beach, now it's all fenced off. The condo builders are making believe it's theirs, the beach, but it's not. It's just, to get there, you got to cross their stinking property and they won't let you. That's Peek's job, his number one job, making sure nobody crosses their fucking property to the beach. Making sure nobody falls in one of their stupid canals.

So we're driving to the gate, and what do we see? Blue lights and red lights, cop-car lights. Camille says, Oh shit, and I slow down, and already a cop is coming over, he's waving us back. I stick out my head? And say we're just here to pick up the night watchman? But it's like the cop don't hear me, he keeps waving us back, saying turn around, sister, and go. Then guess what, Rita? Guess who it was, the cop? It was Paulie Kosakowski! Honest to God, it was Paulie, and I go, Paulie?

I go, Paulie? and he goes, Holy good shit in heaven! He goes, What're you doing here? I said, Paulie, I just told you three times, we're here to pick up the night watchman, what's going on? He says, Oh, just some guy's body. They found some guy's body, on the beach. It washed up. And zoom! Camille's out of the car, right? She hears dead body, she jumps out like maybe it's Peek's. And Paulie says, Hey! Paulie says, Hey you, girlie, stay right there. He's kind of sharp with her, you can tell he's been a cop twenty years. Twenty years, but he's still wearing a uniform. You'd think by now, I don't know, he'd be a detective, or something. Maybe he's a shitty cop, I don't know. He sure was a very shitty drummer.

So he goes to me, Franny, how you been? How you doing? Like we just bumped into each other at the Pathmark. Then the ambulance showed up and I had to move my car off the road.

Yeah so, what happened? This guy's body, it was a black guy's body, washed up on the beach, and Peek found it. So he had to, like, talk to the cops and stuff. But Paulie was cool, he said it'd be okay if we waited, long as we waited right there. Stayed put. It was kind of weird, but. We watched them put the body in the ambulance? in a bag? and you want to know something *really* weird? The ambulance people? All women. I swear to God, Rita, three women. Camille and me stood there smoking, and it was really buggy down there, lots of mosquitoes, I still got the bites.

Paulie went away and came back. Said he seen Peek for us. Told him we were, like, waiting. That was nice. Paulie was always pretty nice. Then he goes, Franny, I didn't know you were still living around here. And I said, Oh yeah, I own a house, I own seven houses. He says, You own houses? He still rents, he's kicking himself. He says five years ago he could've bought something decent for ten cents, now he can't buy shit, it's all so expensive. I say, Yeah, who could've figured, right? Jersey City. And then he says, Hey, you'll never guess who I seen last week up the Square. He says, Spangler! He goes, Bobby, no shit. The Bob is back.

And Rita, I swear to God, I felt lightheaded. I really and truly did. Goosebumps all over the place. And it's June. But you know the first question I asked Paulie? The very first? How's he look. He look good? Not, What's he doing back. Not, Where's he been. Not, How's he doing. How's he look. I go to Paulie, I go: He look good?

*   *   *

So Rita? You'd die. You ready? Spangler still colors. You really and truly would die. Coloring books all over his father's house. In the bathroom, even—these ninety-nine-cent coloring books. Like, probably the first thing he did? When he got back? Was go to McCrory's and buy a whole bunch. Huey, Dewey and Louie. He-Man. Chip and Dale, the chipmunks. And he still colors neat, very shrewd. Very nice. Says he can sit and color for an hour, it's cheap therapy. And I can tell, he *is* a bit edgy, always rubbing his fingers together. He don't smile all that much, either. And he's turned real quiet. He looks good, but. He put on some weight, his face looks rounder, but he got all his hair. Bobby and his crayons.

Remember in high school? Always there'd be a coloring book rolled up in his pocket, loose crayons in his shirt. What it was then, it sure wasn't nerves, was a trademark. Down Asbury Park, on the beach. Coloring books. Up Trutone Sound? Crayons and coloring books. And there they still were, crayons and coloring books, all over his father's house.

But his father, my God. To see him, Rita, it's spooky. I mean, he's not even that old. He's almost seventy, I guess, but geez, so's

my mother. It's that big disease they're always making sad movies
about on TV—that Rita Hayworth had. What a shock. There he
was sitting in the parlor in his bathrobe. His bare feet all wrinkled.
I said to Spangler, You couldn't put his shoes and socks on, at least?
And Spangler goes, Yeah, I do that, he walks out and disappears.
He's been doing that a lot, Spangler says. Once he got clipped by
a car. Spangler says he should've got run over, he should've been
killed. And maybe so. He just sits there, this poor old guy. Remember always the chewing gum? He was always chewing gum? Now
he got a glass of flat Seven-Up on his snack table, this plate of
dried-up cheddar cheese, and a box of no-brand tissues. The television's going, and the color is putrid, green faces. I go to Spangler,
Couldn't you get a better picture for the old guy? And he says the
TV's shot, and what? he's gonna buy a new one? I go, Well, couldn't
you shave him? Then Spangler got real testy, and I shut up. Except
I go, Hey, Mr. Spangler. But he didn't remember me. He just sat
there in his winter bathrobe, watching TV, and I felt sick. Thank
God, Spangler said let's go in the kitchen. And later? When I left?
I left by the back door.

There was nothing to eat except Mint Milano cookies, but there
was a gallon of burgundy, so I got a little drunk, and Spangler starts
to color—in this *101 Dalmatians* coloring book, he's got a deluxe
box of Crayolas handy on the table. And finally I go, Bobby? So
how come you didn't call me? How come I had to call you first? I
mean, what if I never seen Paulie? I go, You weren't gonna get
in touch? He says he would've. He says he would've. Sure, he
would've. So then I said, I don't know if you know? But Clare died.
You know that she died?

He said yeah, he knew about Clare. Coloring these puppies that're
jumping through a hole in the wall.

I should've asked him how he heard, but I didn't. I don't know
how he heard. Somebody told him, I guess. Maybe even Paulie.
But listen. He goes, yeah, he knows about Clare, then he goes, She
had a pretty shitty life, didn't she? Then he goes—he goes, But I
never liked her much, Franny. You know how come? And he looks
at me, and he's holding a red crayon between two fingers, like a

cigarette, exactly, and he goes, She never took the records serious. *That's* how come. Clare never believed in those songs, Franny. She never did. She was never a girl like you. You were a great girl. Shit, you were sixteen for eight good years, twelve straight through twenty. You were a great girl, he says, and it startled me, Rita, like a shade flying up. Because I knew what he meant, because it was so true. What Spangler was saying was so fucking true.

*   *   *

And I been thinking about it, ever since. Which I don't usually do. I don't dwell, you know that, Ma. But ever since Bobby Spangler said that? I been thinking. About me and Rita and Clare and Denise Rodhy and Marilyn Findlay and Chrissy O'Donnell. The girl pack? You always made fun of us, all the makeup, all the fixing our hair and learning new dances. New dance every week. American Bandstand. And I had to be home by eleven, you said. On the dot. But I never was. '62, '63, just before the Frantastics. Friday, Saturday nights, walking around Bayonne in belted skirts and shell blouses. Little transistor radios Made in Japan, when Japan meant junk. Soldier Boy. Playboy. Johnny Angel. God, I loved those songs, those songs about boys. We all did, even Clare. Clare did, too. Brenda Lee, Shelly Fabares, the Crystals, the Orlons. The Marvelettes. Ruby and the Romantics. Our Day Will Come!

And we'd stop at Lenny's candy store on Avenue C and Fourth Street, where that Shop-Rite is now, and hog the phone booth, trying like crazy to get through to WABC. Cousin Brucie? This is Franny Tolentino? From Bayonne? Could you play I Will Follow Him? My Boyfriend's Back? She's a Fool, by Lesley Gore? And we'd haunt the record stores uptown, buying new singles and getting our club cards punched. And we'd chew Wrigley's spearmint gum and smoke any brand and always we carried Kleenex tissues, the little dime packs. And we'd pass the same bunches of cute boys every couple of blocks, every twenty minutes, half an hour—we'd see them coming toward us and my stomach would just, just *cramp*. Lesley Gore. Little Peggy March.

I'll tell you something, though. Bobby's right, Ma. He's absolutely right. I *was* a great girl. I was a truly great girl. And that's how come those records we made are so great. Still. They're perfect as anything. Some crazie could stab me tomorrow on the Greenville bus, so what? So what? They're still perfect, always will be. And they're all mine, till the end of time.

*   *   *

My cousin Clare? It's maybe true, what Spangler said. Maybe it's true, Camille. Because you know something funny? She had two kids, she never told them she made those records. I did, I told them. It was up to me, I had to tell them. Not that they were super-excited or nothing, they were still kind of young, but still. She never told them. Those eighteen, twenty months, they didn't mean nothing to Clare. Jesus, I think of her a lot, you know? Thirty-five years old. Cerebral fucking hemorrhage. Can you believe that? And what's so awful? Her kids found her. They tried to wake her up, they tried for three solid hours. All alone in that shitty little house in Country Village with Clare's dead body. Her husband wasn't living there. Everybody knew, but Clare wouldn't admit it. She'd always say he was out of town, that he had a spiffy job that kept him traveling. You know what Peter did? What Peter does? What he's always done? Sells wine, Gallo wine. Some spiffy job.

In the last two, three years of her life, I didn't see much of Clare. Nothing in common no more. She was the only one of us that kept singing, though. Clare was. Sang in church, in the choir. And with a local band that did weddings. She was always kind of large, but she never got fat. She kept singing. And she got real religious— she was something called a charismatic Catholic, whatever that is. I seen her once on Broadway? In front of Woolworth's? Handing out these pamphlets? Pro-life stuff with pictures of unborn babies in a dumpster. I was embarrassed, Camille. She had a glassy look. I just said hey and took the stupid pamphlet and got away quick. That might've been the last time I seen her.

She was the first of my friends to get laid. And the first time she

did it? She did it with Peter Hogue. That she later married. He was
her first and only. The only guy in her entire life, I'd bet money.
There we were traveling with Del Shannon, Gene Pitney, who was
really, really cute, the Ad Libs, Cannibal and the Headhunters, our
pictures every week in some teen magazine, and Clare had her love
pledged already to that dim bulb from Zabriskie Avenue, Bayonne.

So maybe Spangler is completely full of shit.

*   *   *

That girlfriend? That you met Peek on account of? You ever see
her? You don't have to tell me about how it is, I know. I know all
about it. Like Rita? I hardly *ever* see her anymore, either. We talk
on the phone, just. And, like, I've known her since third grade. I
guess we're still best friends, but I never see her. Maybe twice a
year. This year not once even, so far. She don't drive. She will not
drive a car, I don't know how she can manage. I mean, she lives
down Point Pleasant. How can you live at the shore and don't drive
a car? But she don't, and she won't.

You walk in her house? It's a wreck. It's filthy, it's pathetic. She
collects vinyl ponies—they're everywhere. Some are unicorns, some
have wings, and they all have colored manes. Some manes are
silver and some are purple. Some ponies look real and some look
just crazy, impossible. These blue ones, these green ones, these
polka-dot ponies. And she's got, like, a pony stable, a pony castle,
like even a pony beauty parlor, all this pony stuff she collects. And
there's Rita, surrounded. I couldn't live like that.

I remember when we were on this tour, this Dick Clark thing?
Clare roomed with one of the Kettles, and me and Rita roomed
together. I couldn't stand it. We'd be there ten minutes and the
place was already a pigsty, makeup and tissues and hair spray and
blouses, all over. I'm not saying I'm the neatest person in the whole
wide world, I'm not saying that. You can just look around here,
I'm not so neat and fussy, but Rita. She got pig genes. She very
definitely got pig genes.

We've known each other so long. Always best girlfriends. We used to sleep over each other's house. We were always doing that, sleeping over. There was this one time? We watched something spooky on TV. This was, like, 1961, around there. It was called "Way Out," you wouldn't remember, Camille. But in the show there was this guy that committed suicide, but he was still walking around, he had a bullet hole in his temple. I got the creeps, I got very upset, and Rita turned it off. Then we went to bed. We slept in the same bed and—you think you know what I'm gonna say? You're right. I don't know who started it first, or did what exactly. I mean, we didn't even have breasts yet, not really. What am I thinking? Of course we did. We had to be, like, almost fifteen. But it was nothing, it was over in a minute. The two of us, I guess, embarrassed. It's happened to everybody. Something like that. Something like that must've happened to you, right? When you were a girl? It's nothing. It's not a very sharp memory, but it's a memory. I wish it was sharper, in a funny kind of way.

And I wish Rita was happier. I could see her more, I could drive down there and see her, I got plenty of time, but I never do. Her house is a pigsty. She got this shitty job, in a library. And she's been going with this one guy, seeing him for, like, two years already. This social worker. Ronald. Ron. I tell her, Rita, he makes fifteen thousand dollars a year, he still goes to church, don't do it. She's gonna marry him but, I know she will. One day. She's working on it. It's wasted labor, you want my opinion. This guy Ron. He's kind of stocky. What he is, he's kind of fat. He's kind of this, he's kind of that, he's kind of nothing. His teeth are bad—he couldn't get them fixed? I don't know what he's like. I met him maybe twice.

Rita says she don't want to see Spangler, I don't know how come. Maybe she don't want to be reminded. She goes, Franny, the guy left us flat. Took off to California and left us flat. I said, Come on— it was all over anyway. And I'm the one that should be mad. If there's anybody should hold a grudge, it's me, not you. Maybe she just don't want to be reminded. So fuck Rita, if she really feels that way.

*   *   *

Don't bother with any of those real estate sharks, Bobby. I mean, it's a frame house and there's no good detail or nothing and it's not exactly in a prime location, with Ocean Avenue right up the block, but I'll bet you can get at least ninety. Oh sure, maybe more. I'll tell you what to do. If you want.

Why shouldn't I know something about real estate? I own enough, don't I? I should know. Me and Donald Trump, right?

All together? Seven buildings, all together. Three on this block, three on Astor, and a big tenement down the end of Park. I used to own more, but I sold a couple houses last year. Listen, I got those in '79, one I paid six for, the other I paid two. Six thousand and two thousand. I'm not shitting you. City auction. Nobody wanted to live here then, you could get anything for nothing. It was like "Monopoly," at "Monopoly" prices. So that's what I do, Bobby, I own buildings. And when I need money, I fix one up and sell it. The two last year? I got one-twenty-nine for one, the other went for almost ninety-seven. I do okay. Look, I haven't had to work any dumb jobs in almost five years. That's doing okay. I just manage my property.

I can't take all the credit, though. It was this guy that got me thinking about it, this guy I met in a bar in Bayonne. Nice-looking guy, real confident, super-serious, and we're talking for about ten minutes and he goes, You haven't asked me yet if I'm Jewish, and I say, All right, are you? And he goes, You just had to ask that, didn't you? Weird guy.

So we're drinking stupid drinks with dopey names for about three hours and he ends up taking me home. His home, not mine, to this real shitty neighborhood in Hoboken. This is, like '77, '78. Real shitty neighborhood, lot of Puerto Ricans, lots of big radios. I bet you I hadn't been in Hoboken for ten years—my Aunt Rose used to live there, we used to go visit her at Easter time, when I was a kid.

So this guy? We park his car and we're coming down his block?

And he's going, I own that place and I own that place and I own that place, too. Like, this guy was buying up every place in sight. Dirt cheap. That place, he goes, and this place and this place too, and that one there. I couldn't keep track.

Finally we come to his house, big brownstone on a corner, and there's graffiti on the stoop, but inside it's just gorgeous. Red carpet on the stairs, red drapes on the windows, this big sofa with claw feet. Lace on the tables, and gas fixtures that worked, in the hall. Really beautiful. I go, This is neat, and he says thanks, then he says he'll go over my finances with me sometime, tell me what kind of house I can afford, make some recommendations. He says there's still time. Not much, but some. And I go to him, What the hell do I want with a house? I mean, I always lived in apartments, that was fine with me. I was working at Bayonne Hospital then, making pitiful money. In the admitting office. Yeah, it sucked. But hold on, I'm telling you about this guy. I go to him, What do I want with a house, and he's shocked. He's shocked. I mean, he's literally shocked.

It's a piece of property, he says. It's an investment. There's a tax thing. It's income-producing. He's rattling off these reasons. And I could live there, too, he says. For next to nothing. And then he asks me what kind of salary do I make. And then he says he don't have herpes. I'm still thinking about the tax thing, but he's way past that already. A house, I kept thinking. Why should I buy a house? Grown-ups buy houses. I was over thirty years old, Spangler, and still I'm thinking why should I buy a house, grown-ups buy houses.

So that was the guy responsible. He's how come I own this place, and the one next door, and 114, and 91 Astor, and 93 Astor and 108 Astor and that tenement down Park. He's how come I don't do nothing no more, except collect rent and spend a day every other week in landlord-tenant court. They know me at the Planning Board.

When I started, I couldn't afford Hoboken. Back then, brownstones in Hoboken went for about fifty thousand. Today they're getting half a million. Can you imagine? Half a million! Three-quarters of a million. But I couldn't afford fifty thousand bucks in

1978, so I came here. That's what I'm doing in Jersey City. My mother was real upset, still is, but even she can see it was smart. Now she can. When I first moved here but, she thought I was crazy. So many blacks. She goes, Franny, you weren't raised like this.

Well, it wasn't Bayonne, I got to admit. It was crummy all right, and didn't change overnight. It stayed crummy, I put up with shit. Those buildings across the street? With the names chiseled over the doors? The Hillcrest, The York? Apartments there rent for eight-fifty now. Eight-fifty! Two years ago it was still all black and Span-ish, Carter Cubans, and the rent was, like, five hundred dollars cheaper. No kidding. I'm not kidding. People were still hanging bed sheets out the windows. Today it's skinny blinds. The steps were loud at night with kids, fistfights—I remember this one big fat lady showing up there at three in the morning, in the rain, screaming her head off, threatening murder. But now things are changing fast.

I could sell this place tomorrow for one-eighty-five. These people from New York are nuts. They'll buy anything, pay anything. They're dying to get in. You should see this neighborhood on Sunday after-noons. They're all over the place, they got the real estate section of the *Times*, they got their checkbooks. Every other house has balloons on the stoop. Open house. Quarter of a million dollars? They'll buy. If they see you out front, they smile and ask if you know any buildings for sale. And the real estate people! Let me give you my card. Let me give you my card. If you decide to sell, give me a ring. They give their cards to anybody. They give their cards to ten-year-olds with beat boxes on their heads. The neigh-borhood's changing real fast, week to week. When the brickface cleaners come? The gutters run red.

It's crazy. I mean, we bust our chops for two years, we have three hit records, and what'd we earn? Three, four thousand apiece? I thought we were gonna be rich, and we come out the other end with beans. With nothing. And here I am now, I could blow up some balloons tomorrow morning, be rich tomorrow night. It makes me crazy. I'm not complaining, Spangler, but it makes me a little crazy. If I think about it.

* * *

Six o'clock, somebody starts jamming on the bell. I'm in the bedroom downstairs sorting laundry, making piles. It was the night you and Peek seen the Pretenders, so I know it's not you, you're at the Meadowlands. So I figure, This time of day? Either it's some tenant come to bitch, or it's UPS.

I been shopping the catalogs, I don't know why. It started out, a blouse twice a year, then pants. Then I'd buy a sweatshirt, then I'd buy a T-shirt. Now I never go shopping, except for, like, food. I use the phone, my Visa, but it's so bizarre. The stuff is pretty good, it's quality stuff, but I don't know, I feel funny. It used to be, I'd get the paper every day, I'd read that. Now it's catalogs. I don't keep up with terrorism, but I'm hip to all the latest trends in designer eye-masks.

Anyhow, my guess was, it was UPS, but I never just open the door. Not ever. It might be a tenant, it could be anybody. At all. Always I look through the window first, out of sight, and spy. I can see the stoop.

Well, it was Bobby, it was Spangler. Wearing his usual jeans, and this green scrub shirt, this doctor shirt? God knows where he found it—it's got a laundry stencil on the pocket. And he goes, Franny, you wanna help me do something? Not even hi. And I go, Help you do what? and he goes, I can't find him, meaning the old man, of course. The old man is gone again.

So we take my car, Spangler don't have one, and we drive. Cruise just, all over. First down Garfield, to Spangler's neighborhood, then up and down side streets. Then Ocean, then Martin Luther King. I go, You wanna stop and ask somebody? And he goes, Ask who, the guys in the fucking skull caps? I say, Why not, they got eyes. Maybe somebody seen him. But he goes, Let's just drive some more. Spangler hanging out the window, looking for his father. I used to buy sneakers, he says, right over there. Right over there? It's Akba's Steak 'n' Burger now.

Martin Luther King is such a pit. Touch of Class Ballroom and Bar. Brite-Spot Laundrette. Nothing's hardly in business no more, and every bank we passed? Boarded up. Where my mother used to work? Boarded up. Spangler goes, They should bulldoze it. He means the whole street. And start over. But I go, Won't happen. It's not convenient to New York. It's too far from the PATH. Then I say, Spangler, how long we gonna keep this up?

Say, Spangler, maybe we should stop, you should call the Medical Center.

Say, Spangler, What're you gonna do for the rest of your life?

What? He goes, What? And pulls in his head.

I said, You heard me. I'm just wondering. You sell your father's house, you going back to Florida?

He don't know. He really don't. Camille, here's a guy, almost forty-two, he can sum up the past twenty years in half a minute, not even. The next twenty get a shrug. He goes, I sell the house, I don't see a penny. I gotta turn it all over to a goddamn nursing home. That's what they're telling him. They want every dime, soon as they got a bed, which is maybe six months. We're talking December, January. And I don't think Spangler can hold out that long. Without some job. But what can he do? He says, What can I do, work at McDonald's? I go, They got racetracks here. He goes, Yeah, racetracks. Forty-one years old, he's a hot-walker still. A groom. He says, I don't like horses even, it was just something I found. Here's a guy, Camille, was a magic boy. Could walk into a nightclub at eighteen, get us on stage in half an hour. What happened? He goes, The rest of my life? Franny, don't make me crazy. Turn at the next corner. So I turned.

And Spangler says, Stop! I thought he seen him, seen his father, so I pull over. And he gets out. We're in front of this Spanish deli. Giant bananas in a bin, the window is filled with Joy detergent. And Spangler says, I'll call. Then he says, Who should I call? I say, Call the Medical Center. Jesus, who should he call?

He goes in the deli, and I'm thinking, Bet they don't even got a

public phone. Then I'm thinking, Thanks a lot, Spangler—you
leave me out here sitting by myself. Sanctified Church of the Living.
The Roxy Food Center. Black girls squealing and chasing each
other, and flirting with boys in baseball caps on sideways, on backwards, like the stupid guy in the Dead End Kids always wore his.
Loads of bars. Cousin's Hi-Life Lounge. All these crummy bars and
bad air, so I rolled up the windows. Outside it's eighty degrees, but
I roll up the car windows.

In high school? Me and Clare and Rita used to go over the Village
a lot, just to walk around. So one night? This black guy and his
girlfriend come up to us, they go, You ladies wanna be in a film?
They don't say movie, they say film. Guy says, guy with big bushy
hair, guy says, All you gotta do is come with us, won't take an hour,
no pay. You'll be in a film. So we went. We did. To the East Village.
This old, I guess, factory building. And the guy paints our faces
like Comanche Indians, and we sit on the floor, he films us. At
least he pointed his camera at us. I couldn't testify there was actually film in it. And his girlfriend? She wore a wig. And under the
wig? She was bald. She showed us. And we sat there and they
filmed us, then we left. I never seen the film. If there ever *was* a
film. But the point I'm making, the point is, I never used to be
scared. Black guy comes up to me, I went to his loft. Sure. Okay.
That's the whole point I'm making. Now, Christ, I'm sitting in my
car, I got the windows rolled up. And outside it's June, it's eighty
degrees. Black guy walks up to me now? I'd shit. Everybody on
Wall Street's a crook. Eleven o'clock news, they cover their faces
with hand-tailored jackets. And I collect rent. More every year,
hundreds more, for the very same linoleum, the same flaky ceilings.
And buy everything, even underpants, from the Land's End catalog.
And you. You're creaming to get married, no offense, Camille. I got
nothing against marriage, Camille, it's just that you're creaming.
That's my whole point.

Anyhow. Spangler comes back with a brown paper bag. He takes
out a pack of Vantage, a can of Coke. And potato chips. I had to
laugh. Really. I didn't know they even made that size anymore,
that baby size. When it was just me and Clare and Rita and Bobby?

We always had potato chips. Bon-Tons. And whenever you finished
a bag? Spangler had to blow it up, hold the top, punch it with his
fist and pop! He'd do everybody's, you couldn't do your own, you
couldn't pop your own yourself. He had to do it. If you popped it
yourself, he got mad. He got so mad, if you popped it.

So I go, Did you call? and he goes, Yeah.

So? What happened?

And he goes, Yeah, they got him. He's at the Medical Center.
He's all right.

He was all right, Camille, the old guy. But somehow? His head
got cut. He must've fallen down. He's always falling down. And
Spangler? I go, Spangler, I'll drive you there. Okay? We'll pick up
your father. Okay?

But Spangler don't say nothing, not right away. He's swigging
on Coke and scarfing down chips. Meanwhile smoking. Then he
says, You want some? And I go, No thanks. Then he finished the
bag, then he popped it. I was waiting for that. And I said, Spangler?
Tell me your thoughts.

He didn't look surprised. That I asked him such a thing, like all
of a sudden. But he didn't answer me, neither. He wouldn't tell.
Sometimes I wonder if Spangler does think. Or if that's all he does.
He don't talk much. He used to. Always going on and on. Talking
like if he stopped, he'd lose control. Of the conversation. Saying
we'll do this, we'll do that. Just leave it up to me. But he's turned
so quiet. It's the biggest single change. The single biggest change.
He sat there in the car just breathing beside me.

*   *   *

Couple, three times he's been over. Just shows up, Ma, never calls.
He was always doing that, remember? Showing up in the middle
of supper, Sunday dinner, sitting down in the parlor, coloring? He
still does it, he's doing it again.

He was in California, then Florida. He worked in a stable, at a
racetrack. Is what he says. I think he's broke, not that he's asked
me for money. I just think he's broke. I get that impression.

I do, I keep telling him I wish he'd call first, he keeps saying he will, then doesn't. It's no big deal. I don't really mind.

Like, the other night? I was outside doing the hedges, and there's a car stopped for a light, the corner of Summit and Astor? Radio blasting, and what's it playing? He's All Mine, I swear. So I just stand there and listen, and I'm thinking about that tiny studio in West New York, I could remember what I had on, I had on a brown jumper and a white blouse. I had a cold sore on my lip. And Clare was screaming that somebody put a cigarette butt in her can of root beer. We done the song, like, six times and finally had it perfect. Or thought we did. He's all mine, he's all mine, till the end of time. And Bobby's coloring, he's coloring Woody Woodpecker with a flesh-colored crayon, which is, like, all wrong—he's coloring, then he starts shaking his head. Says no. He says, No good, we do it over, and Rita says, What're you, crazy? What's the matter, it's great. And Bobby says, I got a better lyric. And he goes, He's all mine, is that a *crime*? And we all groan, but Bobby says, We change it, we're changing it. What I'm saying is better.

And you know something? About ten years later, about fifteen years ago, I'm reading this interview with John Lennon? And he mentioned that song, and he mentioned that lyric. And he said it was good. He's all mine, is that a crime? John Lennon!

So I'm standing there the other night with the hedge clippers in my hand, and the light changes and the car peals off down Summit toward the Junction, and our song gets fainter and fainter and fainter, and finally I can't hear it, and three minutes later, I'm not kidding you, Bobby shows up. Like three minutes and nine seconds later. Three-oh-nine. That's a joke, Ma. He's got a pizza pie and he rented some movie, and I should've been annoyed, but I was happy to see him. I was so happy.

*　　*　　*

Oh come on, Spangler, you didn't know I was married? Jesus, I guess how could you? Well, I was. For two and a half, almost three years. '70 to almost '73. After I came home from Los Angeles, after I said fuckit, after that.

I met Lenny in college, don't you just love it? I guess I'd decided to grow up. But gradually. So I took a few courses. Never finished. College was so bizarre, those years. Leaflets, people locking themselves in classrooms, big demonstrations, everybody and his brother had a bullhorn. But I skipped all the rallies, and went to class, if it wasn't canceled. Big demonstrations, and foreign movies with subtitles. Twice a week you could see *The Seventh Seal*, some club was showing it. Or *Wild Strawberries*. Movie, coffee, doughnuts, discussion. It was great.

The first time I seen Lenny was at one of those free films, something Japanese—he was stirring non-dairy creamer into a cup of coffee with a wooden stick. A cigarette in his mouth. The smoke getting in his eyes, making him squint. He wore glasses. And he wore regular shirts. No slogans, no comments. No buttons. He looked like you, a little, before you looked like a Martian. Before you grew your hair and disappeared.

I went over and grabbed a hot cup, then a packet of instant, then checked out what was left in the Dunkin' Donut box, and Lenny suddenly reached across in front of me, for the sugar, and our arms collided, making an X.

I still expected people to recognize me. I'd been on "Shindig," I'd been on "Batman." But he didn't. He didn't recognize me. Two years had passed. A million years had passed. So I smiled and he smiled, and dear Christ, I checked his gums. I'm a riot, no? To see if his teeth were plaque-free.

Hey, speaking of "Batman," hey Bobby? You know Channel 5 shows "Batman" reruns every day, like four o'clock or something? But I don't think I could stand seeing that episode. Seeing myself as a twenty-year-old. I looked sharp in that leotard, but I was in pretty rough shape. I was in very rough shape. You were gone and Clare had quit and got married and Rita was down the tubes, and I really, really didn't know what the fuck it was I wanted. I should never've signed with that Curly Marschall. I mean, I knew I couldn't do it by myself. That my voice was no great shakes. That I was no good by myself. But what was I supposed to do? You were gone by then. Fuck you. And Curly said get seen, get around, get on TV, do TV, I said all right. I don't ever hear of Curly Marschall anymore—for a while in the seventies, you seen his name at the end of those dopey sitcoms, but I haven't heard of him since.

I called you, you know, when I was doing that "Batman." I called you. Don't hand me that crap, Bobby. You got the message. San Francisco to L.A., what's that—a few hours? You could've come. You just sucked, that's all. I looked good in that leotard, but. I was a great-looking kitten. You know, that Julie Newmar was beautiful. She was a beautiful Catwoman. Amazing body, amazing boobs. You never see her in anything anymore. She's not dead, is she? She was real nice to me. It's so funny, that I was on "Batman." That I was one of the Catwoman's kittens. Yeah, four o'clock every day.

Channel 5. How many times you planning to ask me that. Channel 5, Channel 5. Right after "Superfriends," right before "The Dukes of Hazard."

*   *   *

Here they come again, Camille. See that girl nearest the fence? Don't stand up—that's Darlene. If you seen her up close, you'd know her, she's always around. She can't be more than sixteen. Or maybe she's older. Maybe she is. But she don't look sixteen, even. She's real pretty, though. You know who she reminds me of? DeeDee Sharp. You know that song, Slow Twisting? Well, there was a song called Slow Twisting and the girl that did it was named DeeDee Sharp. We knew her, she was on the Dick Clark tour with us, the Caravan of Stars. Mashed Potatoes?

It don't matter, what I'm saying is that girl Darlene reminds me of DeeDee Sharp. She has a great ass, but her stomach's a little round, a little fat. She has two kids already, one of them definitely Nosy Brown's, maybe both. Yeah, right, *Darlene*. Now you know who I'm talking about. Nosy Brown's girlfriend. Her older kid? Say he's four: then she can't be sixteen, can she? Well, I guess she could. I suppose she could. But she's probably not.

She seems like a real quiet girl, but once? Once I heard all this commotion, all this shouting—this was before you moved into the neighborhood—and I looked out the window and she was right down below, and Nosy was screaming at her and she was screaming back. This guy Kenny was over, and it was around two in the morning. Nosy hit Darlene, I seen him, so I told Kenny, Do something. He should do something, I'm saying. He wouldn't, but. He said call 911 if you're so upset. We weren't undressed or nothing, we'd been over New York and were just having coffee. Darlene was screaming and crying. So I went downstairs myself and Kenny wants to know what I'm doing. He got real angry, but still he wouldn't do nothing. Said, Mind your own business. I should've, but I didn't.

So anyway, there was this trowel? This garden trowel? Lying in the front hall? And I picked that up. Later on, I realized I'd picked it up for a weapon, but when I did it, I wasn't thinking. I went outside and stood at the top of the stoop. My heart was going nuts, I couldn't breathe, I'd never done nothing like this before. I mean, like go out and play citizen, that's what I mean. Do man's work. My heart was nuts. I seen Nosy hit Darlene again. And I swear, I seen a tooth go spinning away in the streetlight.

Here they come again. That's her, that's Darlene, with the girl with the radio, under the streetlight.

So—I seen that tooth go flying? I seen a tooth and started yelling Stop! Said I'd called the cops, which I hadn't, and Kenny was in back of me but halfway up the stairs, hissing like a radiator, going, Get the hell inside and cut out this shit.

I looked back at Nosy and Darlene, and Darlene was sobbing, her face was in her hands, then I seen for the first time that her kids were there, both kids, standing by the hedges. They were right over there, holding hands.

So Nosy looks at me. He don't say nothing, but. I really expected him to, I really expected him to abuse me, but he didn't. He only said something to Darlene, like he was disgusted with her, and then he starts to walk away, shaking his head, and all of a sudden? All of a sudden Darlene says, Wait! Don't go, she says, and then she says she loves him. I'll never forget it. Never. And me standing there with that trowel. I got so mad. What do you mean, how come? What do you mean, how come? I was angry. I been willing to defend this twit and she turns around and tells him that she loves him. Then a cop car came by, but it never even slowed. I was so mad at her and at Kenny, and Kenny was mad at me, and he got his coat and he left. I was really, really pissed.

I seen her next day in the Neighborhood Deli, and we both ignored each other. She was buying two packages of Twinkies and a quart of Clorox.

That's her, that's Darlene, she's lugging the radio now. That's Darlene.

*   *   *

So you met Mr. Brown. Well, don't let him bother you. He says stuff like that to all us sow-bellies. I'm only kidding, Spangler, jeez. But so, what'd he say to you?

I've heard worse. But look, Spangler, don't call him that. All right, my sixties are showing, but I'd rather you didn't use that word. Don't get offended, it's not just you. I know it's not. I hear it more and more. People that never used it before, they're using it now, saying nigger. I hear it all over. These niggers were standing outside all night. Niggers had another party at the Friendship Lodge. Like that.

Call him crazy, that's okay. Because he is, I guess. I guess he is. If you live here, you see him every day. He's always around. See him prowling in his red-checked shirt. That way that he walks. That way that he stares. One morning last winter? Every car on the street had its headlights smashed. I heard it was him. I don't know, but I heard. So don't say nothing, Bobby. Promise, okay? Don't say nothing to his face. They're gonna gut his building. The sign is up. By Christmas, he'll be gone.

He's never bothered me, though. Never has, except for a couple of sex remarks. He says he likes my ass. Well, he does! So he likes my ass. So what's wrong with that? You used to, didn't you? Didn't you?

*   *   *

They want to tear down the Loews, the beautiful Loews, and put up an office building. So there was a big shootout at City Hall the other night, I went down with Camille. You know—who rents the apartment upstairs? I told you about Camille, Ma. She's kind of cute? The cute redhead? Who lives with the guy that was in jail?

So anyway, I drag her down to City Hall, the place is mobbed. You got these developers with their plans. You got, like, a hundred fifty people saying don't do it. You could go up and make a thirty-second statement. So I figured, why not, and I went up. And said, You gotta be kidding, you're gonna let this guy come in here, this Hartz Mountain guy, and tear down our beautiful palace? I did. What're you so surprised about? Hey, Ma, I'm no stupe. I'm a grown woman. I can get up in front of people, it's no big deal. I used to get up in front of people all the time, don't forget. Left and right.

Anyhow, this went on all night, and it was, like, after midnight when it was over. What do you think, they actually made some decision? Don't tease me, this is city government. They didn't make no decision, but I bet you it gets the ball, I bet you they wreck the Loews, I bet you next year you'll see another white office building up Journal Square. Some day I'd like to know what all those people do in all those white office buildings.

So me and Camille get in the car and drive home. But it was such a cool night, so nice and cool, I didn't wanna go in right away. Me and Camille sat on the stoop. She had to hang around anyhow. She picks up her boyfriend at one.

So we're sitting there and along come these five or six black girls, and they're all talking together, talking all at once. Two of them sound like they're arguing, but I can't really tell. And they pass by and disappear around the corner. Five minutes later, here they come again. I guess they were just walking around the block.

And the same two girls are still arguing, only now they're really going at it, and the other girls are egging them on, having a very good time, and now they got a radio. Usually you don't see girls with those big radios, maybe they're too heavy. Usually it's the guys. But these girls had a great big radio, turned up loud. It was that rap shit, and I was thinking, except for that rap shit it was just like me and Rita and Clare, walking around and around, arguing about boys, arguing about hair spray. I remember once Rita wanted to kill me 'cause I stole her very best hair spray, I just took it from her house and she found out. She found out 'cause Clare told her, is how she found out. Those girls are just like me and Rita and Clare, I'm thinking.

But the third time the same girls went by? I seen the two that're still arguing? They're both pregnant. They had stomachs out to here. I could see their stomachs in silhouette.

So they weren't like us, not exactly. Because we never got pregnant. I mean, we got pregnant, but we never got pregnant. If you know what I mean. Not me, personally. I'm just talking about us girls. Rita got pregnant twice. You knew that. Oh come on, Ma, you did too. You never did? I find that really hard to believe. Twice: once in sophomore year, that guy who's, like, assistant Hudson County prosecutor now, I used to see his name in the paper. And once when I Got a New Boyfriend was number seventeen. I remember that. The day we broke into the charts, she tells me. Ruined that happy day, all right.

The first time she went to a doctor in Weehawken. Oh, Christ, was that ever awful. She was bleeding for days and we thought she was gonna die. The second time was a piece of cake. We told Bobby and Bobby arranged for her to go to somebody in New York, a high-priced guy up near Central Park. I remember, I went to the zoo while I waited. And I got recognized, some kids in the park recognized me, and I think I probably signed a couple of autographs, and meanwhile Rita was having her scraping. I forget who

was the father. I must've known, but I forget. She must've told me,
I must've known, but I forget. How long's it been, that abortion's
been legal? You remember? I forget.

*   *   *

I met Spangler in 1963, in the fall, in October. Seen him the first
time at a Holy Family dance. No band, Camille, just records. No
refreshments, no band, just records. No decorations, nothing on
the walls. Just records and chaperones—girls' fathers in the four
corners, talking. Not mine, but. He'd never chaperone—I wouldn't
ask. He lived over a bar on Second Street, he'd call Ma at three in
the morning, angry about something. Something different all the
time. He was a mechanic. Then he owned an Esso station. Then
he lost it. Then he was a mechanic. He'd see me on the street?
He'd wave and smile, treat me like a neighbor. Sundays, though,
he came for dinner and was always very polite. Not always, I guess.
But usually. Sundays only. He's better now, it was a blood chemical
thing, too much of something, or maybe not enough. But I never
see him. My mother's never divorced him, either, they're still married. They're married still. They still receive communion, at different masses, but.

Anyhow. I had on a red dress, a bright red dress, and I seen this
boy I never seen before going through records at the table by the
stage. Saying he wanted this one played, he wanted that one. And
getting what he wanted. Whatever it was. The Crystals. Little Eva.
Loco-Motion.

He seen me staring. He had good skin, thank God, and a green
sport coat. He was tall, one of the tallest boys there. And he seen
me looking, but he wouldn't smile. He had lots of 45s he was
holding. Orange labels. Cameo records. The Orlons. He looked at
me direct, he wouldn't look away. But I did. And he kept passing
singles to this girl in charge of the record player. Christine Larson.
It was always Christine Larson in charge. Big glasses, fingerprints,
great big glasses with fingerprint smudges. She was good at bas-
ketball. And she played everything that Spangler wanted, all by

girls or girl groups, even when other kids complained. Said play something slow. Play Roses Are Red. Play Walk Like a Man. Some kids got sore. I kept thinking, We like the same songs. Me and that boy.

Then—I was standing with Rita? And wait a second, what's this? Stranger on the Shore? That, what was that? was that a clarinet? Mr. Acker Bilk. And I looked around, down the gym, and Spangler was gone. But I didn't know his name was Spangler. It was just that cute boy that was picking out records. And now he was gone. Mr. Acker Bilk. Stranger on the Shore. Slow song. Last dance. Lights on. And Rita said, What's the matter with *you*? And I said, Nothing.

It was only eleven o'clock, not even. Friday night. There was a crowd on the Boulevard, waiting for buses, and we seen some Marist boys heading down toward the Bayonne Bridge, to hitch a ride to Staten Island. Well, you know. You grew up down there. And me and Rita and Clare and a bunch of our friends? What we did, what we always did, we walked to Broadway, to the Eighth Street diner. You must've spent half your life in that place, yourself. Right? But it's funny. You must've been, like, only four or five. There you were, not even five, comfy in your bed, tucked up comfy. Little Camille. In 1963. It's funny. And here we are now. We're girlfriends. So we all walked to the diner, after the dance.

There were old guys on the sidewalk, in aprons, selling papers, and cops going in and out for coffee, and tons of kids, tons of kids, and no free booths. Instead of just standing crunched up in the vestibule, us girls went around behind the diner, to the parking lot, to smoke cigarettes. Cigarettes, just. It was 1963. And it was cold, it was October. We smoked cigarettes and huddled together, and stood somebody's Jap radio on the hood of a car. And if something good came on, like He's a Rebel, like She's a Fool, we sang. All of us, at first, then not all of us. After a while, just me and Rita and Clare and Denise Rodhy. You Can't Sit Down. Playboy. Even Deep Purple. Deep Purple, even. Then just me and Clare and Rita, 'cause Denise seen her uncle come out of a bar across the street and she went over. Then the other girls went back inside the diner? To see

if there was a table? But we stayed out in the cold, singing, and
finally we didn't use the radio, we didn't need the radio. There were
too many songs that sucked. Surf City? That sucked. Blue Velvet?
That sucked. Washington Square? No vocals. So we just sang by
ourselves, like we always did, like we usually did, walking First
Street to Fifth Street, Fifth Street to First.

And I looked up at the diner, and who's inside? At a booth by
the window? But that same cute boy I seen at the dance. Watching
us. And when I seen him? I got embarrassed, but he smiled. Finally.
Then he opened his mouth and said something. He was talking at
me, but I made believe I didn't understand. But I understood. Not
heard, exactly, but I read his lips, like. He said, I'm coming out,
okay? I'm coming out. Wait there. And I seen him get up and then
I seen him grab his coat from the hook, and then I said to Rita—
I go to Rita and Clare, Let's walk, I don't feel like the diner. Let's
walk just. I said, Let's just walk. Because, see? I was gonna make
him follow us. Make him follow us, make him catch up. If he hadn't
smiled, I'd've gone after him myself. But he did, he smiled, and
now he had to pay. I had to make him pay. I had no other choice.
There was nothing else for me to do.

*   *   *

I only went to Bermuda that time with Rita to make her happy. I
hate resorts, honest to God, but I sure have gone to enough. I don't
go anymore, though. When I was married? I went. Twice. And
once after. But not anymore. I don't go anywhere, anymore. I don't
take vacations. Why should I? It's not like I need one, it's not like
I even work. Sometimes I think I'll go someplace, but then I don't.

Anyway, Caribbean resorts I hate especially. They're always so
full of the biggest jerks. How about some prime beef—the buffet
table's straight this way. Gimme a break. You were never as crude
as that, were you, Spangler? If you were, I forget.

But Rita wanted to go, so I said, All right, yeah I'll go with you.
She never been before. Well, she'd only been single three months,
something like that. This is five, six years ago already. Right after

she threw out that clown Stuart, the King of Sheetrock. He was a Sheetrock guy, he put up walls. But you know what his favorite thing was, Stuart's? Watching "The Honeymooners." And he liked to camp. Can you imagine Rita in the fucking woods? He took her camping, like, every July. And you know who he dumped her for? A checker at the Pathmark, a little ball of fat with the most pornographic mouth I ever seen on a girl, to this day, excepting maybe Carly Simon's. I'm sure that's what got Stuart interested in the first place, started him flirting across the laser beam. Plus this checker was only twenty-two. That had to be another factor.

Anyhow. We flew down on a Friday afternoon, out of Newark. And on the plane? I read *The Shining* in paperback and Rita drank tropical punch, one right after the other. Oh, she's even worse now. I know she used to, you don't have to tell me how much she used to, but now she's worse. She's even worse now. I mean lately. I seen her fall down last year? I seen her get up and fall flat on her face, chip a tooth. But I don't want to get into that.

We got a white bungalow. From the window, you could see the water, it was nice. Rita bounced on the beds, she bounced up and down. She turned on the TV to make sure it worked. Then she checked out the closed circuit listings for adult movies. Tells me she never seen one, not once in her whole life, which I didn't believe. She says it'd be fun to watch some movies like that, and I said, Rita, just don't get a disease, okay? And she goes, What, from dirty movies? And I said, You know what I'm talking about. I go, Since you been married? Disease has come along. Always ask, all right? And as soon as I shut up, she says, Let's go drink something out of a pineapple. Let's go drink something out of a pineapple, she says, and puts on this clingy white blouse and leaves off her bra. Don't get herpes, I go. There's still no cure. And don't let nobody ever turn you over on your stomach, ever.

It was only a little joke, Spangler.

So we had our pineapple drinks, me and Rita, and Rita made eye contact with half a dozen phony-baloney Tom Sellecks from the greater metropolitan area. Everybody in these places, don't ask me how come, is always from either New York, New Jersey or

Connecticut. Once in a blue moon you meet somebody from Maryland.

Anyway, two of these hairy mustached apes finally grace us with great big fuck-happy grins. They stroll over to us? At the bar? Which is naturally made out of bamboo. And they go, You girls—girls, they call us—you girls ever seen Skip Lacosta, the comedian? They tell us this Lacosta guy is really a riot, a really funny guy. Really funny. You like Belushi, they go? Try Lacosta. They actually talk this way, Spangler, I'm not making this up. I'm not exaggerating. They go, This guy Lacosta? He throws rubber chickens and shit. So what do you say, girls? We're thirty-five years old, it's girls this, girls that. Hey girls, you wanna come with us, we're gonna catch the early show. Well! I mean, how could us girls resist such entertainment? A guy who throws chickens and shit.

So off we go with Michael and Joseph. I'm Joseph, he's Michael. I'm Michael, my not-so-good-looking friend, here, is Joseph. I'm telling you, Bobby, I wasn't thrilled. My guard was up. Because guys that want you to call them by their full first names? Are generally, in my experience, big, nasty pains in the ass. The smarter ones are lawyers, mostly, that specialize in personal injury claims, and the dumb ones? They work for mortgage companies, or something semi-shady like that. But smart or dumb, they're real pains. Joseph, Michael. Richard. Lawrence. Christopher! If a Christopher won't let me call him Chris, I walk. I just like to keep my distance from guys that won't let you shorten their names. That make a big fucking deal out of it. Joseph, please. I prefer to be called Joseph. Or Michael. Smug? I'm telling you. Not only that, they treat you like dirt. The only exception to this rule is men named Charles who want you to call them Charles. They're usually all right. And I have no explanation for that. You never wanted to be called Robert, did you? You're no Robert, no matter what it says on the piece of paper.

And Spangler? I can testify that Skip Lacosta does, indeed, throw rubber chickens as part of his act. And he rings bells, too, and squirts seltzer water, and he's got this one routine with a Sylvester Stallone hand puppet. What an act! It was like seeing five minutes of the old "Ed Sullivan Show" stretched out to forty-five. I guess I was cringing, I guess I was rolling my eyes, 'cause finally? This guy Michael turns to me and goes, You really don't like him? Really? Then he goes, Finish your drink.

What'd I tell you about a Michael? Finish your drink. Next thing, if I wasn't careful, it'd be, Suck this. What's the matter with you, you're not much fun in bed.

Rita caught my eye and gave me this look. Like, don't spoil it, please? Don't be a bitch. So, for her sake, for Rita's, I tried being pleasant. I let her do most of the talking, though, and, typical, what's she talk about? Computers. Says, Do either of you guys make use of business computers in your line of work?

Rita loves blabbing about computers. It makes her feel, I'm only guessing—very current? From the way she talks, you'd think she was the queen bee of IBM. She works in this library down Monmouth County someplace, and part of her job is typing book titles into a computer. She thinks it's fascinating, or at least she *says* she thinks it's fascinating, that what she types ends up in a memory bank in the Midwest. It's so funny. But it's kind of sad, too. I mean, she makes less than twelve thousand a year, and she's real unhappy, no matter how she acts.

But oh God, when I think of what Rita used to be like! When we were doing His Car Is Cool, you remember? First time in a genuine recording studio, no more two-track mono machines. What street was that? In the Forties somewhere. On Broadway, we were making a record on Broadway, New York! So great.

And right downstairs? remember? was that place, the Metropole? That old topless place? I remember, we'd been doing the vocals over and over and over, take after take, and you were coloring with your crayons, being a real slave driver, a real prick in your leather sport coat and black glasses, those wraparound glasses, and we were all crazy tired. Well, not you, maybe, but us. I can tell you that. We were. Us girls were.

And suddenly we looked around, you and me—and where's Rita? No Rita. So you sent Clare out to find her? Oh come on, you do so remember this. You got to. You sent Clare, you were pissed off, this was costing money, so then I went? So then I went looking for them both?

And there was Rita, goofing on guys trying to peek in the Metropole, trying to see a tit free of charge. Clare was real embarrassed, and there was Rita doing a whole routine, seventeen years old doing the bump and grind, right there on the sidewalk, ten o'clock at night, arching her back and sticking out her big chest and laughing all over the place. That's how Rita used to be, always goofing, always flip. She had a very sharp mouth. Some of her lines? Really outstanding.

It's funny, I always had this reputation for being the Mouth—in the Holy Family yearbook? I was Best Talker, as well as Celebrity Grad. But once upon a time, it was Rita, Rita was funnier. Rita had the better mouth, she had the cooler attitude. For a while, she was a better girl than even I was. Then we broke up and then she went nuts and then she got married and now she's divorced, she's on that stupid computer every day and she never says nothing funny on purpose. She's even kind of dense. Don't get my jokes half the time. What she is, I guess, is serious. Rita's turned serious. And she's put on a lot of weight. Too much dope, too much vodka, too much Stuart. I keep telling her, lose twenty pounds. You'll feel better. . . .

So after Skip Lacosta retrieved all his chickens and thanked everybody for being such good sports, shoveling that pious Don Rickels bullshit, all kinds of people started going up on stage, people from the audience—because now there was a lip-sync contest and you could win a bottle of wine. This shrink from New Haven? Who looked like Peter Yarrow? Did Emotional Rescue. On purpose, to be funny. He says, I'm a shrink from New Haven, then he does Emotional Rescue. From Peter, Paul and Mary, that's Peter Yarrow. And this other guy, he's a general contractor? He does Another Brick in the Wall. And four separate women, all of them looking sad as Mary Magdalene, did The Rose. Four of them. I nearly lost my mind. If you want my opinion, Spangler, that's one of the dullest records ever made, right up there with Sukiyaki. The Rose, Sukiyaki and The Most Wonderful Summer. The dullest records ever made.

So, I'm sitting there making this mental list. The Rose. Sukiyaki. Most Wonderful Summer. Raindrops Keep Falling on My Head. When all of a sudden, Rita starts yanking on my arm, saying, Franny, you want to? Come on. She's actually trying to drag me to my feet. I looked at her, like—get away away from me, you Martian! But she's serious. She's dead serious. She wants us to go up there, she's saying, We could do it better than anybody. Geez, she goes, We should—we only did it for three years. She's going, Let's see what records they got, maybe they got some oldies, maybe they got—but right there, Spangler, I cut her off. I knew what this was all about. Don't think I didn't. In two seconds, she was going to be telling the Hardy Boys just Who We Were. Who we used to be. And I didn't want any part of it. No fooling, they'd say, that was really you? And meanwhile—meanwhile, their two little pea brains would be crunching numbers like one of Rita's computers, going '64 to '74, '74 to '80, '81. Holycatzolis, seventeen years ago. How old are these broads anyhow?

So I told Rita, Forget it. I told her to sit down and shut up or else go lip-sync herself. I said, They probably got 9 to 5. Go ahead, Dolly. Yeah, says Joseph, go on up there, Dolly. And Rita shook her head and says to me, she looks me straight in the eye and she says, No. No, she says, I'm only a background singer. I made like I was playing the violin, and Rita stuck out her tongue. Then Joseph says, Let's say we get out of here, people, and go for a swim. He started pulling beads apart, to pay for our drinks.

Rita looked stricken when I said I didn't feel like the beach. She probably did severe damage to her back teeth, clenching them like that. We're getting up to leave, right? And these two Swedish-looking babes start doing He's So Shy, the Pointer Sisters? Who learned everything they know from girls like me and Rita, from the Chiffons, all the rest. So there's the Pointer Sisters, making hits, and here I was, trying to give the brush-off to a Weickert realtor from Succasunna, New Jersey. Hey Frances, he goes, trailing his stubby fingers across my tush—Frances, don't be a stick-in-the-mud. You're on vacation. Come swimming with us. I informed him that I didn't like being called Frances. Fran or Franny would do nicely, I said. Then I walked away and left poor Rita. I guess she'd pissed me off. We could do it better than anybody! Geez, we should, we only did it for three years!

Two years, darling. Just two, I felt like reminding her. The first thing that goes is your stomach. Then your boobs. Then your memory. It was two years, honeybunch. Only two. 2 years, 3 hits, 4-ever. Christ, Franny, that's really cute. How old are you, sixteen?

I only wished.

Yeah, sure. We'll take a drive down Point Pleasant sometime, we'll go see Rita. We'll go. Definitely we'll go see Rita some weekend. She'd like that, I guess.

*   *   *

. . . So it was, like. It must've been, like, the first or maybe the second week in October that we met, at that dance. When Spangler followed us all around downtown Bayonne and finally caught up. Fourth Street, corner of Trask. And he got all our names, mine and Rita's and Clare's, and we talked about songs and he said he knew this guy. That went to Seton Hall? And this guy he knew that went to Seton Hall? Who was getting, like, a hundred bucks a week writing songs for some music publisher—in New York? He'd had two little hits already. This guy named Worm. And that's all we talked about, Bobby never asked for nobody's phone number. He said it was nice meeting us, he'd see us. And left. And Rita thought he was interested in *her*. She goes, You think? She goes, I think. But I never said nothing. But I knew, Camille, I knew.

Then he called me up, the very next day, said he'd called four different Tolentinos? Just looking for me. And he said there was this party. Next Friday? I should come. It was at this guy's apartment, near Lincoln Park. I said no, then I said okay.

I took the bus to Jersey City all by myself, never told Rita. I wore black corduroy jeans and a fuzzy green sweater, a navy pea coat. My hair was long then and I had it stuffed under a watch cap.

Spangler's friend? I forget his name, was an older guy who'd already finished high school and was working. It wasn't his place, though. You could tell he still lived with his parents. There was, like, this combination TV/hi-fi in the living room, there was wall-to-wall carpeting, there were a couple of truly awful palette paintings on the wall. Street scenes of Paris. Remember palette paintings? People used to have them.

About ten kids were there when I arrived, but only two other girls, and I didn't know either of them. I didn't know anybody, period, guys included. The girls both wore a lot of mascara, a lot of eye shadow. I wasn't wearing any makeup at all, nothing. Wipe Out was playing. Then Louie Louie. I didn't see Spangler, but somebody said he was around. Around where? I threw my coat on the couch and went straight to the kitchen and drank one drink after another. Mixing whatever was there with Seven-Up. I was real nervous.

So I go in the bathroom? And I'm on the toilet? When I realize some guy's passed out in the tub, some guy with pimples and horn-rimmed glasses like Buddy Holly wore. I pull up my jeans and run. And there's Spangler in the hall, he's waiting, and he goes, You feel okay? You want to lie down for a while?

What a seduction, right? What do you say, Camille, was that a seduction and a half? Nobody smoother than a seventeen-year-old boy, right? Do I wanna lie down! I wasn't dumb, I knew what was going on, but I was game, not totally but a little, so we flopped down together on the bed, which was piled with coats. It was thick with coats. He starts kissing me, right away the tongue, then he's feeling me up. Then he tries to get my sweater over my head, but I ask him, So what do you think you're doing? And he goes, Nothing, then he turns on a lamp. It hurt my eyes. I don't think we need that, I go, and he goes, Yeah, but I want to see you, and then what I'm feeling? I'm feeling a very definite pain in my stomach, like a knife stab. Spangler looked way too serious, and it scared me.

I want to make love to you, he goes. The door is locked. Nobody can walk in. And I say, No. Just like that: No.

But he says, Why not?

And I told him he's got to be kidding.

He gave me this look? this quick frown? It was funny. But not really. Then he starts digging through the coats. And I figured, Jesus Christ, he's gonna grab his and leave me. I felt definitely excited by that, that he'd grab his coat, like in love comics, and go. Go for right now, but then call me up tomorrow.

What he did, but, he found his coat and pulled out this coloring book! This coloring book! And a box of crayons. Sits down in a chair. I'm looking at him, my hair's all messed, and my sweater. He starts to color, it's Mighty Mouse. Legs crossed, coloring book on his knee, he's coloring fucking Mighty Mouse! Then he starts talking about that songwriter again, the one making a hundred bucks a week, and it's like he never tried to zap me. It's like he never said, I want to make love. I was confused, all embarrassed. For myself, not for him. For myself. If he'd grabbed his coat and left, I could've handled that. I knew a few things. But this. I was completely thrown off.

Spangler goes, he could write songs. He goes, he never has, but he could. It's no big deal, he figures. Then he looks up and says, this is Spangler talking and he says, I understand the mechanics. I don't know shit about music, but I understand the mechanics. The mechanics? I'm thinking, What a funny word to use, mechanics. Mechanics of what? He's coloring, he's talking fast, he says, I'll write songs, I'll get a tape recorder, a band together. You and your girlfriends? You three can sing. We'll make money. Girls love boys. It'll be easy. Girls love boys more than boys love girls. That's the secret. If you listen close enough to songs. And finally I say something, I go, I can't *sing*. He says, I'll write a few songs, get a tape recorder. Then he put off the light and I let him feel me up with my sweater on, and I let him hump me with our clothes on till he came in his pants. I think I got mad, but I can't, can't really remember.

                              *   *   *

You remember how Daddy used to call you up, say where was his money, his cash? Say you took all his clothes, and his stupid favorite lighter? Say you'd stolen it, you were a thief? When he got so bad, when he called you all the time on the phone? And remember, like, how he'd show up sometimes at the house? And just stand there on the porch with his arms folded, always so angry? After dark, just. Late at night. Like a vampire. A werewolf. Daddy the zombie. And we couldn't walk out? You'd say, He'll leave, Franny, he'll get tired soon enough and just leave. But sometimes he'd be there, like, all night? I don't know how come nobody called the cops, Mrs. Cuff or somebody. *You* wouldn't, but Mrs. Cuff or somebody. But nobody did, and he just stood out there? Angry about whatever. About whatever he was angry about? Remember, Ma?

Now it's Spangler, only different. He's not angry or nothing, at least I don't think he is. But maybe.

What happened, I didn't even know it. Camille told me. What happened was, the other night? Jacky Peek came home, I don't know what time, but late. He went out around one-thirty in the morning, to see his other girlfriend. And he comes home, maybe three, three-thirty. And there's somebody on the lawn. What do you think, you see some guy on the front lawn, three-thirty in the morning? You're gonna get jumped, is what you think.

It was Spangler, yeah.

Camille told me, next day. She says, Peek seen this guy? He's on the lawn? By the fig tree? Like he's hiding. And Peek goes, What do you think you're doing, or like that. I said to Camille, Did Peek have his gun? Peek has a gun, you know. For his job. Camille says no. But still. Still, when she told me? I got all nervous, for a second.

Peek says, What do you think you're doing? To Spangler! And Spangler wants to know who *Peek* is. Peek's a jerk, but I probably wouldn't've said nothing, too. Meet a guy standing on your lawn, you have to answer questions? So Peek figures, I give him credit— he figures the best thing he should do is go inside, quick. So he goes up the stoop backwards, Spangler watching him. Then Spangler says, Where do you think *you're* going? Where do you think *you're* going? Like that. Like, *Peek* was doing something wrong, going into his own house. He must've been drunk, Spangler. I mean, he knows about Camille. That Camille lives upstairs. He *knows* I don't use the whole house. He knows. He even met Camille once. He must've been drunk, or something.

Well, Peek almost called the cops, but Camille looked out the front window and seen it was Spangler. And said don't. She figured he'd just come out of my apartment. But when she told me? I couldn't believe it. Spangler hadn't even been *over* that night, I hadn't seen him for a couple of days. I got really creeped out. It was too much like Daddy.

Sure, I talked to him about it. I called him right up. And he says—he says he just took a walk, ended up here. He didn't want to bother me in the middle of the night. I said, Spangler, you just hang out on my lawn? I go, You could've got mugged. He says he can't stand it being home. His father sees things. I mean, that aren't there. He's really off it, his father. And it's kind of grim, I can believe Spangler, but three o'clock in the morning? He walks from Stegman Parkway, all the way here? I'm almost kicking myself we ever got back in touch. Almost.

*   *   *

. . . So this one time? This is a riot, Camille, also very weird. This girl wanted his sperm? She came to Walter's apartment? Just showed up, like you'd show up at somebody's door, you want cocaine or an ounce of grass. He lived downtown, not far from Hamilton Park.

I'm up his place, all weekend I think, we're sitting around on Sunday reading the papers. Half-watching an Abbott and Costello movie on Channel 5. The doorbell rings—or, I guess, somebody just knocked. It wasn't a buzzer building, it was an old brick heap, but the rooms were big, and he had four. Four big rooms, all to himself.

Anyhow, in come these two girls—these women. The one talking was maybe thirty-five. The other was Oriental, a teeny little thing with round tinted glasses: she reminded me of that character in *Doonesbury*? That's always with Uncle Duke? Honey. She looked

like Honey, from Red China, in *Doonesbury*. She was in her twenties. The older one had black, black hair, a black cashmere sweater,
black jeans. Black, black, black. She was pretty but thin and her
skin was pale. Like Joan Jett—that look. Punky. But thirty-five.

Walter don't know either of them, okay? They got his name from
somebody. The Joan Jett one did, at least. Her friend just came
along. So she got Walter's name, now she wants Walter's sperm.
She'll pay fifty bucks, cash. It's the perfect day, she goes. According
to her, the egg has landed. Marge. Her name was Marge. And I'm
thinking, This is very weird. This is very weird. I felt like somebody
from the planet Zorkon. Earthlings are strange. I had the funnies
on my lap. I'd been reading *Prince Valiant*. I remember: they were
all out in the hall talking, and I was listening, but with one eye still
on *Prince Valiant*. The color orange kept jumping out at me from
the page. Dark orange.

So Walter leaves them and goes out to the kitchen. Just leaves
them in the hall. And so they peek in the parlor, and you can see
they're both surprised to see me. The Chinese one looks a little
embarrassed. Not the other one, though. Not Marge. She's a real
stone-face. She's here on business. I smile and go, You want to sit
down? They say no, thanks, and finally I get up and go looking for
Walter.

He's in the kitchen, he's rinsing out a lidded jar, like a spice jar.
Not a jelly glass, Camille. Very funny. A little thing, a spice jar,
like for cardamom or ginger. I say, What're you gonna do? He says,
Make fifty bucks. Easy. Fifty easy bucks. Nothing to it, he goes.
And I go, Yeah, I guess not. Simple mechanics.

So he goes in the bathroom and jerks off. Didn't make a sound,
not a single sound, not so much as a grunt. All I heard was the
medicine cabinet open and shut. I guess he used baby oil. Be my,
be my baby oil. It takes a minute, maybe. He's a real pro. And he
gives this punky thirty-five-year-old woman the jar and she hands
him two twenties and a ten. Nice doing business.

So they leave, the two women leave? And Walter goes back and
sits down, starts watching Abbott and Costello, that scene in the

haunted house where the candle moves back and forth on the table. He sat there looking at the TV, I sat there looking at Walter. I felt funny. Even though sperm is blood, and people sell their blood. Even so, I felt funny. Earthlings are strange. And I'm thinking about Marge, about her racing home with this spice jar, lid on tight, and how's she gonna do it? I'm wondering will it work? And how come I never got pregnant, not once, how come I never wanted to. And how come, in all my life, I never lost sleep worrying about it, one way or the other.

So if Peek keeps stalling you, Camille, there's always Walter. People like Walter. Plenty of Walters in this world. In the modern world. I'm just saying. I'm only making a joke.

*   *   *

It was 1964, April. May? No, it was April. The Supremes were big, the Dixie Cups, the Shangri-Las. But we were still local girls. Spangler dumped the first band we'd been singing with, these kind of good friends. One was, like, even Clare's boyfriend. He just dumped them. And got a bunch of new kids from different high schools, one kid from Prep, couple kids from Snyder. Paulie Kosakowski, that cop you met? He went to Snyder. He played drums. For shit, but he had a good set. And one guy that was going to St. Peter's College. Bobby put a whole new band in back of us. Rehearsed us till we puked, school nights included, up his father's house. I had to take a bus from Bayonne, me and Clare and Rita together, all of us lying to our parents. She's at my house. And I'm at hers. They'd've killed us, we said Jersey City.

At Spangler's, we'd fool around with this little two-track machine, doing Shirelles. Doing Ronettes, doing Martha and the Vandellas, a few of Spangler's songs. He was getting better, but still he wasn't what you'd call very good. And we were making, like, fifteen, twenty bucks apiece every weekend, and it was fun. Playing high school dances, bowling alleys, Kiwanis things, Knights of Columbus, stuff like that. We had something almost every week, every other weekend, thanks to Bobby. He couldn't get us into bars, though. 'Cause we were all underage, except maybe that guy from St. Peter's, and maybe even him.

Then Spangler got this idea, I think he read something. About this club, in New York? The Candy Bar. West Forty-third Street. It was supposed to be a cool place, like the Peppermint Lounge had been a cool place, and Bobby decided to get us in. He was gonna fix it up, we'd get in, we'd sing. Just us, not the band. Us just. Clare and Rita thought he was full of it, but not me. If he said he'd get us in, I believed him. I was Bobby's Girl.

So this one night? We all showed up at Spangler's, and he takes out maybe twenty bucks' worth of cosmetics from a little white paper sack, stuff that he bought himself. All this liquid makeup, lipstick, perfume. He'd even bought denim skirts. And these matching white sweaters? I'd never worn nothing so tight in my life. And stockings. Black stockings. I was impressed. Bobby, when he got that way, when he got so intense, so in charge, could be a little bit scary. More than a little. He scared Clare to death. But I was impressed. I was very impressed, Camille.

So me and Rita put on the skirt and blouse. And Bobby stayed right there, he stayed right in the cellar. Didn't even turn around. But Clare wouldn't change in front of him. Not Clare. She couldn't. She sneaked off behind the furnace.

Then we drove through the Lincoln Tunnel, and Bobby parked in a parking garage. He was spending money. He didn't care. We went right into a parking garage. It was the first time I'd ever been in an underground garage. Leave your keys in the car. It was so bright. It was great. We looked like what we were, a group, all dressed exactly the same, hair teased, our matching makeup, green Cleopatra eyes. Bobby had on a shiny blue suit with skinny lapels, one of those electric-blue jobs like Dion used to wear, pointy shoes and white socks.

Spangler had on white socks, pointy shoes, and that shiny blue suit, and he took us right up to the Candy Bar, and as we were coming toward the door, he lit a cigarette. Sure he did. There was a guy at the door, an older guy, gray hair, it was curly. And he looked at us, and Bobby looked back, like daring him, just daring him to card us. And he stepped aside, this guy, and we walked in. Walked right in.

The walls were mirrored, there were gold veins in the mirrors, like at a catering place, like at a wedding reception. And there was even one of those reflector balls? That too. And there was a fat guy playing records. It was like the junior prom, almost. The Holy Family prom with a wet bar. A little record player, and the fat guy was playing 45s. Compare that to now, right? And just twenty years ago. Listen to me. Just. Like twenty years is nothing.

A band was setting up, nobody special, the house band. It was the middle of the week, don't forget. Bobby stood us at the bar, he just left us there and went to work. Clare was chewing her lips. Rita and me, but—we were, like, thrilled to death. I bet we could've bought drinks. But I couldn't think of nothing to order. All I could think of was scotch and soda, and I didn't want that. Besides, I didn't have money. Not a dime. None of us did. Bobby hadn't let us take our purses, since they didn't match. If he'd just left us there, we couldn't've got home. But of course he didn't leave us. Not then. He went to work.

I seen him talking to a man with silver hair. Up three steps where some tables were. Then I seen him talking to this other guy that was hooking a cable to a speaker. Then I seen him hand a fuzzbox to somebody else, and he was still talking. I seen his mouth go, his hands move. He was working. He knew the mechanics. He was doing the job.

Maybe ten or fifteen minutes went by, maybe a lot more. Then he came over, Spangler came back and said it was all set. And Camille? Let me tell you, I jumped up and down, which, I guess, wasn't the coolest thing to do in a nightclub that got mentioned in Jack O'Brien's column in the *Journal-American*. But I did it. Spangler bought us Cokes. He'd done magic. He was a magic boy. We did Twist and Shout. Twist and Shout and Please, Mr. Postman. Please, Mr. Postman, then Will You Love Me Tomorrow. And the whole time? Spangler leaned so cool against the bar. Spangler. I seen him take out his shades and put them on in the dark, and my heart swelled up like bread.

*   *   *

It's creepy as anything up here, and that insulation—don't breathe too much, Spangler, it'll kill you. It's true. What, you never heard that? It's fiberglass, it's death in your lungs, it'll kill you. Just don't go away and lock me in. I'd go off my rocker.

Hey, lookit this: the Platters. I loved the Platters. Lookit this cut glass. There's always cut glass in somebody's attic, it's a rule. I bet you, we dig long enough, we'll find some plates with pictures on them. A church, and like that. Boy. Your father never threw nothing out, did he, Spangler? You ever seen such stuff? It's great. Box of books, box of books—lookit all this *Reader's Digest* condensed shit. I loved them. My mother subscribed, I read a bunch. I remember *The Agony and the Ecstasy*. About Michelangelo? One summer I read that, I loved it, I still remember the last page, him an old guy dying? I cried and I cried. It's funny, but when I was girl? I figured that was a great book, the first grown-up book I ever read. I heard since that it's trash. The guy who wrote it? He's supposed to be a trash writer. I thought it was great, but. I should read it again. No, I shouldn't. If you find a copy of *The Agony and the Ecstasy*, Spangler, give it here.

We'll clear this place out in no time flat. When you're trying to sell a house, you can't have too much clutter. That's a rule. I know all the rules. Wash the windows, put out flowers, clean the attic.

Hey, you know what? You should have a yard sale. The weather's nice, it's the best time. You and me, we can tag everything. Be fun. We can stand outside. Get a table, find a table and stand outside. The books, the cut glass, the oldest blender in creation, that set of picture plates we're bound to find. We'll get tags, price everything cheap, to move. We'll do it all day, pick a Saturday.

You remember when we used to spend *every* Saturday in a different record shop? When people came to see us? And we'd sign labels? Remember at Sam Goody, that time? When some guy stole one of Rita's barrettes and took a bunch of hair with it? I wonder if anybody still got stuff we autographed. Franny T. Franny T.

Franny T. I always wished there was an *i* in my first name, so I could make a circle over it, instead of a dot. I always wished I had Rita's name, it used to drive me nuts she only made dots. I always liked Rita, I always liked her name. You always like Rita? The name Rita?

I liked it so much I thought we should be Rita and the somethings. Rita and the Candy Bars. I forget all the other somethings. I never liked the name Frantastics—who came up with that? It wasn't Clare, I think you're wrong. She wanted to be the Clare-Alls, remember? The Clare-Alls! But there was no way. And it wasn't just we'd get sued, she was—she was the third girl, just, the balance. No way we'd ever name the group after her, right?

I never liked the name Frantastics, but. We swiped it from that musical. The *Fantasticks*, there was that hit song. Try to Remember? Really sucky song, but it was a hit. And we swiped it from that. We did, too! The name. Oh, we did. It did so come from that. You just don't remember.

Oh, Spangler! This is so cool! Spangler, remember this jacket? There's a picture I got, I think I still got, you in this jacket. And when you got your gums cut and drained? You wore it.

You had your gums cut, you wore this purple jacket. One Saturday morning. Are you listening, Spangler? It's a good story, you don't know it, so listen.

I seen you the Friday night before, we done a Prep dance, you were swallowing pus, worried sick about your mouth. All night long you chewed aspirin, gum with aspirin. I never seen your lips so tight, I never seen you so quiet. Rinsing your mouth. And I liked you so much, it broke my heart.

Saturday, I called the dentist, your dentist, to see when you were supposed to get there. And I made sure I got there first. He had a girl's name for his last name, Dr. Marilyn. At Journal Square, above the Orange Julius. I stood across the street, by the Trust Company. I sat on a bench. The bench was near some discount bins. Beach towels with lion faces. Alarm clocks. Hand towels. Face cloths. I seen you get off the Bergen Avenue bus. This purple jacket, unzipped, some coloring book in your back pocket rolled up in a tube.

You were by yourself, you didn't see me, you walked different. Just like everybody else walked, there was no roll. Your shoulders were down. There was no roll. I stuck my wrist in my mouth, I liked you so much. You walked just, you just walked straight into that brick building, it's not there no more. Dr. Marilyn, neither. Now there's a big white office building.

I go to myself, He's upstairs now. He's inside. A fish tank, last summer's magazines. Now he's sitting down. I seen you in my head. I gave you five minutes, it was ten past ten—it was ten past ten, and I go to myself, The dentist is packing his mouth with cotton. I liked you so much, I could feel your eyes stinging at the corners, your heart in my chest, your white hands. I'm looking at my feet, my shoes, at the curb, in the gutter. Now I'm stooping, for a soda cap. It was a Canada Dry. And a piece of broken bottle, green broken glass, another piece, another cap. And because I liked you, Spangler, I put all that shit in my mouth. The bottle caps, the glass, the green broken glass, everything. And I can't swallow, I couldn't swallow. If I swallowed, I'd die. It was. It was fucking insane. But you were across the street, up the stairs, your mouth wired open, cotton in your mouth, and fingers, thick fingers but clean, and something to cut. Something cutting. You wore this purple jacket.

Spangler? Don't.

Side Two

So why didn't you come? You said you would. I waited, and when you didn't show, I didn't feel like going by myself. But then I said, what, just 'cause you don't show, you don't call, I'm gonna sit home on the Fourth of July? Who are you? Who the fuck are you? And besides, when it got dark? Everybody was going on the roof, where you can see New York, the Statue of Liberty. You know me and fireworks. If you remember.

So I took a shower and put on jeans, white jeans, and a T-shirt, and I didn't wait for my hair to dry, or even brush it. That's what so good about keeping it short. And I wore sandals. I looked at myself in the bedroom mirror and said, All right. I said, Fuck you, Spangler. I said, Not too bad. Then I turned around and looked at my ass. It also looked okay. I been told, as a compliment, that I got a black girl's ass. I forget who by. The way it sticks out. Going to a party with my hair still damp. What a youthful thing to do!

So I leave, and there's Jimmy. This guy that lives next door, he's out doing lawnwork. He's our age, you probably seen him: thin guy? wears glasses? He used to be a programmer, now he owns buildings. At least half a dozen on the hill. He's been here way over ten years, long before me. Moved in when all the old houses were still carved up into flops. You'd probably like him. You'd probably

like Jimmy, you two guys might get along. You two guys had vision.
Maybe not the same kind, it sure wasn't, but it was vision, what
you both had. See? I'm not mad. I'm saying something nice. That's
a compliment. You didn't wanna come, that's your business.

Anyhow. Jimmy waves and goes, You been swimming? On account of my wet hair. Which was funny, that he even noticed. And
that he'd say something like that. He's just a friend, Spangler. Not
even, he's just a neighbor. A guy in the neighborhood. The new
people don't like him. They think he's crude. Which he is, maybe,
but his apartments? Are the last ones with rents under five.

So I'm going down the walk, and Jimmy unravels a hose, he
turns on the water and starts wetting his lawn. That summer, that
real dry one? Couple years ago? You weren't around, but there was
a drought and you could've got a big fine for watering the grass
just. But Jimmy watered. Every single night he was out. He didn't
care. He wanted his lawn nice and green. You'd like him, Spangler,
I bet you. So listen. He's wetting his lawn, and all of a sudden? He
swings around the nozzle and squirts my heels, like a boy would.
And laughs when I jump. And I laughed too. What I did, I guess,
was squeal. And I hated myself. All the way down the street, I hated
myself for doing that.

But so, this couple? That had the barbecue? It's an old Victorian
job they got with a nice backyard. Where they keep finding syringes
that junkies toss down. There's a brick tenement next door. And
every time that Patricia finds something? Like needles? She calls
the cops. And the cops come, maybe, and if they come, they drop
the stuff in plastic bags and they look up and shrug at the tenement.
What're they gonna do? I know what Patricia wants. Them to get
out the riot guns, make a door-to-door search. She says it's bad
enough, but now there's AIDS. Like, she might walk out one day,
step on a needle. Next thing you know, it's death by pneumonia.
Everybody tells her, sit tight, the place is going condo. The sign is
up already.

So I had to pass this tenement, and there's, like, firecracker paper
all over the sidewalk, and blobs of white ice cream, bags of garbage
at the curb already and the next pickup not until Monday. A dozen

kids out front, and older guys in cars with North Carolina plates. I been living here longer than any of those people. They still got North Carolina plates. But still I feel like the new girl walking by. My neck tickles. Always. But those people, people like Nosy Brown? Endangered species. And they know it. One of the things I always wonder is, like, where they gonna go?

So at the barbecue? I heard one solution. Where the black people all gonna go? Down the sewers. No kidding. And the guy that came up with this bright idea, he's a magazine writer. He's divorced. He's from Minnesota. His stuff's been in *Rolling Stone*. That's what I heard. God, there's tons of writers around here now, and actors galore. I got one tenant was in a Broadway show. *Three Musketeers*, that bombed.

But this guy? This writer? Says they're all gonna end up down in the sewers. He giving away this real good plot, anybody wants it. He goes, It's not my kind of story, but anybody feel like beating Stephen King at his game, here you go. Take the idea. Free of charge.

He was sitting on the back porch with a plate of carrot salad on his knee, a bottle of beer in reach. Keeping one eye on his small bald daughter toddling around in a diaper. He had some carrot in his beard, but nobody told him. He says, It's a good idea! I'm talking popular fiction, he goes. A four-ninety-five paperback! All these welfare people, screwed by Reagan? The underclass, that's fucked? They start living in the sewers and they come up late at night to, I don't know, rob and kill. I'm just talking popular fiction. Then he jumps up and runs after his daughter who's wandering through the badminton game. And I was thinking maybe I'd just go home and skip the fireworks.

But then Patricia comes over wagging a cassette in my face. Says 1964 on the label, and I smiled, but I really wished she wasn't gonna do what I knew she was. I didn't want to make any big deal, though. Come off looking silly.

So out comes the chamber-music tape and in goes 1964's greatest hits, starting with Rag Doll. I decide to get up, I need a soda. Next song is I Get Around, then Do You Want to Know a Secret? And then it's His Car Is Cool, and Patrica's walking around the yard, telling everybody what's what, pointing back at me, and I feel giddy, for a second I feel blank, and almost sick to my stomach. His car is cool, it's candy red, he goes to my school, he goes to my head.

People I don't know, never seen, are smiling at me, and I realize that most of them? Probably were *born* around 1964. People just out of college, or out a couple years and making tons of money, who spend it on health clubs and real estate. But they all know that song. They all did. It's a classic and you're damn straight I'm proud. You're still proud, aren't you, Bobby?

Look, I'm not vain and I never did any of those revival shows. Never. And I had a lot of chances, these guys used to call me up, but I always said no. Once, Rita practically begged me to. Rita needed the cash—she goes, We'll hire somebody, she can be Clare. But I said no. I got my pride—but hey Bobby? We made a classic record. We made three classic records.

So Patricia played it four more times, five altogether, and listen, I was embarrassed, but I'd be lying to you, Spangler, if I didn't say it was kind of neat, too. I'm human. I still watch the Academy Awards.

Anyhow, this writer guy. From Minnesota. Sticks to me like glue for the next three hours, asking me questions. You wanna hamburger? Get you a beer? You don't sing anymore, not at all? He can't believe it, he goes. That I own a bunch of houses, that's it, that's what I do. You don't sing at all, not ever? He says he seen Ronnie Spector with Southside Johnny, and I go, yeah, so what? He says, well, he just seen her, she's still in the business. I love that: *in the business.* And finally I told him, I said, Look, I wasn't any great shakes voice, believe me. There were three of us, we were, like, sixteen, seventeen years old, we had this guy that put it all together. It wasn't a career. Just big-time adolescence. It happened just.

And then I asked him if he ever heard of you. You ever hear of Bobby Spangler? I go. And I'm sorry, Spangler, but he never did. The asshole. He should've heard of you. I mean, he says he knows all about sixties music, he's talking about Phil Spector and shit. He

should've known you. He was a jerk. Not Phil Spector, this guy
from Minnesota. But maybe Phil Spector, too.

Then he starts asking me about the other girls, he don't know
their names. But he wants to hear what happened, blah, blah, blah.
I told him Clare was dead, and Rita's down the shore, that she
works in a public library. Then it clicked: this guy's a magazine
writer. I don't wanna end up in some whatever-happened-to-Franny
Tolentino piece of garbage, I don't need it. She owns property. Like,
I'm real with-it in the Eighties. Look how she's grown up, everybody. Small-time real estate operator. Screw that. It's not important
I grew up. What's important, I was a girl. That I was a girl maybe
the last time it was cool to be one. Cool and safe and all right.

So, I go, let's talk about something else. Like, where do you come
from in Minnesota. But he don't want to. He's a real pest. I forget
his name. What do you care what his name was? I haven't seen
him since. Yeah, right, I went out with him. Of course I didn't go
out with him. He was a jerk, didn't I just tell you he was a big
jerk?

So finally it's almost dark, it's almost nine, we go up on the roof,
twenty people. To watch the fireworks. But there was no railing,
no parapet, just a flat tar roof, absolutely flat, and I got a bad case
of, what's that fear? Of heights? I was afraid that I'd fall and break
my stupid neck, and I stood by the chimney and held on. Everybody
talking real estate. I am not exaggerating. Everybody was. Always
it's real estate, real estate, who got robbed and real estate. Mortgage
rates, gut jobs, all that stuff. These are very hard-nosed people,
Spangler, bet you they even talk FHA screwing in bed. Nine point
seven, ten point six. It's pure sex. And I'm standing up there scared
silly, not saying diddly, waiting for the sky to light red, white and
blue. So I can say that I seen it, and go home. And I look around?
And I can look right across the alley and through an open tenement
window, and there's Nosy Brown. At his kitchen table, drinking
soda from a can. Sitting there with his shirt off. His big shoulders.
And I don't know why, I never thought so before, but now I think
he looks like Sam Cooke. But heavier. And not so happy. God,
Spangler—Sam Cooke.

You wanna hear something funny? Whenever I have people over? Usually I don't, but say I do? I'm always nervous wondering what I should play, 'cause I don't buy records, so usually I don't play nothing. But if somebody says put something on? I play Sam Cooke, and everybody says, oh man, that guy. He's still cool. His stuff is, like, twenty-five years old, he's dead, but still he's cool. Yeah, I know he got shot. So what? So he got shot. It don't matter. You Send Me is still great. Wonderful World. Another Saturday Night.

So I seen Nosy Brown, in this crummy-looking kitchen. One wall is, like, a public school building, it's all spray-painted. His refrigerator is spray-painted, the cabinets. He don't need a coloring book, Spangler, he got his kitchen.

I don't think he could see me. Could see any of us. He could probably hear us, but, going, Lookit that. Going, Ahh. Cooing at the fireworks. Then somebody touched me, Spangler. In the dark. On the roof. On purpose, I'd swear. Brushed against me. Definitely on purpose, definitely male. It could've been anybody. And I just stood there, Spangler, holding on to that chimney.

You could've come. I waited. I called. You said you'd come. Then never showed. Same old Spangler. Same old Spangler. Same old shit.

I should get a dog. I should. I know I should. All these burglaries. Like, just yesterday, at 111? The whole door kicked in. Last week, it was 79. And last Christmas? Couple days after Christmas, a woman got raped, just three houses down. I paid a thousand dollars for a steel door, after that.

Five o'clock in the afternoon, abducted at gunpoint. I say abducted, I mean it. Like in Lebanon. She's on the stoop taking her mail, guy sneaks up. Drags her down the steps, down the walk. And throws her in a car. Like it's done in Lebanon, except that he raped her. Maybe that's done in Lebanon, too. I don't know. All I read is headlines.

I still get the *Jersey Journal*, but only on Wednesday. I give Camille the coupons. She comes down here, we talk. I help her clip Pathmark coupons, and we talk. I spread out the paper, we both cut. She brings her own scissors. If I forget to buy the Wednesday paper, I'm mad at myself. I'll even ask Jimmy if he's done with his copy, can I have it. I stoop that low. I like it when Camille comes down. She's company. And she reminds me of me, a long time ago.

But you're right, I should get a dog, a big dog. But a dog you have to walk, so what's the point? You buy one, you own a dog to feel safe, and what do you do? Go out at night to walk it.

I like cats. Sure, I know cats are useless, I'm just saying I like them. I had one. Named Pearl. I named my cat Pearl. I found her on the street. What she did, she found me. And I took her home and gave her milk. I had her spayed. It was the biggest mistake. She gained I don't know how much weight. Ballooned right up. Her health went to pieces, her shit always smelled. She got ear infections, nothing helped. Her ear just rotted away. She was always scratching it. Then shaking her head—she'd spray the walls with bits of skin, this bloody pus. Finally, I couldn't stand it, I had her destroyed. I still wonder if I did right, if I did the right thing. I guess my conscience is pretty clear. I mean, if that's what bothers it.

This was. It was a year ago this coming-up fall. Election Day. This guy Kenny stayed over the night before. I got up early, an hour before I usually did, but I let Kenny sleep. It was chilly in the bedroom. And as soon as I got dressed, I went over and felt the radiator, afraid that I'd find it cold. I worry about my furnace like some people worry about tumors. It's just as serious, just as sickening, it makes me wretched when something goes wrong with the furnace. Goes wrong in the house. It's my house, I'm responsible. But I wish I could just call somebody, a landlord, my mother, somebody, anybody, and say the furnace conked out, there's a flood in the basement, you fix it. But I can't. I got to deal with it. And I hate it. This is not the kind of life I wanted for myself.

Anyhow, it was okay, it was warm. The radiator. Just barely, but that was good enough for me. I lived, I still do, in dread of some house calamity. A leak in the water-stack. A window blowing in. Termites. I hate having to deal with those things, Spangler, I deal with them badly, I lose my temper. I got an answering machine. Tenants call, I never call back. I got this reputation for never calling back. I hate contractors, plumbers.

But I was telling you what I did about Pearl.

I let Kenny sleep and went downstairs, boiled water for coffee. There was a bunch of papers, compositions, spread on the table. Kenny was still teaching high school. Compare Hamlet and Claudius. I read a few. Hamlet was the good guy, Claudius was the bad guy. Mostly everybody got that right. Claudius wanted to make it with Gertrude, so did Hamlet. A couple of boys called her Trudy, I guess to be wise. Hamlet didn't get drunk on Saturday nights, Claudius did. Hamlet believed in ghosts, Claudius didn't. Kenny taught all boys. Hudson Catholic. The grammar and spelling were pretty wild, but I guess I shouldn't laugh, I shouldn't make fun. I was pretty bad, myself, I was rotten. You know who was good at that stuff, but? Clare. She used to be in honors English, she had to read a zillion novels. All the time on the bus, her reading *A Tale of Two Cities*, reading *Call of the Wild*. *To Kill a Mockingbird*. Me and Rita looking at *Sixteen* magazine, reading comic books. Betty and Veronica.

Kenny hated teaching, it's how come he finally went to X ray school, he's a technician now. The boys he had to teach? Were real zeroes. Coming in stoned, Catholic boys coming in stoned to school, or else they worked full-time jobs and slept at their desks. He couldn't teach them nothing, he said. They didn't care. We were the same. We weren't the same? Oh, come on, Spangler, I cared about Hamlet? Hell, I did. I cared about songs, I cared about songs and clothes and fixing my hair. And later on? I cared about you.

So I had coffee and I'm breezing through Kenny's composition papers, and Pearl jumps on the table. I could tell, she wants me to chuck her on her throat. But her ear was disgusting. It was all blown up. The stink was wicked. I pushed her off the table and she ran on the back porch, started thumping to claw at that ear, and Jesus holy Christ, I couldn't stand it, I couldn't stand the guilt. I had to leave. I just got up and left the kitchen. I walked out on her.

And when I woke Kenny? I was talking all in a rush, upset as anything. He slept in his T-shirt. I got him out of bed, and he goes in the shower, and I'm standing in the bathroom talking through the curtain, saying I gotta take Pearl to the vet, but I'm scared. I'm scared what the vet's gonna say. I'm always scared of hearing bad news. I'll do anything, almost, not to.

Like, when Clare wanted to quit and get married? She kept saying we got to talk, Franny, and I'd say, Sure, later. Sure, later. Later. And when I got these stomach pains, a bunch of years ago? I knew something was wrong, something real. Pains in the same spot every single day is something for real. But day after day I kept making believe they were nothing. I didn't want to admit nothing. Ended up in an ambulance. That's what this is from. My beautiful, beautiful scar.

And when those people at Mercury had those tapes? And they kept holding them? And wouldn't return your calls? It drove you crazy, remember? I knew what was gonna happen, I knew they were gonna say they didn't like it, they wouldn't release it. I knew it was all over. Three songs and you're out. Meet the Beatles. You kept calling and I wouldn't tell you, but I was happy nobody talked to you. I was glad of it. Glad not to hear. And, like, when Paulie Kosakowski told me you were gonna go to California—like, I could've went to you and said, Are you? But I just put it off. Later, later. I'm like that, Spangler. Later. It's a crazy way to be, it's limbo time, but I always been like that.

Pearl wasn't getting better, she couldn't get better. Eventually, the vet was gonna say it. But I didn't want to hear. Didn't want to be told. I wanted somebody else to deal with it. Be told. Face the music. Make decisions. So I begged Kenny. He said, he gets out of the tub and starts drying off—he's drying himself off and he goes, She's your animal, Fran. You take her, Fran. Drop me at school, he goes, and bring her to the vet on your way back home.

What *is* this stuff we're smoking? Don't touch me. I'm talking.

I'm still talking. About Pearl. And Kenny wouldn't take her. How can you color stoned? How can you color so nice, how can you stay in the lines like that? Aren't you high? I never get high. Nobody gets high. Nobody smokes. I wouldn't know where to buy it, I don't know anybody that sells it. Nosy, though, I bet you he sells it. That's nasty. That's racist. You're racist, that's new. Everybody is, all of a sudden again. All of a sudden everybody's racist again. No, wait, I'm not rambling. Don't touch me, just leave me alone—all right?

You were saying I should get a dog—you were, too. That's what you said, that's what started all this! You were saying I should get a dog, I was telling you about Pearl, and about Nosy Brown. He was there. What do you mean, who? I just told you. He was there, at the vet's. With that big dog of his, he got a German shepherd, could tear out your throat. He's sitting in the waiting room when I come walking in with Pearl.

Nosy Brown, for crying out loud. I told you seventeen times, Spangler. Listen. You listen to me, Spangler.

I had her wrapped in a bed sheet, a white twin sheet. All bundled up, like a baby. And he looked at me, Nosy Brown did, and gave me a nod. Like, hey, I know your face. His dog was stretched out on the floor, well behaved. You could tell he took good care of that animal. It looked healthy. Probably it was in for shots, just. A male dog, testicles big as plums. Yeah, so I noticed. And on the walls were these pictures? Of dogs and cats and farm animals all dressed up like people dressed a hundred years ago, in derbies and checkerboard suits, in checkerboard vests. Playing poker in a saloon. The ladies, the female dogs, in fancy plumed hats. Taffeta gowns. What a crazy picture!

I went with Clare once, long time ago, to a pediatrician. She was taking her youngest kid? And in that office was the same kind of picture, almost. Only instead of dogs, it was babies. Two babies standing at a bar. A boy and a girl. You could see their faces in the back bar mirror. The boy baby had his hand on the girl baby's ass. She was dressed like Mae West, he was dressed like Al Capone. I took a poll. I checked everybody's face when they walked in, when they noticed that picture. Everybody thought it was funny, they

thought it was cute. I thought it was dumb, I thought it was even
a little bit sick. Which surprised me.

Anyway, it's my turn, I take Pearl in, and the vet goes, Again?
Like, you again? And I go, Yeah, us again, and so he checks Pearl,
and I could tell by his grunts he was gonna say it's hopeless. And
he did. She's suffering, he goes. And tells me how much it'll cost
to put her to sleep. Explains the whole thing. Goes, It's very gentle.
She just shuts her eyes. And then he goes—I don't think he meant
to be insulting, but he was—he goes, You could, if you want, take
her to the SPCA. They charge thirty dollars less. I didn't care about
thirty dollars, I was just pissed he thought I had to watch my budget.
I was ticked. Do I look poor? So I took Pearl and left, and Spangler?
Outside? On the street? I just broke down.

It was ten-thirty on a sunny fall day, beautiful out, there's people
all over, and I'm standing with my cat, she's wrapped in a bed
sheet, I'm shaking like I'm freezing. Maybe I should've let her escape,
let her go run into West Side Avenue, get creamed by a truck. But
I couldn't. No, I don't want to smoke anymore. How can you? How
can you still color? *Why* do you color? You're so good, but what's
the big fucking thrill, for Christ's sake. For God's sake. Why don't
you draw your own pictures? And color those?

Anyhow. I'm standing, all right? On West Side Avenue, sick to
my stomach, crying like a stupe. And Nosy Brown comes out, got
his dog on a leash. And he stops. I didn't expect him to. He stops,
but, and says, What's wrong? What's wrong, girl. Calls me girl.
What's wrong, girl. And I told him. And he says, You want me to
take him? And I go, It's a her. And he smiled. Goes, You want me
to take *her* down? He meant the SPCA. He knew where it was. He
said he'd take Pearl. If I wanted. If I can't do it myself. And Bobby,
I said all right. To this day I can hardly believe it, but I said all
right. To this guy I seen punch his own girlfriend, right in the face.

I took Pearl in my car, and he drove down in his, with his dog.
And I gave him the money, it was twenty bucks, and he went inside.
He took her inside. I stayed in the parking lot. Standing next to
his car, this blue crummy Nova. His dog watching me through the
windshield. Across the street is this place that collects glass, crushes

it up. You can see hills and hills of broken glass, mountains of it. And when Nosy came back? When Nosy came back? He gave me the sheet, and kept saying, You gonna be all right? And me sniffling the whole stupid time. Like I'm sixteen, like my boyfriend and me just had a big fight. Like we just broke up, like my heart's in little pieces. You gonna be okay? You gonna be all right, girl? And finally I got fed up—it was only a fucking cat, that's all she was, it's not the end of the world. I got totally fed up, for crying, and jumped in my car and drove home. Calling me girl, I'm almost forty years old.

And the next time I seen him? It was just like we'd never met, like he'd never been kind. I was on Astor Place, he was coming around from Park Street. Didn't even look at me. And the time after that? I was wrapping the fig tree, I was wearing jeans, my ass sticking up in the air. And he walked by and stopped. Just stood there. And made some remark.

*   *   *

Of course I know. You don't? I don't believe that. If you sat down and you concentrated, you could, you could so remember. Oh, you could. Don't make me crazy.

Seven. It's seven. In my history, it's seven. That's not a lot, is it? Seven. Rita wouldn't think it's a lot. Not that I ever told her. Not that she ever asked. In fact, she'd be surprised, I bet. She probably would. She probably thinks it's higher. She remembers, like in our late twenties? when I used to flirt and flirt and flirt. She probably thinks I fucked every one of those guys. So it's funny. She probably wouldn't think seven was a lot, and especially she wouldn't think it was a lot for me. But I'm. But I'm.

But it's seven.

Some of them still live around here, the ones that haven't done, I guess, so great. I see one guy half a dozen times a year. I see him over on Kensington Avenue, he must live around there. I'll be driving toward Bergen, I'll see him walking toward the park. He limps. Of course I don't talk to him. It was twelve, thirteen years ago and it was maybe two or three times, and he took me to the old Copa and I still have the ashtray, it's right there. He don't look like he's doing too hot and I notice that he limps.

One guy went to prison for drugs and one guy is dead, and one guy's a doctor in Bayonne and he's married to a girl I knew at Holy Family. She's a doctor too. I seen his picture in the paper last year. I think he was appointed to the school board, or maybe he's something at the hospital, maybe it's the hospital board.

Seven is not a lot, I think.

There was nobody before you, then you, then six after you. Seven in twenty-four years. That don't sound like a lot, does it? Of course, I was married for three years, almost three years, and while I was married? I was true. I was a faithful, thankful girl.

*   *   *

I can't believe you don't remember taking that picture.

We were over Paulie's house, Paulie's garage—this was, like, just before you went to see that guy Worm. So, that's, like, two, three months before we did I Got a New Boyfriend. We were over at Paulie's. There was me, Rita, Clare wasn't there, Marilyn Findlay, Casey, Eddie Anderson, and that guy Steve who played electric organ for a couple of months. We were in the garage, just fooling around. We were singing New Boyfriend, we were doing that one over and over, practicing for a Prep dance we were going to play. I got a new boyfriend, he's better than the last. He spends a lot of money and drives his car real fast. So tell us more, tell us more, tell us everything he does. . . .

Eddie Anderson had that awful wine, you remember? Him and Casey went over Staten Island, and they had, like, five bottles of that wretched stuff, but we drank every drop. Tell us more, tell us more, and Casey kept interrupting, starting to sing the Peppermint Twist. You know what happened to Casey, just by the way? He's living in a sheltered boarding house, just by the way.

So, Paulie's mother finally said we had to stop because she was having a club meeting, all her friends were coming over. And you took me home, and nobody was there, and we started messing around. The Polaroid was out, because—because it was March. The Amazing Franny, what a memory. It was March and the Polaroid was out because I'd just got it, got it for my seventeenth birthday. And you took a picture of me on the couch. I was wearing only my bra and underpants just, and when the picture dried, I looked so blowsy, like a real living tramp, my eyes were half-shut. And I loved it, I loved that picture, it was so awful, but I made you tear it up. And you took another picture and another and I kept tearing them up, I kept tearing them up.

And then I took off all my clothes, because you said, Take off all your clothes, and I brushed my hair—I think I even brushed my teeth—but I brushed my hair, for sure, and I put on lipstick and I sat up straight. On the couch. I was just sitting on the couch with my hands on my knees, and you took the picture. And when it came out, I felt like crying. I looked so pretty, my hair looked so pretty and my face looked so pretty, and my breasts, you said, looked so pretty, and I couldn't tear it up. I told you to keep it, but never to show it. To anybody. I trusted you. And you promised. You promised so fucking solemnly. You fucking promised. And you really don't remember?

You really don't? It was the only one, ever. Of me like that. The only one.

*   *   *

Spangler: You got to promise you won't say nothing. Or else I can't tell you. I'm serious. I'm really, really serious. You got to promise, you got to cross your heart. I'm not supposed to say nothing. She'd kill me. She'd kill me, but you know Camille? Upstairs? You can't say nothing, Bobby, honest—but you know what she does? I don't mean that, I mean besides. I know you know where she works. *Besides* that. The thing is, even Peek don't know, what she does besides. That's how come you got to promise.

She calls people up and talks dirty. I mean, for *money*. She's like a subcontractor. It's a little business. Like, this guy up the street got a type shop in his cellar. He got a computer, he sets type. Well, Camille got a phone, she talks dirty. But promise you won't tell.

What happens—there's this, I guess, company in New York, it's got operators and all, standing by. Guy sees an ad, like in a skin magazine? Calls up, they get his charge account number, the expiration date, all that stuff. Like he's buying from Land's End, a pair of pants. Then they call up Camille? And she calls the guy back, collect. It's very efficient. She don't even work all the time. Just, like, three nights a week, seven till maybe ten. Or eleven. She makes eight bucks a call, she makes. She puts it all away, socks it all away, she wants to get married. She wants to buy a house. Get pregnant. Rent a share at Long Beach Island, in July. That's a lot of dirty talk. A lot of call-backs. But she goes, I don't mind. Either it's this, she goes, or work double shifts at Roy Rogers. She goes, Hi, blank, this is blank. And Peek don't know. If he knew, Camille don't know what he'd say, so she keeps it a secret. It's her secret. But she told me. We're girlfriends.

Well, she's got this ring-binder? It's a regular ring-binder, but what it's full of? It's full of scripts. Got everything she needs, all prepared. She goes—she calls a guy back, she goes, Hi, and says the guy's name. It's right there in the book. Hi, then fill in the blank. Camille fills it in. Like: Hi, Joe, I'm blank. I'm Trudy, I'm Terry, I'm, I don't know what, Joanne. Whatever she feels like calling herself. She don't say Camille. And she goes, We got five to seven minutes. What's your favorite kind of sex? And depending on what he tells her? She finds it in her book, in that ring-binder. With plastic tabs, for speed. Whatever the guy says, it's right there. All prepared. There's maybe twenty pages, maybe not even, double-spaced. All the basic stuff, for every single occasion. She takes it serious. She does a good job. That's what she says. She dims the lights. Hi blank, this is blank.

Is that a riot, or what? Is that a riot? Like: Hi, Bobby, this is Franny.

* * *

Spangler, you sleeping? Bobby, wake up. Wake up, all right? Just wake up. Just . . . be awake. I had a bad dream, I don't wanna go right back to sleep. You took me to a movie. In the middle of the week, in the middle of the afternoon. It's not what I figured we'd do, in the dream. I don't know what I figured we'd do, but it wasn't that. But I liked it. I kept saying I hardly ever go to movies anymore. And so we're sitting there, but it's a gross-out picture, where the babysitter gets stabbed, the boyfriend, all her girlfriends, and suddenly—Spangler?—you're on top of me, crawling on top of me, smothering me to death, I can't breathe, and I look under your arm? At the screen? And somebody's bleeding from the mouth. Her face is, like, blue.

You wanna feel old, Spangler? It was twenty-two years ago. Can you believe it? Twenty-two years ago this summer. He's All Mine was a hit song twenty-two years ago this summer. He's All Mine twice an hour on the radio till even I got sick of it.

When we left New York that June, on the Clark tour? It was Pick Hit of the Week. And when we got to Ohio, it was already on the charts. Top 40, top 20, top 10. We jumped from being middle of the bill right to the top. And working our way home, doing state fairs, doing one-nighters, doing twenty minutes, singing three songs to prerecorded music, it kept climbing higher and higher. It was a monster. And we were making fifty bucks a show. Who cared, but? We got our rooms paid for, and our clothes, all our makeup. We were being taken care of. We had spending money. I just loved it.

Me and Clare and Rita were the only white girls on the bus, the only white act, period. This was the first time that ever happened— usually there'd be at least two or three other white groups, but not that time, not that summer. We knew everybody, though, from tons of other shows, all that Murray the K stuff, and everybody got along, playing cards, swapping comic books like we'd always done, swapping lipstick. But it wasn't like before. You could feel something different. You could feel it. Everybody was still friendly, but something was definitely off. Something definitely had changed.

And you know what it was? Spangler? It was all that stuff in the

South. The police dogs, the fire hoses. All that stuff. Civil rights.
Voter registration.

At night? I'd walk into somebody's room? And see all these sol-
diers on TV, big angry crowds, people running like Godzilla was
back, wet streets, George Wallace—I'd hear Negro demonstrators,
Negro demonstrators. And I'd turn around and walk right out again,
feeling . . . Feeling, I don't know, pissed off. I guess pissed off, all
that stuff going on when we were number one. Spoiling it. I wanted
parties, to celebrate. And everybody with us was black, was *Negro*,
and talking about sit-ins. And I'd call you up long distance, say how
much I missed you, say that I loved you. Or write you a long letter
sealed with a kiss.

That first week in July was so hot. It was ninety degrees, every
day. Ninety-five, a hundred. I was so glad we were coming back
home. I couldn't wait to see you again. You could tell us how much
money we earned, how many records we sold, and I could stare at
your face and see for myself how happy I'd made you.

We'd been all through Pennsylvania and came back into New
Jersey on the third of July. To do that one last show at a county
fair at a lake up there, in a ballfield, then straight home. We stopped
at some town, like four in the afternoon, for something to eat. What
I wanted to do first was call you. Just get to a phone and call you.
Chaperones saying as we filed off the bus, Behave yourselves, behave yourselves, act like ladies and gentlemen. And I ran across
the street to this little cigar store, it had a wooden Indian out front.
Rita's with me, Clare's with me. I claimed first dibs on the phone.

But when I got to the booth? At the back of the place? This guy
Myron—Myron, Spangler, remember Myron Raleigh? From the
Wonderfuls? Fucking Myron's in there, he's dialing. And he's got
maybe three dollars in dimes on the counter. What's he calling,
Alabama? Ah shit. I go, Shit on a stick, then lean on the booth, and
make a real pest of myself. Finally he puts the receiver down,
unfolds the door and says he's gonna be a while, it's his booth. Go
find my own. Very snotty. And I always liked Myron, he was always
a funny guy—I mean, good for jokes and stuff. Nice-looking guy,
had a choirboy face. Like Frankie Lymon's, like Sam Cooke's. But

now he got this attitude, saying he's gonna be a while, get lost. And he slams the door and I gave him the finger, only I don't think he seen me do that.

So I got to wait, and we only have twenty minutes before the bus leaves. I was really—I was pissed. When was the last time the fucking Wonderfuls had a number-one song? Fuck Myron, fuck the Wonderfuls. So I start walking up and down, up and down, and Clare's twirling a rack of paperback novels, par for the course, and Rita—Rita's down at the front of the store, and when I go over there, saying how pissed off I am at Myron, what's she doing? Looking at a bunch of coloring books—like, she'd already picked out three to buy. But soon as she seen me, she only shrugged, acting like she was just looking—to, like, pass the time. I got very upset. I knew she was writing to you, I knew all about that, Spangler, and I went back to the phone booth and Myron's still talking and I start pounding on the door, saying, Hurry it up, for Christ's sake, would you? Saying there's other people in the world besides you, and like that. And he looks like he's gonna kill me. Like he wants to murder me. And him usually the nicest guy in the world. So he turns his back and just goes on talking, and then I guess I really started pounding on the door, using both hands. Clare said, Cut it out, Franny, come on. She was always such a wimp, such a fucking pill.

But I wouldn't stop, I'm making this ridiculous scene—I want the phone, I wanna call my boyfriend! And finally Myron comes out and starts screaming at me. Calling me all kinds of names. Calling me a stupid girl, saying stupid girl, big-mouth stupid girl. And like that. And I guess I called him some names myself, but I never said nigger. I never used nigger, I never said that. Him telling everybody later on that I did. Well, I didn't! I never said that. I never did. I never was that kind of girl. I never used that word. Never. And him saying I did!

And when I got you, when I finally got you on the phone, you saying, Franny, what's the matter, calm down. But I was so mad— Mr. fucking Wonderful calling me stupid girl. I said, Spangler, I said, Bobby. Going, Myron hurt me, he grabbed my wrist, he had no fucking right to even *touch* me. Saying, I wanna see you tonight. Drive up, take me home. I'm your girlfriend. Saying, Myron hurt me. And you saying you'll try to come, but there's something you gotta do first, then saying, Is Rita there? Put Rita on. Like—what, she could give you the lowdown? Sort out the facts? Rita! Rita smoking grass in a corncob pipe every night, just waiting for us to break up. Writing you letters, sending you postcards. I was gonna put Rita on? I said, Be here. Remember? Like a threat: Be here. And hung up.

And when I came out of the booth, Clare was standing there, and Rita, they're both staring. Clare staring like a nun, like I ought to be ashamed. And Rita saying, Well, that was really stupid. And I thought she meant having that fight with Myron, but she didn't. She meant telling you to be here. Telling you what you should do. Like, if now you didn't show, *then* what? I seen a little smirk and I almost smashed her face in.

So we get back to the bus? And shit, it was like in twenty minutes? I'd gone from being Franny Tolentino to being Lester M. Maddox. You should've seen how everybody looked at me. Or wouldn't look at me. Looked out the window. Looked past me. Looked through me. And, like, I stood there, I wouldn't go sit down—I just stood there at the front of the bus and I said, All right, somebody wanna say something? Somebody wanna say fucking something? And the chaperones? Even the chaperones were black, and this black woman chaperone that always wore a church hat with fake flowers, she goes, Sit down and try to act like a lady. Lady. Screw lady. I was pissed. And I was ready to argue, I was ready to *demand* that Myron tell me exactly what lies he was spreading—but Clare pushed me into a seat and said, If you open your mouth again, Franny, I'll knock out your teeth. I couldn't believe she said that—Clare? And it surprised me so much, I just, I sat down and shut up. But I was burning. I was burning, Spangler.

That county fair: Christ, what a sleazy job. About fifty tents, game booths, bunch of rides so old-looking I'd be scared to death to go on them. And a stage where, when we arrived? There was a corn-eating contest—all these people eating corn like they do in cartoons—back and forth, back and forth, turning it like a type-writer roller.

Like we did before every show, we got off the bus and sold records. They had a table set up for every group, and anybody that bought a single, we'd sign the label or sleeve, whatever they wanted. Cost a buck apiece, so we didn't have to make change. A buck apiece, and I was glad to go do it, go sign records. This big sign at our table: MEET THE FRANTASTICS. NUMBER-ONE SMASH: HE'S ALL MINE. We got swarmed, it was great. It was *Hi-Teen* magazine come to life. I got asked ten times if I thought Ben Casey was cute.

And after we sold every record, we just walked around, killing time till eight o'clock. And we ended up going down to these, like, trailers? Where they actually had freaks. You don't see freaks no more. Even the circus don't have freaks, but there were freaks in these trailers, cost a dime. Each different freak cost a dime. The fat man, the rubber man, and like that. And there was this one sign that said: IS IT A WOMAN, OR WHAT? But when we tried to get in? Guy stopped us. Guy in a white suit like a medic wears. Said it was only for men. Try that stunt now, they'd get sued in a minute. Try that stunt now. That men-only stuff. I wonder what it was, though. Was it a woman, or what?

Anyhow, after that we crossed the highway. We weren't supposed to go too far, but we did—we crossed the highway and cut through this, like, graveled parking lot and hopped some railroad tracks and went on the beach. Some guy was snorkeling in the water. There was a big tree in the middle of the beach, the bottom of it was whitewashed. And I said to Rita, I said to Rita and Clare, When Bobby gets here, he's gonna, like, *lynch* that fucking Myron from that fucking tree. I only said it to shock, I only said it 'cause I was still so pissed off and hurt. I didn't really mean it. But Clare thought I did, she got mad and said I was acting like a real shithead, and Clare hardly ever said words like that. A real shithead and a bitch. I said, Fuck you, Clare, and she told me I should drop dead. Drop dead, Franny.

But Rita, Rita just looked at me. Then what, she folds her arms and shakes her head and smiles. And how she smiled, I didn't like

how she smiled. It was, like—that smile was like: Franny, you don't
know, but *I* know. Know what? And I said, What're *you* fucking
smiling about, but she turned around and walked away.

Anyhow. We were top of the bill, so we sang last. Usually I
watched, but that night I didn't. Wouldn't for nothing. I couldna
cared less. Fuck Myron Raleigh. Fuck everybody. I was waiting for
you. You were coming to get me. In that cool red Corvette. You
were driving through Newark, through East Orange. You were on
Route 46. I seen you in my head, I seen the bugs on the windshield,
coloring books on the shotgun seat, the radio light, seen your finger
changing stations. I seen your lips moving, you singing every song.
You'd come, I knew you'd come, you had to come. You knew the
mechanics. I knew the rules.

I was standing over at the bus, we'd already changed. Tight
sweaters, tight skirts, black stockings. You dressed us, Spangler,
and I looked like Rita, she looked like me. And the two of us looked
like Clare. We stood there together in the purple light from the Tilt-
a-Whirl, and just stared at each other. But I was waiting for you,
Spangler. You were coming. You knew where we were, you knew
where to turn, knew where to park. We'd go up on stage, start with
New Boyfriend. Then His Car Is Cool, then finally He's All Mine.
And I'd look down and you'd be there, Spangler. I'd be able to pick
you out. I'd smile, I'd nod, I'd pick you out of the crowd. Nod in
Myron's direction, let you take care of the rest. You knew the mechanics. He'd hurt my wrist. Called me a stupid girl.

And all the acts went up, did their three, four songs, bing, bing,
bing. No musicians, just tape. Finally it was our turn. I guess it
was around nine o'clock. Our turn on the stage. The number-one
act in the world. Number-one hit. Three straight weeks in a row.
Perfect girls. We were perfect. We were one girl, we were every
goddamn girl, every goddamn white girl in the whole fucking country. I got a new boyfriend, he's better than the last. His car is cool,
he drives real fast. He's all mine, is that a crime? Is that a crime?

They loved us, Spangler. We were number one. We were number
one. Three weeks in a row. But I looked around and you weren't

there. I couldn't pick you out, I couldn't smile at you, I was alone. You didn't show, you son of a bitch. I could look over the heads of a hundred kids in front of that shitty little stage, see the hot dog haze in the air, and way down the end of the field? I seen Myron, with his back turned to me. His back turned to us all. He's at a game booth with these plates and saucers and cups and jars stacked on shelves, and he was pitching baseballs, hard. I couldn't hear the sound, I couldn't hear them smash, but I could see them tumble, I could see them break into little pieces, every time he threw another ball.

And I should've seen you go up to him, Spangler. I should've seen you stand behind him, wait till he turned. Then I should've seen you talk, seen you move your hands, then I should've seen you go ahead and shove him. But I couldn't see you, Spangler. You never came. I seen the bugs on your windshield, I seen your hands jabbing buttons, then I seen nothing.

*   *   *

Well, it says right here: *and guest*. It says right here, Rita: *and guest*. But if you don't want me to bring Spangler, that's fine, that's it, I won't. Who knows if he'd come anyway, right? Nice fucking invitation, though. Cocktail hour one-fifteen, very fancy script. What'd those invitations cost you? Even the little map to the church, you thought of everything. You're doing it right, everybody's doing it right again, the cocktail hour, the fancy script, the little fucking maps. Even the stamp, Rita. I caught that, the little Love stamp on the reply envelope. Very cute, very correct, very fucking eighties. You wearing white? Hey Rita, you wearing white? You and Ron: well, Jesus Christ, Rita, congratulations. Congrats! And better luck this time. You deserve it, sweetheart.

But speaking of Bobby. Hey Rita, speaking of Bobby: I always wondered but I never said nothing. About the two of you. You two. Spangler and you. I wondered, but I never said nothing. And who the fuck cares, now. Right? Could even give a shit.

*   *   *

Is there some chance of getting anything back, anything at all?
Any chance? Or am I just being stupid, hoping that? I mean, *tell*
me. Come on, Paulie, tell me: Is everything gone for good, or is
there a chance? Is there some chance? You cops ever catch anybody? You ever catch any bad guys, or is it all a big joke? Ah shit,
Paulie! Everything! Lookit! Everything good I have is gone. Not
only my fucking VCR, the rental tape! Now I gotta pay for it, I gotta
buy it. I gotta pay for that fucking *Scarface*, the new one. And I
didn't even *rent* it, Spangler did.

Insurance, right. You know what the woman's gonna say? She's
gonna say, you got receipts, you got proof, you got pictures of
everything? Yeah, sure, like I went around taking pictures of my
fucking VCR, fucking television. What, you go around taking pictures of your clock-radio?

But it's not just what's gone, Paulie, you seen the door. You seen
it. I mean, what'd the guy do, use a bazooka? That was a metal
door! What if I'd been home? I could've been. Very easily I could've
been home. I'm usually home, I never go out. You think the guy
was watching? How'd he know I was out? I bet you he was watching, just standing someplace, watching the house. Like, right across
the street. What, because I'm white? I'm telling you. Because I'm
a woman? I'm telling you. I'm telling you, I should move the fuck
out. I hate this city! I hate this neighborhood! What am I doing
here? I should stay here by myself, let some fucking maniac, black
fucking maniac shoot a fucking bazooka at my door?

All right, I'm assuming. I'm assuming he was black. Right, I got
no evidence. It could've been the fucking white guys up the street
that work for CBS. Sitting around saying, hey, you wanna steal a
clock-radio? Right. It could've been. Or hey, it could've been Spangler, even. Sure, why not? Only Spangler wouldn't need a bazooka.
Spangler has the key. Let's get real, Paulie.

I tell you, though—I had a dog, this wouldn't happen. Tear the
fucker's throat out. I should get a big dog or something. You live

in this world, you need protection. A woman very definitely needs protection in this fucking insane world. She's not safe. I could've been home. I could've been murdered, Paulie, for a clock fucking radio.

No, I haven't. I haven't told him yet. When he hears, though, Jesus. He's gonna go off like a bomb. Wait'll he hears. Spangler's gonna go off like a fucking bomb. Like once, maybe you don't remember—but this one time, some black guy really got nasty with me, grabbing me and shit, ³and Spangler? Spangler nearly killed him. Got him up against a fucking tree and nearly killed the guy. He can be like that. Well, you know. He hasn't changed much. He hasn't changed much at all. It's the same old Spangler. So wait'll he hears about this. Wait'll I tell him.

*   *   *

When I seen you talking to Nosy Brown, it was—I got a funny feeling. I seen you as soon as I got out of the car, the pair of you standing in front of his building. And I thought you were laughing. I thought you were being friendly, the both of you, laughing over something. I thought—I thought I even seen you smile. Well, it's possible that you did. But I thought I also heard you laugh. Then Nosy musta said motherfucker fifteen times in ten seconds. And you saying son of a bitch. You did.

I'm not criticizing you, Bobby. I don't care *what* you called him. Everybody *knows* he's the one, *one* of the ones.

I got scared, though. Him saying motherfucker, you saying son of a bitch. And when he pulled that knife, Bobby—God! Calling *you* crazy, and what's *he* do, pulls a knife. Calling *you* crazy—well, *I* would've called him a thief, too, only I'd be too scared to. Everybody *knows*. People seen him. Hanging out, just watching. I even seen him once, going around the side door at Jimmy's house. Fuck proof! Fuck the law, the law don't work, rules don't work. Not anymore they don't.

And fuck Paulie too. I should be grateful, but I didn't like the way he talked to you. I'm glad he pulled strings and shit, but I really didn't appreciate him calling you stupid, in front of people like that. I mean, how could the cops even *think* of arresting you?

If it wasn't for Paulie, but—Jesus, can you imagine? What, they were gonna stick you in jail? For what? For *what*? Nosy pulled out the knife, he stabbed you first. If it wasn't for his knife, there wouldn't've *been* a knife. So you stabbed him. What were you supposed to do? So you stabbed the fucking guy. What were you supposed to do?

And were you right, or were you right? Is that my clock-radio, is that my TV, or isn't it? And where'd the cops find it, down the sewer? Or did they find it in that fucking guy's apartment? Imagine that little tramp of his saying it was hers, that Darlene. Imagine Darlene screaming like that. Stupid girl. Well, if she loved him so much, she wouldn't've let him go around robbing people's houses. You do shit like that, you get what you get. She'll find somebody else, but. She probably already *got* somebody else, already. Girl like her.

It was self-defense, Bobby. I seen that. I'll swear to that. You gotta go to court, I'll swear. All you *did* was tell him that you knew, you knew what he done to me. It was *him* that pulled the knife, it was Nosy Brown that said motherfucker fifteen times and pulled that knife. Not you.

Does it hurt? Lemme see, Bobby. Just lemme see. It's only a nick, it's not deep, you'll live. My hero. I'm serious: my hero. He called you a motherfucker and you called him a son of a bitch. Jesus, though. Women get dragged into everything, don't they?

*   *   *

Spangler? Not for a couple of weeks, but he's busy, he'll probably call tonight. He's been real busy. First with the fucking county prosecutor, every other day he gotta go talk to somebody there. You'd think fucking Nosy Brown was, I don't know, fucking Jesse Jackson, for Christ sake. So that's a big pain. That's taking up a lot of his time. Plus, he found a place for his father in Bloomfield, some nursing home called him back. It's run by the Sisters of

Charity. Bloomfield. They'll take the old man August first. So that's good, that's settled. He'll probably call tonight, though. Definitely. He said he'd call, maybe even come over.

But wait'll you hear this one, Camille. You'll drop dead. I'm gonna buy the old man's house. Just a temporary thing, I'll turn it right around, but Spangler needs the money now. He needs it up front. He needs a car. He needs some clothes. Some spending money. Maybe a lawyer, if this Nosy Brown stuff gets really stupid, gets out of hand. If there's, like, a trial, God forbid. A trial! It makes me sick. You know what somebody's trying to do, some fucking trouble-maker? Wants to sue Spangler for, get this, violating Nosy Brown's civil rights. Gimme a break. First they want Spangler thrown in jail for murder, now it's civil rights. They don't have a prayer, but. I'll testify. I'll say what's what, I'm not scared. I'll get up in court, I'll get up in front of anybody, it's second nature.

Palmolive soap. Save fifteen cents on two. Also good on a four-bar pack. Camille? Should I clip? Is that the phone? Camille, is that the phone? I thought that was the phone.

But anyhow, Spangler needs some money right now. So I'm buying his father's house. It's the simplest way. It's the least I can do. Maybe it's not the greatest investment, but it's not bad. I'll turn it around. I'll make a profit. I'll make something out of this. I'm paying more than I think it's worth, but you know, it's Spangler. It's Bobby Spangler. And we go way back. We go back a long way together.

Where We'll Never Grow Old

(2028)

Hey to everybody, but especially hey to Jane Teaneck and Alkali Rose, to Eulamae Nutley and Joanie-Joanne, to Grinner the Fish and Myer and Noochie and Triple-A Nancy—hello! how are you? it's me, I'm Joy. Gonna tell you a story, okay? It's all true, I promise it is, so just listen, then pass it on when the Tape Worm gets back. And let him know what you think, all right? If you liked it or not. All right? But you gotta be honest. Be honest.

On the last tape in the bundle, that's me singing, and playing the stones and the pots and making those neat, I think, spit sounds. On guitar that's *not* me, that's a girl who used to live up here too, called Tragedy. Isn't that a great, great name? Tragedy Ringling. And it's about Tragedy and me that I'm gonna tell you about, that's my story. If you like it, don't tape over it, okay? Just mark the label and pass it on, okay? And I'm not asking for pity or anything. All right? I mean, I've been *practicing*. I'm not bragging on myself, but I've been practicing day and night, talking at the wall. Still with me, guys?

Like I say, my name is Joy, and before everything happened that I'm gonna tell you about, I was living in a house on the shore of this green lake called Sunburn Lake. It must've been, like, a hundred years old, maybe older, and it was made of logs, and the roof was red and the logs were black with cement in between. We had a field-rock patio with a tree in the middle. I don't know one tree from the next, but it was big, it was a big old tree, I couldn't put my arms around it. In January and February, when it always turned sticky, I'd sit under that tree, in the shade, taking swaps of water from a bottle and humming to myself. I liked that tree. Boy, I liked that tree. I'm real sorry it's gone. I'm sorry the whole *house* is gone, too, and everybody in it. Well, *mostly* everybody I'm sorry is gone.

Anyhow. Up until last August, I lived there with my mother, whose name was Loretta, and with Dick Idea, that pig, and with Dick Idea's son. Flyboy was fourteen, I was fifteen, but now I'm sixteen. I'm pretty sure.

And then there was Kerwin, this guy Kerwin, who was maybe twenty. I never asked him, but he was twenty maybe, or twenty-one. Kerwin didn't *live* with us really, but he came up to the house a lot, almost every day, because he liked me. Yeah, *that* way. He liked me that way.

Me and Kerwin, we'd walk around TenEyck Springs smoking cherry twigs, or we'd carry pails to Weaverhouse Cove and pick different berries, whatever was growing, or sometimes go looking for the Prowler, not really hoping to find him, and I don't know to this *day* if there *was* such a person as the Prowler, and almost every other week, on Thursday, me and Kerwin took my canoe down the lake to the Circle, to the casbah, to get food and batteries and old sinus pills (for Dick Idea) and clothes and stuff, whatever Loretta thought we needed, and that's when I'd swap with the Tape Worm, if the Tape Worm was there.

And I got to tell you that Kerwin was real handsome, he was real muscular, he had black hair and brown skin, and last winter he never wore a shirt, not one day that *I* can remember—he didn't wear a shirt November till May, and even sometimes in May, before the gray blizzards blew in from Netcong, he didn't. Wear a shirt. He didn't, really! And even though by that time I was pretty sick of him *always* being around, always wanting to touch me, always grabbing my wrist, always wanting *something*—even though I just wanted him to leave me alone by then, I still kind of liked to stare at his shoulders and his back when he was walking ahead of me.

I used to like to stare at his neck, his neck was kind of pink in places, where he'd got bit when he was a dog boy, and I used to like to stare, even, at the hard skin like old shoe leather on both his elbows. His elbows I even liked. I used to like to stare at him. I used to like to sit on our dock and watch him fish with a stick and a piece of string and a safety pin and a ball of pressed bread. I guess I won't ever forget Kerwin. And he didn't wear shoes, either.

But I got sick of him 'cause he wouldn't leave me *alone*, ever. I *liked* being alone, I liked being alone so I could listen to stories. When I had a story to play, I didn't have to think about Dick Idea and Loretta and everything else. I *liked* being alone, but I was lonesome, too. That's possible. You don't think that's possible? It is.

Anyhow, this one day last July it was raining hard and the wind was blowing like crazy, and everything outside looked green and white, and I was trying to listen to Joanie-Joanne's story about that guy Michael Dzikowski, about him thinking he could just make himself King of Paramus, what a joke! That was such a cool story, except I didn't like the ending—somebody should've *killed* that guy Michael. So anyhow, I had my headphones on, but the tape was dragging, and Joanie-Joanne sounded like she had *palsy* or something 'cause my batteries were low.

Flyboy's little Sony used the same kind of batteries, it used double-A's, but I knew if I asked him, he wouldn't give me the four I needed, 'cause then *his* machine wouldn't work. Or else he'd give me them, but then I'd have to give him something back, like do whatever he said for a couple of days, like probably go to his mass and receive his goofy holy communion, and I didn't feel like doing *that*. So I was miserable.

And then, of course, everybody else was miserable, too. Well sure, it'd been raining for seven days straight, a real hard rain, and the house was leaky, it smelled musty, and coffee cans and paint cans were catching drips, and up in the sleeping balcony, where I slept, all the bedding was soggy and the floor was puddled, and I was starting to worry that maybe the whole thing would just collapse on our heads any minute. Kill us dead.

Kerwin had come over the night it started to rain, so he'd got stuck there with us, but at least he was spending most of the time playing cards with Dick Idea, and he left me alone, pretty much, for once. Loretta was in a really *horrible* mood, though, on account of her bad teeth, which were *killing* her. And Flyboy stayed downstairs in the bathhouse, mostly, saying his rosary and praying for the souls in purgatory, and doing whatever *else* it was that he did.

So anyhow, we were in the house and it was raining, not a *white* storm, thank God, just a regular one. We were cold and damp, but there was no, like, *danger*. I kept going to the front window to look at the lake. It was all whipped up, and I couldn't see Blueberry Island. That was just a blur. Usually, you could see the island, and you could see the house on it where Dick Idea killed my father, but not in *that* rain you couldn't. It was, like I said, all a blur.

Then Loretta came running in from the kitchen, saying there was a *bat*. That did it. Dick Idea was just waiting for that sort of excuse, you know, and him and Kerwin jumped up from the dining-room table and grabbed whatever they could, a broom and a rake, or maybe a rake and a shovel, I forget what exactly, and they started chasing around, running after that bat, which I never did see, myself—running around like two crazy people, trying to smash it. Then Flyboy banged up through the trapdoor in his cassock and his alb and his chasuble, wanting to know what was going *on*, and then it was what you'd have to call sheer pandemonium.

Jane Teaneck, if you're listening to me, what happened in our house with the bat, if there *was* a bat, is like what must've happened at your house when that dog got in, or whatever it was, that fox? and everybody went flooey in the dark chasing it? It must've been just like that, except nobody here got hurt.

But even though nobody's bones got broken *here*, it was just as crazy, I bet, Dick Idea and Kerwin and then Flyboy all running around and Loretta cringing by the window seat, and I couldn't take it anymore.

I snuck into the spare bedroom and squeezed under the twin
bed and stayed there with the dust. I found a book of matches on
the floor and lit a couple, but then I got scared I'd set the mattress
on fire, so then I just laid there.

Finally, I seen Kerwin—I seen his bare feet and his lumpy toes
sticking under the bed, and I reached out and squeezed his ankle,
and he jumped like he'd been *bit* by something. We have rats too,
Jane, we have rats too, Alkali Rose, we have great big rats around
here, too.

I laughed, then Kerwin got down on his knees and stuck his
face under the bed. Says, You little rat. See, he *did* think it was a
rat! And then he says, Move over, and I did, pressing against the
log wall and sawdust came trickling out and Kerwin squeezed under
and started kissing me hello and playing with my hair and I didn't
like that, but what could I do. He pulled some dust out of my hair.
Then he started squeezing those blue scars on his chest, squeezing
them between two fingers and rubbing them, like dog boys do to
show off.

I asked him, Did you kill that damn bat? and he says, Nope.
Then he says, What're you *doing*? and I told him, I said, I can't
stand it when people act crazy.

And he said, You gotta learn to ignore something if you don't
like it, be here and *not* here at the same time. He was always saying
that, I guess since I was *always* ducking away to hide when Dick
Idea started screaming at Loretta or being a bully to Flyboy. Kerwin
said that was something I had to learn to do, switch myself off like
I was a human tape machine. It could make the difference, he said,
between going crazy and staying regular.

He used to live in Paterson before he came up the lake, before
he was a dog boy, and he says that's where he learned that switch-
off trick. In Paterson, when he was younger than I am *now*, when
there were Chartists and Cristianos and white newsboy gangs
and black crackers and different militias all *over* the place, and
people had machetes, they had *machine guns*, Kerwin said, and
lots of buildings blew up and burned down, and you could be

kidnapped for no good reason, and he said he could just turn himself off, be not-there, it saved his life. And he said I should do it, too.

He kept on saying that, but he never taught me *how*. That's what I *especially* didn't like about Kerwin, and about everybody else. Nobody taught me *nothing*, which is how come I've always loved getting tapes every other week from the Tape Worm.

So me and Kerwin were under that bed and then Kerwin put his hand down my pants and in my underpants, making me short of breath, but I had to laugh—did he really think we could *do* something? We had no space and our heads were touching the wooden slats and the bedsprings, we couldn't *move*. Or maybe he didn't want to do something *really*, just play with me a little bit with his fingers, but I'll never know, 'cause I told him to stop. Stop it, I told him. Which I could *only* do with Kerwin, I couldn't do that with Dick Idea. You couldn't say no to Dick Idea, ever. You said no to Dick Idea, it was all over, believe me—you could ask Loretta, if she was still around.

Anyhow, Kerwin stopped when I told him stop, but he makes a face, like I'm really a stupid *chunk*, and he goes, So what do you *wanna* do, then?

And I told him, Well, if it stops raining, you wanna go down the Circle, it's Thursday, and he laughs. It's not real *likely* to stop raining, he says, and even if it *does*, who's gonna *be* there? There can't be no casbah in the *mud*. Like that, he says. Maybe the Circle, he says, is under two feet of *water*, and I guessed that was possible, so we just laid there, and l heard Dick Idea go to Loretta, This lamp is out of kerosene. We got any kerosene? Loretta was in charge of the food, she was in charge of the kerosene. Well, fill the lamp, says Dick Idea.

Then Kerwin moved closer to me, squeezed up against me and he swallowed, and I watched his throat bob. His neck was real strong. I almost felt like kissing him, then I *did* feel like kissing him, so I did. Then he says, he's whispering to me, touching my ear, his chin was stubbly, and he said, Did you know Loretta's supposed to have a baby?

And I said, yeah, I knew that, and it's really making her nuts. But how'd *you* find out?

Says Dick Idea told him. Who else? Then Kerwin said, And Dick Idea says she got to get *rid* of it. He asked me if *I* knew how to do it. That's pretty funny, don't you think, Joy? Then Kerwin said— we're talking about an *abortion*, okay?—and he said, You can't do it, can you?

And I tell you, everybody, it surprised the lights out of me. Do an *abortion*? *Me*? On *Loretta*? Who's my *mother*? I'm supposed to give my own mother an *abortion*? I thought that was pretty sick. But I didn't let on it's what I thought. I only said, no, I couldn't do it, I didn't know how.

Kerwin didn't talk for maybe a minute. Then he whispered, Dick Idea heard about somebody living in Andover could do it, but that was, like, already last *year*.

Then I had this great thought, and I said, But I bet we could maybe find a *tape* that would tell us how. Maybe we could even find a videotape that could *show* us. I bet if we asked the Tape Worm, I said, *he'd* know if there was something like that. Bet you if we found a videotape like that, Josephine would even let us use her generator and we could watch it on *television*, then you could see how it's done, and you could do it for Loretta yourself.

And Kerwin said, *I* don't wanna do it. But what I'd said got him thinking, I could tell. And what he was thinking, I bet you, was that if he *did* do this thing for Dick Idea, this abortion on Loretta, then maybe Dick Idea would let him come live in the house with us, which is what Kerwin wanted most.

See, Dick Idea'd kept telling Kerwin no, for, like, *months*—saying, No, Kerwin, you can't stay with us, there's not food enough. And don't ask me again.

We had a garden and all, but lots of times the rains washed that away and then we didn't have hardly anything to eat. I don't want to *tell* you some of the stuff we used to eat, me and Loretta and Dick Idea and Flyboy, but I guess *everybody's* eaten some pretty funny stuff this year and last year and so on and so forth. You ever eat squirrel?

Anyhow, Kerwin just laid there next to me, thinking, thinking probably that Dick Idea would be, like, more *inclined* to let him stay with us if he got rid of Loretta's problem, if he did that favor for Dick Idea. It wasn't that Kerwin was *scared* of living on his own, moving from one empty bungalow to another, but the dog boys *were* after him, and it'd be a whole lot safer to just live in our house. Not to mention he'd get to be with *me* every single day. You got dog boys? The ones we had up here weren't rabid, just stupid and filthy and wild, but they weren't rabid yet. They kept trying, though.

So whatchamacallit, Kerwin laid there and thought for such a long time with his eyes closed tight that I was about convinced he'd fallen *asleep*, but he hadn't. At last he opened his eyes and smiled, then he wiggled out from under the bed and then he was gone. I blew at a dust ball, up close it looked almost like a bug, then it looked like a cloud, and then I felt hungry.

And so half the day passed and then, guess what? The rain stopped, yes it did, and as soon as it did, Flyboy took all the credit. He would. He went parading around the house with his headphones on, the ones with the orange ear sponges, and he said his prayers had been answered. Him and his stupid prayers.

He'd almost died last year, it was awful, he could hardly breathe. His lungs filled up with gunk, and every time he tried to swallow, you'd hear this bubbling sound. It was pneumonia or something. At first we'd thought he'd caught the rose, but the rose never bloomed, and Flyboy got better, and ever since then he'd been real religious.

He used to say he'd even died for a little while and floated around, floated as high as the ceiling, which is, like, twenty feet above the floor. He said he seen me sleeping on the balcony and Dick Idea cleaning his rifle and Loretta saying wait, and then he said he could've gone straight through the *roof* if he'd wanted to, but he hadn't wanted to. It wasn't his time yet, he said, he still had a mission, he said, something he still had to do. And because he was always talking so much about floating away, that's how come he got that nickname Flyboy. His real name was Kenny. But Dick Idea started calling him Flyboy, to make fun. And Dick Idea said that me and Loretta had to call him Flyboy, too, so we did.

He was all right, Flyboy was, except he could sometimes be a pain, and the weirdest thing was, every couple of days he made believe he was a priest and set up an altar on the patio or down in the bathhouse if the weather was bad—he'd set up an altar from a gateleg table. He'd spread it with a white beach towel and put out candles that Loretta wouldn't let him burn, and then he'd say Catholic mass. He'd found a missal in a box of moldy books hid away behind the old furnace downstairs that didn't work. That's how come he said *Catholic* mass, it was a *Catholic* missal, sixty years old. He genuflected a lot and he mumbled a lot. I'd made him his priest stuff from clothes we'd scavenged at a cottage in French's Grove. I seen a how-to-sew video cassette when I was a kid. I must've watched that thing fifty times. Loretta made me. That was when Raymond was still alive and we lived on Blueberry Island and had a battery TV. Raymond was my father.

So there was Flyboy saying we should all thank him for the rain ending, and Dick Idea started teasing him, pulling out his shirttail and stuff. But then Flyboy got annoyed, and told Dick Idea to leave him *alone*, which was very, very stupid. It was, like, *dangerous*. And Flyboy realized that, right away, and apologized. Get out of my sight, says Dick Idea, and Flyboy went back down through the trap into the bathhouse, and the next thing we heard from Flyboy was Holy, holy, holy, Lord God of hosts, like that.

Then Dick Idea went over and shut the trapdoor with his foot, then he sat back down at the dining-room table, where Kerwin already was, and they started playing cards again.

He was awful fat, Dick Idea, and he had a square head and a big black beard, and Loretta used to trim his beard every once in a while, and when she did, I'd sit across the room, kind of watching, kind of hoping she'd just stab him in his fat neck with those scissors. Sometimes they did get into arguments while she was cutting his beard and his hair, but she never stabbed him. She was too good.

So I walked out on the patio in my bare feet and the cold water went up past my ankles. I stood by the wire fence and looked at the lake, and beyond the lake I could see a green-and-yellow smear in the sky. Over on Blueberry Island, a lot of roof shingles were floating in muddy puddles, and water was gushing down from the blocked gutters on the gray house. The air was clean and nice. I breathed and I breathed and I breathed, then I heard the screen door open and shut behind me.

It was Kerwin, holding out a chunk of white cheese that he'd cut. I took it and ate it whole, and he said, well, he'd told Dick Idea about there being maybe a special kind of tape, like we'd been talking about, and Dick Idea had told him so why don't you and Joy go *see* about that. And I got real happy real quick. We were going to the Circle!

Kerwin had a nice strong neck, and I hugged him around it and I liked him again, almost, then I seen Loretta watching us both from behind the screen door. But I couldn't see her expression or nothing. Then she turned around and went away.

So we said we were leaving, and everybody started telling us what they wanted, what to look for, like beans for soup, and Loretta said if anybody had a packet of yeast, get a packet of yeast, and stuff like that. Dick Idea said look for sinus pills, he always did, 'cause he had this totally crazy idea—Dick Idea's idea!—that if you took sinus pills every day, you wouldn't catch the rose. I don't know where he'd picked *that* one up. And Flyboy shook an imaginary bell, and I promised him, yeah, I'd look for a real one, but I knew that I wouldn't. Loretta gave us a lot of rhubarb wrapped in a dish towel. We could barter with that, she said. And then she gave us a head of lettuce in a basket and a bunch of plum tomatoes that looked gross.

Flyboy walked down to the dock with me and Kerwin and he blessed the canoe, like he almost always did, and helped us slide it off the grass and into the lake. Then there was a wild flash of lightning behind Cooley's Mountain, it was *ferocious*, and I looked at Kerwin, and he'd turned pale. I thought for a second he was gonna tell me it wasn't such a great idea after all, going to the Circle. But he only knelt down in the stern, and I knelt in the bow and off we paddled like a couple of Indians. I seen a lot of dead fish, sunnies mostly, belly up in the water, and I seen a dead bird, too. Passing Blueberry Island, I shut my left eye so I wouldn't see it too up close, which was stupid, I guess, but that's what I did.

I used to live there. I said that already, but I did. Me and Loretta and Raymond, all three of us, in that gray house built on a boulder, till Raymond, till Raymond. First his gums bled, then he got hoarse, then he got dizzy, then he couldn't even get out of bed, he couldn't stand up, he could hardly *see*. And the rose bloomed then, on his throat, and those blisters broke out, and those black dotty marks, and all. We lived there till I was twelve years old, on Blueberry Island. From when I was nine till when I was twelve.

Anyhow, we come into the channel and we're going down the lake, but Kerwin kept looking up at the sky, and I said, Relax, storm's over, but who could be sure. Well, you know, I don't have to tell you. I don't have to tell you guys about the crazy weather.

Like, we had a white storm last April? And it blew away a little kid that lived in Cabin Springs, and we never seen her again. I was down Sandy Beach with Kerwin swimming and stuff, and suddenly—there was this guy named Bruno, and Bruno shouts Look! and there's that mist coming down the mountain, and, like, ten seconds later, *whoosh*! The wind was screaming, and if I hadn't hung on to a tree I don't know *what* would've happened. My skin felt like it was being splattered with bacon grease, and my hair got plastered down, and when it passed, when it just *stopped dead*, one of the Sullivan girls was gone. I forget her name. Gone, like— just *gone*, like *that*!

Anyhow—anyhow, I didn't think it was gonna rain again, but Kerwin was still pretty worried, I could tell. And he kept looking so much at the *sky* that he didn't pay much attention to steering the *canoe*, and what happened was, we kind of drifted toward the eastern shore. Then all of a sudden, smack, I got hit in the neck with something, a rock or something, and it really *hurt*. And when I looked around, it's three dog boys sitting naked on the spillway, and Kerwin said, Oh, *shit*, and backpaddled, dog boys all barking. Chucking more rocks now and barking like mad and pinching their scars. Then one dove off the wall. I jumped up, rocking the canoe, and lifted my paddle, all set, all ready to crack him in the head if he got too close. But Kerwin told me, You're gonna tip us, get down, and I did. And the dog boy in the lake just turned over and started floating, his toes showing, his arms straight out, and he spit water like a whale, and both his friends laughed. Then *Ker*win! *Ker*win! they all called, and Kerwin looked kind of sick.

I don't know how anybody can be a dog boy. I know what they say and all, but it's just crazy. I don't think you got to be an animal to stay alive. I don't think you got to be an animal at all. And I'd never give up talking, like they're all supposed to do. And I'd never let a dog bite me on purpose. You should've seen some of the bite scars on some of those dog boys we used to have up here.

Anyhow, we got down to the end of the lake finally and tied my canoe at a catwalk in back of this old pink building that used to be, like, a store or something. Part of the catwalk is under water and the rest of it's rotted and you have to be careful where you step. I climbed out first and right away I heard *tick-tock, tick-tock,* so I went and peeked in one of the store windows. Most of them were stuffed with rags but this one had glass, and I seen two kids inside playing, I swear to God, Ping-Pong. There were bedrolls on the floor and piles of garbage. Then Kerwin took my elbow and walked me around the building to the front and we crossed these railroad tracks, which are rusted as anything.

I never seen a train. I don't think there *are* trains anymore, are there? I got a tape a long time ago—somebody telling a story about a ghost on a train going from Baltimore to Chicago. It wasn't a great story, I don't believe in ghosts and stuff like that, but it was all right, this ghost kept ripping heads off women and throwing them out the window and they'd roll down embankments and always it was a little boy that found them, that found the heads.

The embankment down there is all cinders and weeds and there's a lot of broken glass. A ways up the tracks is a crossing signal but the lights are missing and the gate is broken off. And past the tracks is the Circle, full of white gravel, and a wall of field rock at the edge of Highway 206.

Kerwin was saying it looked like a pretty shitty casbah today, and it sure did. Only about twenty blankets were out, but I guess it could've been worse. Going over the tracks I seen the Knife Guy and the Bullet Guy, and the Aspirin Lady, and a lot of people with vegetables and some with clothes, some guy had a carton of dish detergent in yellow plastic bottles, and there was a table heaped with old kid toys, mostly broken, and the Hostess Guy was there with his cupcakes. Loretta always told me to stay away from the Hostess Guy 'cause his stuff was, like, *years* old. She'd heard he'd found a warehouse full of Hostess junk, this stuff was like *antique food.* And there was a guy with a blanket full of light bulbs wrapped in toilet paper, but I didn't see the Tape Worm, and I was real disappointed.

I seen a lot of people I recognized from around the lake and from the Tamaracks, and I seen a whole family called the Gleason family from down the road. They live in this cinderblock building that says Lakeland Rescue Squad over the garage door. There's a fire truck inside. Then I seen one of Josephine's men come walking up the tracks with a bucket of blueberries.

Josephine was this woman from Laurel's Point, it was just her and her daughter Emmy in this bungalow on stilts, but outside these four men—Loretta called them Josephine's husbands—lived in huts and tents and lean-tos. Josephine had a generator, she had electricity, and she grew amazing things in her garden. She never came to the casbah herself, never. She always sent one of her husbands, and what they mostly bartered for was light bulbs. Carrots and lettuce and strawberries, and sometimes marijuana, for sixty-, seventy-five- and one-hundred-watt light bulbs. You always seen one of her husbands shaking bulbs to make sure they were still, you know, good.

Anyhow, the Tape Worm wasn't there, so I walked over to the Aspirin Lady. She was sitting in a canvas chair and she had a pad of paper on her lap and a pencil in her hand and she was drawing. The funny thing about *her* is, she's *always* drawing, you always see her doing that, drawing, so you naturally think she's drawing what she's looking at, which is usually the crab apple trees that separate the Circle from the shell of the old 07821 post office, but that's not true. That's not so. On her pad? All that's there? Is heads, people's heads in profile, and the people have their mouths wide open and there's spit flying. They're awful crazy, her pictures, but she draws them calm as can be. I don't know how old she is, maybe sixty? She's a big old thing, a big woman, big breasts and gray hair—not *totally* gray, there's some brown left still—and her hips are as wide as a door but she's got a pretty face and not a wrinkle on it. And she smells like camphor, don't ask me how come.

She doesn't barter *only* aspirin, that's just, like, *part* of it—she usually got crèmes and ointments and stuff, stuff she found in drugstores and bathrooms, I guess, Band-Aids and wart medicine and Mercurochrome and stuff, everything spread out nice and neat on a beach towel with a faded picture on it of a lion. That day her towel was sopping wet. So was the Aspirin Lady's hair and clothes. What does she wear, but army fatigues. I never seen her in nothing but army fatigues, the kind that's mottled for camouflage.

How're you this afternoon, Joy? she asks me, and I said I was pretty good, I guess, happy the storm was over, and she nodded and looked past me at Kerwin, who was showing that rhubarb to the Knife Guy and pointing to a little gravity knife.

She *always* kept an eye on Kerwin, and not just her, *everybody*. 'Cause he used to be a dog boy, see? 'Cause he had all those bite scars on his neck, and the colored-in scars he'd made across his cheeks and chest on purpose a couple of years ago with, I don't know, maybe a razor blade. Every dog boy *I* ever seen had those same exact marks, dyed exactly the same blue.

It was kind of not fair, Circle people still being so suspicious of Kerwin and stuff—I mean, they all *knew* he was okay now, that he wasn't a dog boy anymore—but I guess I can understand it. Like, you can't be too careful, and stuff. And besides, Kerwin still had that dog-boy habit of rubbing his scars, and squeezing and pinching them.

I squatted down and picked up a bottle of Anacin and shook it. There was only a few pills inside. Then I said, You seen the Tape Worm? and the Aspirin Lady said no.

I didn't see hardly anybody on the road today, she said. I didn't expect to get here myself.

Me neither, I said. And then I said, Where were you during the storm?

I was just being friendly, but all of a sudden she looked like I'd asked her something too personal, and I felt bad, so I made believe I hadn't said it and picked up a tiny dropper bottle. It was ear medicine, clear stuff, just the least tiny bit left at the bottom. I guess I don't need this, I said. But you got anything for Dick Idea?

Not this time, she said. Maybe next time.

So I shrugged and looked around again for Kerwin. He was talking with the Battery Guy now, and picking through a shoe box full of loose C's, the crummy kind that leak. I walked over there and put my chin on his shoulder and said, I could use four double-A's, sweetheart, and he laughed. So he got me my batteries, and we just stood around the casbah listening to people talk about the storm. I heard somebody say that his roof fell in, right during the worst of it, and he had to find another house and it turned out to be a place where a couple of dog boys had taken shelter. But I didn't get to hear the end of that story, 'cause then I heard a rattling sound from 206 and five seconds later I seen the Tape Worm's old yellow taxi cab pull into the Circle.

The Tape Worm is so cool. Isn't he? I mean, *nobody* has a running car anymore. Almost nobody. But there he is. He got one and he keeps it. It's a mystery how. You got a running car, you got a working electric car, you figure somebody'll try and *take* it from you, correct? But nobody takes it away from the Tape Worm. You ever wonder about that, wonder how come? If you didn't know him—just make believe you didn't know him and somebody told you about him, about this guy with a car, you'd figure he'd be nine feet tall, right? and half as wide with teeth like nails, but there he is, nothing *like* that. Skinny as a picket with a little pot belly and I don't guess he has one strong muscle under that milky skin of his. How's he manage it? Any of you tapers know? I mean, yeah, sure, he got shotguns and junk, but so do a lot of people.

Anyhow, here he comes, here comes the Tape Worm in his dirty yellow taxi cab, number seven on the trunk, and I seen him sitting there behind the wheel, just looking at everybody in the Circle, maybe counting heads, and he's wearing his green shades. Then he lifts them up—his shades?—and looks at everybody with his little squinty eyes. That's really cool, too, isn't it? That one eye is brown and one is gray?

Then he got out of the cab, and he must've been, like, eating while he was driving 'cause now all these crumbs—not like bread crumbs, cookie crumbs—and cellophane wrappers just fell in the puddles. And he bent over and brushed off his bluejeans. Sure, he had his suede gloves on. And he was wearing a gold-colored T-shirt, and that button of his, his button pinned on that says Listen Up.

And then, and this is what, like, *surprised* me: the back door of the cab opened. There was somebody riding with him! I'd never seen *that* before. How about you guys? He's *always* alone, right? But that day he had somebody *with* him. Just like it was a real honest-to-God taxi cab. The back door opened and this girl climbed out.

She was older than me but still a girl still, eighteen or nineteen, right around there. Tall and black-haired, long black hair, and her chin came to kind of a point. She had on black pants and a black vest, and I thought for a second that nothing was under that vest but *her*, but I was wrong. It just looked that way. She really had on a beige T-shirt that I mistook for skin. And she turned right around again and reached back into the cab and pulled out this blue traveling sack that was just bulging with stuff, a traveling sack and then a bone-white guitar.

I seen the Tape Worm lean over and say something to her. Whatever he said, she must've thought it was pretty funny. Her face cracked open into a big smile, and she laughed. What I mean is, it *looked* like she laughed, only no sound came out of her mouth. Nothing at all. Then I seen the long scar on her throat. When she tossed back her head to laugh, I seen that raggedy scar, and it ran from one ear to the other, almost.

Then the Tape Worm noticed me, and he waved and said, Hey

Joy, how you been? And I put my hands in my back pockets and went over to see him.

Kerwin didn't come, which was funny 'cause a couple of times he'd said he wasn't gonna leave me alone with the Tape Worm anymore. He hadn't liked it when I'd told him about giving the Tape Worm—about getting in the taxi with the Tape Worm and doing stuff for him when I didn't have anything specially good to swap for a story. You know what I'm saying? But it was only now and then, and with our clothes on, and it wasn't *regular*. It was, like, only now and *then*.

Kerwin had got really mad, though, when I told him that, only I'd made him *swear* he wouldn't say anything, ever, about it to the Tape Worm. I didn't want the Tape Worm getting mad at *me*. And Kerwin promised, but he said, That's a good way to get the rose, jumping in the car with that, that. He couldn't think of what he wanted to call the Tape Worm. He just said that, that. You don't know anything about that, that. Where he's been or who he's been with. And I said, Don't worry. If I'm not worrying, don't you. But I got to admit, I *did* worry, a little bit, only nothing ever happened, so why even talk about it, right? Right.

So anyhow, I went over to see the Tape Worm but Kerwin didn't, so I guessed I'd have to ask him myself about that special sort of tape, which probably didn't *exist*, it was just what I'd said to get down there, like I already told you.

He'd unlocked the trunk and was sorting through some stuff he thought I might like. He kind of knows my taste by now, although I can surprise him sometimes. Like the time I took the one supposed to teach you how to hypnotize yourself? And the one about how to fix a car engine? A *gasoline* car engine! The Tape Worm thought it was a riot, me taking that one. And the time I took home those *poems*? By that guy Tyriss Prasad? The Tape Worm was *real* surprised when I took that one home, but I got to tell you I didn't like it much, or even know what the heck it was all about, even. But if the stuff in those poems is *true*, that guy Tyriss should have his hands cut off, just like he done to those people in that place Union.

So I gave the Tape Worm back Joanie-Joanne's story about the

King of Paramus and he looked to see how many check marks I'd
put on the label (I'd put two, it was *good*) and then he showed me
some new stuff. He had a Glen Rider story, and he had that last
one of Helen Scurvy's—the one where she says she's going to press
Stop and kill herself and then it just stops, so I guess she killed
herself. But I'd heard that one already. I took the Glen Rider, though—
it was the one about the old man with the rose who just starts
infecting people *on purpose*. And I took the tape those five zombies
made together—those zombies from the Van Buskin homestead?
And that Don Wirth tape, I took that, too—about when he met the
mayor of New York City at that free clinic in Montclair. Know that
one? I took that one, too. Then I bent over the trunk myself to see
what else was in there.

There was a bunch of blank tapes lying around, and I picked up
a package of four, TDK D90s, and I stood there thinking about it.
The Tape Worm put his hand on my shoulder, and just like he was
reading my mind, he said, Yeah, you really ought to. I bet you got
a few good stories you could tell.

I laughed and bet him he wouldn't even listen, and he said, Bet
you I would. He says he listens to *all* his tapes. What do you think?
You think he does? *All* his tapes? He got a player in that taxi, so
maybe so.

At the back of the trunk, squeezed in on both sides of the spare
tire, was a whole bunch of videotapes, and it was on the tip of my
tongue to ask him if he had one that might show us how to get rid
of Loretta's baby, only for some reason I couldn't do it. I couldn't
ask him. And I kept looking over my shoulder to see if Kerwin was
coming, let Kerwin ask.

But Kerwin was still talking to the Battery Guy, they were having
quite a conversation. Their arms were flying this way and that, and
Josephine's husband had gone over and was standing alongside
them. He'd already got rid of his blueberries, and he had a big
spotlight in the pail, plus a couple of wrinkled black shirts slung
over an arm.

And all this while, the girl who'd come in the taxi with the Tape
Worm was leaning against the field-rock wall with her arms crossed,

just leaning there watching me. I knew she was watching me. And when I caught her staring, she didn't look away, like a stranger usually would. She just kept staring at me with a little smile on her lips.

I always was, I got to admit, a big sucker for a nice smile. So I smiled back, and what's she do then but walk over and reach in the trunk and pick out a sixty-minute tape. Tries to give it to me, shakes it a little, meaning I should take it. I generally went for ninety-minute ones, unless the tape sounded too good to let go. I liked more sound. But I looked at the label anyhow, and it said Bread and Butter String Band, and there were only a couple of check marks beside the name, so it hadn't circulated much, or else it had but nobody much liked it.

I said, Good stories? and the girl tipped her head to the side, and the Tape Worm, who'd been doing a little business with Donny Gleason from the Rescue Squad, looked at me and said, That one's songs, Joy. That one ain't stories, it's all songs. Then he looked at the girl and said, Right? And she nodded, gave a little shy nod.

Now, I didn't really *want* a bunch of songs, songs are all right but stories are much better, but I tell you what I *did* want, I wanted that girl to like me. Don't ask me how come. I know it's kind of stupid. For all I knew, she was gonna hop right back in the Tape Worm's car and that'd be the last I ever seen of her, *forever*. But it didn't matter. I wanted her to like me, even if it was for only five minutes there in the Circle.

So I said, Well, I like songs, songs are good, and I offered the Tape Worm a little can of something that Loretta had stuck in my knapsack, a little can of something that might've been tuna fish or it might've been cat food. It didn't have a label and it might've been twenty years old. But the Tape Worm always goes for that kind of stuff—right? Well, you know. He's a gambler, right? Isn't that what he always says? And he took the can and shook it, and there was something solid in liquid inside, and he said, Okay. All right, he said, okay.

Then he looked at me and the girl, and he grinned a grin that I recognized the meaning of but didn't like especially. In my head I

seen a picture of him grinning like that and then grinding his teeth
and then I seen his eyes shut tight in pleasure. He said, Joy, this
is Tragedy Ringling.

That sounds funny, don't it? Joy, this is Tragedy. But I'll tell you
something that's *really* funny. I didn't hear her name as a word
meaning something awful. I heard it as a word meaning *her*, this
girl, if you get my drift. I didn't think, Here's a girl whose name
means trouble. I heard the sound Tragedy and right away I matched
it with this girl, and the name and the girl fit, and the name didn't
mean *anything* as a word. Am I making sense? Joy, this is Tragedy.

And I said, Nice to meet you, and stuck out my hand. Only she
didn't stick out hers, she nodded just, and I tried my best not to
look at that long thick ugly scar on her throat.

By then, some of the lake people had come over and were nosing
around in the taxi's trunk, so I said good-bye to the Tape Worm,
smiled at the girl, this Tragedy, then drifted away on the white
gravel. I was hoping she'd come along with me. The girl? It'd be
nice, I was thinking, if she'd follow me, and we'd get to know each
other, get to be good friends, get to be *great* friends, best girlfriends,
and like that. I was always thinking I'd like to be great friends with
a girl my age. A girl like me, or even a girl *not* like me, just a girl
my age. It was just something I was always thinking about.

And then she *did* come, she came, she followed me. And I know
it's crazy, it's stupid, but it made me so happy.

Because I hadn't done what I was supposed to do, ask the Tape
Worm about that abortion stuff, I didn't want to bump into Kerwin
again, not for a while at least. So when I seen him still talking to
the Battery Guy, I went and sneaked off through the apple trees,
and Tragedy, lugging her stuff, came right behind.

And over there, on the other side of those trees, is that old post
office and this big long wooden building, used to be a restaurant.
It's burnt down, and you can see timbers sticking up black and
puffy, and the pitched red roof is full of chopped holes. Still smells
like a fire, and it was already burnt down when *Loretta* got here.

Anyhow, I'm walking around that old restaurant, just to walk, and all of a sudden I remembered the time, a year ago maybe, that I'd come down the lake with Loretta in Dick Idea's rowboat and we'd gone through the casbah, getting what we needed, and we were making a swap, strawberries for anti-itch powder, with the Aspirin Lady when somebody started to scream.

I figured at first it was Tiny Douglass, this guy that wears a white uniform like somebody that works in a hospital, only it's filthy. He's a real loony, always screaming, but it don't mean nothing, he's harmless. He's been screaming since his man-friend died of the rose, that's what people say. It don't mean nothing, his screaming, and I thought it was just him again, Tiny, but then I realized it was a woman's voice, and it gave me the creeps.

The Aspirin Lady seen me keep looking back toward the crab apple trees and finally she said, Just relax, Joy, it's only some woman trying to have a baby. And Loretta said that from the *sound* of it, she was trying real *hard*, but none of us laughed.

Then a few minutes later, everybody started folding up their tables and blankets and beach umbrellas 'cause a bunch of dog boys were heading this way from down around the point. There was maybe a dozen of them, and they had some of their bulldogs with them, and they had sticks, and they were fooling around like they always did, shouting and whistling and pushing each other, getting their dogs all excited. The dogs weren't on leashes, either, which is *really* what made everybody at the casbah turn jumpy so fast and hurry up to leave.

Loretta pulled me by the arm, only she didn't pull me back toward the rowboat, she pulled me instead over toward the trees and the post office and the burnt restaurant, and there we found this Spanish-looking woman, her hair was all tangled and full of dirt and gravel, and she was lying down on a green and bloody woolen blanket. There was a man there too, I'd seen him around the lake, but didn't know his name. An old guy still with pimple scars from when he was a kid. He was hunkered by this woman, wringing his hands.

When he seen Loretta, up he jumped, saying, You gotta help, I don't know how to do this, I don't even know who she *is*, and like that. Loretta knelt right down, and the woman was flopping around, banging her fists and kicking her heels, and screaming, and her big stomach was heaving and rumpling, and her dirty filthy dress was pushed up around her waist, and I had to leave, I didn't want to *see* anymore.

So I just walked away, and looked down the highway and up the highway, but there was nothing to see. There never was any cars, except the Tape Worm's car. Never was, never is.

Then I sat on the wall, put my feet up on the wall, and there went everybody streaming out of the Circle, going one way, heading toward Netcong, or the other way, toward Andover and Newton, moving fast, leaving before the dog boys got a chance to start trouble, to grab whatever it was they felt like grabbing. They always just grabbed, they never traded. Who was gonna argue, they had those animals. And what did they have to trade? Nothing anybody'd want.

Anyhow. I kept hearing that woman scream, her screams got louder and louder and wetter-sounding, and a couple of dogs went charging around the Circle barking, and a bunch of dog boys started looking at me, kissy-lipped, and I got a sharp pain way deep down in my stomach. But they left me alone and walked over to where Loretta was, and I sat on the wall and chewed my stupid tongue.

When Loretta didn't come back after a long, long time, I got scared. I mean, *really*. What if the dog boys were *doing* something to her? What if they'd already *done* it? So even though I didn't want to, I jumped off the wall and crossed the Circle and ducked between the trees again, but all I seen back there at first were dog boys, ten, twelve dog boys saying ah and oh and laughing, smooching their lips and rubbing their scars. And one tried to bite me on my neck, but I gave him a jab in the ribs. I was scared, but I gave him a pretty hard jab anyhow.

Loretta was still kneeling down, leaning over that woman who was still lying on her back, who was still flopping around, and her face—the woman's face, not Loretta's face—was so pale and it was covered with sweat. Big drops on her flat nose, and little beads on her chin.

And I'll skip all the gory details, except to tell you that Loretta's arms were bright red to the elbows when it was over, and the baby was red too, the baby was all bloody, but the baby was dead. I seen its little penis. It was born dead, which is a funny thing, if you think about it. I mean, can you be *born* dead? If you were born *dead*, were you ever *born*?

Loretta pulled a shirt out of the satchel she'd brought—she'd just swapped something for that shirt, but now she pulled it out and wrapped the baby. The dog boys were acting especially crazy by then—one of them was saying how much he loved that little dead baby, he loved it so much, he loved it more than anything, he kept on saying till somebody told him to shut up, quit talking.

Then with a big long sigh, Loretta stood up and looked around at the dog boys, and at me, and she didn't have any expression except tiredness, then she walked straight across the railroad tracks and down the catwalk. I followed her. And somebody followed *me*, and when I looked around, it was a dog boy with dark-brown skin.

He just stared at me and tried a little smile, but I didn't want his smile, dog boys *stink*, and I whipped around again and caught up with Loretta. And that was the first time I seen Kerwin, and the next time I seen him was, like, two days later, and he was standing down below the steps at our house. Well, he stood there and he stood there, he stood there almost all day long, till finally Dick Idea went down with his shotgun, but Kerwin said he wasn't a dog boy anymore. He swore to God he wasn't. And after that's when he started coming around so much, and that's what I was thinking about, remembering, walking past the burnt-down restaurant with Tragedy.

I was thinking about that woman and that baby, and I can't tell you what happened to the woman, or even what happened to the baby, but I kind of guess the dog boys took it, maybe they took the mother too, but I bet you they took that baby. They loved funerals.

I remember about six months ago. I was going home to my house, I was taking the path along Strawberry Point and I seen a bunch of dog boys in a fisherman's rowboat and there was a body floating behind it in the water tied by a rope. They were dragging it to this island that don't have a name, with lily pads around it. I seen other dog boys on the island and they'd already started a fire.

It used to give me the creeps, their funerals, but it didn't bother me anymore. You just get used to anything. And Dick Idea used to say the dog boys were doing us all a big service, kind of. If *they* didn't burn the bodies, he said, somebody else would have to. Somebody always got to burn the bodies.

And now I'm thinking about when Dick Idea wanted to burn Raymond's body, but Loretta said no, so he buried it. But I don't want to think about that, so I'm just going to talk about what happened after me and Tragedy walked past that restaurant, okay?

And what happened was, we went down to the lake, right down to the edge of the lake and sat on the beach, looking across the water to French's Grove, and it was funny, but even though I *knew* she was still a girl, not twenty for sure, there were age lines in Tragedy's face, especially around her eyes. Up close sitting next to her, I could see them. She was sitting with her legs drawn up and her hands on her knees.

It was funny, I. She couldn't talk, that was pretty clear, and she couldn't probably on account of whatever'd made that scar on her throat, so I didn't know *what* to do. I couldn't ask her any questions, except yes-or-no questions, nod-your-head-yes-or-no questions. I couldn't ask her, like, where you from or how'd you meet the Tape Worm, and I didn't know yet if she wanted to hear anything about me or anything, so I just—so we just sat there together by the lake.

Then I said, I finally said something, I said, This is where I've always lived, all my life, and she smiled, watching a tiny snapper turtle swim past a big-mouthed jar half-stuck in the mud. And then I said, I'm probably always gonna remember that you sat right here and looked at that jar and that turtle, and instead of laughing at me, which she could've easily done—I mean, it was such a crazy thing to say—instead of laughing, she only nodded, then we heard a rumble, still far off, and the sky flickered and there was a jagged branch of lightning, you could smell it.

I didn't want to be caught down that end of the lake in a storm, and I knew I should get up and go find Kerwin, but I couldn't just leave Tragedy. It was that feeling again. That I wanted her to like me. I got so antsy trying to figure out what to do that I pushed my fingers through my hair—what hair I had. Loretta always cut it so short there was hardly anything left, just soft fuzz. Now it's long, though.

But that day it was just soft fuzz, and I could see the sky turning yellow-green, and if it storms again, I was thinking, where could she go? Where could she go where she'd be safe? I sat and watched Tragedy's eyelids, they flickered with the lightning, and her eyeballs gleamed. She stared so hard across the lake, I kept thinking something was happening over there, but nothing was.

Then she loosed the rope at the top of her traveling sack and worked the pleats open, then she took out a steak knife and a tiny harmonica and a cellophane bag full of yellow apples freckled with bad spots. And. Well, this next part is a real tricky part to tell, but here goes. She starts to give me an apple, like more as a gift, I could tell, than 'cause she thought I was hungry, and I said thank you very much, but instead of me just taking the apple, I grabbed the apple and Tragedy's hand, the apple and her hand both, and the first thing that happened, I seen her flinch. She flinched, then pulled back, like I was trying to *capture* her. Then all of a sudden— I'm just gonna tell you *exactly* how it was, all right? All of a sudden, I felt panicky and behind that panicky feeling was, like, it's so hard to *tell* it—a tight plug of anger. Saying it was a tight plug of anger is the best I can do.

I touched her hand, and that's what I felt, then my tongue went and pressed itself against my teeth, only my tongue felt different, thinner, and so did my teeth, my teeth felt *smaller*, and you know how if there's one thing a person knows good, it's the feel of her own teeth. Well, my teeth didn't *feel* right, not like my *own* anymore, then instead of me looking at Tragedy, I'm looking at *Joy*, seeing just how *awful* those clear little moles look on *her* cheeks. On *my* cheeks. I was looking at myself from *outside*, and I'm thinking, or *somebody's* thinking, Oh yes please God her, it ain't such a long drop. Two seconds, then done, and the apple goes splash in the shallows. Two, three seconds and done.

Tragedy'd turned big-eyed, and I couldn't tell if she was angry or frightened or both, and I felt like I'd just thrown up, weak all over. You know how you feel when you just threw up. Like that. Like you been wrung out. But I said—I reached over and got the apple, and I shook it off, shook off the water, and dried it with my shirt, and I said, I'm gonna keep this for later, if you don't mind. Just like nothing happened. I'm gonna keep this for later, I told her, then her eyes closed some and then she nodded and then she put away that little shiny harmonica and the steak knife and the plastic bag of apples. Just like nothing happened.

Then I heard another clap of thunder, much closer, and I don't know if the idea came right then, maybe it did, or maybe it came on my way back to the Circle—but anyhow, I jumped up and told Tragedy, Wait here, *please*? Thinking: It ain't such a long drop.

Most everybody at the casbah was looking toward the west by then, at the sky, and some traders were packing away their goods. The Tape Worm had his taxi's hood braced up and he was tightening something inside with some kind of tool. He seen me and waved me over, but I was looking for Kerwin then, so I just waved back.

When I found Kerwin, he looked unhappy and nervous. You ready? he said. You talk to him? Meaning the Tape Worm. I said, I didn't get a chance, but then Kerwin seen the new tapes that I'd got for myself and stuck in my satchel, where I'd just stuck that apple.

What do you mean, you didn't get a chance to? he says.

And I said, Well, there was people all around.

So? he says? So what?

And I said, Well, I just couldn't ask him with all those people around.

Kerwin made a spit noise, and, Well, he says, you gonna ask him or not?

I smiled, even though I could see the muscles in Kerwin's face move around and I knew him good enough to know that his mood was changing. He was shifting from kind of nice to not so nice. Maybe I haven't mentioned he could be not so nice sometimes. Well, he could, and he said, I shouldn't listen to you, he said, and I said, What'd *I* do?

You forced me to come here, he says, and now we got a storm and we ain't got that tape.

We ain't got one *yet*, I said, meaning both the tape *and* the storm, I guess.

Then he fingered his scars and said, I could just kill you. I could really kill you, he said, then he shoved me.

Don't you kill me, I told him. Don't you kill me, Kerwin, or I'm not going home with you.

He couldn't help it, he laughed. What a stupid thing, he said. You hear what you're saying, Joy?

If you kill me, I said, I'm staying right here. With her. I hadn't meant to say that, but since I did, I lifted my arm and pointed at Tragedy, way down on the beach still, sitting on the sand at the edge of the lake.

What're you talking about? says Kerwin and his face muscles moved around some more, and he was all right again. Not exactly nice, but all right. At least the Dick Idea had left him. Who's that? he says, talking about Tragedy, but I didn't answer him right away. Things had shifted a little bit, and I wanted to keep the shift to my side as long as I could. But then I said it, I said, That girl down there? She can do an abortion.

How do you know? he says, and I said, She can, I *know*.

And I *didn't* know, not for sure, of course. It was just my way of getting her back to the house with us. Understand? So Tragedy'd have someplace to stay if another storm blew up. Don't you think that was smart of me, kind of?

You saying you *asked* her? says Kerwin. That what you're saying?

And I said, I'm saying what I'm saying.

I felt a couple of raindrops, heard another clap of thunder, and the sky turned even greener. Then there was a bright flash of lightning, and Kerwin said, I think I best go see her myself, and I just shrugged, meaning go ahead.

So Kerwin started down toward the lake, and I went with him, but only a short ways, 'cause then he stopped. You wait here, he says. Something's funny. I wanna talk to her myself. You stay right here, Joy. And just like that, he wasn't so nice again. He gave me a nasty look, and I didn't want an argument, so I said, Okay.

And I don't know *why* I didn't tell him that Tragedy couldn't talk herself, but I didn't. Let him be surprised. And I wasn't worried that she might shake her head no when he asked her could she do what I'd said she could. She'd nod yes. I *knew* it, I knew that she would. She'd understand and nod yes. It's hard to explain what I'm trying to say, but it was, it was. Just trust me. Like Kerwin said, something was funny. Something was funny, all right.

I watched him go jump the railroad tracks, then I heard a loud honking, and looked behind me. The Tape Worm was back in his car, behind the wheel, his window down, he's honking. Joy! Come here, he says, come here! Where's the girl? he says.

And I pointed. But she's not leaving with you, I told him. She's staying here.

And his eyebrows lifted up, and he laughed.

How long she been riding with you? I said.

Oh, he says, just today. You know Hackettstown? I was in Hackettstown, he said, I was staying with some people there. Then he said, You know Alkali Rose? And I said, You stayed with *her*? and he said, Yeah. During that storm, I stayed with her.

And even though I wanted to ask him a whole bunch of questions about Alkali Rose, I mean I've listened to all of her stories—all *your* stories, Rose, if you're listening—even though I wanted to know about Alkali Rose, I asked him instead about Tragedy. I said, Was *she* living there, does *she* know Alkali Rose?

I don't think so, he says. I just found her, he says. On the front seat of my car. Just curled up here, out of the rain. And that cassette you got? he says. The one I told you was songs? *She* gave me that, he says. She gave me that, I gave her a lift.

Then he squinted and his lips bent up at the ends. She's staying with *you*? he says.

I told him, That's right, and right then he kneels up on his seat and leans over it and goes hunting through this carton of tapes in the back of the taxi. Well then, he says, still looking for something, you got to take home this Triple-A Nancy, you *got* to. Then he finds it, Triple-A Nancy Number 4, and flips it at me through the window. If that girl's staying with you, he says, you'll wanna give a good listen to Nancy Number 4.

I said, How come, and he said, Just give a good listen.

Then I watched him pull out of the Circle, heading north, up toward Andover and Newton, and whatever comes after Newton. Pennsylvania? Pennsylvania, I guess.

But wait. I forgot something important.

Before he left, before he said he had to go and then left? The Tape Worm says—last thing he says, he says, Joy, so you gonna have a story for me next time I come back? And I looked at my feet, I guess I was embarrassed, kind of, and I gave a little tiny shrug and said, I don't know. I'll think about it, but nothing's ever *happened* to me. I was being modest, and he said, Well, now something *has*, and I said, What? and he said, *Her*, then he rolled up his window and drove away.

How do you like that for mysterious? Well, *kind* of mysterious. I knew he meant Tragedy, but still. It was kind of mysterious, don't you think?

Anyway. So now he's gone and I hadn't asked him about that special tape, which probably didn't exist, and practically everybody else at the casbah was gone too, and the rain was falling pretty steady, but still there wasn't too much of a wind and the sky was moving so quick that I'm thinking maybe the storm is gonna pass over.

I hurried across the Circle, feeling happy, expecting to see Kerwin and Tragedy together on the beach. But then I stopped dead, 'cause I didn't see *either* of them. Well, I got almost sick to my stomach. Where'd they go? *Kerwin!* I called, I called Kerwin's name a couple of times. Then I ran over the tracks, but stopped again, 'cause finally I seen him. I seen Kerwin. He was still on the beach, only farther *up* the beach, leaning against a tree. His face was against the trunk, and his back was turned.

But still I didn't see Tragedy, but then I did. She was on the bridge, there's a bridge that crosses the lake, did I tell you that? This wooden footbridge? And she was walking over it to the other side, to French's Grove.

What happened? I'm thinking, what *happened*? And I didn't know *what* to do. I didn't know where to go first, if I should go see Kerwin or run after Tragedy, so I just stood there like a big stupid chunk on the railroad cinders. I yelled Kerwin's name again and that time he turned, and there was blood all over the front of him. All over his middle, and lower. Then I seen his bare feet were covered with blood, and the sand, and the tree was all smeared. And the next thing, he fell to his knees and his whole body shook, he was holding his stomach, then he fell on his face. When I. Everything was still twitching when I got there, but he lifted his head up a little and I looked in his eyes, and it was like, it was just like Raymond's eyes, like Raymond's eyes when he was so sick in his bed and he'd looked at me and Loretta and knew we were leaving him, we *had* to, that we couldn't stay 'cause he had the rose, and I remembered stepping back from Raymond's bed and Loretta stepping back, and Raymond just pleading at us with his eyes, pleading stay, and it was like that, exactly, with Kerwin, he was just pleading.

Then something went out of his eyes, and his head dropped, and there was nobody else on the beach, nobody in the Circle, and I jumped up, and out on the middle of the bridge Tragedy was looking back. I couldn't see her face good, it was too far away, and the sky flickered and there was another crash of thunder, and the rain came harder then, hissing down, and I was soaked to the bone.

Then I started running up the steps to the bridge, concrete steps, and I seen it. Her knife on the beach. I went back and picked it up, and the handle was sticky, and the blade, and sand was mixed in with the blood, and the lake was all riled up with raindrops, a billion rings, and the bridge started to sway, and I got splinters 'cause I wasn't wearing shoes, and I got closer and closer to Trag-

edy, closer, and she turned away from the railing, that traveling
sack on her shoulder, guitar in her fist, and her vest all spattered
spattered spattered with Kerwin's own blood.

Well, I'm back. Didn't know I was even gone, did you? But yeah,
it's been three weeks yesterday since I taped that stuff you just
heard, about Kerwin being stabbed dead and all, and me on the
bridge. Three weeks yesterday afternoon. And if my voice sounds
different now, a little throaty? a little bit hoarse, it's only 'cause I
had a bad cold. But I'm almost all better now. I been gargling with
salt and water and my throat's better, it was sore as *any*thing, and
I hardly even have the sniffles. I'm feeling okay. I'm feeling pretty
good. I can swallow. It's me, Joy! Back at the mike.

It's funny, though, what happened. Not really, but there I was
sitting in this chair I always took from the house to the dock, it's
a ladderback chair that somebody tried to scrape the paint off, once
upon a time, but quit before he finished, so it's partly white and
partly stripped, but even where it's stripped there's some white still
in the grain. It's my taping chair, and there I was sitting on it
talking about Kerwin being killed, and it was such a beautiful sunny
day and the lake was like glass, and I pressed Stop, and went
swimming, thinking I'd wait till it got dark to finish telling that
part of the story, that part with me and Tragedy on the bridge in
the rain after Kerwin got killed. I was thinking I'd make it better
if it was dark when I told it, but you know what? I wasn't being
honest. With myself, I mean. So what if the sun was shining, or
wasn't? That wasn't it. It wasn't the sun shining why I'd broke off
right in the middle, it was something else, and I knew what. Down
deep I knew what.

So I came back from swimming and already I was being honest
with myself, and I picked up the tape recorder again but still I
couldn't finish that part of the story. I rewound it and listened, but
when I got to the end, to spattered spattered spattered with Kerwin's
own blood, I just watched the tape counter count and the tape hubs
go round, and I couldn't say what I'd practiced. I couldn't. That's
all. Couldn't.

Finally what I did, I went in the house and got out Tragedy's tape of songs, that Bread and Butter String Band, which I never gave back to the Tape Worm, and I played it through, all the way, listening with headphones and Tragedy's voice was so high and airy, but not pretty and sometimes it cracked, it cracked singing in that beautiful home where we nevermore roam, in the land where we never shall die. Never grow old, and we'll never grow old, in that land where we'll never grow old.

And I listened to every song, all seventeen songs, then I went to sleep and woke up later feeling muscle-achy and my face all hot and I couldn't swallow. I stayed inside for almost a week, and all that I ate were some blackberries—there's no blueberries on Blueberry Island, what do you think of *that*? I ate some blackberries and drank lake water, made tea with lake water, stayed inside, and when I felt better, I got down Tragedy's guitar, I keep it on the mantel, but still I couldn't do chords, I'm not—my fingers can't remember, plus I bet it's out of tune.

And what do you care, you're saying, if you're even still *there*— you're saying, This Joy can't tell a story straight through, what's the *matter* with her? Blackberries, blueberries! What happened on the bridge after Kerwin got stabbed, *that's* what's important, that's what you want to hear about, not blackberries. So all right, you want to know what happened on the bridge? I'll tell you. I'll tell you.

Nothing.

Nothing happened on the bridge, so help me. Except—I'm coming at Tragedy, running with the knife, and already the blood on her vest is washing away, the rain is doing it, and she gets this. Her black hair is sticking wet to her head and her cheeks, and she gets this, she got this funny expression, like *what's the matter*? Like, why are you charging after me? Like surprised. Almost like— it's funny but I think of it now, she looked almost like Loretta looked, all puzzled and stiff, the time the Kerosene Guy went running after her, calling Loretta! and what it was, she'd just forgot her gallon of kerosene, she'd left it on his table. Tragedy looked at me, like, *did I forget something*? Like that.

Then she seen the knife, and she takes a big step back, toward French's Grove, and right then I stopped, and we're looking at each other, maybe six steps apart, and the rain's not so much rain anymore, it's, like, sleet, hard little balls. And I liked Kerwin pretty much but he was dead, and I know what you're thinking, you're thinking if I was the kind of person worth hearing a story about, I'd've stabbed her then and there, it's the way of stories worth hearing, or *tried* to stab her, at least, 'cause Kerwin was family, kind of, and Tragedy wasn't. She was nothing but a stranger. Like Eulamae Nutley using that clothes iron to kill the stranger that took away her husband to army camp. Get that story if you never heard it, it's good, and Eulamae's good, and I'm sure that it's true, Eulamae's right, to do what she did, but I couldn't do nothing but throw away that knife, over the railing it went. I liked Kerwin and all, but he was dead. So I followed Tragedy across the bridge.

Over in French's Grove the sleet wasn't too painful, it didn't hit us too hard 'cause there's so many trees, but I'll tell you about something that *was* painful, my *feet*, with those splinters. I could hardly *stand* it, and I was limping like an old lady, and that's what Tragedy noticed, me limping, and what she did then I took for a sign of true friendship—she threw down her sack and laid her guitar against it, then she unlaced her shoes and pulled them off, then she pulled off her socks and stuffed them in the shoes, and then she went barefoot like me.

After that, she walked slow as I did, slower, chomping her teeth every time she stepped on a rock that wasn't flat and smooth. I watched the sleet bounce off her shoulders and bounce off her traveling sack, and the shiny body of her big guitar was slick and wet, but I seen for the first time there was no strings on it. Then I went from walking behind her to walking beside her to walking ahead of her, a little ways ahead of her, and if you're wondering just where we were going, well, I was too. So I asked her, You know anybody up here?

She shook her head, no.

Well, I said, maybe we should go inside somewhere, till this all stops. Talking about the sleet, I mean. Till *that* all stopped.

She nodded, and I told her, I said, Come on then, I know a good house.

And the house I was talking about was this log house on a hilltop, not far, where I'd lived with Loretta and Raymond and my older sister Patrice till she died and we moved to Blueberry Island. I didn't know if it was empty for sure, but I hadn't heard about anybody new coming up and moving in, and if we were going to stay anyplace in French's Grove till the storm passed, I felt that place should be it.

So we kept on walking, barefooted and both of us limping, and we didn't see nobody, who'd be out? And I was *glad* we didn't see anybody, 'cause most people that live down that end of the lake are kind of strange, most of them. There was this one family called the Murphys. I don't know much about them or where they came from, but they had about nine kids, and when they'd first showed up I thought I'd play with some of them, the ones my age, but Mr. Murphy didn't want me around. He'd heard about Patrice.

I didn't know if the Murphys were even still there, but they might've been, and just past where the road forked was a house with these *religious* people living in it. Called the Host of Heaven. They were even too religious for Flyboy, those people! He'd gone over there once, to visit? But they'd wanted to keep him, they *did* keep him, wouldn't let him leave, and Dick Idea had to go get him back. Dick Idea had to get this guy Hirth and this other guy Smokey to come help him get Flyboy back. That was crazy, and those people were still around. Least I hadn't heard they'd left or died or anything.

Lots of houses were burnt down in the grove, and that's 'cause six, seven years ago, a lot of roses bloomed there and squatters from up the other end of the lake kept going down there with gasoline. I'd heard they'd even burnt some houses with people inside that *didn't* have the rose, I'd heard Raymond tell Loretta that once. We'd moved out just before all that happened, though. Patrice died just before all that happened.

So like I say, there wasn't too many people in French's Grove anymore, and me and Tragedy didn't see even one single person that day, didn't see even any squirrels or nothing. And we just kept walking, followed the road around a couple of turns, then up a short hill.

Before we got to that hill, though, I said to Tragedy, I said, If we're gonna see anybody, we'll probably see the Prowler, I said. She looked at me, and for the first time she moved her lips. She didn't *say* anything, but I could see her lips move around the word *Prowler?* And I laughed. So she *could* talk to me, in a way, and I said, Yeah, the Prowler. If you see anybody with a red-and-black flannel shirt on, run. She closed her eyes a little bit, squinted, not sure, I guess, if I was being serious. I laughed again, then I, then I thought about Kerwin, and felt I shouldn't laugh, it wasn't right. I shrugged, saying, But I don't know if there *is* a Prowler. I just heard about him. People got little stories about him looking in windows and hiding behind trees, but I don't know. He's supposed to wear a red-and-black flannel shirt, I said.

Then I pointed and Tragedy looked, and there was the house at the top of the hill, and to get there you had to climb up twelve, I remember when I was a kid counting—twelve wooden steps, then you had to go around a little bend and there was five deep cement steps there, the cement all busted up, then eight more wooden steps to a redwood deck. We were on the last few steps when I stopped. The sleet was still coming down but it wasn't that hard anymore, and I tried to listen, but the sleet made a lot of noise, and what I was listening for was sounds of people, voices and stuff.

But I didn't hear nothing, so I crept up the rest of the steps and there was a gate at the top, but it wasn't locked, it stood open. I stepped on the deck and looked through a window.

First I couldn't see nothing, so I cupped my hands and looked harder. I seen pillows and blankets on the floor, and pieces of firewood lying around, a pile of T-shirts and underpants, a couple of kerosene lamps, and there was a mattress sticking part way over the window. You could tell *somebody'd* lived there since we'd moved out. Of course, I'd *known* that, even known the family—I'd seen them over at the casbah. It was a family of three women, but they all died, that was four years ago, and it looked like nobody'd lived there since.

So I said to Tragedy, I turned around and said, It's okay, I think we can get in here, and I went and tried the door. It wasn't locked, just stuck. Then I walked in, and the house had that sad cold smell of nobody being there for a long time. I stood in the middle of the front room, remembering there'd been a rug that Loretta had brought up to the lake from the Bronx, New York, but that was gone, it was just the wood floor. I looked at the fireplace, and the spark screen was gone, and the andirons and shovels and things, all gone, and there was a lot of charred wood inside it, and I heard a squeaking sound, mice and stuff up in the chimney, the ceiling, the bedrooms, whatever.

Then I sat down on the couch, lifted up one foot and twisted it and started picking out splinters, the ones I could. And I said, I used to live in this house, until I was about nine. About nine, I said. Pretty nice house, I said. I live way down the other end of the lake now, I said, and Tragedy nodded. I really wished she could talk, I really did.

She walked around the room, all the way around it. Then she found a piece of shirt, just the sleeve, blue sleeve with snaps on the cuff, lying in the corner, and first she dried her guitar with it, then she dried her hair, and I kept picking out splinters. Could hear sleet ticking on the windows and ticking on the roof.

And I said, Loretta lives down the lake with me, I live with Loretta. She's my mother, I said. We used to live here, then we used to live on a little island, I said, just talking. We don't live on that island anymore, though. We live right across from it, with somebody named Dick Idea. Isn't that a stupid name? I think he made that up. And Dick Idea got a son named Kenny, I said. I didn't say Flyboy, I said Kenny. And he lives with us, too, I said.

Then it was so crazy—after I said that about Kenny? I almost said, I *didn't* but I *almost* said, And there's this other guy named Kerwin that comes to visit. It was so crazy! It jumped in my head to say that, like one girl to her special girlfriend, about this guy that came to visit every day 'cause he *liked* me. I'd almost forgot that Kerwin was dead, but then I remembered.

And then I stopped talking and got up. I'd only pulled splinters from my left foot, but I jumped up anyway and walked into one of the bedrooms. It used to be Loretta and Raymond's, and I poked around in the closet, opened the dresser drawers. In one of the top drawers was a litter of tiny pink mice.

I didn't find anything good there, but in the kitchen I found a yellow bug light, and the filament wasn't broken. I took it with me back to the front room. I could get corn and lettuce for that light bulb from Josephine. Tragedy was bringing me good luck already.

So finally I looked at her again and what she was doing was stringing her guitar, tying a string around a nut and pulling it tight. I watched her. I never seen anybody do that before. She was tying a string around a nut and turning the peg, and when she finished, I reached down and plucked the string, then I wondered if I asked her, if she'd teach me how to play guitar, but I was afraid in my throat to ask.

She did two more strings, taking her time, and so wrapped up in what she was doing it was like I wasn't even there. She never looked at me. She kept stringing and tuning, and outside the sleet changed back to pouring rain, then it tapered off, and in the meantime it got dark.

I hated the dark, just hated it, and usually what I did when it got dark, since I hated it so much, I played one of my story tapes. I'd get in bed under the sheet, or under the sheet and a quilt, nothing on but headphones. A voice in my left ear—I always turned the right channel off—could make it so I wouldn't think my own thoughts. In the quiet dark, I was liable to think scary thoughts, thoughts that started out as some little scrap of memory and then went crazy.

Without a voice in my ear, I could think about pulling weeds that morning on the patio and before I knew it, I'd be weeding with Patrice, the both of us little girls, and then I'd go with Patrice to visit Mrs. Ahern up the road, instead of *not* going with her, which is what happened in real life. And Mrs. Ahern would give us both

toast with cinnamon and Patrice and me would play with pony dolls
that belonged to Mrs. Ahern when she was little. And we'd both
kiss Mrs. Ahern good-bye, and later on we'd both get sick, then
run a fever and bloom and die. That would get my heart knocking
so loud I could hear it. A quiet dark was the worst. I'm not like that
anymore, now I can sit in the quiet dark all the time. But not then.

Anyhow. All I wanted to say was that a voice in my left ear was
something I needed come dark, so when it got dark that afternoon,
I wished I had a tape to play. That's all I wanted to tell you. I had
tapes, I even had new batteries, but I didn't have a tape player.
And I sure wished I did.

Tragedy kept stringing her guitar—I think she must've strung
it and *un*strung, then strung it again. She was finicky. It reminded
me of how careful Flyboy covered his chalice with a flap torn off
a cardboard carton, during his masses. His chalice was nothing but
a heavy beer glass with a coat of arms stenciled on it, but during
the consecration he raised it slowly, serious as a real priest. Tragedy
strung her guitar that seriously.

When it got so dark that I couldn't even *see* her anymore, Tragedy
began strumming the guitar—she'd strum it a few seconds, then
stop, then start again. It took a while, but finally she played a couple
of songs straight through, more rhythm than melody, and I didn't
recognize a single one. Then she stopped playing, so I said, Are
those songs on the tape you gave me *yours*? You in the Bread and
Butter String Band?

I didn't get an answer. If she moved her head, I couldn't see,
then she was playing guitar again, and I shut my eyes and listened,
and still I didn't hear anything I knew the words to. And with the
rain and all, and the couch pillow, I fell asleep and dreamed a
bunch of short dreams, my regular kind of short nothing dreams.
Like in one, I was shutting a window and I seen the Prowler right
outside and it spooked me. Then I was down along the cove and
seeing Loretta on the lake in her rowboat. But she didn't see me,
or if she did she pretended not to, and just rowed away. All that
kind of regular dreaming, and I woke up twice, it was still raining,
Tragedy was playing still, and I wondered if the rain would ever

stop, and I turned over both times, not caring what happened, and went back to sleep.

Then the funny dreams began, ones like I'd never had before, and I don't mean funny like they made me laugh, I mean *strange*.

In the first one? I was crouching next to a basement window, only it wasn't a house basement, it was, like, a building. Like that old restaurant at the Circle, only it wasn't *that* building, it was another building, of brick. And I was all fussed up inside, worried. I knew I was waiting for somebody but I wished they'd hurry up and come. Then the window opened, it swung toward me on hinges, and a crate of soda bottles, filled ones not empties, came sliding out. Green soda bottles that were all dusty, and I took the crate and pulled it next to me, then Tragedy wiggled through the window, and we each took one end of the crate and hurried up this, like, alley way. Then I stopped and seen where I was, and got scared and tried to wake up. I'd never seen that kind of place before, or dreamed it, either.

There were houses, but squeezed close together, and sidewalks, and a road in front that was black like Highway 206 but not as wide, and standing on one of the porches were a lot of people. I noticed two especially, two bearded guys that didn't have any clothes on. Blue scars on their chests, which they rubbed with their fingers in little circles.

All together, there was maybe a dozen people just standing around, but only two didn't have any clothes on. Were dog boys. And seeing everybody, I got scareder than I was already, but Tragedy kept me walking by walking herself and lugging her end of the soda crate, the bottles clinking. I could hardly breathe, I was so scared, and Tragedy said, It'll be all right, and then I seen that she was leading me right over to that porch and those people, and I groaned so loud I woke myself up.

It was a quiet dark, and first thing I did, I flinched, and brushed up against Tragedy. She was lying alongside me on the couch, asleep. I felt her vest and some knobs of her spine, and the rain was still coming down, beating on the roof and plinking in lots of places around the front room. I made myself lie real still, waiting for my heart to quit knocking, but it wouldn't, and I fell asleep again with it still knocking, which I never could do before, and it was knocking when I said, I don't feel so good, my voice all quivery.

And Tragedy said, Take an aspirin.

I wouldn't, though. I said, They make me sick to my stomach, which wasn't true, I took aspirins all the time, when Loretta let me have them. But in my dream I said they made me sick, and Tragedy, who was stringing her guitar again, said, We'll just do half an hour, you can't say you're sick, we *promised*.

I said all right, and followed her down some creaky stairs in a house and into a dark curtained room filled with people sitting on couches and standing around the wall. I seen one of the naked dog boys from the last dream, his belly soft and covered with black hair, and I seen his long red penis, longer and redder than Dick Idea's, and it didn't have a cap at the end, it was just closed like a drawstring bag.

Tragedy sat on a wooden chair, and there was another chair just like it next to hers that I took. Lights stopped flickering on the dirty wallpaper. It got quiet. Somebody put a kerosene lamp on a table in front of us, turned up the wick, then stepped away into the dark. Right then I felt a twisting pain in my stomach. Tragedy was playing her guitar, and I knew I was supposed to sing, but I didn't know the song, I didn't know the words, and she kept on playing the same rhythm part, and finally I got mad and said, Play the stupid *melody*, and I heard people talking, and Tragedy gave me a look with her bottom lip pushing up the top, and I shook my head, apologizing but still mad, and she started to sing by herself, singing I once loved and courted a fair beauty bright, I courted her by day and I courted her by night, and I knew I was supposed to know that song but I'd never *heard* it before, and I got more and more upset, feeling hot in my face, then hotter, and finally I stood up and walked away, bumping into people and looking for the door so I could breathe some fresh air, and Tragedy behind me singing, Her parents said no, they would not agree, they locked her in a tower and threw away the key. Then somebody snatched me around the waist and pulled me up the stairs, and I let myself go, almost grateful to be led, and up the stairs and down the hall, it smelled bad, and into a room and hands on me and hardness inside me till it was light, and a bearded face above me, yellow teeth, blue scars on his chest, and I was hit in the side of my head. I felt sick and burning. And Tragedy's voice outside, just outside the door, saying, Let me *see* her, and me getting hit with that big hand again but not caring, I was burning. Then I seen Tragedy come through the door, after somebody she'd pushed. Tragedy saying, Leave her alone, and somebody hitting me again and again, bearded man saying, She *killed* me, look at her rose, she *killed* me the bitch! And burning so hot, I seen Tragedy struggle toward me, trying to get at my side, and then I seen blood on her throat, then I felt a pain that made it so I couldn't breathe. But even before that killing pain could scare me, it was quiet dark, and Tragedy was stirring on the couch, one shoulder moving.

And I laid in that quiet dark, hearing the rain slack off, trembling from the dampness and with the recollection of those two connected dreams. After the rain stopped, the dark faded minute by minute, till it was gray and the first birds started. I climbed over Tragedy, careful not to wake her, then went and sat where she'd sat last night. I stayed there till the sun came through the front window. Then I walked outside.

The wood deck felt spongy. Up that high on the hill, I could see the lake, and part of the bridge and part of the beach. I wondered if my canoe was still where I left it, or if somebody took it. I couldn't see that old store, not from the deck. And I was still standing there at the railing when somebody called me from the road, by name.

It was Hirth, this fat guy named Hirth, and he was looking up, saying, Joy, what're *you* doing there? Hirth in his white hat like a jungle hat and a bathing suit and a white towel jacket, and his beach hamper in his hand. Joy? he says again, and starts up the hill, like he might come all the way up the steps. Finally I called hiya Hirth and ran down to meet him. Not glad to see him or anything, it was just I didn't want him coming too close to the house.

Hirth was just this fat guy that Dick Idea knew pretty good, and if you want to know what he was *like*, his personality and stuff, the best thing I could say is that he was cranky. Most of the time he just made cranky remarks, about everything. I never heard him say anything good. Always complaining. But he could be funny, too. Sometimes he was just cranky, but sometimes he was cranky and funny.

Like, once Hirth was over the house and so was Kerwin, and Hirth kept saying stuff about Kerwin, about not liking his brown color and not liking his high-pitched voice, and telling Dick Idea that he shouldn't ever let Kerwin come inside. I don't care if he's *not* a dog boy anymore, said Hirth. He *used* to be, said Hirth. And Kerwin kept trying to be friendly, kept saying, I just want to be your friend, and finally Hirth said, I already got plenty of friends. You got to wait till one of them dies.

And everybody thought that was pretty funny, even though it wasn't true. About him having plenty of friends. He lived with his sister, who was *really* fat, twice the size of Hirth, and they shared this pink bungalow in Cabin Springs with two men, one with brown freckles all over his face and the other one bald. Those two men and his sister, and Dick Idea and Smokey—those were all the friends that Hirth had. That's not a lot. But it was funny, anyhow, what he said to Kerwin.

And now there he was, standing on the steps, pushing out his lips, saying, You here by yourself?

I was at the Circle, I said. Till it started to rain.

So then he asked me again was I there by myself, and I said, No. I said, I came down the lake with Kerwin. Then I said, You going over the bridge? I gotta get my canoe, I left it at the beach.

And Hirth said, Is Kerwin in the house?

I don't think he is, I said, and ran down the steps, saying, I'll walk you over the bridge, if you're going. All right? Okay?

You just left your canoe? says Hirth, huffing and puffing behind me. You just *left* it? That was stupid, he says. Then he made a sound of disgust, 'cause he'd just splashed through a puddle deeper than he'd figured and got mud on his towel jacket. He called the mud a son of a bitch. He was such a funny guy. Sometimes I could almost like him.

He'd come over Dick Idea's house a lot with clear whiskey to drink in Mason jars, and him and Dick Idea would sit at the table and get drunk, talking about themselves like they used to be, Dick Idea talking about when he used to work in a store and sell uniforms, like for nurses and firemen, and Hirth saying he didn't miss driving a truck, he just missed there *being* trucks, period, and Dick Idea would say after he left, That Hirth is out of his skull. But Dick Idea liked him.

And I think it might be true, that Hirth was out of his skull. Some things that he did! Like, I seen him once up Cabin Springs stark naked, and he stopped when he seen me and we talked, and we're still talking and he starts to piss in the dirt. He turned away a little, but still, he took a piss right there while I was talking to him.

And this whole business with the beach, him with that beach hamper and dressed like he was on his summer vacation, that was another crazy thing. He'd walk to the Circle Beach and empty out his hamper, six beer cans that he stuck in the sand. Just the cans, they didn't have beer in them, they were old and scratched up, he probably got them at the casbah. And he had a cigarette pack, it was white with red and gold and black stripes, but just the pack, no cigarettes, and he laid that next to his blanket, and he had a potato chip bag filled with berries or pieces of bread, and a little transistor radio that he'd turn on, but all day long it played nothing but static.

He'd sit in the sun and never go near the water, making believe he was on vacation. You'd see him, he'd say, Only three goddamn days left. Or he'd say, Only two goddamn weeks a year you get, and what happens, you end up with only four goddamn sunny days. And I could never tell if he was serious and crazy, or just pulling my leg. He had those beer cans and that empty cigarette pack and that transistor radio, and right there in the hamper he also kept his blue pistol with the white grip.

Sometimes his younger sister, called Mooney, went with him,

but not very often. And if she went, she didn't wear a bathing suit, only pants and a gray sweatshirt, and she'd dump herself on Hirth's blanket and never move, her legs were like trees. She smiled. That's all she did, smiled. She never spoke a word.

Anyhow. Me and Hirth took the path that led to the bridge, and Hirth was saying, So there was a casbah yesterday? and I said, Yeah.

I was thinking of going, he said, but I didn't know if there'd be one.

I nodded and said, Yeah, there was one. But not so big as usual, I said, and Hirth nodded, glad to hear it. Then he asked me how was Dick Idea, and I said all right.

Still talking about his protective association? says Hirth, and I said, Yeah, I guess. Then I stopped walking and said, Hirth? Something happened yesterday.

But Hirth just kept going, slapping his hand on the bridge rail, good way to get splinters, slapping it down and picking it up. I said, Hirth! I said, Hirth, the dog boys came around yesterday before me and Kerwin left the casbah.

And Hirth said, Well, they come around again. Sons of bitches, he said. And pointed across the lake. That's *my* beach today, he said, talking under his breath, mostly to himself. Sons of bitches, he kept saying, goddamn sons of bitches. No way I'm letting them stay there, no goddamn way. Person got a right to spend his goddamn vacation in peace.

My heart shriveled up, seeing those dog boys on the beach right where Kerwin still was, five of them, couple of black dogs running around, and I said, Hirth, Kerwin's dead.

Hirth still wasn't paying me any mind, though, he was still carrying on about those goddamn sons of bitches, and like that, and I said, Hirth, *they killed Kerwin*, they just stabbed him in the stomach, I said. The dog boys did.

Finally Hirth stopped grumbling and says, What? What? he says. Then me and him just stood there on the bridge and watched the dog boys drag Kerwin's body up the beach to the catwalk and dump it in my canoe. Sons of bitches! says Hirth and his face turned bright red and he ran across the bridge so fast that it swayed.

Before he reached the other side, though, he stopped and went pawing through his hamper, those empty beer cans flying every-whichway and rolling on the planks. Then he found his gun and fired a shot at the dog boys on the beach. They all ran, they scattered up the tracks in the direction of the spillway.

But one of their dogs stayed behind, snapping and barking a blue streak, and Hirth reached over the railing of the bridge, stretched his arm straight out and fired. The dog just dropped over on the sand.

It's hard to tell you exactly what I was feeling when all this was going on. I felt safe 'cause Hirth had that gun, and I was glad the dog boys had run off, and I guess underneath it all I was *real* glad they'd been there in the first place. It just kind of confirmed the story I'd already started telling. Maybe somebody would say, Well, how come they didn't just take Kerwin's body after they killed him, but I could say back, Well, it was sleeting and they had to find shelter. They left Kerwin till the sleet stopped. That made sense. That was believable. So things were working out okay.

I stood beside Hirth, and his face wasn't so red anymore. I guess he felt better for having shot that dog. He was smiling.

Anyhow. The dog boys that'd been on the beach and catwalk—they were all gone. But the one that paddled away in my canoe with Kerwin's body—me and Hirth looked for him, and he was just about to pass under the bridge on his way to Strawberry Point. So Hirth reached out his arm again, only before he could squeeze the trigger, the dog boy stood up and jumped overboard. The canoe almost tipped, then Hirth fired, and I could hear the bullet hit the lake, go plip.

I could've jumped off that bridge and grabbed the canoe and pushed it to shore. I could swim, I'm a good swimmer, but I just watched it drift under us. There was some breeze and the lake was riffled, and the canoe drifted past, keeping to the middle of the lake, the back swishing just a tiny bit.

Hirth kept moving from one railing to the other, looking for that dog boy that jumped in the water, and finally we seen his head break the surface. Hirth fired again, but right away, the head ducked back under water. About twenty seconds later, farther out, down toward the Point, the head popped up again, and Hirth fired again, and down the head went. Then up it comes again, dog boy's head, but too far away then for Hirth to shoot and hope to kill.

After that, the dog boy stayed put, treading water, waiting for the canoe to drift toward him. Which it did. Then he held on, kicking his feet and pushing my canoe ahead of him. Me and Hirth watched him go down the lake, turn the point and disappear.

Hirth stuck his gun in the pocket of his towel jacket, it made a big lump, and without saying a word, he picked up his beer cans and put them back in his hamper. Then he looked at me and said, I *told* you you'd lose your canoe. You can't leave nothing behind, I *told* you. Sons of bitches steal everything, he said, and walked down the steps and onto the beach. I went with him.

He looked at the dog that he'd shot, there was a bleeding hole in its head. Then he scuffed out all the footprints and paw prints in the sand and took out his blanket and shook it and spread it down. I stood watching him take out the beer cans again, take out the potato chip bag, the transistor radio, and he took out a pair of dark-green sunglasses. Then he plopped down on the blanket and pulled out an old magazine, one with shiny paper and lots of color pictures. Move a little to the right or left, he said. You're blocking the sun.

Well, I could've kicked him right in his fat stomach! Who'd he think he was talking to? But I stepped to the left anyhow, so I wouldn't block his goddamn sun, his stupid goddamn sun. Well, he said, since you gotta *walk* home now, maybe you should get started, and I said, I'll leave when I feel like it, thank you very much. I'll leave when I feel like leaving, I said, thank you very much, and he snorted and kept looking through his magazine. I seen him looking at pictures of telephones, shiny color pictures of telephones, wasting his time looking at shiny stupid pictures.

Then I felt like crying, 'cause Dick Idea was *really* gonna get mad that I'd lost my canoe. And I say *my* canoe, since it was the one I always used, but Dick Idea figured that everything attached to his house was *his*. So it was *his* canoe I'd lost.

I fretted a little longer, then told Hirth, Well, I'm going now. If you see anybody, you tell 'em that Kerwin got killed by the dog boys. And Hirth said, Maybe I won't want to tell anybody anything, why should I tell anybody something? And like that, being a real bastard.

So I just walked away and started back over the bridge, thinking about how good it'd be to wake up Tragedy and see her again. But then I thought maybe I *shouldn't* wake her up. Then I asked myself, Why not? How come? Why shouldn't you? Then I pictured myself shaking her by the shoulder, and I guessed *that* was it. Somehow I was feeling maybe I shouldn't *touch* her. I tried getting rid of that feeling by hurrying up, but then I got another splinter and slowed down.

I never got to the other side, 'cause before I did I looked up the lake and seen a rowboat, and who was in it but Dick Idea and Flyboy and Loretta, everybody. They'd come looking for me! All three of them together! Usually, Dick Idea made sure that somebody stayed home all the time. He always said, even if you locked the house up tight, you could still lose all your stuff by the time you got back. But there they all were, all three of them, they'd come together, they'd taken that risk, they'd come out together looking for me.

Well, I couldn't just go off and not talk to them, since they'd come out together looking for me.

So I waved and I called, then I went back to the beach. But once I seen their faces up close, I didn't feel so good anymore. They all looked mad at me, like I'd done something wrong. And Loretta said, Where the hell you been? And Dick Idea said, Where's Kerwin?

I said, It's not my fault! Then I said, I was at the casbah and I was talking to the Aspirin Lady. Then it started to rain, but I couldn't find Kerwin, so I asked somebody and he said Kerwin was down on the beach, and he was, but so was a bunch of dog boys, and I just stopped on the railroad tracks, I couldn't make myself go.

And then I said, Oh, I forgot! I met this girl, she came with the Tape Worm in his car, she's really nice, and it was her and me on the railroad tracks, it was us together.

And Dick Idea said, Where's Kerwin?

And I said, Well, this girl and me were standing on the tracks and it was raining, but I wouldn't let her go on the beach after Kerwin, either. She said, Let's go get your friend, but I said, Not with those dog boys there, and then the—and then it started raining pretty hard, I guess it was already sleet, and I seen the dog boys run away. And when they were gone? I went on the beach, and this girl came with me, and we both found Kerwin, but they'd stabbed him in the stomach. The dog boys did. It was like they always said, You couldn't leave the pack. It was like, well, *you* know how they always been after him.

I stopped, truly crying, and Dick Idea finally stepped out of the boat. His pants were rolled up, he had scabs on his legs, and he said, Shit. He walked past me and said, Hirth! And Hirth lifted up his sunglasses, and Dick Idea said, Hirth, you hear this? And Hirth said, I did, but I got the shorter version.

Then Loretta was squeezing my wrist, saying, So where have *you* been since yesterday? and I said, Well, it was all that sleet, and I just went someplace to stay. Loretta said, Where? and I said, French's Grove, where we used to live, and Loretta took a step backwards. You went *there*? she says, and I said, It was *sleeting*.

In the meantime, Flyboy had took out his little gold cross that he always kept in his pants, and he kissed it to his lips, mumbling a prayer. I guess for Kerwin. And Loretta made a screeching sound, like she couldn't stand it, and she walked up the beach, and I said, Oh, shut up, you, but Flyboy went right ahead mumbling his prayer, little gold cross sticking out between his thumb and his first finger, little gold cross that he'd plucked off a rosary.

I seen Hirth offer Dick Idea one of his beer cans, and Dick Idea took it with a funny smile on his face. Then he stood there talking with Hirth, but I couldn't hear what they were talking about. Then Dick Idea came back, shaking his head and looking at me. Goddamn, Joy, he said, saying goddamn just like Hirth. Goddamn, Joy, you lost the canoe.

I said, I didn't lose it, they *stole* it. They put Kerwin's body in it and *stole* it.

Well, what happened, Dick Idea went and said something to Loretta, and she came over and said, Let's go get your things and we'll come back here and go home, and I said okay, and we walked over the bridge together. Flyboy came too, but Dick Idea stayed behind with Hirth, each of them rolling a beer can between his hands.

When we got to French's Grove, I said to Loretta, This girl I met's waiting for me at the house. She's real nice. She's a couple of years older than me, but already we're best friends. Loretta shut one eye and looked pale.

What's her name? she said, but I didn't answer right away 'cause it was such a funny name and I didn't want Loretta to make a face. But then I said, Her name is Tragedy, and Loretta didn't make any face, and I said, She can't talk. Then Loretta gave me the face I'd been expecting to see after I'd told her Tragedy's name.

So how're you such good friends, if you can't even talk to each other? says Loretta.

I said, People don't always have to talk. We just get along nice.

Then I said, I was thinking, and stopped, and Loretta said, Thinking *what*? real cold.

And I said, I was thinking maybe she could live with us.

And Loretta said, No, just like that. No.

I said, But she could work in the garden. She could, she could do things. I don't think it'd be safe for her to be on her own.

Loretta said, That's not my problem.

And Flyboy said, Is she pretty? but I didn't answer him.

We took the path to the road, and by then Loretta's face had turned to stone. When we came to that hill just below the house, she looked sick. Well, go on up and get your stuff, she said, and run straight back.

I said, My friend's up there.

Loretta said, Just get your stuff. We're leaving.

But she's my *friend*, I said, then Loretta slapped me in the face, not hard, and Flyboy came up the stairs behind me.

I ran across the deck and through the door, but there was nobody in the front room. I didn't see Tragedy's guitar, I didn't see her blue traveling sack, and my heart fell into my stomach. I called her. I called her ten times, throwing open every bedroom door and looking in. My satchel was on the floor next to the couch, and I grabbed it up, I dumped it out, thinking she'd maybe left me a note, but there was just my tapes, those batteries and that bug light.

I squeezed my eyes shut and sat down on the couch, and I was still there with my fists on my legs when Flyboy walked in. He'd been waiting outside on the deck, because he'd spotted a garter snake and got fascinated. So you coming? he said.

I said, Go away, but he wouldn't leave.

He said, Where's your friend?

I said, She's gone.

He said, This another of your make-believe friends, Joy?

I don't *have* any make-believe friends, I said. I'm no baby, I'm no little girl. This is a real person. She was here.

He nodded, then he looked at his shoes, then he looked at me, then he said, Maybe she was an angel.

And I called him a name, called him a chunkhead, but he said, No, no, really. Hey Joy, he said and his face was serious and waxy all of a sudden. He walked across the room and sat on the couch with me. Joy, I can tell *you*, he says. I can tell you, he says, but don't you tell anybody else. Last night in that storm? I looked out the window?

And what? I said. Seen the Prowler?

No, I didn't see the Prowler, he says, like that was ridiculous. I seen angels of God, he said, bright blue angels of God and they had swords big as a person, and you know what that means, Joy? When you see angels in the sky in a storm? I seen them.

Then he picked up my satchel, and we went down to the grove and met Loretta, then we crossed the bridge, and Dick Idea was still talking to Hirth, they were laughing. Then Dick Idea stuck his beer can back in the sand, he gave it a little twist, like he was screwing it in. Then he said to Hirth, So after supper? And Hirth said, Yeah, sure, be nice.

I got in the rowboat and Loretta got in, then Flyboy, and Dick Idea rowed us up the lake. The sun was hot, but it felt good on my face. Where'd she go? I kept thinking. What happened? I kept looking from side to side, hoping to spot Tragedy on one of the shore paths, but I didn't see nobody. I didn't see one single person. Dick Idea said, Joy don't seem too broke up about Kerwin, and Loretta said, Be quiet, people can feel sad lots of different ways.

I appreciated that.

The rest of the morning and most of the afternoon, back home, I felt like you do just before you get sick, like just the day before, all achy and foggy, and my eyes burned. I'd think about Tragedy and think about Kerwin and right away be afraid I was going to throw up. It was an awful day.

I spent most of it out in the big garden behind the house. It was so big you could get lost in it, almost, so deep and so long. I filled a bushel basket with sweet corn, another one with tomatoes, taking my time, and later on when it cooled off, Loretta came out.

She had on her straw gardening hat, she had on green gloves, and at first she didn't know I was there. She started watering some of the herbs she grew, and some of the rhubarb. Then I ripped the husk off a corn, and she said, Joy? She was squatted down.

Seeing her from the side, she looked old. Her chin wasn't too separate from her neck anymore, and the skin below her ears was loose and slack, and there were lines in her face. She said, I seen you brought some tapes home.

I said, Yes, and she said, You get that tape you and Kerwin went down there to look for?

What tape? I said.

She looked at me. I heard what you went down there for, she says.

I took a breath. Then I said, I don't think there's any tape like that, Loretta. I just told Kerwin that. He didn't want to go to the casbah. I didn't even ask the Tape Worm.

Loretta said, You should've, and my stomach folded in two.

You don't wanna have this baby, Loretta? I said, and she gave me a nasty look.

I said, But so how're you gonna get rid of it?

She says, Don't you worry.

And I said, You really gonna get rid of it? You know somebody can do it?

She said, Don't you worry.

And I said, You know, if you had it, I could help you take care of it, but she only snorted.

So I got mad and started to leave, but Loretta said, Don't. Then she said, You should've asked the Tape Worm.

And I said, I didn't get a chance to, and Loretta watered the garden some more, and we didn't talk for a while. Then she said— I guess she'd been looking through my satchel, and she said, Where'd you get that yellow bulb?

Found it, I said. In the house down French's Grove. I was thinking I could bring it to Josephine's.

Then Loretta said, I'm sorry about Kerwin, I'm sorry you had to see that.

And I said, I'm sorry too, but it ain't the first time I.

Then I stopped and we looked at each other, and I said, I'll go over to Josephine's.

I ran back in the house and got my tape player, then I put the new batteries in. I took that Bread and Butter String Band tape, wrapped the light bulb up in a piece of paper and stuffed both things in my satchel.

Dick Idea was on the patio using a saw. There was a glass jar full of nails sitting on a flagstone beside a hammer, and mismatched pieces of wood everywhere. Flyboy stood looking down at Dick Idea, who was making some kind of trap. And Dick Idea said to Flyboy, You think you could drive a nail in here without breaking your thumb? And Flyboy said, I think I can do that.

Then Dick Idea said, Where you going, Joy?

I said, Josephine's, I got something to swap. And he said, She got any of her strawberries, whyn't you get some of those, and I said, I'll ask. Then I went down to the lake path and followed it out to the road. I could hear the saw sawing, then I put on the headphones and pressed Play.

At first there was nothing on the tape, then there was a guitar playing simple chords, and I recognized the tune, it was something I'd heard Tragedy play the night before. Then I heard a girl's voice singing, and I walked up the road listening to the song, about standing by a window and seeing a hearse. And I was feeling extra blue by the time I left the road at Laurel's Point where there was a shingle of wood nailed to a black tree. THE MCGUIRES was painted on it in black enamel.

I walked through the brush, keeping my eye out for sumac, then came to a flight of wooden steps going down a hill. Eighteen steps. At the bottom were Josephine's cats playing in a sandy area, cats and kittens. Beyond there was kind of a boundary of metal drums, and strung from tree to tree were pennants made of colored plastic. It looked like there was going to be a party, but those things were always up. And then there was Josephine's tiny white house, beautifully kept, red curtains in the windows. Beyond the house were a couple of orange tents, and beyond those was Josephine's garden, best garden at the lake.

Right away I seen a few of her husbands. Carl was painting the bottom of big rowboat that looked solid enough for the ocean, splashing on green paint and smiling. His chest was speckled green, and his hands too. Bailey was standing at the rabbit pens, holding one rabbit by its neck, rabbit's legs were churning a mile a minute. Other rabbits had their pink noses at the pen doors, poking through the mesh. Timothy, the husband I seen the day before down at the casbah, was straddling an exercise bicycle alongside the house. There was a long cable that ran from that bicycle across the grass and up the side of the house and through a window.

As I got to the front porch, Timothy stopped pedaling, and his fatty chest heaved and jiggled, and his whole body was covered with sweat. He was a long-haired guy with blurry tattoos. He had asthma and couldn't smoke any of the dope that Josephine grew, and of all the husbands that Josephine had, he seemed the least happy.

Anyhow, he pulled a towel off the handlebars and blotted his face with it. His calf muscles kept quivering. He said, Joy, I heard something about Kerwin. I hope it ain't true.

I said, It is. My mind came to a complete stop for a couple of seconds. Then I finally asked him what he'd heard.

That Kerwin got killed, he said. That's true?

I said it was.

I can't believe it, he said. This must've happened just after I talked to him.

I said, Right after the rain started. The dog boys killed him, I said, and Timothy looked at me funny.

Dog boys? I didn't see any dog boys yesterday, says Timothy. I thought you were gonna tell me it was that girl he was with. That came with the Tape Worm.

I hadn't thought about anybody else seeing Tragedy. I'd never thought about that, not once. My tongue got dry.

I said, They were on the beach.

He says, You *seen* dog boys? Yourself?

Before I could answer him, though, a voice came through the open window, saying, Hey! what happened? What happened to the TV?

And Timothy leaned back and fitted his feet to the pedals. Don't get excited, he says, it's coming back! Then he hunched over the handlebars and started pedaling again.

I said, I'll see you, Timothy. His face was red already. I went up to the door and knocked.

Come in, said Emmy, that was Josephine's daughter, and I walked in. The room was sparkly clean, like always, red curtains blowing in all the windows, and shiny tables and upholstered chairs of mahogany. There were pictures on the walls, and different calendars from different years.

Emmy was lying stretched out on a daybed, the only thing that was knotty pine in the whole room. And she was staring at a small-screened TV on a table not ten inches from her face. There was nothing but snow on the screen, like a white storm in a square.

Emmy was about my age, maybe a year older, horsey-faced and covered with freckles. She didn't look a thing like Josephine, and I kind of wondered if maybe she wasn't Josephine's *real* daughter at all. And it wasn't just *me* that wondered, either. Dick Idea used to say when he was drinking with Hirth that Josephine and Emmy shared the same bed half the time. Maybe they did, but the other half the time Emmy probably slept right there on that couch, staring at the TV.

It was usually run by the big red Honda generator that Josephine had, the TV was and so were the lights and stuff, but that day it was being run by a small black generator stuck away behind a big plant in a washtub and connected by cable to fat Timothy's bicycle.

Emmy finally looked around and said, Hi Joy, and I said hi, thinking like I always did when I went to Josephine's that I should be better friends with Emmy than I was, 'cause she was my own age. But there was something about her, I could never feel too close. I just couldn't.

We used to be all-right friends a couple years ago, but that was when she was still agreeable to going for walks farther than her garden. Now she hardly went out of the *house*. Josephine even did most of the gardening by herself, Emmy had got so housebound. That's what Carl told me.

Hey Emmy, I said, and she turned back to the TV screen, waiting for something to come on. That's all she did, wait.

And you know how come? 'Cause just around the time that Flyboy got so sick last year, everybody at the Circle one Thursday was talking about this TV show that was supposed to've come on suddenly a few nights before. Nobody at the Circle had actually seen this show, but they'd all heard about it. So there must've been something to it. Emmy got so mad that she'd missed it that she almost never went out again.

Emmy said, Mommy's in the kitchen, and I said thanks, and walked down a little hall with framed pictures behind glass hanging up on both sides. And I heard still another one of Josephine's husbands talking, then a thumping sound. And when I got to the kitchen, what that thumping was, was Josephine at the kitchen table kneading bread dough. Her fingers all sticky. She was a big large women with a shiny face and dark red hair. Like always, she looked as happy as a picture of a doll in a storybook. She had on a housedress and a white apron.

Her fourth and latest husband sat at the end of the table. One of Josephine's old diaries was open on his lap, and he was reading from it out loud. One or another of her husbands seemed always to be doing that whenever I went over there. Reading from a diary in the garden when she was planting, or beside the house if she was lying in the hammock, or at the picnic table if she was having lunch or supper. Josephine had a bookcase full of diaries, some of them had flowers on the covers, some of them were plain-covered, some of them were black, each one from a separate year.

When I was younger and went over there to see Emmy, I used to listen sometimes, and what she'd written in those diaries from a long time ago was real interesting. It maybe even got me started liking stories—I never thought of that before right this second.

Anyhow, Josephine seen me and said, Hello Joy, sit down, be with you in a second. Then she looked at her newest husband, I didn't know his name, and she said, Keep going. I stood against the wall, and the newest husband picked the diary up closer to his face and said, December fifteenth, Monday, went to Debbie's in the A.M. Had tea and came home. Started to snow around 9 P.M.

Whump! Josephine turned over that dough and kept kneading it.

The husband said, Tuesday, December sixteenth, snow amounted to nothing. Took money out of the bank to give Jack's mom for Christmas. Had my piano lesson and stayed for a bit of the figure class. Then went to Bloomfield and had pizza with my mother. Stopped at Mrs. Crosby's on the way home. Had a long talk with Jack last night. Went to bed early.

Then the husband said, Nothing for the seventeenth of December, and Josephine smiled. Then he said, Thursday, December eighteenth. Jack didn't get up till 7:50, but somehow he was only a few minutes late for class. Went to the p.o. to mail Christmas

cards, then had lunch with Debbie and napped in the afternoon.
Friday, December nineteenth, Jack out to do last-minute Christmas
shopping in Bloomfield. Went over to Debbie's in the P.M., had a
Christmas drink and exchanged gifts. Came out of her house into
a heavy snow. Drove to the Pathmark to get Nicky a record, my
last gift, and to buy some food in case we can't get to my mother's
for dinner. Driving a nightmare. Jack didn't go to EJ's party, even
though the snow had stopped. Had a drink.

Then Josephine turned the dough over again and beat it with
both her fists. Then she said to husband, You can stop now. That
was nice, thank you. She looked at me and said hello again, and I
said, I got you something, Josephine.

Well, let's see it, she said. I took out that light bulb and unwrapped it. She wiped off her hands on the apron, took the bulb
and shook it next to her ear. This is nice, she said. Then she said
to that husband, Isn't this nice? For when we sit outside at night,
it'll keep those bugs away.

He smiled and shut the diary, then Josephine said to me, So
what should we give you for it? Then she said, Wait a minute, Joy,
I think I know something. She finished wiping off her hands and
went out and down the hall and into a bedroom. She came back
with a couple of T-shirts.

They were still new-looking, real white. These'd fit you, wouldn't
they, Joy? She says, Emmy outgrew them.

I'm sure they would've fit, and they looked nice, but if I'd took
those shirts, Loretta would've called me selfish and worse for the
next ten days. The clothes I had were just fine. So I told Josephine,
I don't need any shirts, thank you, but Dick Idea was wondering
if you had any strawberries.

I seen her make a face at just the mention of Dick Idea's name.
They weren't talking, those two, and I never could understood what
that was all about. For a while, I thought Dick Idea might've stolen
one of her marijuana plants, but Kerwin said he bet it was, like,
sex. That, like, maybe, Dick Idea had turned her down when she
wanted him for a husband, or something. Anyhow. Whatever. I
seen her make a face, but then right away she said, Oh sure, there's

strawberries. Then to her husband, she said, Why don't you go find a pail for Joy and fill it? He got up and went out the back door. I seen his head move past the window. Josephine started rolling her dough again, and I remembered that I'd promised Loretta yesterday that I'd look for some yeast, but I hadn't.

Josephine said, I heard the bad news about Kerwin. That kind of thing just keeps happening, she says. Last week it was Russell Rhodes.

Last week? It was six months ago, at least. And Russell Rhodes hadn't been killed, exactly. It wasn't the same thing that happened to Kerwin. He fell out of his boat and drowned. There'd been some talk that his wife pushed him, but it probably was an accident. Russell Rhodes used to be a United States congressman from New Jersey. Any of you guys ever hear of him?

But like I say, it was six months ago that he died, at least. Not last week. Josephine had a weird relationship with time. She told people she was forty-five, but she had to be in her sixties. Some of her *diaries* were almost forty years old. She kept saying she was forty-five, though.

It was a joke at the casbah. Whenever a new husband showed up there with pies or breads or produce, people would ask right away how old Josephine had told him she was. The new husband would always answer, Forty-five, and everybody would laugh.

Anyhow, Josephine said, Last week it was Russell Rhodes, then she said, I always worry every time I send one of the men down to the Circle. She called her husbands the men. I'm always afraid he'll get robbed, she says. Or bit by a dog. I'm still thinking of building that wall, she says. She'd been thinking of doing that for years and years.

You remember I used to talk with Raymond about building that wall? she said. I said, Vaguely. And she said, *He* told me to go ahead and build it. Well, he had the same pessimism as me about where things are headed.

I said, Like a *stockade* fence? And make it like a fort in here?

Yeah, like a fort, she said. Only it might not be worth all the trouble to build it, she said. Here we are sitting on the side of a hill. If somebody wanted to, they could do me a lot of mischief from above. So I don't know if I'll ever build that wall. She laughed. I've been going on like this for ten years, she said.

I smiled, because it was true. Then I said, Josephine, I met this girl yesterday at the casbah. She's come up here to live. She's kind of a skinny girl, a little older than me.

Josephine said, What about her? and I said, Well, I was with her and then we got separated. And I'm kind of worried about her being by herself. If you see her, tell her where I live, would you? And she has this long scar on her throat.

Josephine said, All right. And I said, She has a guitar, the strap has flowers, and Josephine said all right again. Then she asked me the girl's name and when I told her, she made a face and said, Is she a *news*girl? I said, Newsgirl? No!

Josephine said, Don't newsgirls have names like that, like Death and Disease?

I said, That's mostly a lot of baloney, Josephine, then I told her about that tape called Nora Speaks, where Nora tells all about being a newsgirl herself. Where she said that newsgirls kept their own names, blaming Grinner Fistick and his story called Freaks' Amour for making up that entire business about newsgirls calling themselves by gruesome names. Josephine didn't seem that interested in what I was telling her. I said, Well, it's just her name, she's not a newsgirl.

I didn't know for *sure* that Tragedy wasn't a newsgirl, but I couldn't imagine her being the kind of person who'd poison reservoirs and stuff. Here I was thinking that, and meanwhile I *knew* Tragedy had killed Kerwin without any reason that I could tell. It sounds crazy. But still, that's what I thought. She *couldn't* be a newsgirl, I thought, no matter if her name was, I don't know—Plague.

Josephine took out her bread pan, and I said, Well, I'll just go get the strawberries.

Leaving by the front door, I told Emmy that I'd see her. She turned the station knob one position toward the window, and said she hoped it would be soon. Then I noticed that her chin looked kind of puffy, she'd put on some weight. See you, Emmy, I said, then went out and took the strawberries. I said bye to all of Josephine's husbands, and started for home.

Then I'm halfway there, just about halfway, moping along through the woods—I'd took a short cut—when suddenly something rustled behind me. Let me tell you, I got so scared, my heart felt gigundus, and I couldn't swallow. I was afraid it was some tramp, then I was *certain* it was the Prowler, and if I turned and looked, I'd catch a glimpse of red-and-black plaid. So I ran and kept running, and when I got back to Dick Idea's house, I could hardly breathe, my lungs were so burned. Then I thought, What if it was *Tragedy* back there? and then I was angry at myself, for acting like Red Riding Hood, for God sake.

Everybody complimented me for getting such good-looking strawberries, though, and ten minutes later I completely forgot to stay mad at myself.

We ate supper on the patio, just lettuce and cucumber and tomato with basil, and water that had little flecks of rust in it. The rust got Dick Idea upset, and he said we should be drawing our water from the pump at Cabin Springs, the drinking water at least. Loretta said it was three times as long to walk to that pump, and besides Hirth might not like us using it.

Then Dick Idea said, Hirth wouldn't mind. Then he dipped a finger in his water glass and tried to catch rust flecks. Flyboy asked if he could have some strawberries, but Dick Idea said they were for later when the guests came. Unless you can say a prayer and multiply what Joy brought, he says.

Flyboy squirmed on the bench instead of saying something back and causing trouble. He wasn't such a bad kid. He could be all right. Sometimes I miss him.

At dusk, bats started flying around the patio, and Loretta went in the house. Then Flyboy went in, and I wanted to go with him, but was afraid to. Leaving just then might've started Dick Idea complaining that nobody treated him nice, or appreciated him. What am I, not worth keeping company? He might've said something like that. So I stayed, and Dick Idea swallowed another sinus pill, his third and last of the day, washing it down with rusty water. Then he said, Joy. He said, Kerwin told me something about you two looking for a videotape? It was so phony, the way he said that. Like he'd *vaguely* heard something about a videotape.

I asked about it, I said, but there isn't one. Least the Tape Worm doesn't know about one.

And I wished right away that I hadn't changed my story again. I'd already told Loretta that I *hadn't* asked for that tape. I was glad it was almost dark, so Dick Idea couldn't see me. I probably looked guilty and fretful.

What do you think about the position I'm taking on this whole thing? he said then. And I'm telling you exactly what he said, in his own words. Position he was taking. I said, It's not my business. Talking about my half-sister. Or half-brother.

I just think another person to feed is too much, he said. And a baby needs to have shots and all, or else it gets sick. Plus I have strong feelings against anybody being born right now, he said. Then he took a bite of a cucumber and chewed it. I'm not just being mean to Loretta, he said, is what I'm saying.

I said, I know what you're saying, and our conversation ended right there, 'cause Hirth and the rest of his household came tramping up the steps just then, somebody swiveling a flashlight. All together, it was Hirth and his sister Mooney, and those two other guys that lived with them, one called Ed and the other called Wilson. Wilson's first name was Fred, but nobody called him Fred, 'cause then it would've been Fred and Ed, and that sounded stupid. So it was Ed and Wilson, and Ed was the one with freckles. Wilson was bald.

They came on the patio, Hirth complaining about a root he'd just tripped over down below, he could've broken his neck. Mooney giggled. Which was about the extent of the noise that ever came out of her. She giggled, or sometimes she made a little grunt, being agreeable to something. I already told you she never talked.

Wilson was carrying white liquor in a plastic gallon jug.

Dick Idea said, Should we go inside? and they all did. I stayed out, watching the bats swoop, a lot of them were spinning around the chimney top. Our house had a pitched roof. I leaned back and patted my hands on the arms of my chair. The sky was purple.

Well, Dick Idea and everybody, they all sat in the dining room, then I heard glasses clinking, and Loretta passed around the colander full of strawberries, and pretty soon they were playing Monopoly by the light of candles. Their voices stayed low for a while, then started getting louder, then there was some laughter. Loretta even laughed at something Hirth said.

Finally I went inside and got my tape player, but on the way back out again, Flyboy stopped me, his cassock and surplice slung over his arm, and he said, I'm going downstairs and say a mass for Kerwin, you want to come?

I said, No, thank you.

He said, You should come, we can both celebrate the mass.

And I said there wasn't nothing to celebrate, and he said, That's just what they call it, you *celebrate* a mass. It's an expression, he says. But I told him I didn't care what it was called, I was going back outside, and I did.

Then I listened to some more songs from that Bread and Butter tape, and gradually got the feeling, then felt for sure that it was Tragedy's voice singing most of those songs—it was the voice I'd heard singing in my dream the night before. That song was on the tape, even, that one about loving and courting a most fair beauty bright. There was that song, and one about a pilgrim and a stranger, and another one about memories that linger like smoke.

There were seven songs on the first side, I listened to all of them a couple times apiece. I decided to leave the other side for tomorrow. The other songs. Why rush? That way I'd have something to look forward to.

It was so dark by then I couldn't see past my own face. The patio disappeared, and the treetops, and the lake, and Blueberry Island. I couldn't even see the bats anymore. So finally I went back in the house, and the loud talk had changed to grunting, and the laughter had died completely. Ed landed on Boardwalk. Says, Boardwalk! Does anybody own it? And Wilson said, Yeah, you do, Lady Ed. Ed laughed and said, Well, I'll buy a house, then. But Dick Idea said,

You can't, you don't own Park Place. Then Hirth said, Is anybody besides me bored with this game? Loretta said yeah, she was, too. Wilson rolled the dice. I sat in the front room and looked through the arch. Community Chest, said Wilson. The candles had burned way down, two were guttering. It was like a séance, everybody sitting around those wobbly flames—it was like that story of Joanie-Joanne's, when Joanie's friend Angus starts talking in a woman's voice.

Anyhow, like I knew he would, Dick Idea got nasty. He couldn't drink without getting nasty.

It started when Loretta was sent to jail, and instead of paying her fine she decided to stay there till she rolled doubles. First Dick Idea said, That's a chicken way to play. Then he said, You're ruining the game. Then he said, That's your third roll, Loretta. Now you got to pay the fifty dollars. You can't stay in jail anymore.

Loretta said she could too, if she wanted. She'd stay till she rolled doubles. Long as it took.

Dick Idea said, You can't. Then he said, Somebody read the rules. And Ed took out his little flashlight and shined it on the rule book. But Loretta said, I quit, and stood up. Dick Idea said, You can't just quit. I'm quitting, she says, I don't feel so good. Then she told Mooney, who hadn't been playing, just sitting there next to her brother—Loretta said, Mooney, come out on the patio. I want to ask you something.

Hirth said, Ask her what?

Loretta said, Mooney? And Mooney went with her. They walked right past me in the dark, they didn't even know I was sitting there, I bet.

Dick Idea said, Just throw her money back in the bank. And her deeds.

What's the matter with Loretta? said Hirth. She really don't feel good? You feel her glands lately? She looks a little thin.

Dick Idea said, She's all right.

Then I heard the patio gate open, and I thought that Loretta was going for a walk with Mooney, but it wasn't them going out, it was Smokey coming in. That was another friend of Dick Idea's. He was almost a freak of nature, Smokey was. He stood seven feet tall. Well, maybe not that tall, maybe six and a half feet. But real tall and skinny. In daylight, his face was yellow. Smokey had lived at the lake his whole life, he wasn't a plague squatter. And he always had on a white T-shirt and army pants, and he wore an overseas cap, like a baseball cap with camouflage. I guess he must've been around thirty. But skinny? You'd think he had cancer, but he wasn't sick, and he was always working. Smokey was a carpenter.

He talked to Loretta on the patio for a minute, then knocked on the screen door and called inside, Anything left to drink? Dick Idea told him to come in, which he did, and when he'd sat down, somebody poured him a glass of whiskey, and Hirth said, Try those strawberries. They're from Josephine.

Smokey asked around how everybody was doing, then he said, There's a big fire on that island off Strawberry Point. On the way over here I seen it. The dog boys are burning something, he says. I wonder if it's Kerwin.

Everybody'd heard about Kerwin!

Probably is, said Dick Idea. Probably *is* Kerwin. Then he said, I don't know how you guys all feel, but I'm getting tired of those kids. I'd hate to get torn to bits someday by one of their, and he said *fucken* animals. Their fucken animals. He hardly ever said that word. Do you happen to know if they're *breeding* those dogs? says Dick Idea.

And Wilson said, Of course they are. Half of them are wild already. Bud Friendlich found three of them on his back porch a few days ago, just before that long storm we had.

Well, said Dick Idea, that could turn into a major problem.

Then he said, You know, Kerwin told me some things about those dog boys you would not believe. They sit around jerking off, for one thing. Together.

Then Wilson said, Are we finished playing? Or what?

That's when I got sick of listening to them, and climbed to the sleeping balcony, but it was stuffy up there, and besides I could still hear Dick Idea talking about the dog boys, and what they did that was so disgusting. Half of them don't talk at *all* anymore, he says, and like that. The same old stuff he'd been saying about dog boys for a couple of years already.

So I took my tape player and stuff and went back down the ladder and into the spare bedroom. I crawled under the bed, where it was always cool. And I liked the smell of dust.

Then I kept fitting tapes into the player and listening for a couple of seconds, trying to find that Triple-A Nancy. It was so dark I couldn't see the labels. I finally got it, though, and listened.

Now, I don't know if you guys ever heard any of the tapes that Nancy has made—Hi, Nancy!—but if you never did, she tells these short little stories that other people told *her*. Nancy Number Four is like all her other tapes, short little stories, and I listened to every one on the first side, they're only about five minutes apiece, but there was no story about Tragedy, which is what I was waiting for. Why else would the Tape Worm have give me it?

I turned it over and started playing side two, and there's a funny story on there about a girl from Ringwood who just decided to start delivering people's mail for them. That one filled almost twenty minutes, though, and there was only about ten minutes left, and I wondered if maybe the Tape Worm gave me the wrong tape. It was possible he'd grabbed the wrong one. Or got one tape mixed up in his mind with another one.

But then Nancy said that her good friend Jeebo had told her a sad story just the other day about these two girls he'd known. Children shouldn't listen, Nancy said. Children shouldn't listen to Jeebo's new story, she said. And in case you don't know, Jeebo is this friend of Nancy who keeps on going back into rose gardens taking pictures. He says it's important to keep a record and stuff. For later on, he says, when there'll be magazines and books again. Stuff like that. He thinks he's immune.

Anyhow, Nancy says Jeebo told her a story about these two young girls, and right away, I got like an electric shock in my stomach. I pressed Stop, then didn't know why I'd done that and pressed Play.

Jeebo said he'd met these two girls at a pack house in Hoboken, a house that used to be a church rectory, so it had stained-glass windows. It wasn't strictly dog boys there, it was mixed, Jeebo said.

Dog boys and some actors, and the pastor of the church, an old black guy with an English accent. The actors used to put on plays in the church basement. Jeebo went there on a visit and decided to stay awhile. He took a lot of pictures and wrote a lot of notes, he got people talking into his tape recorder. The actors put on a play called *The Hole in the Wall.*

And while Jeebo was living there, these two girls showed up one day lugging a wooden crate of soda. They used that to get something to eat, and later they sang songs, they both were singers, they both played guitar. Tragedy Ringling was one, and her friend was Margaret Lowell.

Anyhow. They stayed at the rectory, doing a show every night, and the actors did skits, and so on, and the dog boys living there behaved themselves. But then these two *other* dog boys showed up. And these new ones were a lot more wild than the ones already at the rectory. They didn't wear clothes, for one thing. Jeebo told Nancy that their personal habits were foul, which I guess meant they shit on the floor, but I don't know.

They were wild and acted like chiefs, bossing everybody around, and it was getting so bad that Jeebo was thinking of moving out. Then this horrible thing happened.

When I heard there was going to be a horrible thing, I stopped the machine again. Horrible thing. *What* horrible thing? But it didn't take me five seconds to realize what it was gonna be. I'd already *dreamed* it. I'd already dreamed *everything* so far in Jeebo's story, only in different order. Like, in my dream those two naked dog boys were on the porch when I went over there carrying that soda crate. In Jeebo's story, those dog boys weren't even *there* yet when that happened. Otherwise, it was the same story.

And knowing what the horrible thing was gonna be, I wasn't too scared to hear about it. I was mostly curious if anything *else* in Jeebo's story would be different than in my dream. So I went ahead and finished listening, and what happened, one of those new dog-boy chiefs decided he liked Margaret, so he just took her upstairs one night. When he woke up in the morning, though, his face felt like it was on fire. That was because it was pressed against Margaret's shoulder. She had a fever, and the rash was on her throat, and the dog boy started making such a racket with his screaming and furniture breaking that he woke up everybody in the whole house. Nancy said that Jeebo said. And she said that Jeebo went running upstairs with his camera. Can you imagine? If I heard some crazy boy screaming, I might grab a club, but I wouldn't grab a camera.

But he did, and ran upstairs, and Tragedy Ringling was there hollering to be let in the bedroom. Dog boys kept pulling her back, but she threw herself against the door, and crashed it open. Jeebo got a picture of that. And a picture of Margaret tangled in bed sheets, soaked with blood. Then somebody slapped at his camera—Jeebo didn't say who, but I bet it was the old pastor. His camera got broken, so he couldn't take any more pictures. But he seen Tragedy have her throat cut from ear to ear, just for trying to help her girlfriend, who got killed anyway.

Jeebo said it was a terrible, horrible thing, the worst thing he'd seen in a long time. And even before it was all over, he picked up his broken camera and went back downstairs, then he took his other cameras and his tape recorder and left. Then Nancy said that was all the story she had room for, then she gave the address again of her wine shop, 909 East Main Street, North Plainfield, and the tape ran out.

After my heart stopped thumping, I folded my arms and snuggled my face in an elbow, ready to fall asleep. Please don't be gone for good, I said to myself, and maybe to her, it was possible. Come back, I said to myself. I didn't leave you, really. I just went over the lake for half an hour.

Then I fell asleep hearing Dick Idea blab but not hearing what he said, and woke up later when the door opened. Dick Idea's voice was coming from a different place then, from on the patio. Somebody came in with a lamp, put it on the dresser and sat down on the bed. Then it was Loretta whispering, I'll help you, I'll show you what to do. But shut the door. And the door shut.

Loretta said, It's all right, then somebody else sat on the mattress, causing the slats to bow and the springs to creak. If the bed collapsed, I was in big trouble.

Loretta said, I'll just lie back here, and you can do it, okay? With this. It'll be fine, she said. Don't worry, she said, and the mattress moved. I heard a zipper scratch down. Let's do it right now, said Loretta, then she gave a groan, and there was some rustling around.

Loretta said, You're not hurting me, just do what I told you. It's all right, she said, it don't hurt, she said over and over. You're doing all right, you're doing good. Then the other person said something at last, she said, Loretta? You're bleeding.

It was Mooney, not that I'd ever heard Mooney's voice before, this was the first time ever. But whose else could it be except Mooney's voice? And Mooney said, You're bleeding.

Loretta said, A lot?

It feels it, said Mooney. She sounded like she was going to cry any second.

It'll stop, said Loretta. If you're finished, you can go now.

I *think* I'm finished, Mooney said.

Then just go, said Loretta. And you don't have to go telling everybody.

I hardly think I will, said Mooney.

Anybody asks you where I am, says Loretta, say I went to bed, I wasn't feeling so great.

Then Mooney left, not shutting the door all the way after her, and I heard Dick Idea still out on the patio, saying, A protective association, like all for one and one for all. Saying, It's worth a try. We could have officers. Nothing too formal, just officers. Like president and sergeant-at-arms.

Who'd be president? said Hirth.

I don't want to be president, said Dick Idea, all huffy like he'd just been accused of something. I only wanna be a member. Everybody laughed, then it got quiet on the patio, and quiet in the house, and quiet on top of the bed. I laid on the floor a long time, and heard it when Dick Idea and the rest of them came back in the house, Ed or Wilson saying, I'm not unfriendly to that kind of association. But who do we protect, exactly? Just us? And who against? The dog boys? Or the dog boys and the Host of Heaven? Who exactly?

Smokey said, The Host aren't so bad. I'd let them join. It'd be good for us to know them better.

Dick Idea said, Good for you, you mean. Then he said to everybody else, They got nine women and four men. Hirth laughed and said, Smokey'd have to convert. Then Dick Idea said, Where's Loretta, and Mooney told him, She went to bed.

After that, the talk petered out. Somebody said, I'm falling asleep, and nobody answered him. Then it got quiet again, and stayed quiet, but I couldn't fall asleep. Finally it got too uncomfortable, so I slid out from under the bed, and swept my tape player and tapes after me. The room was so dark that I couldn't see nothing, it could've been a cave.

I took one step, and Loretta flinched. Says, Mooney? I didn't answer. Loretta said, Mooney, thank you. I opened the door and went out.

The front room was pitch black, too. There were no lamps or candles burning, and I could hear somebody really sawing a log, and somebody else smacking his gums, then somebody else cleared his throat. I took care moving across the room, but Dick Idea stirred anyway, and said, Who's that? But he sounded more asleep than awake, so I didn't answer him, either. Then I felt the window seat, and faced left toward where the front door had to be, and went outside and down to the boathouse. I sat on the cement wall with my feet in the warm lake.

All sorts of thoughts kept coming into my head, I couldn't stop any of them—I must've been pretty tired. But one thought that kept sneaking back at me from different directions was a good one, and I even tried to hang on to it whenever it showed up. It was a long wish of a thought, kind of a story. Me and Tragedy fix up the house on Blueberry Island, we clean it with brooms, scrub the floors, mix up whitewash from a sack of lime. The rooms are sunny all day, like Josephine's. Even brighter than Josephine's—we don't hang any curtains. And I stay there. I even call across to Loretta, who's standing on shore. We can visit back and forth, I tell her, but I'm living here now. Flyboy rows over to see us, and Tragedy plays guitar and I know all the words to all her songs, and I sing them. My hair grows long and I have to keep brushing it off my face while I'm singing. Flyboy claps. Flyboy says, You could've rolled into the lake and drowned. Get up, Joy. Get your shoes.

Sometime or other, that wishful story had turned to a dream, and I was curled up on the boathouse dock. When I first cracked an eye open, I seen mist rising from the water in early daylight. Then I lifted my head and seen the house on Blueberry Island, and it still was dismal, missing that dream coat of whitewash.

I said, What do I have to get my shoes for? But then I looked at Flyboy, and there were flecks of white at the corners of his mouth and his shirt was misbuttoned, his hair was sticking out, sticking up. I thought, Shoes! Are we being attacked, do I have to run? But Flyboy said, You gotta get your shoes 'cause you have to come with me. I can't go without you.

I said, Go where?

He said, With Dick Idea, and everybody. Just get your shoes. Joy? Would you? Tell me where they are, I'll find them for you.

I said, Go *where* with Dick Idea?

He says, Strawberry Point. They're going over and tell the dog boys they got to leave the lake for stabbing Kerwin. And if they won't budge, we're supposed to shoot them. Smokey says shoot the dogs first. Then Flyboy started pulling me to my feet. You could tell he was all panicky, saying, Dick Idea says I *have* to go with them. I don't *wanna* go, he says—just like how Eulamae Nutley's husband must've said it, not wanting to go to Fort Dix and join the New Jersey Army. I don't *wanna* go, says Flyboy, and I said, Well, then don't.

He's *making* me, says Flyboy. Dick Idea is making me.

He can't make you, if you just disappear. I told him either disappear, or shut up and go to Strawberry Point.

Will you go with me? he says.

I thought for a second, then said, All right, and we both went back to the house. I expected to find everybody all set to leave, but nobody was there except Dick Idea. Smokey and Hirth and the others had all gone home to get their rifles and stuff. They were going to meet back at Dick Idea's house soon as they could.

What are you doing awake? says Dick Idea when he seen me.

I said I never went to bed, then I asked him, So are you president?

He looked all grizzly and one eye was closed more than the other. He frowned, but then he smiled. Not yet, he said. But I will be. Then he said, You coming with us, Joy? Kenny tell you what we're doing?

Kenny. Get that. He called Flyboy Kenny.

I said, Yeah, he told me. Is it all right if I come?

Dick Idea said it was fine with him.

I said, Then I'm coming, but couldn't remember where I'd left my shoes. Under the bed! That's where. I'd kicked them off under the bed, which meant to get them I had to see Loretta. I almost couldn't do it, I almost didn't go to Strawberry Point 'cause I was chicken about seeing Loretta. What if there was blood all over? Mooney said she was bleeding. I almost couldn't go in the spare bedroom, but Flyboy seemed so pitiful and I'd already promised him, so finally I gritted my teeth and went.

Loretta was sleeping on her side. I watched to make certain she was breathing. I seen a stain on her checked blanket, but it was pretty small. I stooped down and felt under the bed and found my shoes.

Then Loretta sat halfway up. Her face was pale and her eyes had bags, she looked awful. What're you doing? she says.

Getting my shoes.

What time is it? she says.

I guess not even seven.

What're you doing up? she says.

Go back to sleep, I said.

I feel crummy, she says.

So just go back to sleep, I said. I was losing my patience. I just wanted to *leave* already.

But she keeps talking. Did everybody go home? she says.

Everybody went home, I said, and ducked out of there. Right then I hated her more than I felt sorry.

Hirth came back with a shotgun, Ed and Wilson each had a rifle, Mooney had stayed home. Then we had to wait for Smokey. When he finally showed up he was dressed all in army clothes, he'd even run smudges under his eyes with burnt cork. Hirth made a wise-crack, but didn't say anything else once Smokey turned around and glared at him.

Dick Idea said, All right. We're all set. Let's go see if this new association of ours is protective or defective.

Smokey frowned, and said, The best way to get there is through the fields with the old chicken coops.

Dick Idea said, There's no need to surprise them. We're official. Let's go straight up the road.

Smokey said, The best way to get there is through the fields with the old chicken coops, and Hirth said, I think Smokey's right.

Dick Idea said, If that's how everybody wants to go, that's how we go. I'm just one member.

So that's how we all got to Strawberry Point—we took the back road to where it teed with the main lake road, then cut through a field of high weeds and up the hill behind a maze of chicken coops from one million B.C. Those coops were so overgrown you practically couldn't see them. And passing by there, I remembered that story of Grinner Fistick's, the one that's eight tapes long, remembering how he told about this bomb hole in the ground full of trees and plants, like a jungle, and about how he said it was kind of his hiding place when he was a kid. And then I remembered how I used to have that same kind of hiding place, only mine was right there in that field, in one of those chicken coops. I'd cleared it out, but left the vines in front, so nobody could see me. That was just after we'd moved up to that end of the lake, just after Patrice died. Before Raymond did. I sat in my chicken coop and had long conversations with myself. Sometimes I made believe I was talking to Patrice, or to these two other girls that I made up, Jackie and Gina, but I always *knew* I was talking to myself, really. Except one time, Flyboy sneaked up and heard me talking like that, and that's how come he asked me if Tragedy wasn't real. Just in case you were wondering about that.

Anyhow, we got past those chicken coops, and Flyboy was already sweating. It wasn't even full daylight yet, it wasn't even eight o'clock. It was real buggy in that tall grass, you couldn't help breathing midges, but it wasn't hot. Even so, Flyboy's shirt had bubbled-up air pockets on his back and shoulders and pot belly. He swung his arms when he walked, and since I was next to him, I kept being whacked with the barrel of his pistol. I finally took it and threw it in my satchel.

In front of us, Dick Idea and Hirth, the two fat guys, were arguing about the protective association. Dick Idea was saying, Why *can't* we be more cooperative?

Hirth said, First it was protective. Now it's cooperative. Next thing, you'll be calling holidays.

Oh come on, says Dick Idea. My well is giving rusty water. Why *can't* I use your well?

Because it's mine, said Hirth. If your water is rusty, it's not the water, it's the pump. Take it apart and clean it.

What if I can't get it back together again? says Dick Idea.

Ask Smokey, says Hirth. He can tell you what to do.

And what'll he want for helping me? says Dick Idea.

Probably Loretta, said Hirth.

Dick Idea didn't think that was so funny. That's exactly why we should have an *official* association, he said. That's *exactly* what I'm talking about. So people can't ask that kind of stuff anymore.

Hirth said, I don't think anybody else is half as much interested in making things official as you are. Not now, at least.

Dick Idea said, Well, how long are we gonna wait?

Hirth said, What's the hurry?

Then they both stopped walking, since they'd caught up to Ed and Wilson and Smokey. Then me and Flyboy caught up to Hirth and Dick Idea, and where we'd all come to was a ledge behind the pack house, behind it and maybe twelve feet above it. Right below was a fenced-in junkyard full of dogs, some walking around, some of them asleep. There were car tires, and wooden chairs with the legs chewed up, and trash, and scrap, and a lifeguard's bench lying on its side, and life preservers, and piles and piles of dog shit, some black, some bleached white, all over the place.

Smokey said, Try to shoot them in their heads.

We're gonna shoot them? says Wilson. Wait a second. I thought we were just supposed to kick everybody out of the house.

How're you gonna kick out a dog? says Smokey. It'll take your leg off if you try. And he stepped to the ledge, aimed his rifle down, and started firing. I don't know what made a bigger noise, his automatic rifle or the bulldogs howling. For a little while, probably the bulldogs howling. I stayed back with Flyboy, crouched. Dick Idea and Hirth and Ed joined Smokey. Wilson didn't use his rifle at all. He just stood between Flyboy and me, and the others, with his teeth clenched tight and his jaw sticking out. He was mad at what was happening. Seemed like Dick Idea's protective association was off to kind of a shaky start.

Finally, the guns stopped and there were no more sounds from the dogs, then there was some whimpering. Then Smokey said in a loud voice, It's been decided that your group has to leave the lake this morning. I couldn't see any dog boys from where I was, but they must've come outside, 'cause Smokey was saying, It's been decided by our group that yours got to leave. Then he said to Dick Idea, What's the name of our group? And Dick Idea said, The Sunburn Lake Protective Association.

And Smokey said, The Sunburn Lake Protective Association.

Hirth Maybry, recreation director, said Hirth.

Ed laughed, but then a small red hole appeared above his left eyebrow. Nobody caught him, and he fell like a bag of cement. Then Dick Idea and Hirth and Smokey started shooting again like they were in a real war, and Flyboy, still bent over, turned and ran away, and I chased after him.

He didn't know where he was going, and kept falling, scratching his hands bad and moaning. I grabbed his shirt and made him stop. We were practically back at the chicken coops. I had to keep telling him, We're safe. There was still gunfire.

Then it got quiet, and before too long, we heard grass being swished aside, and me and Flyboy crawled under a hen house. It was Wilson, stumbling around and throwing up. I let him go by without saying we were there.

Then Flyboy said, I'm not going back to the house, and I didn't know which house he meant, Dick Idea's house, or the dog boys'. I said, So don't.

Joy, you want to come with me? We could get to the Abbey. I met a kid from Andover. He said there's people in the Abbey, it's like a regular house of people. Everybody works on a farm.

I said, *What* kid from Andover?

He said, There was this kid at the spillway.

I said, the Tape Worm says there's nobody *at* that Abbey. I *asked* him, I said. And that was true, I *had* asked the Tape Worm about Saint Paul's Abbey, once. And he'd said it was empty. If there'd ever been a farm there, he said, it broke up. Nobody was living there.

But Flyboy said, This kid swears there *is* a farm. I'm not making it up. I don't lie.

Well, good for you, I said. I could get sick real fast of him being Christ on earth.

So will you come with me? says Flyboy, and I said no. Then I started bellying out from under the hen house. Flyboy said, You going home? You going home? he says, and keeps asking me that even when he could see I was going back toward the point. So then he came after me, saying, Joy, you still got my gun? Like, I might've thrown it away! He says, Can I have my gun back? But I wouldn't give it to him. He says, Can I have my gun back—please? But I wouldn't give it to him.

So what happened? What happened was like that story by Karim, by that guy Karim, about that whole drug tribe being killed in the Detroit of Michigan. I guess everybody knows that story. Last time I got Karim's tape, there were so many check marks on the label I could hardly squeeze in mine. And stars. So many checks and stars. What do people mean when they put a star instead of a check? You guys know?

But anyhow, it was like that Karim story, except it was dog boys

shot, ten boys and eight dogs. And when I came to the ledge and
looked down, Dick Idea and Hirth were walking around in the
junkyard, and Smokey had just come out of the pack house. He
was swishing a tennis racket that he'd found. He swished it a few
times, then twirled it by the grip and threw it back in the house.
Through the doorway. There was no door.

I think we should tell people, said Dick Idea. And Hirth said,
Well, I don't. And Smokey said, If people find out, they find out.
They ask you, you don't have to say nothing. But right now I think
you should decide who to bury. If you're gonna bury anybody.

We have to bury Ed, says Hirth. Everybody else, go screw.
Where's Wilson?

We can't just leave these kids lying here, said Dick Idea. What
about disease?

Hirth said, You wanna get a shovel, be my guest. Then he looked
up the rock to the ledge, and seen me, and said, Well, do you feel
avenged, darling?

But I didn't say nothing. I didn't feel I had to answer a smart
crack like that. Dick Idea asked me where was Flyboy, and I said,
Right here. Right there, but a little ways in back of me, stooped
beside Ed, making signs of the cross with his thumb on Ed's forehead and lips. He's right here, I said, and Dick Idea said, Well, tell
him to come down here, and you, too.

He says to get down there, I said, and left Flyboy to finish giving
last rites to Ed, which is what he was doing, you know. Giving last
rites to Ed.

Anyhow, anyhow. It was real gruesome and I hated it, being in
the dog boys' yard with dead bodies, already there were big green
flies. And nothing much else happened for a while, we all just stood
around, and Flyboy didn't come down. Then Dick Idea said, I think
what we should do—he was looking straight at Hirth, and not
blinking while he talked, saying, I think what we should do, we
should take everybody in the house, and the dogs, and just burn
it down. That makes more sense than just leaving them out here
to stink.

Smokey said, I'll go along with that, and turned to Hirth and said, Will you go along with that?

Hirth thought for a second, and didn't look happy, but finally he said, All right. Dick Idea's face broke into a big stupid grin, then he got started picking up bodies, him and Smokey. They're carrying this filthy bloody dead kid toward the house, and Dick Idea says, I think you should be sergeant-at-arms. You wanna be sergeant-at-arms? Smokey said, I don't care.

Hirth found a shovel inside a little shack, then he climbed back up the rock, picking his way toward the ledge. He passed Flyboy coming down. And he said to Flyboy, You can be chaplain. Then he laughed and went to bury Ed. At least, I *think* he went to bury Ed. I don't know for sure that he did, and I never seen Hirth again, not from that morning to right this minute. He could still be around, I guess, but I never seen him. Or Wilson. I never seen Wilson again, either. Or Mooney, either, for that matter.

Anyhow, Hirth went up to the ledge with a shovel, and Flyboy came down, and when he looked at all the bodies, when he *seen* them all, his bottom lip began to shake. I thought he'd be sick, but no. He just rubbed his thumb knuckle over his mouth, and stood still for half a minute. Then he went bouncing from one dead boy to another, stooping beside each of them for two seconds to cut a ritual cross in the air with the blade of his hand, then moving on to the next.

Dick Idea stood that for as long he could, which wasn't too long. He said, Kenny, you think you might help us? You too, Joy.

You too, Joy. You too, Joy. What a pain in the ass!

He seemed rocky on his feet, Dick Idea, then he squeezed his head between his hands. I feel sick, I got such a headache, he told Smokey when Smokey came out of the house. I got such a headache.

Smokey nodded and touched his own head. I could make better shine myself, he says.

So why don't you? says Dick Idea.

I'm a carpenter, says Smokey.

So what's that mean? says Dick Idea. So you're a carpenter. I was a uniform retailer, so what? What's being a carpenter got to do with it?

Smokey looked puzzled, like he'd missed some part of the conversation, like he hadn't been paying that close attention and now he wasn't quite sure what Dick Idea was talking about. He went down off the porch, and Dick Idea followed him.

I *know* you're a carpenter, says Dick Idea as they both take hold of still another dog boy, Smokey taking the legs, and Dick Idea the arms. That don't mean you're *just* a carpenter, he says. You could do other things. Do you know anything about plumbing? he says. You know anything about pumps? Hand pumps?

What do you mean, anything? says Smokey, going up the porch steps backwards.

Do you know how to take them apart? says Dick Idea, then they went in the house and I couldn't hear the rest of it.

Flyboy had finished playing Father Kenny and was standing against that little shack where Hirth had found the shovel. Beside his head was a square dirty window, and through it I could see a black lunch pail on a shelf. It's funny I remember that. That lunch pail. This was already quite a while ago.

Anyhow, Flyboy stays leaning against that shack, but his head turns so we could look at each other. You think I'm a priest? he says. I mean, really? I felt like I was, just now.

How about *right* now? I said. You *still* feel like one?

I don't know, he says.

I think it'd be all right if you considered yourself a priest, I said. That's probably how anybody gets to be anything. You just say that you are.

He smiled. So or nutso, he said, Kenny is a priest, and I smiled back, the two of us sharing an old joke.

Before Flyboy got religious, he used to write poetry. Not serious stuff, funny stuff. And he wrote this one poem once that I always thought was a riot. It was called So or Nutso. And it went, like, So or Nutso—We are happy in our home. Nutso! So or Nutso—the rose is a beautiful flower. Nutso! So or Nutso—Dick Idea loves us

all. Nutso! You could make up anything you wanted, and me and
Flyboy, when he was still Kenny the poet, used to mock on each
other, using so or nutso. Like, he'd say, So or nutso—Joy is good
at Chinese checkers. Nutso! And I'd say, Kenny is cute. Nutso! It
was just a stupid joke.

So that's what *that* was all about. Flyboy saying, so or nutso,
Kenny is a priest. I smiled, and said, I'm gonna help out here. And
Flyboy grabbed a wheelbarrow from inside the shack, and together
we loaded dogs. But he never said the last nutso! What a stupid
dumb poem.

I rolled the dogs around to the porch, then Flyboy helped me
carry the wheelbarrow up the steps and into the house. It had three
rooms, one after the other. In the first room, there was garbage
everywhere, dried-up corncobs and filthy socks and underpants,
and junk like the hoods from a couple of cars. Over in one corner
was a table. On top were drinking glasses built into pyramids.

In the middle room was where Dick Idea and Smokey had been
piling all the bodies.

Past there, through a doorway, I could see Dick Idea talking to
Smokey in the kitchen, Dick Idea's elbow going up and down as
he talked, pretending to prime a pump.

I rolled the wheelbarrow into the second room, and I don't know
what it was—maybe it was seeing all the dog boys lying on top of
each other, I don't know, but all of a sudden I felt icy cold and my
stomach moved around like a fish. Flyboy caught me dropping. And
brought me back into the first room, then sat me down on a cable
spool, facing me toward the front door. Deep breaths, he said. I'll
be right back.

I felt better almost right away. I don't know *why* I'd passed out
like that, it wasn't as though I'd never seen a lot of dead bodies
together in one place before. So maybe it was the bad smell.

I looked around, and Dick Idea was bent over some dog boy,
trying to light his pants with a stick match. The match went out
before the clothes caught fire. Then Smokey said, Maybe they have
some kerosene, and he left by the kitchen door. Dick Idea said to
Flyboy, What are *you* looking at? I couldn't see Flyboy from where

I was, the wall blocked me. And Dick Idea says again, What are *you* looking at? Then he says, You wanna stare, go stare in a mirror. Then he went out after Smokey.

I sat on that cable spool, trying to breathe just through my mouth. Then Flyboy stuck his head around the doorway and said, Joy! He says, Joy, but he's whispering. Joy, there's somebody under the floor. There's somebody hiding down there, he says. Come here, he says, and I did, then he points to a big square in the floor that cut across two planks. Lots of houses around the lake have trapdoors like that. To, like, a little crawl space.

There's somebody *in* there, Flyboy says. Then he bent over and worked his fingertips into the trap grooves, speaking to the floor, saying, Kid! You have to get out of there, kid, they're gonna burn the house. You got to get out and run!

Flyboy starts pulling up the trapdoor, and even before I could say don't, which I would've, that bulldog was on him, tore out his throat like nothing. I couldn't believe how quick it happened! If that dog had turned on me, I'd be dead now too, but it kept going after Flyboy, snapping at his fingers. He was flat on his back, Flyboy was, staring at the ceiling, but that dog kept snapping at his fingers. I killed it with Flyboy's gun, and I'm just lucky it fired. I didn't know *what* I was doing. I'd never fired one, even *aimed* one, before. But it fired. Just point and aim, that's all you do.

Anyhow, Smokey burst in through the kitchen with his gun up, and another lucky thing was that he didn't shoot me. He seen Flyboy, though, and his face paled to what comes after white. Then he says, What'd you do, Joy, bring in a dog still alive? Right away ready to blame me!

I said, It was in the crawl space. Flyboy let it out, *I* didn't!

I was almost glad Smokey said what he did, though. That way, I got angry, and being angry was better than standing there like a zombie, especially once Dick Idea came back in and seen Flyboy with his throat torn open. He kept saying no, each time it was more a groan, saying, No, this didn't happen. Then he just exploded, and started kicking the bulldog. Smokey couldn't make him stop, and finally he quit trying and just splashed down everybody on the floor with kerosene, pouring it from a couple of small cans. Finally, Dick Idea wore himself out. Then it seemed like he didn't know *what* to do next, so he closed his eyes.

I left and walked down to the tip of the point. From there, I could see the island where the dog boys had their funerals, and just a speck of the Circle bridge, pretty far off. Pretty soon, I heard the house burning, and a while after that, these flakes of ash came blowing over my head and into the lake. The heat bugs were clicking so loud you couldn't hear yourself think. My canoe was there, tied up with three others to a stump.

Smokey came down to find me, or maybe he just found me by accident. Anyhow, he showed up. I think you probably should go home, he says. People might come to see what's burning.

I said, Is Dick Idea still here?

He left, says Smokey. And I'm leaving now. You should, too.

He watched me go sorting through a jumble of paddles, to get mine, then he watched me climb in the canoe, then he said, I'll see you in a couple of days. Tell Dick Idea I won't forget about his pump.

I drifted out into the cove, then turned the canoe around and looked at the pack house from there. It didn't seem like the whole house was going to burn down, the fire looked like it was burning itself out already. There were still flames licking up the side walls, and the porch roof had collapsed, but there was no way that house was going to burn to the ground. No way.

It took most of an hour to paddle home.

And before I tell you what happened next, I got to jump back and tell you first that after Raymond died, after Dick Idea shot him, Loretta closed herself in that spare bedroom in Dick Idea's house and wouldn't stop bawling, and she wouldn't eat, and finally Dick Idea made her get out of bed, he yanked her out. Then he made this big announcement. He was wearing a gray sweatshirt with a hood, the hood bunched at the back of his neck. He said, Starting now, nobody talks about Raymond anymore. And nobody cries, either. Enough of crying. Starting now, he said, I'm Loretta's husband, and Kenny, you treat Joy like a sister. That's that, he said.

Loretta's eyes were red and puffy, but she'd stopped crying, all right. That's that, says Dick Idea, but Loretta stands up from the couch where he'd sat her down. No thank you, she says, but thank you all the fucking same. She said fucking. Thank you all the fucking same. And Dick Idea slapped her openhanded on the side of her head.

I expect you to be faithful, he says. I haven't had relations for some time, so you don't have to worry. He said that right in front of me and Kenny. Flyboy was still Kenny then. Right in front of us, Dick Idea said, I haven't had relations in some time. Then he said, And I'll be faithful, that's my part of the bargain.

Loretta said, Bargain? and I thought she was gonna say more, but she didn't. She backed down and became his wife—they didn't get *married* or anything, but you know what I mean. And she stayed faithful, so far as I know. And we never talked about Raymond again in Dick Idea's house. Or cried about him, either.

And I'm telling you guys all this so you can know, so you can *appreciate* how upside-down it was, when Dick Idea became, like, grief-stricken after Flyboy died.

Here was the same guy that said Loretta couldn't be sad anymore for Raymond, here he was staying in bed, himself, for days on end with his eyes open and wet. You could hear him groan every couple of minutes. I swear that's what happened. He'd always acted like he *hated* Flyboy. But now that Flyboy was dead, he curled up in a fat ball, hugged his knees and carried on. That was the biggest shock of all the big shocks I'd had since the day before. Dick Idea practically lost his mind for grief. It's what happened. I know it don't sound like Dick Idea, but it's what happened, he went all to pieces.

And Loretta never comforted him. She stayed in the spare bedroom, and never got up, complaining that she felt rotten, sometimes she ran a fever and had hallucinations—like, once she started ripping apart spider webs that weren't there. I made tea, and got Loretta to drink some. But Dick Idea wouldn't so much as sip any of his. I kept trying, though. What crazy days! I was all by myself with two sick people. This would've been a great time for Tragedy to show up again, I was so lonesome, but she didn't.

Life got especially boring, so I listened to the other tapes I'd got from the Tape Worm, to that Don Wirth tape, and that Van Buskin zombie tape, and that Glen Rider—Glen Rider has a really great voice, I love it.

And I listened to Tragedy's songs, too, over and over. The first one I learned through and could sing all the words to, was that one about a heart stained in anger, about the altar boy that's been hit by a local commuter just from walking with his back turned to the train that was coming so slow. You can hear me sing it on the last tape you should have, if you got the whole bundle. But whatcha-macallit, after I learned that song, I learned the rest of them real easy, real fast, and when I wasn't singing them, they were going around in my head, the tunes and the words.

It was clear, cool weather for the next full week, and when it was casbah day again, I left Loretta sitting propped up in bed against two pillows—she was feeling better, but her face looked different than before, shinier, her complexion real coarse—and I took the canoe down to the Circle. I brought a bunch of figs, we were swamped with figs, nobody eating them but me, and I brought back all the tapes from last time, including the Bread and Butter String Band. But the Tape Worm didn't show up.

That was annoying enough, but almost worse, everybody at the casbah treated me like I had loose teeth and a swollen neck. I wasn't stupid, I knew it was all connected to what happened down at Strawberry Point, how come they ignored me. They never even *looked* at me, and nobody wanted my figs, which meant I couldn't get any batteries or yeast, I remembered Loretta's yeast. But nobody came right out and *asked* me about Strawberry Point, and I didn't bring it up. It was real chilly at the casbah that day.

Anyhow, I waited on the wall for the Tape Worm a long time, and when I got tired of waiting, I decided just to go home. I mean, it was real chilly how the people treated me, but it was also chilly *cold*. It was the third week of August, Baby November. I had goose-bumps from hanging around waiting for the Tape Worm. So I'm thinking, If nobody wants to talk to me, all right. Nobody wants to swap, fine. I'll go home. I don't need these people. Half of them were from the Tamaracks, anyway, real hillbillies. Who needed them? Who needed the Aspirin Lady?

So I started back to where I'd left the canoe, but then Carl—Carl from Josephine's house? Carl was coming down the railroad ties, and he told me to wait up. He said, I hoped I'd see you. Josephine says to tell you, your friend came around.

He was going on about somebody raiding their garden every night, but my ears had closed and were sizzling, it sounded like. I said, You seen her?

Emmy did, says Carl. Out the window. She says it was a girl, at least. But maybe it's a different girl, says Carl, maybe it's not your girl. We thought it was some animal, at first.

I said, I'll wait for you, I got my canoe.

So Carl went around to all the tables and blankets at the casbah, and I sat in the canoe eating figs. I ate so many they finally turned my stomach. So then I dumped out the basket, and watched the figs bob like corks till they sank. Then Carl came back with a bolt of cloth, some chocolate bars, and a bottle of pink liquid medicine that I'd seen before on the Aspirin Lady's table. He said—I'm paddling us away under the bridge cables, and he says, What did people ask you about the dog boys?

People didn't ask me nothing, I said. People didn't talk to me.

Carl said, You know what people think? They think Flyboy joined the pack, and that's how come it happened. Somebody seen Flyboy's body in there. It *was* Dick Idea, wasn't it?

I said, The house never burnt down?

It's burnt down now, Carl said. But it was the Murphys that did it.

I said, How come everybody's mad at *me*?

They're not mad at you, he says. It's Dick Idea. They're scared about Dick Idea.

I had to laugh. I just had to laugh, if people were really scared about Dick Idea. Dick Idea sat around. He'd got out of bed finally, but now he just sat around. In the house, I mean. He never even walked out on the patio. So it was funny, people being scared about

Dick Idea. But I guess if you didn't know, like me, you might be scared.

Carl said, People didn't like him very much to start with. And was that ever the truth. He'd been told to his face that he should send Loretta or me to the casbah and not come anymore himself. He was always getting into fights, and being caught trying to steal something.

I said, Well, they didn't have to act mad at *me*.

I left the canoe tied up at this dock people called Zeman's dock, and me and Carl walked to the road, then up twenty steps to Josephine's house. Her rooster was flapping around in the gravel, and one of the cats was watching it flap. Carl says in a loud voice, Josephine! I got chocolate—Josephine? And I met Joy!

I looked toward the house, expecting Josephine to come out the front door, but she'd been over at the garden, and I jumped a little when she said in back of me, So you met Joy. Then she says, Joy, you letting your hair grow? It looks nice. Then she says, That skinny friend you were telling me about, does she have black hair?

I said, Yes.

And Josephine said, I think she's living at Funcheon's house.

Funcheon's house, I said to myself. Which was that one? So I asked her, and Josephine said, With the statue on the lawn? The cart and donkey? She pointed up the hill. You know that white house with the thermometer on the wall? It's the one right next to it. Barometer, thermometer, whatever it is, says Josephine.

She's there? I said. At Funcheon's house?

I think it must be her, says Josephine. There's somebody just moved in up there, and Emmy seen a girl that sounds like your friend in my garden. It's probably the same person. She's probably up in Funcheon's house, your friend, says Josephine and I told her, thanks, I'd go look right now. I appreciate you telling me, I said, and Josephine said, Wait a minute. Let me send one of the men with you.

I said, I don't need one of the men, but Josephine says, Carl? Carl? she says. You mind going with Joy?

Mind? Not Carl. He didn't mind. He passed Josephine his shoulder bag. There's some chocolate in there, he said. Then he said to me, Well, let's go have a look, Joy.

We squeezed out between the metal drums and took the stairs up to the high road, that's called O'Shay's Road, then we crossed it, and right there on the elbow where it turned was the white house with the big thermometer. Only it wasn't on the wall like Josephine said, it was on a porch post. It was a big metal thermometer, all rusted. Small white house.

And right next to that house was an even smaller log house on stilts, with a black tar roof. Out front was a little planter, a donkey in harness to a cart. Carl says, Why don't we just call her? See if she's home. What's your friend's name?

I told him, and he laughed and said, Let's just knock, then. He went up three wooden steps and knocked at the back door. I waited at the foot of the steps. But there were some yellow jackets, they started circling my head, big huge yellow jackets, and one landed on my hand. I shook it off and moved. Carl put his face to the door glass. Your friend have a blue bag, he said, like a backpack?

That's hers, I said. You see it? Open the door, I said. Is it locked?

Well—no, says Carl. You wanna just walk in? Call her first.

So I called her, but nobody answered, so I went up the steps and reached in front of Carl and opened the door. It was the kitchen, a real old-time kitchen with a white sink on legs and a washtub, and a round table with two chairs. Tragedy's bag was sitting on one. There was a pile of unshucked corn on the seat of the other chair. Well, said Carl, she's our thief, all right.

I said, What, you guys are the only corn growers?

I hated it when people just accused other people of something, right off the top of their heads.

There were just four tiny rooms, but Tragedy wasn't home. I seen her guitar, though. It was lying on top of a blanket in the smallest of the rooms.

When I went back to the kitchen, Carl had opened her sack, and was digging through it. Hey you, I said. Hey Carl, you shouldn't snoop in other people's property.

I was against that. I always hated it when Loretta poked through my satchel. I said, Hey you, Carl, stop. He wouldn't, though. He took out a paper bag with a wet bottom, and right away an odor of something overripe, half-fermented, plums maybe, filled the air. Then Carl took out some crumpled posters. I said, Can I see? and he laughed.

Look who's curious now, he says. He was teasing me, and my guard went up. You got to be careful when somebody starts teasing you. 'Cause next it'll be a touch, and then you got to make all sorts of decisions, fast. Kerwin used to tease me, when he first started coming around. Anyhow. Carl says, Look who's curious now, but I took the posters.

They were like things I used to see tacked on trees, like when somebody had something to swap or he'd lost something, or was looking for company, for somebody that liked to play cards or Ping Pong or play pool or read books. These posters from Tragedy's bag were like those, with hand printing, only they had old dates on them, different dates, and they had blurry Xerox pictures. You know Xerox? It's when you get paper copied, that's called Xerox.

In some of the pictures, there were five people, Tragedy and a girl and three men. Everybody had either a guitar or a little mandolin. There were a few posters with only three people in the Xerox picture. Tragedy and that girl, and a guy with a square face and a long beard. On half of the posters, though, the Xerox picture showed just Tragedy and the girl. Tragedy always looked the same, she even had that black vest on in every single picture. The other girl was smaller than Tragedy, and she had long straight hair, probably blond but you couldn't really tell. It could've been, like, reddish-colored hair, I guess. It was only a Xerox picture. Her hair was long and straight, though. I bet that was Margaret.

I put the posters back, and Carl asked me, So what're you gonna do? He'd finished snooping. Mostly there was just clothes in the traveling sack. And some candles. A jar of peanut butter. More guitar strings. And some green chilies.

So what're you gonna do? Carl says.

I told him, Wait a while.

He says, Want me to wait with you?

I said no, but he stayed anyhow. I put the corn on the table and sat down. Carl strolled through the house and came back. He said, Look at this, and I had to get up from the table and look in the sink, and there were these black wasps crawling up the drain, one right after the other, crawling out the hole, then flitting around in the bone-dry sink. A dozen, at least, and more just kept coming, it was really creepy.

Carl said, Maybe we should wait in another room. He touched me, on the arm, to turn me away from the sink. What'd I tell you? It starts with teasing. I said, Maybe we should wait outside. I hate wasps, I said. I didn't see a single one fly out of the sink, they just climbed up the drain and wobbled around in there. It was really creepy.

Outside, the treetops shook in the wind, it was nippy, and the sky was churning gray and black. Carl studied the moving clouds, trying to decide, I bet you, was it just colder air moving through, or was it another storm. We waited and waited, but nobody came except finally Emmy, who called across the road, Is everything okay?

Carl laughed and said, And what if it wasn't? Josephine sent *you*?

Emmy said, I sent myself. But Josephine says if everything's all right, she needs you to carry in the picnic table and stuff. In case we get rain.

Yeah, all right, said Carl. Then he says, Joy, you gonna stay?

I said yeah, a little longer, then Carl said, Well, if she comes back, this friend of yours? Tell her Josephine says to leave her garden alone. All right? says Carl.

Josephine says to tell you. Josephine wants you to know. Josephine says to say. Boy, was she like the queen bee! That's what Loretta used to call her, the queen bee. Always sending messages. Carl says, You'll remember to tell her what Josephine said? and I promised.

He crossed back over the road, and Emmy crossed it the other way, and came to where I was sitting on the porch steps. She'd really put on some weight, really. Her waist had bulges, and her stomach pressed against her shirt. She had shorts on, and her legs looked flabby and white, they were like old-lady legs.

What're you doing out? I asked her.

She looked shy, like embarrassed, but for only half a second, then she looked all offended. I go out, she said. I go out a *lot*. Everybody thinks I don't go out. I go out. Then she said, Sometimes, and we both smiled. So, she says, you ever walk down to Netcong anymore? You ever see those kids?

Me? I said. No. I'm getting chicken in my old age, I said.

What we were talking about—Netcong? Me and Emmy used to go there sometimes together. Take a walk. Netcong is this, like, little town. We hung out with some kids inside this old IGA supermarket that still had the aisles. We hung out with kids in the aisle that had freezers. I had a boyfriend. Emmy had a boyfriend. We were, like, fourteen and thirteen. I was thirteen. Then some kid hanging out in the butcher department got sick and me and Emmy were scared to death, 'cause we knew him, he used to come around the freezer aisle and talk to us, he wasn't real handsome but he was cute. Emmy was sure we'd catch whatever he had, which wasn't the rose, it was that thing where your throat gets so sore and you sweat and get chills, sweat and get chills, that blue rash thing. Anyhow, we never got sick, but we never went back to Netcong, either. After that, Emmy only wanted to hang around her garden, and we didn't stay friends.

I said, I'm getting chicken in my old age, I haven't been to Netcong since we went together.

Emmy said, I always meant to ask you. Then she walked around the yard. When do you think, she said. And stopped. Then finished. When do you think you might move out of your house? I *knew* she'd wanted to ask me something else besides about Netcong.

I said, I don't know if I will.

Didn't Kerwin ever ask you? says Emmy. Weren't you and Kerwin ever gonna get a house?

Kerwin? I said. Kerwin wanted to move into *my* house.

Emmy said, I think if September isn't too wet, I'm gonna look around and see if I can find a place. You know Reid's Property?

There's a bunch of little houses way back in there. Nobody knows.

You'd have to fix it up, I said.

I could, she said. Or I could get some help.

Whatever you do, I said, don't ask Smokey.

Emmy scoffed at me for even thinking I had to say that, like maybe she didn't know about Smokey's reputation.

I said, How come you wanna move, anyway?

It's too crowded, she says. There's too many people around. Maybe if it was just Josephine it'd be all right.

I got up from the step, it was starting to rain. I'm surprised at you, I told Emmy. I just am. And I was. People were surprising me left and right. First Dick Idea, then Emmy. I told her, I said, I thought you were happy on the couch. Teasing her a little bit.

Happy? she says. Miserable! There's nothing on! If there's nothing on television, there's nothing on anywhere. Which means we're gonna miss *everything*, people like you and me, Joy. We get to grow up when there's a fucking plague. She said fucking. A fucking plague. We're gonna miss everything, she says. I think I should at least get my own place. She was in a dreamworld, Emmy was. Like, where was she gonna find a generator so she could watch TV? And where was she gonna find diesel fuel? She was living in a dreamworld.

It started raining harder, but just a cold rain, no thunder with it. Come on, says Emmy. Come on back to my house. I said all right, but then halfway down the steps, I changed my mind. I think I'll go home, I said. It's not so bad. I meant the rain. I meant it wasn't a storm, it was just raining. See you then, says Emmy, and she ran ahead, then cut sideways through the metal drums, and I watched her go charging across the yard. Timothy was on the porch, and he said, Emmy, you missed it! There was a Mickey Mouse cartoon! Then he laughed, but doubled over when she poked him in the gut, running past him through the door into the house. I guess he meant there'd been a Mickey Mouse cartoon on television, she'd missed *that*. But he must've been only kidding around. 'Cause I never heard anything else about any Mickey Mouse cartoon.

So. I turned around and went up the steps to the high road, but instead of taking it home, I crossed it and let myself back into Funcheon's house. I sat in the front room and waited, looking out the sliding windows, at the rain and the woods, the rain coming at such an angle the windows never got wet.

I kept wondering about how glad Tragedy would be to see me again. I was almost positive she'd be real glad, but not absolutely positive. I sat there for hours, then I got hungry and went to the kitchen and opened Tragedy's sack. I felt guilty for doing it, but I was *starving* and I took out that jar of peanut butter and ate some with my fingers. Not too much. Then I went back in the other room and sat down again.

It stopped raining, and the sky turned pearly, like the inside of a shell. I waited some more, then all of a sudden I jumped up, 'cause you know why? 'Cause I remembered I hadn't put the peanut butter away, I'd left it on the table, I hadn't even put the *lid* on. I didn't want Tragedy coming in and seeing that I'd helped myself to something of hers without asking.

Well, what happened, I just grabbed the jar without looking, and got stung twice, two wasps stung me on the same hand. My right hand. And I know it's stupid and all, that bee stings aren't *that* painful, they're just bee stings, but I screamed like some kid anyway, and without thinking, ran straight out of the house, and smack into somebody on the porch wearing a red-and-black flannel shirt. Almost knocked her over. It was Tragedy.

I was so glad to see her, but she moved away, stepped back down the stairs. My whole right arm by then was pins and needles. Well, it doesn't happen a lot, but sometimes people *can* die from stings, and when I felt my arm go numb, I turned panicky, which only gave me a headache, which for sure meant the poison had reached my brain. I stuck out my arm, to show Tragedy how swollen my hand was, you could see a couple of tiny black dots, they'd left their stingers in. I said, There's wasps inside. I got stung, I said. Just now. Then I said, Don't be mad that I went in your house. I seen your bag. I been *looking* for you, I said. Why'd you leave? I said. I just went to get my canoe, I said. You shouldn't've left.

She stood at the foot of the steps looking at me. Then I seen that

she wasn't wearing a flannel shirt at all. It was a plaid jacket with
a zipper. The zipper was only halfway up, she still had on that black
vest underneath. Her hair wasn't wet. Her clothes weren't, either.

You been living here all this time? I said. Meanwhile, I was
shaking my arm, getting some of the feeling back. I'd panicked for
nothing.

Tragedy nodded yeah, she'd been living there a while, then she
picked up this peach basket that she had that was half-full of wood
and lugged it up the steps. She went inside and dropped the basket
on the table, then chased away the wasps by waving her hands,
and she twisted the lid back on the peanut butter jar.

I was feeling ashamed of myself, but I didn't apologize for eating
her food, or for snooping in her bag. Instead, I asked her, You like
it here? You're all by yourself? Then I said, You should go down
and see Josephine—she lives right across the road and down the
steps. I bet you could play songs for her, she'd give you something
in return. She thinks you been stealing from her garden, I said,
but she won't hold that against you. Unless you don't stop. I'm not
saying it *was* you, I said. I'm just saying, she *thinks* you been
taking stuff from her garden.

And there I was blabbering away, big mouth, and Tragedy listened without much expression, and she never made a gesture.
Just listened to me, and I was saying, She *thinks* you been taking
stuff from her garden. I'm not *saying* you did. Then I said, I liked
your tape. That's you singing, right?

Finally, she nodded, and I said, I *thought* so. Then I said, I know
all those songs by heart already, and she lifted one eyebrow. Like
she was asking me, Really? Or maybe like she was saying, How
come? How come you learned them by heart? I hoped it wasn't
that. If she had to ask me how come, we weren't as good girlfriends
as I thought.

I said, I could even sing them, I learned them so good.

What I said made Tragedy frown, for some reason, and right
away I was sorry I'd said it. She took the basket of wood off the
table and went in the front room, that had the fireplace. I watched
her stoop and build a fire, starting with twigs. It was dusk, but

night came fast. It was pitch black out by the time the fire caught.
I hadn't talked the whole time she was lighting and feeding it. I
wished she'd acted gladder to see me. But at least she hadn't acted
like she wanted me to go away.

Anyhow, the fire took, and I decided to use its light to see those
two stingers, I still had those stingers in my hand, and to pluck
them out, if I could. So I squatted on the floor next to Tragedy, but
she hopped up. I took it as deliberate, like she didn't want me
coming too close. But maybe I was just being oversensitive. She'd
made the fire and now she was gonna do something else. Maybe
she wasn't running away from me at all. Blah, blah, blah. I think
too much, right? For my own good.

So I get out one stinger, and I'm picking at the other one, and
Tragedy comes back with an armload of corn. And a long fork. She
jabs the fork in the stump of one ear, then sticks it in the fire, husk
and all. We both ate one, then I said, I heard a story about you.
Did you know that somebody's got a story out about you, on tape?
About you and Margaret? I said.

Tragedy nodded that she knew it. Then she did a funny thing.
She pointed to the scar on her throat, then drew the fingertip across
the scar, in almost, like, a funny way. Like, *trying* to be funny. Not
quite, but almost. I didn't know if I should *almost* smile. I decided,
Don't.

And said, You gonna stay in this house? You like it all right?

She turned her face to the fire and pressed a hand to her forehead.
Her arm blocked her mouth, but I just knew she was smiling. Then
her arm fell away, and she *was* smiling. I said, I'm fifteen, because
I knew, somehow, that she wanted to ask me that. I'm telling you
the truth, I'm telling you what happened. Somehow I *knew* she
wanted to ask me how old I was.

So after I said I was fifteen, I said, Do you know what's going
on? I said, Girl, are you sending me messages, or what? Did you
just wonder how old I was?

Well, you know what happened then? We both started to laugh,
because it sounded so dopey—are you sending me messages!
We both started laughing and kept laughing till Tragedy sent

me another message, Let's go out. Or maybe it was, like, we both just *decided* to go out at the same time, it wasn't a message at all.

You could see your breath, it was that cold outside, and I didn't have a jacket, just two shirts. I was freezing. We ran to the road, the high grass felt slushy, the rainwater had froze a little. Then we crossed the road and circled behind Josephine's house, then we slid down the hill and came out in her garden. Then we just pulled everything in sight, stuffing our pockets. I looked toward the house and seen a flickering light in the living room, electric light in an upstairs bedroom.

Then we tiptoed away, passing in back of those tents and lean-tos where Josephine's husbands camped, seeing Carl and Timothy and Bailey outside together sharing a pipe. Josephine's newest husband I didn't see. He was in the house, I guessed. That sounded right.

After leaving the garden, we didn't care so much about keeping quiet, and went kicking down the hill to the main lake road. We passed Zeman's dock, but I didn't bother telling Tragedy that my canoe was there. I figured she already knew. She kept walking. I said, You're walking me home, right? You know which way? This way, I said.

When we got to my house, I said, I'll loan you my flashlight, so you can have it going back. Unless you want to stay overnight. There's, like, so much room in my house it's nuts. You could stay overnight, no big deal, I said.

But she wouldn't, she wouldn't come inside, and finally I said, All right, but you got to let me give you a flashlight. I left her waiting below the patio and took the stairs up, two at a time.

Loretta was in the living room, she'd made a fire, and pulled a chair in front of it. She'd been using the fire plus a kerosene lamp to read by. She had a book in her lap. I probably said hello, but Loretta swore that I didn't. You can't say hello? she says. Then she says, Where were you till now? You wet?

I said, I was at Josephine's.

She said, What're you doing?

I said, What does it *look* like I'm doing, I'm looking for something. I'd taken the top off the window seat and was searching around under musty wool blankets for Dick Idea's aluminum flashlight. And I found it.

But Loretta says, Where're you going with that?

I said, I'm loaning it to somebody, all *right*? and went racing back out and down the steps, but Tragedy hadn't waited, she was gone. I put the light on and swished it around, but I couldn't find her. I didn't go after her, though. I knew where she lived. It was okay. I knew where she lived.

When I came back in with the flashlight, Loretta said, Who walked you home? and I said, Carl. Then she asked me if I was hungry and I said no. Then I asked her where was what's-his-name, and she said, Sleeping. She said, You get anything for those figs? And I emptied my pockets of cucumbers and green tomatoes, what I'd stole at Josephine's. Then I went up the ladder to the balcony and laid in my bed and listened to both sides of the Bread and Butter tape.

I was still awake when Dick Idea came out of his room and went over and sat down by Loretta. He kept rubbing a hand across his chin and it made a crackle. Loretta said, You hungry?

He said, I *think* so.

I'd rolled over on my side and was watching them both through the log railing, and when Dick Idea said he *thought* he was hungry, Loretta made a face. You *think*? she says. Well, *are* you or *aren't* you?

All right, says Dick Idea. I'm hungry.

Loretta says, So why don't you go fix yourself something?

He says, You wanna come help?

Loretta says, No.

You wanna come help *anyway*? says Dick Idea.

So I got this sharp pain that turned to a miserable feeling that things were heading back to how they'd been, but of course they weren't. How could they? Everything was changed. Even though Loretta got up and helped Dick Idea make something to eat, and Dick Idea walked out later and took soap and a towel and washed in the lake, and when I climbed down next morning from the balcony, I seen that Loretta had moved back into his bedroom—even though that stuff really happened, things weren't the same, and couldn't be, ever again. I wasn't afraid of Dick Idea anymore, or grateful to Loretta. Everything had changed.

Next morning early, I knocked at Tragedy's door. She was awake, but only just, there were still red lines in her cheeks. When I came in, she was waiting for a pot of water to boil. The pot sat balanced on top of a log burning in the fireplace, and I knew how she was gonna pick up that pot without scorching her fingers. Bunch up one of her shirts and grab the handle fast, then snatch it out, which she did. I'd *known* she was gonna do it that way. The water sizzled.

Tragedy had real tea bags with strings, and a jar with not much sugar left. At first I said I didn't want any sugar, even though I did. Then I said, Okay, if you *really* don't mind, and I took a little, not even a spoonful.

We drank our tea, Tragedy stared at me across the kitchen table, then I said, You like to fish? Even if you don't, you want to come with me while I fish?

She'd never fished.

She used to live in Dover, Delaware.

I just knew.

So we got ready to go out, and I said, Why don't you take your stuff with us? I'll help you carry something. You shouldn't leave it. Really. You want me to carry your guitar? I guess I didn't give her any choice. I mean, I went and *got* her guitar. I said, You shouldn't leave *this*, especially, right? This is how you eat, right? Next time there's a casbah, I said, you should play. Or, I got a better idea. You let me tell everybody you're *gonna* play, then you find a place down the tracks, I know a good place. Anybody that wants to, they can come—but to stay and listen, they gotta give you something. What do you think? I said. You think that's a good idea? There was a guy who did something like that once. Only he had glasses of water, I said, and he played them by rubbing them with his hands, they sounded like an organ. Loretta said like a carousel organ.

Tragedy laughed and let me carry her guitar. She rolled up her blanket and stuck it in her traveling sack, then she hoisted that on her shoulder, and we left. She knew I wouldn't let her come back there again, if I could help it.

She was wearing that plaid jacket again, and while we were crossing the road, I said, You know I thought you were the Prowler yesterday. I mean, you *know* that, right? That's a pretty nice jacket, I said, but I thought you were the Prowler.

She lifted her hand, and clawed it, being funny-scary.

So anyhow, we tramped down the steps to the main lake road, passing Josephine's house on the way, but nobody was out to see us. I heard that big red Honda generator going. I got that generator now. Josephine's house is gone, but I dug around there one day last month and found that generator. I'm using it to make the refrigerator run. I like to have ice. I've been sucking on ice cubes lately, one after the other, it's been so hot.

But anyhow. Me and Tragedy went down the steps past Josephine's house to the road, and from the road we walked straight to Zeman's dock. It was a good blue day. I bailed out the canoe, then took us around to Dick Idea's boathouse. You don't have to get out, I said. I'll be right back. Be right back. And I ran to the house and around to the side and picked up the lattice and grabbed the fishing stuff, two poles just, with simple slow-turning reels, nothing fancy, and a pack of hooks. There was some old bread in a plastic bag, from the last time that Flyboy had fished off the dock. It looked a little green, but I took it. I didn't think any sunnies would notice the mold.

We left the canoe tied up and took the rowboat, and I was careful tugging on the oars, I didn't want to accidentally splash Tragedy's stuff, especially her guitar. Her hair kept being lifted in the wind, but whenever it blew across her face, she never pushed it back. I was looking forward to having hair long enough to push out of my face, you could laugh but I was. Loretta kept cutting my hair short, no matter what I said. She said, You look better with it short. Well, it was my hair! I decided I wasn't gonna let Loretta cut my hair anymore, at all. I decided it right there in the canoe. Not one more haircut, I'd cut my own hair.

I said, You cut your own hair, right? Tragedy nodded, and made her fingers be scissors, then sent them to clip at the nape of her neck. I'm gonna cut my own, too, from now on, I said. Once it grows long enough. Like down to here, I said, and touched an ankle.

So we fished. Or at least I did. I threw out the block of cement we used for an anchor, and fished for about an hour, caught nothing. And instead of the day warming up, it got cooler. I fished and Tragedy sat leaning forward with her elbows on the body of her guitar, looking all around, looking up, her eye would catch a bird and follow it. I just sat and fished.

After I got tired of that, I pulled in my line and laid the pole on the boat floor. Then I dragged over my satchel and undid all the buckles, saying, I don't think I got anything to eat. Do you? Then I said, like I was answering her question, No, I'm not hungry yet. I'm just asking.

Then I showed her my tape player and said, You ever listen to stories? Ever? Or do you just listen to songs? The Tape Worm has lots of song tapes, but I don't go in for them too much, usually. I like stories. Well, I can understand that you like *songs* more, I said, like we were having a regular conversation. I just always liked stories better.

I used to like stories on television, I said. I'm old enough to remember that. Isn't that *weird*, to be old enough to remember television? But tapes are good too. I got this girlfriend, I said, you probably wouldn't like her, she *never* listens to stories. I don't think Emmy's listened to one in her whole life. Not to one all the way *through*, at least. It's weird. I *like* to know what other people are doing, even if it's made up, which a lot of it is, you know. There's some tapers that make, like, a *hundred* tapes a year. Maybe not a hundred, but a lot. And *all* those stories couldn't be true. But it don't matter. I figure it *might've* happened, it still *could* happen, somewhere. And that's good enough for me.

Then I said, You wanna listen to a story, feel free.

I put away the tape player and said, It's right there, if you feel like listening. I got a bunch of pretty good tapes with me.

She pointed a finger at herself.

I said, Yeah, yours too. It's my new favorite, I said, and felt hot in the face. You had enough fishing? I said. The fish must be dead.

Of course on the row back, I just *had* to take us full circle around Blueberry Island, to show Tragedy the house where I used to live. But I hoped she'd be interested, and she was. It was her, even, that pointed to the sand beach. Then I rowed hard, pulled hard, to shoot us up there.

So we were on the island. I almost couldn't believe it. I hadn't been there since maybe a week after Raymond died. Since Dick Idea's big announcement. Dick Idea hadn't actually said we *couldn't* go back there and visit Raymond's grave, we just *didn't* go, me or Loretta. And after a while, a few months, it was just the regular thing, that nobody went to Blueberry Island.

Then one day three women showed up there, they came in a boat with a small outboard engine. They started unpacking things from the boat, grocery bags and suitcases and stuff like that. But Dick Idea went down to his dock and called to them across the lake. He said they were trespassing, he said the whole island, including the house, belonged to a relative of his.

Then one of the women called back that *she* owned the island and *she* owned the house, and she wanted to know who *he* was, who Dick Idea was. She said, I happen to know the owner of that dock you're standing on, and you're not him. Dick Idea said, Well, then, Mrs. Blueberry Island, he called her Mrs. Blueberry Island, all I'm saying is, you ought to know there were squatters living on your property. One of them's buried right beyond the house, you might want to take a look. Myself, said Dick Idea—myself, I wouldn't feel comfortable living in that house you own, Mrs. Blueberry Island.

Well, Mrs. Blueberry Island and her two friends got his drift, and they hollered back, asking him had the rose bloomed among the squatters, and he said yes, and the women got back in their motorboat and went away and never came back.

Anyhow. I hadn't been to Blueberry Island for a long time. There's a shrine just over there, I told Tragedy, just past the house. Then I said, *Shrine*? I couldn't believe I'd called it a *shrine*. I said, I don't mean shrine, I mean *grave*. My father's *grave* is over there, I said. I felt like a real dope, saying shrine. Where'd I get *shrine* from?

We looked for Raymond's grave, but couldn't find it, so we stood respectful in the general vicinity, and I said, Some shrine, and Tragedy smiled. Then she nodded with her chin, and we walked around and looked at the house. I made sure we stood where we couldn't be seen from Dick Idea's patio.

It's a pretty decent house, I said. It's got a wood-burning stove, so that's good. You wanna go in?

There were tears in the porch screens, and brown smelly leaves on the porch, and there was a high smell of wood rot. I hoped the place wasn't in *too* awful a shape. I remembered it as nice and clean and bright. I didn't want to be real disappointed, or anything. Or ashamed.

Well, it wasn't *so* awful. There was a lot of water damage to the walls, the paper in the front room was puckered ugly, like it had leprosy. And there were brown stains on the ceiling, but the floor didn't seem like it had got wet at all. How do you figure that? There wasn't a lot of furniture, only a couple of chairs that Dick Idea hadn't thought worth taking to his house, and a magazine table and a round mirror. There's this room and the kitchen, I said. I have to show you that stove, I said. And two bedrooms upstairs. It's a pretty small house.

I went over and stood beside the front window and peeked out, and there was Dick Idea on the patio, Loretta cutting his hair. Out of habit, I wished she'd go ahead and stab him, while she had the scissors and was behind him. But it was strictly habit, my wishing. I didn't *care* anymore if she stabbed him or not. I'm not lying. It wasn't like they were anything to me anymore, except maybe neighbors I could take or leave. It was like I was already living on Blueberry Island.

Tragedy had looked in the kitchen while I was at the window, then she came back in the front room and dropped her sack on the floor. She started to go upstairs, and when the top half of her body was out of sight and I could see just her legs, for the tiniest bit of time it was Loretta. I remembered Loretta climbing those stairs maybe fifty times a day, whenever Raymond called, or just taking him up something that she hoped he'd eat. Maybe not fifty times, but a lot. When she probably shouldn't've been going upstairs at all. The rose still hadn't bloomed on Raymond's throat, not yet, but he had every *other* sign, from losing his voice to losing his teeth. Loretta went up and down, up and down.

I heard Tragedy pacing over my head, in my old bedroom. Then I heard her go into the other bedroom, and I bit my lip, deep, then wouldn't release my teeth till she came down again. I said, So you like it? Wanna live here?

She smiled, but I could tell she didn't really get the joke. And that's 'cause she didn't listen to stories. If you listen to stories, you know Myer and Noochie, and you know that story of theirs about Manzini the Realtor. So you like it? Manzini keeps saying to every-body. So you like it? Wanna live here? I *love* that story, Manzini's a riot, but Tragedy didn't get the joke. She only smiled, and I said, You wanna go see the rest of the island? It's pretty big. And you're not gonna believe it, I said, but there's a pear tree. At least there was. So you got a pear tree, you got a wood-burning stove, you're all set.

She looked like she was enjoying me talk, her smile kept growing. Then I said, And I can come over and visit you, every day. You read magazines? I know where there's a lot of old magazines. I got some pretty good board games, with pretty much all the pieces. Or we could draw. Or we could go swimming. From here, you can swim out to those little rock islands. You swim, right?

I just knew she was a good swimmer.

I said, You swim, right? Then I said, Or I could even live here, too.

What do you think of that? Me saying, Or I could even live here, too. Pretty blunt. Can't get blunter. But I didn't see any reason *not* to say it. I mean, I bet she already *knew* why I'd showed her *that* house on *that* island. I said, This place *belongs* to me. I lived in it last. So what do you think? Would you *mind* if I lived here, too?

Tragedy gave a little shrug. Like saying, *I* don't mind. Why should I mind? But not being real positive about it. Well, I said, let's think about it, and took her back outside to show her the island on foot. The pear tree was still there, but didn't have fruit, it wasn't pear season. I don't know when pear season *is*. It's never had fruit from then till now, and I been here three months, August, September, October. It was three months ago I took Tragedy here. And showed her around. Showed her the highest point on the island, and the smooth sitting rock. I said, You like to look at stars, this is a great place to sit.

Going back to the house, I heard Loretta call me from across the lake. I was so annoyed! She was on the patio by herself, calling me. I couldn't not answer, so I went down on the dock, and stood where I'm sitting right now, and called back, What?

I want to talk to you, she says, spacing out the words. I. Want. To. Talk. To. You. Like that.

I said, Now?

She said, *Joy!*

I gotta go, I told Tragedy, but I'll be back, okay? Then I had to walk halfway around the island, to get the stupid rowboat. I was so annoyed! Tragedy helped me to push the boat off the beach. I climbed in, but then she did, too. I'll be *back*, I told her. You don't have to come. I won't *strand* you here, I said. I could tell she didn't want to be left there by herself without any boat, but I said, I won't *strand* you here, I'll be right back. She got out of the boat then, and I passed her guitar and traveling sack to her, then I passed her my satchel, then I rowed across to Dick Idea's dock. Loretta was down there waiting for me. I threw the rope at her and she caught it.

She looked better than she had for a couple weeks. She'd even combed her hair. That's the girl you were telling me about? she said. She pointed at Tragedy, standing by the house on the island. I said, That's her. Then I said, So what'd you wanna tell me?

Wanna, she says. Gonna, she says. Haveta, she says. You're starting to talk like one of your half-assed storytellers.

Loretta thought you guys, especially Myer, talk bad. Like, she talked so good, right? No way. I talk how I talk. Everybody understands what I'm saying. That's what counts. Don't all you half-assed guys understand what I'm saying? That's what counts.

Loretta says, Wanna, gonna, haveta, giving me that old stuff, and I said, So what did you *want* to talk to me about? Saying want with *t* to spare. I didn't have to take that old stuff from her anymore, things were different. And I *never* said haveta. I *always* said *have to*. She was a real pain in the ass.

Anyhow. Instead of talking to me right there, she turns around and goes up the steps, and I gotta follow her. Every little thing she did was starting to bother me. I was glad she was feeling better, though. Don't think I'm a *completely* horrible person.

She goes up on the patio, where all these clumps of Dick Idea's hair were blowing around, it was gross. And I said, Where is he, back in bed? But Loretta said, Down at the pump, with Smokey. Then she caught her breath and got a little color in her face. They're taking it apart, she says. I sat down on the bench at the picnic table and folded my hands together and propped my chin on them. So? I asked her, So? What's so important I had to stop what I was doing, to hear about?

She looked at the flagstones. Then she started crying. Just like that. I slid off the bench and stood up. Then I put one hand in my pocket and slung the other arm 'round her shoulder. You still not feeling good? I said, and almost said something nasty about Mooney. But I changed my mind at the last second. Don't do that, I said. Don't cry. Starting now, I said, don't cry. It wasn't very funny, though, my joke on Dick Idea. Neither of us smiled.

She wiped her eyes with the palm of her hand and shook her head. She says, Joy. Joy, she says, I did all I could. At least I made it so you can stay living here. She says, That's the best I could do. She looked at me a long time after she said that. We can get a lot of things fixed with Smokey around, that Dick Idea could never do himself.

Loretta didn't say any more, and I didn't, either. I didn't feel like talking anyhow. My head was spinning, and I almost cried myself, but I wouldn't do that, not on Dick Idea's patio. Smokey around! I could hear the clank of iron tapping iron, and watched some of Dick Idea's hair go tumbling across the patio. Smokey around? Around *who*? I looked at Loretta, seeing her and not seeing her. Then I went in the house and got all the board games that me and Flyboy had collected from bungalows and I stacked them up, then I found a box and stuffed it with my clothes. I didn't even *have* to stuff it, there wasn't that much. And since there was room, I tossed in a green army blanket.

Loretta raised her head and looked over at me when I came out again carrying everything.

So go ahead, she says. I'm not stopping you. I don't know what'll happen, but go ahead.

She turned her jaw to me and I kissed her, then I went down and got in the rowboat and rowed straight back to Blueberry Island.

Well, there was no point in going all the way around to the hidden side, Loretta knew where I was, and Dick Idea would soon enough— so I tied up at the dock. Then I looked around and seen Tragedy watching me from the screen porch. I was glad she'd gone in the house by herself. It meant, at least to me it meant, she was thinking of it already as *hers*.

I said, Change of plans. I'm moving in right now. That's okay with you, isn't it? We're gonna have to figure out some system for getting fresh water. You have candles, right?

She nodded. I'd seen them in her traveling sack, but she already *knew* that I'd snooped, so I didn't feel embarrassed.

Well, we can worry about water some other time, I said. I'm not thirsty. Are you?

That afternoon we played checkers. Isn't checkers a boring game? We played checkers, and after that we played Haunted Castle. I'd already come to realize there weren't too many games you could play without talking. We couldn't play Pyramid 7, 'cause you have to be able to say your chant when it's your turn holding the pharaoh's crystal. And we couldn't play lots of games with questions and answers. It was kind of a shock when I realized that. I'd been looking forward to playing board games with Tragedy. When I was a lot younger, I'd played board games with Raymond and Loretta. Even when I was too young to play them myself, I'd watched Raymond and Loretta play. It's how I learned most things I know about the world before the rose bloomed and the weather changed. We had Go to the Head of the Class, and Raymond would ask me, like, What was the dog's name in the *Derby Dugan* comic strip? Then he'd tell me what a comic strip was, then he'd tell me the answer, Fuzzy. Fuzzy was the name of the dog in the *Derby Dugan* comic strip.

Later on I seen for myself what a comic strip was in old newspapers that I found, but I learned about it first in a board game. And that's how I learned practically everything else about the world before the rose. The only games we ever played at Dick Idea's house were card games, and Monopoly. Money is something, though, isn't it? I wish there was money again.

Anyhow. I'd been looking forward to playing board games with Tragedy, so it was a real disappointment when it struck me that she couldn't play most of them, 'cause she couldn't talk. I finally had a best friend, and she couldn't talk! It's almost funny, but it's not.

I always wanted a sister or a brother, Flyboy had told me after Dick Idea's big announcement. But I *really* always wanted a brother, he said. And I told him, You get what you get. That's kind of my philosophy still, if you don't mind me getting philosophical. You get what you get. Well, I had a best friend now, but she couldn't talk. You get what you get.

Tragedy beat me twice at Haunted Castle, then I made us switch pawns, she was the Frankenstein and *I* was the ghost, but she just beat me again.

Let's do something else, I said. Then, while I was closing up the game board, I said, You know, if I looked at your mouth, I could probably tell what you were saying. If you want to try that. I could read your lips. I could be a lip-reader! Or, I don't know, maybe you wanna teach me sign language? You know any sign language?

Well, I said all that, and got noplace. Tragedy looked at me blank as a sleepwalker. Then she got up from the floor—we'd been playing our games in the front room, on the floor—she got up and started walking out to the porch.

I said, How come I know that the guy who cut your throat had a beard that grew almost to his eyes? That almost covered his face? How come I know that? How come I *dreamed* that? He had a big beard, didn't he?

She turned completely around to face me, but then all she did was shrug. Like to say, I guess so. Or, Who cares. Like that. It made me so crazy, her shrugging all the time. It made me crazy that she didn't like me enough.

Tragedy went out, but I stayed in, sorry I'd said anything about her not being able to talk. And I was real sorry I'd said anything about the dog boy who'd cut her, 'cause you remember that story by Dr. Michael A. Cohen? Anybody know that story? By Dr. Michael A. Cohen—about the guy who kept seeing this same woman every day at the hydrant where he got water. It was a good story. This guy sees this woman, and they smile at each other, then every day afterwards they smile at each other a little bit more, a little bit longer. You know that story, anybody? Where the woman has this open sore on her leg—it's, like, a really bad sore—and the guy keeps wanting to tell her that he's a doctor, but he's afraid to, 'cause he's not sure if he *wants* to treat her, it's a running sore. But finally he decides to do it, 'cause he's, like, fallen in *love* with this woman. So he tells her he's a doctor, but she gives him this blank stare. So then he says, I'm a *doctor*, I can take care of that sore of yours. But instead of being grateful and going off with him forever, she won't even *talk* to him. Like, what happened, this woman didn't even want to *mention* that sore, she didn't want to admit it was *there*. Pretty weird. So, this guy, the doctor, I guess it was Doctor Michael A. Cohen, himself, goes back to just smiling at her every day. But she won't smile at him anymore, then she stops coming around to that particular hydrant. Pretty sad story.

And I remembered it right after Tragedy walked out, and then I could've kicked myself. I *never* should've mentioned anything about her not being able to talk. I should've just ignored it. I really felt like kicking myself. And that stuff about the guy that cut her—that was really stupid to say.

I put the board games on a shelf in this hutch between the front room and the kitchen. Then I just moped around. I looked for a broom, but there wasn't one. So finally I took out a shirt of mine from the box and swung it over my head, beating up cobwebs at the ceiling. Then Tragedy came back with a yellow sand pail full of blackberries, just when I was really starved. It was so great. She even looked at me kinder. And our fingers kept touching, digging out berries. She had bony hands.

Later, I showed her the dugout cellar and the big rock down there that takes up most of the space, half the rock painted silver by somebody a long time ago. Stuck off in a corner was a blue washing machine, with its lid up and all its hoses bunched inside. And leaning against that were a couple of folding plastic chairs. Tragedy shook one open, then brushed off the seat and carried it upstairs. She put it on the porch and sat on it. I said, Don't you think we should clean up the house a little? But she just sat there.

Smokey came later, in a canoe I'd last seen at Strawberry Point tied up at the dog-boys' dock. I walked down to meet him. He had on that camouflage hat and a black T-shirt. It was a *ribbed* black T-shirt and it fitted his body so tight you could see exactly how skinny he was. He was the most emaciated person I ever seen in my whole life. He said, Joy, what're you doing, camping out? I hate Adam's apples that bob, and his went bouncing around like crazy. He said, You camping out?

I said, Does this look like a camp? Camp, I said. I'm moving in over here.

You and who else?

This friend of mine.

He says, Where is she? Saying *she*, so he must've talked to Loretta.

I said, What do you want?

Nothing, he says. I just came to see you. We got that pump taken apart, we're gonna clean it. Then he said, It's a little embarrassing, you moving in here the same day I'm moving in over there. Don't you think it's a little embarrassing? From my point of view?

I said, I was coming here anyway.

You were like, he says.

I said, I don't care what you think, I was. And I don't care about you being embarrassed, either.

He says, I just thought we could be together a little bit more. That's all. We could go to the Circle together, and stuff. But you don't want my friendship, all right. But I'm a person, he says, and I could've laughed in his face. Can you believe that stuff? Friendship. You should've seen him at the casbah. Every single female, including the Aspirin Lady, Smokey stared at. Some of them he invited home, even. Or if they were married already or attached or something, he'd offer a trade, he'd fix a roof or hang a door or build a closet, for one or two nights between their legs. He had some reputation at the Circle, let me tell you. Guy walks around half the time with his business hard in his pants, he gets a reputation, right? Friendship! I knew what Dick Idea had promised him, and it wasn't my friendship. They think I was stupid?

I told him, I said, I'm living over here now, I'm sorry. So if you wanna go away now, I'd like that. I mean, I'm sure I'll *see* you, but I don't think you and me could ever be close friends, really.

He said, What, d'you just like dog boys? Or what's it now, girls?

I said, Friendship? You're not even *nice* to me. Get outta here, I said. You're gross.

He said, By rights, I could leave Dick Idea with a pump he couldn't fit back together.

So leave him, I said. It's not my problem. I won't be using that pump, anyhow.

He tipped his head to one side and stared at me. Then he said, Dick Idea wants his boat.

So let him come and take it, I said.

Smokey stared some more, sulking, then he turned around and walked out to the end of the dock. I didn't say nothing when instead of getting back in his own canoe, he stepped in the rowboat. I probably even half-expected it. He tied his canoe to the back of the boat, then rowed across the lake.

I wasn't too thrilled about that, being stranded, but Tragedy looked—I'd have to say shocked. I went back on the porch, and she had this shocked look on her face. Then she pointed an arm in the direction of shore. It's not like we're *stranded*, I said. We could swim.

Her forehead smoothed out. If anything, she looked even more shocked. I said, Don't worry, I'll get another boat. There's tons of little boats around. I'll find another boat for us. Then I said, It's kind of funny, though. Being stuck here with no dry way to get off. Then I said, Stuck, not stranded.

I finished cleaning up the front room, mostly dusting it, then washing the filthy windows. Slopping them off, really, I didn't have any soap. I listened to that Van Buskin zombie tape while I worked. That is a really strange tape, they're either giving you recipes for soup and zucchini bread, or else they're babbling about this drug they all like, this fish egg. I finally shut it off, and finished cleaning without headphones. I'd taken Flyboy's headphones when I'd been at the house, just before. His 'phones had softer sponges, so I took them.

Anyhow, I cleaned for a couple of hours, and Tragedy didn't help at all. I guess I was annoyed. All she did, she sat on the porch, first crumbling up some dope leaves that she'd grabbed last night at Josephine's, then playing her guitar a little bit.

But later we had peanut butter, hers, on these brown crackers, also hers, so I guess I really hadn't any right to get so angry. I'd cleaned the house, she fed me. It was a good, honest swap.

Then Tragedy got up from the table and looked all around like she wanted something particular, and what it was, she was looking for my tape player. I said, Go ahead, I already told you, any time you wanna use it, be my guest. Talking like she'd just asked me did I mind if she used it. That was happening a lot. Me answering her like I'd heard a question. Go ahead, I told her, but don't listen to that zombie tape, that's a waste. You want something good? I got a Don Wirth. He meets this guy that used to be the mayor of

New York City, only the mayor is off his rocker and besides that, somebody tries to kill them both. It's really good. It's about forty-five minutes.

I went and took out that Don Wirth from my satchel. Then I gave her Flyboy's headphones and my tape player, and she sat down on the porch again, put the 'phones on, and started listening. I'd sneak a look at her every so often, trying to guess if she liked the story. I said to myself, She's probably at the part where there's a fire at the clinic. That was a good part, but when I looked at Tragedy, there wasn't much expression in her face. It was impossible to tell what she thought.

After only ten minutes, though, she took off the 'phones. I could hear Don Wirth's frog-in-his-throat voice for maybe three seconds, then she pressed Stop.

That was the first and last tape of mine she ever listened to. She never played another story the rest of the time we lived together. I wondered then, and I wondered later on, I *still* wonder if maybe she didn't like hearing people's voices.

I figured maybe she couldn't stand to hear people talk, when she couldn't.

Or maybe she didn't like stories. Maybe she didn't *care* how other people got on, like I did. Or maybe stories—maybe stories just *took* too long. Songs take, what, a couple of minutes, that's all. In a song, you get only part of what happened, a snatch, a glimpse, plus how it felt. In stories you get *everything*—not only what happened, but if somebody's fat or skinny you get that, too. And that takes time.

It's a matter of temperament, I guessed, and still guess—whether you like stories better, or songs. Tragedy liked songs. I liked songs, too, but if some altar boy gets hit by a commuter train, I wanna know what he was doing on the stupid tracks in the first place. That's just me. And if somebody's mother dies and they send her away in a hearse, I wanna know how come she died, was she old or just sick. How long was she sick. I wanna *know*. I'm not interested in how it *felt* so much. Feeling is all right. But knowing is better.

She handed back my tape player with the wires and 'phones wrapped around it, and I stuck it away in my satchel. If she didn't like stories, fine. I wasn't gonna try to *convince* her. She could dislike whatever she pleased. So long as it wasn't me.

It turned windy as it got later, Baby November shaking the trees so hard they'd be stripped naked before August was even half finished. It got cold too, and there wasn't a fireplace in the house, just that stove in the kitchen. But we didn't use it, I don't know how come.

After sitting for a long time, I went and got that green blanket I'd brought, and threw it on the floor. Then I stretched out. If I closed my left eye, I could look up at the table and see both candle flames, one right behind the other so they looked like a single fat flame. Next to the flame, I could see Tragedy's cheek, jaw, part of her throat. Her cheek kept bunching and unbunching as she tuned her guitar.

I hadn't talked for a long time, but then I said, We should probably make a list. Like, we need a canoe. We should put that on the list. Or a boat. It don't matter which. A canoe or a boat, either one. And we need to find a pump for drinking water. That has to be on our list, I said. We can't keep stealing from Josephine, and I don't know if Loretta would give us anything. I mean, she said it was all right with *her* that I came out and lived here, but I don't know if she'll give us stuff from her garden. And it's too late to plant. Unless maybe we still can plant pumpkins. I can get hold of pumpkin seeds, easy. But it might be too late even for that.

She'd stopped playing, and I got conscious of my own yakety-yak. I'd already had that thought about Tragedy not liking the human voice, maybe—I'd already decided to stay quiet for as long as I could, talk only when it was necessary, and there I was, yakety-yak. I said, I think we should probably make a list tomorrow, then I shut up.

She went back to playing guitar again. It was that song about the summertime is coming and the leaves are sweetly blooming— it was that one, that melody. About the wild mountain thyme. It wasn't my favorite song of hers, but I knew it. I knew it, I'd learned it, I could sing it. And I could sing the next one, too, about life's railroad to heaven. But I was afraid to.

She did a regular concert, and I kept fidgeting, wanting to sing the songs I knew, but too shy, too scared. Flyboy'd always made fun of me if I sang, Kerwin too, and Dick Idea, saying, Your voice is worse than noise. So I didn't sing, I listened, I just said, Oh that was nice, I like that one. And said, That's one of my favorites, that speckled bird. And clapped when she quit playing altogether. One candle was out, and one looked like it was going out, but suddenly it flared, like somebody dozing off then starting up at a sound.

I rolled onto my side. You know that song about the Knoxville girl? I said. How come he killed her? How come he picked up a stick and killed her? That's the missing part. He loves her, then he kills her. What'd I miss? I said.

I couldn't see Tragedy's face, how I'd turned on my side and was lying there. I expected she was either smiling or staring, though. Most likely staring. I never seen anybody stare as hard at nothing as her. She could stare.

I guess it don't matter, I said. I was just wondering. Then I chuckled spit round and round, till I swallowed it and said, I wonder if there were any words left out. I mean, I wonder if there's more words to that Knoxville song, someplace. Then I folded my arms under my head and fell asleep, and woke up shivering.

The house was cold. My bones ached from being on the floor. It was pitch black. Right away, like always happened in the quiet dark, my heart started to race. And it was like somebody was pouring sand in my ear, that sound. Only it wasn't sand, it was breath.

And you know that story by Clare the Communist called Clare's Cell? The one that so many tapers got so excited about last year and said they taped over, but then copies just started coming around? You know that story?

I got hold of it by mistake. It had the wrong label on it, it said Fakin' Johnny on the label, but when you listened to it, it was Clare's Cell. Anyhow, if you don't know it, there's this part of the story where Clare goes to Newark, but if she gets caught in Newark, she's dead. So what happens? She *almost* gets caught. But at the last minute, she's saved by this woman named Marilyn. And this Marilyn is who Clare was *supposed* to meet in the first place. Pretty neat.

But anyhow, it's a close call, and Clare is pretty shook up. She isn't a *fighter*, nothing like that, she's not even a spy. She's, like, a party leader or something. Anyhow, Clare's shook up and Marilyn takes her home and there's a bed and one thing leads to another. That's what made everybody so upset. Joanie-Joanne kept mentioning it on every tape she made for, like, six *months*.

It didn't bother *me*, that part of Clare's Cell. You get what you get.

Anyhow, I mention that because, you know what happened in that story? How one thing led to another? Same thing happened on the floor. Same thing. It wasn't sand in my ear, it was Tragedy's breath. And if you wanna tape over this story, on account of that, go ahead, I can't stop you. But maybe somebody *else* might like to hear this story sometime. And that's all I'm gonna say about it. Stuff happens. You get what you get. I'm not ashamed. It was just me and my best girlfriend in a cold house. And I'm not embarrassed. I slept good, not dreaming. Or if I dreamed, I don't remember. I was happy.

But in the morning, I thought my teeth were gonna break from chattering. Let me tell you, it was *cold*. It wasn't Baby November anymore, it was practically January. Don't you *hate* that? I can't *stand* it. There was a funny joke I heard once on a Myer and Noochie. I forget how it goes, but at the end, Myer says, Santa Claus, the tooth fairy and the four seasons. Like, the point was, having four seasons in any kind of order was make-believe, like Santa Claus. That was funny. I love those guys.

But anyhow, it was, like, twenty degrees outside, and probably fifteen degrees inside, and the lake already had a crust. It is so *insane*, this weather stuff. Like, whose big idea was this, anyway?

So, I was practically freezing to death. I told Tragedy, One good thing, at least. If it stays cold, we won't need to find a boat.

I got some wood from under the house and made a fire in the kitchen stove. I just helped myself to Tragedy's matches without asking. Even dumped out half of what was in her traveling sack, looking for them. And I found a blue comb besides, and a rabbit's foot, and a wallet full of photographs. The wallet was so stuffed with pictures the clasp wouldn't shut. It was a gray wallet. I didn't bother looking at the pictures. And I never did, either.

Once the stove was red-hot, our biggest problem was water—or something, *any*thing to drink. I was thirsty and it kept getting more and more a pain to swallow. Finally I decided to just drink a little lake water, and to heck with it. I had to break the crust before I could fill an old milk bottle that I'd found.

While I was doing that, Loretta called me from Dick Idea's patio. How're you making out? she calls. You got any blankets? Check the windows, she says, make sure they're all shut tight and locked. I waved and went back in the house. I thought that was sweet, her saying check the windows. And I checked them. And she was right, a couple weren't completely shut at the top. I missed Loretta, a little bit. I hoped she'd come over and visit. I hoped she'd come over and visit and bring us some pump water. But thinking about the pump only got me thinking about Smokey, so I listened to a tape, side one of Triple-A Nancy Number 4. Me and Tragedy never moved more than six feet in any direction from the stove, all morning long.

I asked her once if she felt like playing guitar. I said if she felt like it, I felt like listening, but she only moved her head the slightest bit, no. She was staring at the stove door, where you stick in the wood. She was thinking about an outdoor stage decorated with red and yellow paper, you could see water from on that stage, dark-blue choppy water. And you could see tall buildings in the distance, in a mist. Tragedy was thinking about that stage, seeing that view in her mind. She was thinking about how she'd patted herself all over, looking for a guitar pick, then she remembered looking into the crowd below the stage and seeing a fight break out, three or four men rolling on the ground fighting, and the crowd kept moving away from the men, and then there were six or seven men fighting, and the crowd kept getting smaller. That's what she was thinking about, staring at the stove door. Don't ask me how come I knew, I just did. She was thinking of that, remembering the stage and the water and the misty buildings and the fight and the crowd fading away, then she lowered her head and pushed four fingers across her forehead. I nearly choked on her sadness, I mean suffocated. I couldn't *breathe*. So I jumped up and went and got my satchel, and found the pack of blank tapes I'd gotten from the Tape Worm. I think I'm gonna start keeping a diary, I said, if you don't mind.

She watched me put the tape in the player, but she wasn't really *seeing* me. In her mind, she was walking in a dark hall behind somebody, they both went into a little room. There were folded green and white shirts piled on different shelves. Tragedy grabbed a bunch, and the person with her took something out of a little box, then turned to face Tragedy. It was Margaret, and she was tying on this green cloth mask that covered the bottom half of her face. Tying it on for fun, as a joke, this surgical mask. In some empty hospital somewhere.

That's what Tragedy was remembering while I got ready to start taping a diary. Then I said, This is Joy. This is my diary. Then I didn't know what to say next. I said, It's Saturday. It's August, but I wouldn't be surprised if it snows. The lake is almost hard. Me and Tragedy are hogging the stove. Isn't that a neat name, Tragedy? Tragedy Ringling. I wish she wouldn't be so sad, but I'm trying my best. Then I said, I guess that's all for now, and pressed Stop.

I had her full attention by then. She was looking at me with the kind of frown Loretta used to give me if we were playing Monopoly and I started getting too excited about winning—say if, like, I had a hotel on both Park Place and Boardwalk. Well, you *are* too sad, I said. And I *am* trying my best. I don't care *what* you think. You get what you get, girly. That was weird, calling her girly. Like Dick Idea, almost. He called me girly sometimes.

Anyhow, I said that stuff, and wasn't sorry for it. And it was good I said it, too, 'cause Tragedy changed after that, a little, she wasn't so moody, so lost in herself. And later on, when I got sick of hanging around by that stove and walked upstairs to look in the bedrooms, she followed me, like she'd followed me at the casbah but hadn't followed me since.

That turned out to be the smart thing to do, going upstairs, and you know why? Stupid Joy, I'd forgot that there were these, like, grates in both rooms, you could open them and get heat from the stove. Not a whole bunch of heat, but some. So it wasn't even too bad up there, once we opened the grates. Once me and Tragedy figured out how to open them. And with heat, I didn't have to walk hunch-shouldered anymore, so I could clean up a little bit more.

I started with my old bedroom, which was pretty much a large closet. The bed was still there, but the mattress smelled foul and was damp. It was a twin bed, yellow pine with twirled posts, a pretty nice bed. We got rid of some cobwebs, but that's all we did in there. Then we went back in the other room, into what used to be Raymond and Loretta's room, and turned over the mattress. I looked, but there was no blood on it that I could see. Tragedy seen me look, but I didn't tell her what I was looking *for*. I hadn't told her much about that stuff, about what happened to Raymond and how come we went to live with Dick Idea. Or about Flyboy. Or Kerwin, *Kerwin* even. I should've maybe, but I didn't. Maybe I didn't even *need* to, I don't know.

Anyhow, we turned the mattress over, then looked in the closet and the old dresser for sheets, but there weren't any. In one of the dresser drawers, though, I found a bunch of neat old quartz rocks, and I thought I even remembered when Loretta collected them, over at Sandy Beach. I scooped them up and put them on the dresser, in kind of a fancy arrangement. In a wide circle with the biggest rock in the center.

Then Tragedy went downstairs and came back with our blankets. She threw those on the bed and went out again. Next time she came back, she had her guitar slung on her shoulder and she was carrying our two chairs from the kitchen. She put them down, facing each other, then she sat on hers and nestled the body of her guitar in her lap.

She wanted me to sit down, too, which I did, then I watched

how she played, watching how one hand moved up and down the neck and the other one strummed. I'd have to grow my fingernails long, if I wanted to play, too. That's what I was thinking, and I was also thinking it'd be easier to learn if I stood *behind* Tragedy and watched from there. Soon as I started to get up, though, she shook her head, so I stayed.

And the first song I actually sang a little of was that one about why do you treat me as if I were only a friend. But right away, I screwed up the words, singing what have I done that has made you so cold, leaving out *different* and cold. Then I was embarrassed and quit. But she kept playing the song, till I got up nerve again, and jumped back in, singing sometimes I wonder if you'll be contented again, will you be happy when you are withered and old. Then I said, Don't you know any songs that aren't gloomy, and she laughed. I could've died then, no problem. I was so happy.

And that's when it started, her playing guitar and me singing, and later on, we taped a couple of songs, "Thirty Pieces of Silver" we did, and "Tramp on the Street," and I don't think I remembered those rocks till maybe the next day, or the day after, but pretty soon I was using those rocks, tapping quartz rocks together, which you can hear for yourself how it sounds, when you get to that tape in this bundle, if you haven't already. Rocks, and then I used pot lids.

It stayed cold for days, it even snowed flurries once, and we had to keep drinking from the lake. That did a job on our stomachs, and we got pretty sick of peanut butter and crackers. Then the lake froze hard enough to walk on. That was on Tuesday. I'd found her on Thursday, we'd gone to the island on Friday, Saturday it turned freezing cold, now it was Tuesday. We went to see Josephine.

All of her husbands had moved into the house, on account of the cold weather, the TV was on, playing white, and Timothy was reading from one of Josephine's old diaries. It was smokey inside too, from the fire in the fireplace but also from the pipe full of dope that Carl was passing around.

Timothy said, March 16, Saturday. Went to Montclair and looked at stained glass. Got lost coming and going. The pieces we liked were way too much money. Tried to call Debbie all day. No answer.

Then Timothy said, Sunday, March 17, but Josephine told him to stop. She'd heard us knock and come in, but she never looked at us till after Timothy quit reading.

Then she said, she didn't even say hello, she said, You just missed Dick Idea.

I said, Goody, and Josephine laughed.

Then she says, I couldn't believe it was him at the door. I haven't seen that particular gentleman since Victor was still living here.

I didn't remember any husband named Victor. So I didn't know who Josephine was talking about.

Then she says, He came asking me to join his organization. I asked him if it was gonna be called Dick Idea's Organization. He didn't think that was so funny.

But Josephine's husbands did, they all laughed when she mentioned that.

Then Josephine said, He told me I could be *secretary*. I said I wanted to be a judge, if I was gonna be anything. He didn't think I was acting serious enough. This is gonna be a *serious* organization, he tells me. I said, All right, then I'll be a judge in it. But he says this is just an organization, it's not the government. I told him I'd think about it. Then Josephine said, You joining?

I said, Me? I wasn't asked.

She laughed again, and finally looked at Tragedy. So is this my garden rabbit? she says. Is this your newsgirl?

I said, Neither, this is my friend, but didn't say her name. Emmy had turned away from the television screen and was staring at Tragedy with her eyes almost slits. She'd got so fat that a big bulge of skin appeared below each eye when she squinted, and these tiny eyes stared out.

So I told Josephine that my friend wasn't a garden rabbit or a newsgirl, then I said, But my friend and me wondered if you guys might wanna hear some music. Since everybody's stuck inside it might be good, you think? You wanna hear some music?

That took Josephine by surprise. Music? she says.

I said, Songs. We can do songs, we have seventeen songs we could do. I'm the singer, I said.

Which Josephine's four husbands thought was pretty funny. And which Emmy, I guess, didn't think was very interesting at all. She turned around and went back to staring at the TV.

Right now? says Josephine. You wanna do songs for us right now?

That'd be fine, I said. Or we could come back.

No, says Josephine, go ahead. Now is fine. And she tells her latest husband, I didn't know his name, she tells him to move the coffee table, so that me and Tragedy could stand in the middle of the floor. I never did learn that guy's name. You know how come? You know why? I just realized. She never *called* him by any name. Whenever she talked to him? She looked him straight in the face. That's how come I never learned his name. And I never heard the other men call him by his name, either. I don't think they talked to him.

Anyhow, he moves the table, and while he was looking around for some place to put it, I said to Josephine, I said, Try to think of us as two bug lights, and she laughed.

What? she said.

Anything you wanna give us, I told her. Food is best, though.

Josephine sat back and folded her arms and says, Well, let's see how good you are, first.

I don't know how good we *really* were, but I thought we did all right, and Timothy or Carl kept saying between songs, That's *Joy's* voice? like they couldn't believe I could sing. Everybody *seemed* to like us, and I never forgot a word, and we did thirteen of our seventeen songs. And we only stopped at thirteen 'cause of what happened to Emmy.

She'd pretty much ignored us, me and Tragedy, and didn't even turn around when I started to sing. I don't know what her problem was, but anyway, she ignored us, and kept her eyes glued to the TV. Well, we're just finishing that song about time slipping away when Emmy all of a sudden lets out this *unbelievable* scream. I looked, and from the corner of my eye, seen something on the television, I couldn't see what, just something not all white snow. Then it was gone, and the snow was back.

Emmy was just—I don't know *what* she was just. She'd jumped to her feet and was pointing at the TV, she looked scared to death. Josephine was over there in a flash, hugging Emmy and asking her, What's the matter, baby? What'd you see? What'd you see?

But Emmy just kept trembling and couldn't talk, then Josephine walked her across the floor and into a bedroom. All four husbands were staring at the TV set. Timothy said, Oh shit, and squeezed his face between his hands.

What oh shit, said Carl, real angry. She didn't *see* nothing. You don't have to get the shakes. Don't be a jerk. She didn't see nothing, she's just crazy.

And Bailey turned off the set.

Me and Tragedy went out in the kitchen, and helped ourselves to anything we felt like taking, we filled a half-bushel basket and let ourselves out the back door.

Then on our way home? Walking on the ice? Who do we see coming toward us but Dick Idea. I guess he was going from house to house, about the protective association. When I seen him, my first thought was to cut across the lake right away to shore and just not *meet* him. But before I could do that, Tragedy took hold of my shirtsleeve. My *top* shirt, I was wearing four. Anyhow, Tragedy takes my sleeve and just tugs on it. So if *she* wasn't scared enough to leave the lake right then, I wasn't either.

And what happened was really funny. It was Dick Idea that changed direction, that suddenly turned and walked off at an angle. When I seen that, I laughed, and kept laughing the rest of the way home. He was ashamed! Dick Idea was ashamed! 'Cause I took care of him when he was sick. I made him tea and stuff. He was ashamed, and I was free.

The weather stayed cold a few days more, then started warming up, and by the next weekend, it was like early fall. Cool in the morning, but almost hot in the afternoon. The lake thawed. We got ourselves a canoe from a boathouse in Cabin Springs, a red canoe with a couple of good paddles. The varnish was still golden bright, it was like nobody'd ever used them.

And every day we took the canoe round and round the lake, everyplace except to French's Grove and Strawberry Point, going through houses looking for stuff. But most houses were pretty much picked clean of good stuff. We found a few things, though. We got candles, and more books, and a really ugly hat with earflaps, and some plates with pictures on them. I wanted stuff for the next casbah, and we got stuff, and we went swimming one day when it turned *really* warm, and we talked to some people that lived behind the old part of the lake, people I seen all the time at the casbah. They all said that Dick Idea had been around. But it didn't seem like too many squatters were big on his protective association. They seemed content to protect themselves. I felt the same way. If Dick Idea ever came and asked *me* to join, I would've turned him down, too. But he never asked. He never came.

Me and Tragedy did all seventeen songs for a family named Panter. They gave us a jar of stew that was all congealed and looked disgusting, but when we heated it up, it was fine. Then we sang for these people named Irene and Isabel and Brian that lived together. Isabel had a winter coat I wanted. But she thought it wasn't a fair swap, me singing just seventeen songs and then walking away with a winter coat. So she only gave me this real junky purple corduroy shirt.

A week went by. Almost two weeks. We played for this woman Polera and this guy Tucker, I don't remember their first names, and then we played for a guy named Zim, who kept dogs, but they were spaniels, so it was okay. Zim had a vertical checkers game, and he gave us that, we gave him songs. People kept saying I had a nice voice, they said it sounded huskier than when I just talked. And they liked Tragedy's playing, too, but instead of telling her that, they told me. Like, it was strange, people found it hard to talk to her, I guess 'cause she couldn't talk back. I always told Tragedy later, They liked you. We'd be in the canoe going home, and I'd say, They liked you. And I like you, too. I always paddled, but sometimes I just let us drift. They liked you, I said. And I like you, too. Sometimes we seen Loretta up on the patio, and I waved.

Before going to the next casbah, I got together all the tapes that

I'd borrowed last time from the Tape Worm, including the Bread and Butter String Band tape. I was real reluctant to give that back, but the Tape Worm won't let you have nothing to keep. Well, you guys know that. And I was afraid if I kept it, he wouldn't let me borrow any new tapes, and I was hungry for some new ones. I'd listened to what I had over and over (except the zombies tape and side two of Nancy Number 4), and I needed to hear something else.

Only, when Tragedy seen me stick her tape into my satchel? She came and plucked it right out. It's mine to keep, really? I said, like she'd just said, No, you keep it, it's yours to keep. So I put it aside, and even though I was a little worried about what the Tape Worm would say, I was glad she'd done it.

Well, I couldn't believe it, but the Tape Worm didn't come *that* Thursday, either. He missed two casbahs in a row, and he'd *never* done that before. I kept saying to Tragedy, I hope nothing happened, I hope his car didn't break down, I hope he's still the Tape Worm. And every twenty seconds, I'd look toward the highway, but all that came down it were traders.

The casbah was specially good that week, fuller than the last three or four combined, I guess 'cause the weather had turned nice again. And I wasn't treated bad like I'd been the last time, either. I wasn't ignored. In fact, everybody *wanted* to talk to me. Asking me how was Dick Idea's association coming along. Everybody that hadn't joined wanted me to tell them who did. I said, I don't know of anybody, except Smokey. And then I said, But I'm in my own house now. So I don't know what's really going on with Dick Idea.

I'm pretty sure that a lot of people didn't believe me when I said that, about me having my own house. Even when I pointed at Tragedy, they didn't believe me. She was sitting on the highway wall. She hadn't walked around with me too much. At first she had, but then she just wandered off by herself to the wall and sat down. She looked a little paler than usual, pale and tired, and she'd lost a few pounds, so I got us some nice red tomatoes and some green peppers and this stuff called wheat germ. Wheat germ is supposed to be good for you. Keeps you healthy. It comes in a bag. I traded two plates with blue churches painted on them, for tomatoes, peppers and that wheat germ.

Anyhow. I asked a few lake people if they wanted my friend and me to come by their house some night and sing songs. I got only two or three takers, 'cause I bet you most people thought it was some trick of Dick Idea's. Like I was recruiting for his dumb association. I figured it would take some time before they'd think of me as just Joy, not Joy from Dick Idea's house. I could wait. It would happen, eventually. I could wait.

Canoeing back home, we passed Loretta and Smokey in the rowboat on their way to the casbah, Loretta was rowing. I waved, but neither of them waved back. Maybe they didn't see us. No, they seen us, all right. They seen us.

I stretched out one leg and poked Tragedy with my foot, I wasn't wearing shoes. She was sitting on the canoe floor with her elbows on the seat behind her. I said, Hey, you feeling okay? I got some wheat germ, I said. You know wheat germ? But she wouldn't look at me straight, and I felt a little sick and held still, and we drifted.

And that was the start of it all going bad. I can say that now, 'cause now it's a story and in stories you can say that stuff. *Telling* stories you already know what happened, everything's all finished and you look back and can say stuff like that was the start of it all going bad, but in the canoe, in the canoe it wasn't a story yet, and I didn't *know* it was the start of it all going bad. But it was. That's when it all started to go bad. That afternoon.

Later on, after we got back to the house, she was lukewarm to eating, lukewarm to anything I said we could do—lukewarm, but still she ate, a tiny bit, and helped me lug the mattress outside to air it, then she helped me string a clothesline. She ate and did stuff, but she was back inside herself again. I tried to think if I'd done something wrong, but couldn't imagine what.

Then it got dark and I lit a few candles, and we sat in the front room, like we did every night. I taped a little more diary, saying, Well, we been to the casbah, got wheat germ, seen Loretta, that's all for now. Then I listened to that Glen Rider tape for the ump-

teenth time but kept skipping forward, passing all those parts where
the old man with the rose takes one boy after another into his house
in New Brunswick and one boy after another gets the fever, gets
the spots, gets the bloom—skipping past those scary parts and
stopping near the end, where the old man starts to bleed from his
mouth and lies on his bed sick about what he did and scared of
dying. That part I could hear over and over. I liked to hear about
how scared he was, and how sick at heart.

Tragedy picked up her guitar, but only played a short time, songs
I didn't know the words to, or maybe songs there wasn't any words
to. Then she put the guitar on the table, and got up and walked
out. After a while, I went to find her.

And found her on that ledge of smooth rock, she was sitting with
her legs drawn up and her forehead on her knees. I asked if she
was okay, but she didn't move. Then I sat next to her and stared
down the lake. But it was dark and there was nothing to see. Sometimes I heard a little splash, like maybe a fish jumping in the water.
But I couldn't see nothing, there wasn't even a moon, and I sat
next to Tragedy, who scarcely moved.

A long time passed. I started getting cold. I asked her to come
back with me to the house, but she wouldn't. Then I said, Sometimes I used to sit up here the whole day, I'd bring a blanket and
sit up here the whole day long. Sometimes by myself, sometimes
with Loretta and Raymond, sometimes with just Raymond. And
once? I said. Once, I was up here with Raymond and I asked him
about what he'd done before the rose bloomed and the storms started,
about what he'd done in the Bronx, New York. And you know what
Raymond said? Nothing. Well, he didn't say nothing, exactly. He
just wouldn't say nothing about what he'd done in the Bronx, New
York. He said, It don't matter. What anybody did before don't matter. How we felt before, how we acted, bad or good, it don't matter.
We're here, he said. We're still alive. That's all. And he wouldn't
say nothing else. I already knew from Loretta that he used to fix
big machines, something about sewers, machines that kept the
sewers working in the Bronx, New York—he fixed them when they
broke. But he wouldn't talk about it. It don't matter, he said, and

wouldn't talk about it. Everything's wiped clean, he said. It's either the beginning, he said, or the end, so either way, how we lived before don't count. I guess he was right. But I don't know, I said, what do you think? You think it's the beginning of something, I said, or the end?

Talk, talk, talk, there I was just babbling again, I guess 'cause I was nervous, I guess 'cause Tragedy had turned so secret again, and I said, You think it's the beginning or the end? and I reached over and touched her on the wrist, but right away I fetched back my hand. I sat there a few more seconds, then stood up. You want me to leave you alone, I said, fine. 'Cause that's *exactly* the message I'd got from touching her. She wanted me to shut up and leave her alone. I walked back down the hill and into the house, feeling scared and angry.

Most of our candles had gone out, and the few left were little flickering chunks, that's all, and the house was so quiet, except the stairs creaked by themselves, and I had this thought that maybe I'd just get my stuff together and carry it down to the canoe and go back to Dick Idea's house. But already, Dick Idea's house seemed like the Bronx, New York, had seemed to Raymond. I was here now, with Tragedy, and what happened before she came, it didn't matter, it was like for every step I'd took, the ground had fallen away behind me and wasn't there anymore. Nothing mattered except I was here. I'd got what I'd got. I almost cried.

Tragedy didn't come back, but I stayed up waiting for her. I couldn't sleep alone in the bed upstairs, couldn't, so I brought down a blanket and wrapped myself up and sat at the table. I lit some fresh candles, then listened again to the Bread and Butter String Band. But instead of listening mostly to the words, which I'd always done before, I tried to listen past them, to listen to the music.

I'd watched Tragedy play guitar, seen how her fingers moved on it, sliding like they were greased and pressing down on strings, but she'd never let me try it myself, never showed me how you turned wire stretched tight into melody. Same as Kerwin had never showed me how to be-there and not-be-there at the same time, she'd never showed me how you played music. Never showed me how you could make a sound that wasn't words, but that caused a feeling just the same.

I'd watched her, though, carefully watched, and now, waiting for her to come back to the house, I shoved down Flyboy's headphones and pulled the white guitar by its neck off the table, turned it around and braced it snug in my lap. Then I strummed it, my fingers floundering on the frets, clumsy, stupid, untaught. Then I let both hands drop, and sat there, and squeezed my eyes shut, trying to picture how exactly Tragedy's fingers moved, song after song, going through in my head all seventeen, some too hard, *most* too hard, to remember the chord changes she'd kept making. I'd do a chord then stop, start and stop, stopped and started, then hummed the easiest tune there was, that one where we'll never grow old, never grow old, humming that, in a place where we'll never grow old, searching for the right melody on the strings, but couldn't get it, couldn't find it, you can't hesitate, you hesitate there's no melody, just unconnected sound, vibrations, don't stammer don't stutter, and the vibrations shivered off the strings and through stubby fingers to blood and skinny bone, skinny bone to blood to brain, and you could believe me or not, but I'm not faking, what happened, I seen—I *glimpsed* faces watching me—there, then passed—chins tipped back or chins on folded hands, bodies hunched forward on concrete steps, on chairs, teeth chewing lip, hearing music, an old woman with bread crusts in the lap of her dress, a boy with bruised eyes. And seen, glimpsed, a courtyard with busted window glass that glittered on the ground, fire in a rusted barrel, a field of brown grass stretching to the water's edge and in the far far distance, misted buildings, and pale, worn faces watching me, and seen the Tape Worm's face through a streaked and rain-dribbled car window, and seen my own face, Joy's, Joy's face all frown as she thought, Joy's face smoothing, Joy saying been to the casbah, got wheat germ, Joy's face starting to shimmer away, to blur, then suddenly I felt a tearing inside my chest, and something clenched, I almost threw up, and tasted blood, felt teeth with my tongue, and felt them shift. And was knocking the table over and raving, and stopped running somewhere outside the house, somewhere between the house and dock, and fell down. And laid there with my tongue pressed to my cheek, not letting it go poke at my teeth again, and all I could think of was, I'm dead I'm dead I'm dead. Dead as Raymond dead as Patrice dead as Kerwin dead as Flyboy dead as dead as dead. And flinched when she touched me on the face.

I scuttled away and curled up, rubbed an arm across my nose, but she came over and stooped, and I knew I should've kept moving, *told* her, should've hid, should've jumped in the lake and drowned, should've told her *told* her I got the rose, 'cause *not* telling her made me as bad at that old man in New Brunswick. Talk, *tell* her, but I couldn't. Her hand felt warm against my face, and I leaned against it, grateful and ashamed and dead as dead as dead as Raymond, whose teeth fell out whose gums were bloody whose eyes pleaded don't I'm dead as dead as Joy is dead.

And she laid on the hard ground with me and fitted herself behind me and held me tight, and there was that girl with the white moles on her face drying the apple I gave her, getting up, going away, don't go, go yes go, go away, and there is the girl with the white moles on her face gone away, stay away, come back, pointing at me, who's that, who's this talking at me saying my girl says and my girl wants, *his* girl, him with the blue scars, fingering blue scars saying my girl says and my girl wants and he's fingering those scars saying can you or can't you, can I *what*? Saying what and you can't and don't and don't, but I cut him. And cut him blood on my hands shirt mouth chin, blood.

On my face! There was blood on my face, all over my face, my shirt, and the sun was just coming up over Cooley's Mountain, and I'm just trying to tell you what happened, exactly. We'd slept together on the ground, I woke up first with my lips pressed against Tragedy's neck, and there was blood on us both.

But from her mouth, not mine. Her mouth, not mine.

And it was *her* face swollen, was flush, was *her* cheeks broken out in black dotty marks. Not mine. And it was *her* throat, not mine, where a puffy red circle had raised up overnight, where the rose had bloomed.

I got to tell you, I'm telling the truth, so I'll tell you: the first thing I felt was relief, but it was like some wild thing that went spinning through me, then blew out through every pore with a violence that almost pulled the rest of my insides after it. And left me so I couldn't breathe. It was relief, though, that's what it was.

After it passed, fled, I could breathe again and wasn't dizzy, all I felt, all I felt was angry, an anger that sat on my heart like a stone.

Tragedy's eyes were open. She looked at me, then turned her face against her shoulder and wiped her lips partly clean of blood. Then she looked at me again, smiling, and remained smiling till she closed her eyes. I thought she was dead, but she wasn't. And the stone on my heart stayed there. I wasn't trembling or nothing— it was just a cool heavy stone of anger that sat in place and couldn't be rolled. She'd touched me, laid holding me all night through. What I'd took for kindness, consolation, what I'd took for love, was death. That stepped out of the taxi, was death. That sat on the beach, was death. Was death there lying at my feet, huddled up, breathing shallow.

Without even thinking what I was gonna do, I walked away and left her, went down to the dock and untied the canoe. The sun was white that morning, not yellow, and there was a chop to the water, a breeze. I took the canoe out, took it out far from the island and far from shore, then drifted. I drifted all the way down the lake, past the Circle beach and under the bridge. Drifting by French's Grove, I looked and could see the house on the hill where we'd lived with Patrice. Before I could drift around to Strawberry Point, though, I took up the paddle again, dipped it, keeled it, turned the canoe and headed back up the lake.

I didn't know what to do, where to go, nothing. And that stone stayed on my heart and wouldn't budge.

I kept feeling my gums, poking them with a finger, but they weren't sore, and my teeth weren't loose, and I could swallow all right, I could swallow all right, I could swallow.

But I hated her, hated her more than I'd ever hated Dick Idea, more than I'd ever hated Kerwin for touching me all the time, more than I'd even hated Patrice for going up the road to Mrs. Ahearn's house without me and coming home sick. And I hated her even more than I hated Raymond for pleading at me with his eyes to stay and not to let that man come up and. I just *hated* her.

I took the canoe to these small rock islands about twenty-five yards in the channel off Blueberry Island. They were just big gray rocks, nothing growing on them except crack weeds. The rocks were cold. The day was cold. I sat facing away from Blueberry, away from Dick Idea's house, and after a while there was some lightning. It flickered, then stopped and didn't start again. But that didn't mean nothing, another storm could blow up just like that, like *that*, and there I'd be, stuck on those rocks. Stranded.

When I got back in the canoe, I seen Smokey shingling on the roof of Dick Idea's house, there was a ladder against the wall, then I looked at Blueberry Island. Tragedy wasn't where I'd left her. I looked toward that high ledge, but she wasn't there, either. Then came the first thunder. I started paddling hard, and didn't know where I was headed till the canoe bumped against the island dock. Already it was raining, and it was a burning rain, a blister rain, and all I cared about—till I got there—was shelter.

She wasn't in the kitchen and she wasn't in the front room. I didn't look upstairs. Just slammed shut all the windows, then sat by one, pulling over the chair that I always used. The ladder was still against the side of Dick Idea's house, but Smokey was gone from the roof, and I seen the light of kerosene lamps over there. The rain came in gray sheets. I hadn't eaten all day, and my head ached behind my eyes. I kept poking at my teeth with my fingers.

After a long time, I heard her. Get out of bed, or get into bed— I heard the springs.

The dark came early and the rain kept up. And Don Wirth kept me company. I fell asleep on the chair with his tape still running, and woke up hearing a weak steady hum in my ear.

The rain was over, it was day again, and I'd slept I don't know how many hours straight, twelve fifteen hours straight, and I felt a pain where the seatback crossed below my shoulders. When I stood up, I nearly fell down from moving too quick and being so hungry. I had to eat something, but what was there that she hadn't touched for sure? Nothing but that wheat germ stuff, that tasted like dirt and stuck in my teeth. I ate with my fingers, as much as I could stand.

Then the banging started.

And once it did, it didn't stop, not for a long time. She kept slapping with her hand, or maybe it was her fist, on the side of the bed. That made one sound. Then slapping the wall, that made a different, duller sound. And when Raymond did that, Loretta's elbows would nip to her ribs and her shoulders would move high, and she'd close her eyes, but then she'd stop what she was doing, and go up.

Till Dick Idea started coming over, telling her, Don't, telling her she was foolish, then telling her like he had the right to tell her, You can't. Telling her, Nothing's more important than your own life, you can't. Telling her, Nothing's more important than your own life. You can't. And finally she didn't, and Raymond kept banging, and Dick Idea said, Let me go. Raymond kept banging, till finally Dick Idea went up.

I got my satchel and threw in my tape player and both headphones and all my tapes, but that's all, then I went out. I still could hear Tragedy banging till I was halfway to the dock. It was humid and getting hot, the ground was spongy and covered with leaves that were orange and yellow, some already brown.

I went down the lake to Cabin Springs and lived in a house where Kerwin had stayed. I sat there a day and a half, listening to my stories till the batteries drained and the voices started to drawl.

Then I got in a panic, walking 'round and 'round that stupid house, dragging my fingers down my face. Knowing that when the dark came it would be a quiet dark without stories, and knowing that I couldn't get through it. Knowing that I couldn't get through it with nothing in my head but my thoughts.

I'd taken Flyboy's headphones, but left his machine. I knew where it was, though, his Sony with the batteries still in it. Down in the bathhouse where he'd had his altar and said his masses, and that's where I went that second day after leaving Tragedy, back to

Dick Idea's house, late in the afternoon with a cold mist in the air like a shivering white wall.

I came along the cove and crept up the hill behind his house, then sneaked under the lattice and let it touch down easy. It was hard-packed red dirt under there, and I had to walk stooped, had to walk quiet, 'cause overhead Dick Idea and Smokey were talking, but when I came around the stairs, instead of Flyboy's altar being like it was, with a tablecloth and two never-burnt candles and that beer glass with the coat of arms, his chalice, and the tabernacle that was a cardboard box that said California—instead of it being like it was, it was set with jugs and pots of water and with paper bags full of vegetables from Loretta's garden, and with oil lamps and loose matches and a friction strip, and kerosene in four mayonnaise jars.

Beside the altar was a gray stepladder that Flyboy used to stand on to read stories from his missal, and that's where he'd always kept his tape recorder. It was still there. I almost just took the batteries out, but then I took the whole machine—mostly 'cause I couldn't get the hatch open, but also 'cause I thought that maybe someday mine would stop working, then what? I took his tape recorder, and started to sneak away.

I was, like, almost at the lattice when I thought, You're stupid if you don't take some of that water, take some of that food, it's right there, waiting to be taken. So I turned around and went back, and was throwing stuff into my satchel, when the trapdoor opened, and I ran.

But he caught me.

It was Dick Idea and he caught me, and I wanna finish, there's so little tape left and it's my last cassette, I wanna be done, done talking, finished, and Dick Idea grabs me by the arm and says, I *thought* you might come back today—scared?

Scared? he says, but I kept struggling, but he won't let go, keeps saying, Scared? scared? you can stay it's all right you can stay— scared? And I broke loose and pushed out through the lattice, and started running toward the dock, and I looked past Blueberry Island, across the lake, and seen it, moving this way, a white storm, cloud on top of cloud tumbling over each other, stitched with lightning. And Dick Idea starts pulling me toward the bathhouse again, saying he'll protect me, saying I'd be safe, saying it like he'd said to Loretta, You'll be safe, I'll protect you. And I let him pull me back, like he'd pulled Loretta from the foot of the stairs, like he'd pulled me away from Raymond's bed and Raymond pleading with his eyes, and Dick Idea calling Smokey! and Smokey coming out, 'cause I was struggling again, I hadn't even *known* I was struggling again, and Dick Idea pulling me, saying, She's crazy, Joy's always been crazy, and my head swinging back and forth, and I seen Loretta's face crisscrossed by latticework but she didn't come out—didn't come out to help them drag me in.

Then Loretta's face was gone, and Smokey's hair was a flying tangle, and Dick Idea's mouth was open, and his hand slid down my arm, let go, and the trees roared and glass broke, and the white storm swept in. And then I was like glass, like trees, like boats, like docks, like *things*, picked up and flung like a thing.

And looked down, like Flyboy looking down from the ceiling, and seen Dick Idea's house blow out from inside, and kept spinning up higher, and seen the pretty painted walls of Josephine's house collapse and her green roof slide down the hill in mud, and seen the lake like I'd never seen it, shaped like a dog bone, then I was drowning. I don't remember the drop, but I dropped, then I was drowning. Then wasn't. And was flung like a thing right back on the island. Or maybe *not* like a thing. Not like a thing at all.

I don't know how I made it to the house from that little sand beach where Tragedy and me landed the rowboat our first day on the island, but I did. Everything I tried to grab blew away and nearly took me along, and the rain felt like shot, it was scalding.

And I don't know why the house was even still *there*, but it was, and the door was blown open and the floor was wet, it was slick, the table was lying upside down against a wall. And I looked across the room and through the windows and there was nothing but white out there, and white in back of me, there was nothing anywhere but white, and I knew I was dead, I would be soon, and I knew there was something—and you could laugh, you could say oh, that's the way stories *always* end, with somebody knowing something she never knew before. But I knew that when I ran up those stairs and went in that room, she'd be there still alive, waiting. And that seeing me, she'd never be frightened again.

Going up, I kept hearing bang and bang and bang—bang!—but it was only a shutter or maybe the kitchen door.

And she was still there, still alive, still waiting, her face small and fevered bright, and the storm tore and tore at the windowpanes behind her. I said, I came back. It's me, Joy. And got in the bed and under the blanket and pulled the blanket over us both and kissed the girl with the _____ ∎

FOR THE BEST IN PAPERBACKS, LOOK FOR THE 🐧

In every corner of the world, on every subject under the sun, Penguin represents quality and variety—the very best in publishing today.

For complete information about books available from Penguin—including Pelicans, Puffins, Peregrines, and Penguin Classics—and how to order them, write to us at the appropriate address below. Please note that for copyright reasons the selection of books varies from country to country.

In the United Kingdom: For a complete list of books available from Penguin in the U.K., please write to *Dept E.P., Penguin Books Ltd, Harmondsworth, Middlesex, UB7 0DA.*

In the United States: For a complete list of books available from Penguin in the U.S., please write to *Dept BA, Penguin*, Box 120, Bergenfield, New Jersey 07621-0120.

In Canada: For a complete list of books available from Penguin in Canada, please write to *Penguin Books Ltd, 2801 John Street, Markham, Ontario L3R 1B4.*

In Australia: For a complete list of books available from Penguin in Australia, please write to the *Marketing Department, Penguin Books Ltd, P.O. Box 257, Ringwood, Victoria 3134.*

In New Zealand: For a complete list of books available from Penguin in New Zealand, please write to the *Marketing Department, Penguin Books (NZ) Ltd, Private Bag, Takapuna, Auckland 9.*

In India: For a complete list of books available from Penguin, please write to *Penguin Overseas Ltd, 706 Eros Apartments, 56 Nehru Place, New Delhi, 110019.*

In Holland: For a complete list of books available from Penguin in Holland, please write to *Penguin Books Nederland B.V., Postbus 195, NL-1380AD Weesp, Netherlands.*

In Germany: For a complete list of books available from Penguin, please write to *Penguin Books Ltd, Friedrichstrasse 10-12, D-6000 Frankfurt Main I, Federal Republic of Germany.*

In Spain: For a complete list of books available from Penguin in Spain, please write to *Longman, Penguin España, Calle San Nicolas 15, E-28013 Madrid, Spain.*

In Japan: For a complete list of books available from Penguin in Japan, please write to *Longman Penguin Japan Co Ltd, Yamaguchi Building, 2-12-9 Kanda Jimbocho, Chiyoda-Ku, Tokyo 101, Japan.*